Bootheel Man

A Novel by Morley Swingle

Bootheel Man

A Novel by Morley Swingle

Southeast Missouri State University Press • 2007

Bootheel Man: A Novel
by Morley Swingle

Paper, $19
ISBN: 978-0-9798714-4-3

Cloth, $35
ISBN: 978-0-9798714-3-6

First published in 2007 in the United States of America

Southeast Missouri State University Press
MS 2650, One University Plaza
Cape Girardeau, MO 63701
www6.semo.edu/universitypress

Cover art by Gina Gray
Cover design by Liz Lester
Author photo by David Crowe
Artwork photo by Bric Rothenberger

This book is dedicated, with love,
to Veronica,
currently holding starting positions
as varsity proofreader, research assistant,
and dream-catcher.

Part I

Grave Injustice

The ancient cultures that are brought back to life by archaeologists through the studies of their carefully excavated
artifacts provide critical linkages for Native Americans to
their past. Through the act of reburial, our only hard evidence
of the existence of some ancient cultures will be permanently
expunged from the archaeological record. Are proponents
of repatriation really correct in assuming that future generations of Native Americans will approve of what is transpiring
today?
>—Robert J. Mallouf, "An Unraveling Rope: The
>Looting of America's Past," 20.2 *American Indian
>Quarterly* 1996

Indians often place scientists in the same category as grave
robbers. To them the only difference between an illegal
ransacking of a burial ground and a scientific one is the time
element, sunscreen, little whisk brooms, and the neatness of
the area when finished.
>—Devon A. Mihesuah, *Repatriation Reader: Who Owns
>American Indian Remains?*, 2000

If you desecrate a white grave, you wind up sitting in prison.
But desecrate an Indian grave, you get a PhD.
>—Walter R. Echo-Hawk, Staff Attorney, Native
>American Rights Fund

Chapter 1

If the fall did not kill him, the Mississippi River would.

Joey Red Horse vaulted over the chest-high railing of the Bill Emerson Memorial Bridge and landed on the concrete platform at its very edge. Beneath him, the treacherous water of the heartless river flowed onward in its relentless race toward the Gulf. A man might survive the impact of hitting the surface of the river after a sixty-foot plunge, maybe, but it was a moot point, really. He had never been a good swimmer. He was going to die.

Some things, Joey Red Horse told himself, *are worth dying for.* This was one of them. His death would bring meaning to an otherwise undistinguished twenty-four years of life.

Taking a deep breath, savoring the exhilaration coursing through his body, he pressed the flint-clay figurine against his naked chest and extended the middle finger of one hand at the police officers crouched behind the open doors of two patrol cars. They were pointing guns at him. The hot August sun shimmered off the white cars. Their flashing red and blue lights added a deadly touch to the carefully choreographed final chapter of Joey's life. He felt like the star of a Hollywood movie.

But this was Cape Girardeau, Missouri, and he was not an actor playing a part. He was real, flesh and blood, and he was about to become the most famous American Indian since Crazy Horse. At least, that was the plan. Truth be told, he was not sure how the whole thing would end. But he was not doing it just for the fame. He was making his last stand on this bridge because he wanted to rectify a cruel injustice. He was sacrificing his own life so the spirits of his ancestors could rest in peace. What could be nobler than to lay down your life for the souls of others?

Not one damn thing.

Injustice! *That* was what brought Joey to the bridge. Righting a grave injustice was the last thing he would do in this lifetime. *Angry men make good martyrs.* And he was plenty angry at the Heartland Mound Builder Museum.

Joey stared down at the swirling brown water beneath him. What would it feel like to hit its surface from sixty feet? A belly flop would be like hitting a slab of concrete. Would it be worse to be knocked unconscious or to survive the fall and be pulled underwater by the current? Drowning was supposed to be the worst way to die, your lungs screaming in agony as they filled with water and clamored for air. Joey sucked in a deep breath. He would find out soon enough.

If the fall did not kill him first.

"I'm unarmed," he yelled to the policemen. He held up the stolen relic. "See, no gun! All I've got in my hands is Gazing Woman! No need to shoot. Unless you *want* to become poster boys for the white man's continuing injustice to American Indians!"

The officer closest to him was a good forty yards away, squinting at him over the barrel of a pistol. The cop wore the midnight blue uniform of the Cape Girardeau Police Department.

"Climb back over the rail," the young officer ordered. "You're under arrest!"

Joey grinned. He hoped he looked fearless.

"Stay back or I'll jump. I'll take Gazing Woman with me! You want her back for the museum, don't you?"

Patrol cars and barricades now blocked bridge-bound traffic. Cars were already lining up on both sides of the bridge. No one would cross between Missouri and Illinois for a while.

Joey was making quite a scene. It pleased him. The more notice the world took of his death plunge, the better. As his ancestors said when going into battle, *It is a good day to die.*

He chuckled when he spotted the KFVS-12 television truck careening to a stop near the foot of the bridge. Cory Blaze, one of those familiar talking heads who report the news each night, leaped from the van and hurried toward the action, a cameraman lumbering behind him.

"Hey, lawmen!" Joey yelled. "Better powder your noses. We're about to be on TV!"

An older, blue-clad sergeant yelled to other policemen near the television van, "Don't let that news crew up here. It's just what this nut wants!"

"Nut!" Joey yelled. "Who you calling a nut?"

Joey moved his moccasined feet to the very edge of the concrete ledge. No railing separated him from the river. One careless move would send him hurtling through empty space to the water sixty feet below.

"Don't overreact," he yelled as he slipped his free hand to the belt of his homemade buckskin breechcloth and unclipped his cell phone. "I'm just getting my phone. No gun. Don't kill me yet."

He hit the speed-dial button for the number of the local television station. A few moments later he watched as Cory Blaze, standing on the railroad tracks on the riverbank beneath the bridge, answered his cell phone.

"Hello?" the news reporter said.

"Hello, yourself. I'm the guy on the bridge."

When Cory Blaze looked up, Joey waved at him.

"Who are you and why are you doing this?"

Joey smiled grimly. The reporter's blond hair gleamed in the bright noon sun. This was all going just as Joey had hoped.

"My name is Joey Red Horse. I'm an Osage Indian. I have taken the Gazing Woman statue from the Heartland Mound Builder Museum. She's right here!" He held up the figurine with one hand while he pressed the cell phone to his ear with the other. "You might want to move your cameraman to a position where he'll be able to get a good shot of me, both where I'm standing right now and during my entire drop to the water below."

Joey watched with grim satisfaction as the reporter gave frantic instructions to the cameraman, who was pointing the eye of the big camera right at him.

Joey knew he would look good on television. Trim and lithe, wearing only his buckskin breechcloth and moccasins, his long black hair blowing in the wind, he would present a dramatic image poised on the edge of the towering bridge. The bridge itself was a massive $100-million piece of architecture, its two steel H-shaped towers jutting an awe-inspiring 330 feet into the sky, each connected to the platform of the bridge by 64 silver-colored cables, giving its sides the appearance of a huge, metallic spiderweb. Joey stood on a ledge next to the guardrail, sixty feet above the water, silhouetted by the clear, blue sky. If the camera zoomed in for a close-up, television viewers would notice the war paint on his face, black from the nose up and yellow from the nose down, in the traditional "bluff war" design of the Osage warrior.

Joey let out a whoop of exhilaration. *It is a good day to die!*

"You've lost me, Mr. Red Horse," Cory Blaze said. "What's going on here? Are you really going to jump?"

Joey felt a twinge of impatience at the reporter's stupidity, but then realized he was being given a golden opportunity to explain to the world what they were about to witness.

"Justice! That's what is going on here!" Joey said. "For decades, the Heartland Mound Builder Museum has housed relics looted from Indian burial grounds. Other museums returned sacred items to proper tribes for reburial, but this selfish, craven Cape Girardeau museum refuses to do so. They're no better than grave robbers, making money by encouraging people to gawk at human skeletons and sacred burial relics. I liberated Gazing Woman early this morning. I took her from the museum. She was kidnapped from an Indian grave in Southeast Missouri over one-hundred years ago. I am returning her to the place she belongs!"

Joey could hear anger in his voice. *Good.* Maybe the television viewers would hear it, too.

The police officer closest to him eased away from the open door of the patrol car and moved toward him. He pointed his gun directly at Joey.

"Get back!" Joey yelled. "If you don't, both the statue and I go into the river! Is that what you want? Get back! Right now!"

Joey extended his arm. Gazing Woman dangled from his fingertips over the open space above the water.

The policeman stopped. Now he could see that Joey was unarmed. He lowered his gun.

"Look, buddy, no one needs to get hurt. Just climb back over the rail and everything will be okay. You've made your point. If you turn yourself in now, you'll be out of jail in no time. Come back over that rail, nice and easy."

"I'm not your buddy," Joey said. "Stay where you are or what happens next will be your fault!" He turned his attention back to his cell phone.

"Have you got me on camera now?"

"Yeah, we've got you," Cory Blaze said. "In fact, we're zooming in on your face. What's with the paint? You say you're an Indian?"

Does this reporter even have a brain? Joey struggled to remain patient.

"Osage. My ancestors lived in this country for centuries. This land was our home before the Europeans came. I'm here today to right an injustice. Gazing Woman was dug out of the same grave as Bootheel Man. You know Bootheel Man, don't you?"

"Sure. The famous skeleton with the hatchet embedded in his skull."

"That's right. Bootheel Man and these sacred burial items have made a fortune over the years for the Heartland Mound Builder Museum. But putting them on display is nothing but blasphemy. I couldn't find Bootheel Man this morning, or I'd have liberated him, too. How would you like it if your great-grandfather's body was the main exhibit at some museum? What kind of peace is that for a person's soul?"

"Are you saying Bootheel Man was your great-grandfather?"

Joey resisted the urge to curse. KFVS-12 apparently hired its on-air talent for looks, not intelligence.

"No. I'm saying it is offensive to all American Indians for our ancestors' skeletons to be displayed like trophies!"

Joey turned his attention to the Gazing Woman statuette in his hands. She was twelve inches tall, made of red flint clay. Her beautiful face featured high cheekbones and large eyes. Her nose was broad, but attractive. Her lips were full. Her breasts were naked and exquisitely shaped. With her gaze upturned toward the sky and her hands clasped over her heart, it was impossible not to wonder what deep emotion was producing her haunted expression. She was the most beautiful thing Joey had ever seen.

Joey raised his eyes from the thousand-year-old figurine. On the Missouri side of the river, the buildings of downtown Cape Girardeau covered the hills and valleys near the riverfront. The river itself was separated from the town by a thick concrete floodwall, seventeen feet high and nearly two feet thick. Joey knew the history of the floodwall. Its construction began in 1956 and ended in 1964. Its combination of earthen levees and concrete walls ran next to the river for 7, 210 feet, interspersed with 5 gates and 2 pumping stations. Before the floodwall had been erected, the downtown area regularly flooded. Old photos showed people paddling boats down Main Street. Downtown stores had lost thousands of dollars in merchandise to the whims of the Father of Waters. No more. The descendants of the hearty white settlers who founded Cape Girardeau had conquered the Mississippi in the same efficient, cold and calculated way they had vanquished Joey's people. The difference was that the Mississippi had not been shuttled off to some Indian reservation in Oklahoma. Instead, it had been cut off from the community by a long concrete fortress.

Joey felt a familiar surge of anger as he thought about the actions of the white men who had swindled the Osage Indians out of their 100 million acres of land. Of course, that boondoggle of treaties took place nearly 200 years ago. Still, it made him ashamed of the white blood he carried from the non-Osage branch of his family tree.

A detective in plain clothes joined the uniformed officers near the car. He was a muscular guy. His neck was too thick for his ill-fitting sport coat. He and the closest uniformed officer were moving slowly toward Joey.

"My name's Harry Sullinger," the detective was saying. He spread his open hands to show he was unarmed. "I work for the prosecutor's office. I'm sure we can work out a deal here. No need to jump. No need to harm the statue. Let's just stay calm and talk about this."

"Stay back!" Joey yelled. "I mean it! I'll jump!"

Joey glanced at the KFVS-12 television crew. They were filming the whole thing. He felt a glow of happiness more intense than anything he had ever felt before. He was finally giving meaning to his shabby life. Maybe someone like the late Vine Deloria Jr. would end up writing a book about him!

The detective named Sullinger stopped. He stood forty feet from Joey, staring at him over the bridge's four-feet-high railing, which consisted of a squat concrete wall topped by two metal rails.

Joey waved at Cory Blaze and the cameraman. He was going for a look that combined noble courage with jauntiness. The television people had moved away from the railroad tracks and were standing at the edge of the river, looking up. The eye of the camera was following his every movement. The world was watching.

It was time. Joey murmured a soft prayer for the soul of the artist who had made Gazing Woman and for the soul of Bootheel Man, the prehistoric Native American whose skeleton had lain with the statuette for over a thousand years in a grave beneath a mound of earth in Cape Girardeau, Missouri.

"I do this for both of you," Joey whispered, "as well as for myself."

Joey thrust Gazing Woman high above his head. The foot-tall ceramic figurine was one of the most famous Mound Builder relics in the world. The sun glistened on the smooth flint clay. Joey extended the girl's beautiful face toward the blazing sun. He hoped the television cameraman was getting a good shot.

He spoke into his cell phone again, his voice rising with anger and excitement. "The men who dug up the bones of my people weren't scientists! They were grave robbers! Do you hear me? Grave robbers!"

With a flick of his wrist, Joey tossed the cell phone off the bridge. It dropped end over end, finally disappearing into the river with a tiny splash.

Taking a deep breath, Joey lowered Gazing Woman. Then, like a man throwing a shot put, he reared back and heaved the beautiful figurine into the empty air above the river. The thousand-year-old effigy soared over the Mississippi River and dropped like a rock. Joey watched, mesmerized, as the valuable treasure sped toward the eternal freedom presented by the deep and treacherous river.

Joey heard the plunk when she hit the water and sank into its muddy depths. He felt anger seeping from the pores of his skin, being replaced by peacefulness and calm determination. *Now I belong to the ages*, he thought. *My time on earth is done.*

The big detective was running toward him, but it was too late to stop Joey's grand finale. Everything had gone exactly as planned. Too bad the other twenty-four years, eight months, and sixteen days of his life had not gone so well.

Joey scooted his moccasined toes over the edge of the ledge, extended his arms above his head, straightened his back, bent his knees, and propelled himself into the air, executing what he hoped was something close to a swan dive.

14

He tried his best for a picture-perfect dive. He had practiced a number of daring maneuvers from the highest diving board at the public pool, but he had never attempted anything even remotely close to this. He knew he was being filmed by the television crew. He knew it would probably be the last thing he did in his life. He wanted it to be beautiful. He wanted it to play on newscasts across the country. He wanted people to talk about Joey Red Horse, to debate whether his act of liberating Gazing Woman from the museum constituted theft or justice. Live or die, he wanted to be a martyr for the cause of repatriating the ancient ancestors and sacred objects from private museums all over the country. He wanted to amount to at least a footnote in the history of the American Indian.

As the Mighty Mississippi hurtled with alarming speed toward his painted face, he realized that his feet and legs were tilting way too far beyond a perpendicular line. He was going to do a back flop on the surface of the river from the extreme height of the Bill Emerson Memorial Bridge. It was going to hurt. It occurred to him that maybe he should have simply jumped feet-first.

The back flop would make for good television, he told himself. He would never survive such an entertaining impact, but at least his face paint was waterproof. He would make a handsome corpse.

He fought hard to try to straighten himself. He wanted to look graceful, not ridiculous. He envisioned Olympic judges holding up cards giving him a score of three on a scale of ten. *I can do better than a three!* He struggled to straighten his back.

A sudden blow to his head knocked him senseless, and his soul spiraled into darkness. *So this is it*, he had time to think. *So this is it.*

Detective Harry Sullinger ran toward Joey Red Horse as the young man made his dive. Adrenaline pumping, his focus solely on saving a life, Sullinger raced to the railing of the bridge. As he ran, he stripped off his coat, belt, gun, wristwatch, and tie. The tie was 100 percent silk, a Brooks Brothers striped number given to him by his fifth wife shortly before their divorce. It would not do to get it wet.

He vaulted the railing and landed lightly on the platform recently vacated by Joey Red Horse. Far beneath him, the young man lay facedown and motionless on the surface of the muddy water of the Mississippi, not swimming, but not yet consigned to the powerful depths and whirlpools of the world's most dangerous river.

Tossing his shoes back onto the bridge, Sullinger held his nose and jumped.

"What the hell are you doing?" he heard one of the uniformed officers shout.

He wondered the same thing as he hurtled feet-first toward the water. *Wonderful! I forgot to take my wallet out of my pocket! It's got my cash, credit cards, driver's license, photographs of my ex-wives, prosecutor's office business cards, and . . .*

With a whap and a whoosh, he knifed into the water with the precision of an ice pick. In an instant, he was deep beneath its surface. His world was suddenly silent, cool, murky, and brown. The water was so muddy, his hands were invisible in front of his face. The opaque water above him was softly tinted with fingers of sunlight. Underneath, all was dark and ominous. With powerful strokes, he swam for the surface.

When his head broke free, he gulped fresh air and jerked his face from side to side. Where was the jumper?

Sullinger had aimed his leap to land right next to him. But the guy was nowhere to be found. From the heights of the bridge, he had been able to see the body just barely above the waterline, but down here, all Sullinger could see was sunlight gleaming off the wide expanse of water. Everything beneath its surface was invisible in the murky depths.

He glanced up at the spot from which he'd jumped.

Parker, a uniformed officer, was pointing downstream.

"Behind you!" Parker yelled, the distance making his voice faint. "He's already gone under the bridge!"

That makes sense, Sullinger thought. *The current was carrying him downstream even while I was dropping through the air.*

Sullinger turned in the water and swam under the bridge, desperately trying to spot the jumper. This was a lot harder than fishing kids out of the public pool during those long-ago summers as a lifeguard.

He looked up at Parker, who had crossed to the south side of the bridge. Parker was pointing to Sullinger's left. He veered that direction, constantly scanning the water near him.

Finally, he caught a glimpse of light reflecting off Joey's naked back a short distance ahead. With the sure strokes of an expert swimmer, Sullinger sped in that direction. His forward progress was aided by the current.

"Hurry!" Parker yelled. "He's gonna sink!"

The still form of Joey Red Horse floated facedown in the water, his arms dangling loosely at his sides, his face under the surface.

Years of life-saving training kicked in. Sullinger approached Joey from behind and slipped a powerful arm across Joey's back. He grasped Joey's limp body and rolled him over so he was face-up. He clasped his arm across the boy's chest. After a few kicks and strokes, Sullinger was propelling them both through the river, their heads well above water.

Sullinger noticed the black and yellow war paint on Joey's face. He also noticed that the young man was not breathing. *Great! I'm gonna have to do mouth-to-mouth on a face that looks like a Halloween mask! What the hell is that stuff, anyway?*

Sullinger was not sure he could do mouth-to-mouth in such a powerful current. He had never tried it. Holding himself upright with strong frog kicks, Sullinger cradled Joey's head in his hands. With one hand on Joey's glistening forehead and the other on his chin, he tilted Joey's head back until the strangely painted face pointed toward the sky. He pinched Joey's nostrils closed and covered Joey's mouth with his own. He took a deep breath and blew air into Joey's mouth.

Sullinger saw Joey's chest rise. *Good*, he thought, removing his lips and taking another deep breath.

Before he could give a second blow, the powerful current caught Joey's legs and pulled Joey's head underwater.

This isn't going to work! Sullinger yanked Joey's head back above the surface. He repeated the process, but once again Joey's face was dragged underwater.

"Hope you can wait until we get to shore," he said into Joey's ear.

He put Joey back into the cross-chest-carry position and began a steady swim toward the Missouri riverbank, following the pull of the current.

Sullinger watched with relief as three men on shore piled into a motorboat and started toward him. As they drew closer, he saw two firefighters and a uniformed policeman in the rescue boat. The cop was Jim Price, one of his favorite guys. Sullinger swam for the boat, Joey Red Horse in tow. He reached it quickly.

"I don't know if he's alive or not," Sullinger said, clutching the edge of the boat with one hand.

"Let's find out," one of the firemen said. "Heave him up here."

Sullinger turned the unconscious Joey Red Horse toward the boat and lifted Joey's slender but surprisingly heavy body into the air with a big heave. Sullinger's head went completely underwater, but he could tell he had successfully shoved Joey's torso far above the waterline. Two men on the boat grabbed Joey and hauled him aboard.

When Sullinger's head broke the surface, he called out, "He wasn't breathing a minute ago. I don't think he's breathing now."

One of the firefighters had already started mouth-to-mouth.

Jim Price caught Sullinger's arm and helped him crawl into the boat.

"I hope the kid makes it," Sullinger said.

"You gave it your best shot," Price said. "If he lives, it's because of you, Harry."

Sullinger frowned. "If he's dead, I ruined a perfectly good wallet for nothing."

Harry took the soggy leather wallet out of his back pocket.

"What a shame," Price said. "I so enjoyed looking at the pictures of your ex-wives and hearing your tales of woe."

"Well, I've still got the tales of woe, anyway," Sullinger muttered as he examined the water-soaked contents.

"What's with this guy's face?" the firefighter doing mouth-to-mouth said between blows. "Looks like a drowned bumblebee."

"Maybe he's got jaundice," Jim Price suggested. "You had all your shots, Harry?"

"Just get me to the shore," Sullinger said, "and get him breathing. I can hardly wait to arrest him."

Chapter 2

Allison Culbertson answered the phone call from the Cape Girardeau Police Department with great curiosity. "This is Allison Culbertson."

"Hello, Ms. Culbertson. Harry Sullinger, from the Cape Girardeau County prosecutor's office. I'm here at the Cape Girardeau Police Department. We've got a suspect in custody who wants to talk to you."

"Who might that be?"

"Did you happen to see the newscast about the guy who stole the Indian artifact from the Heartland Museum and did a high dive off the bridge?"

"I not only saw the story, Detective Sullinger, I also saw part of the excitement from my office window. The commotion was a long way off, but I could make out lots of flashing red lights and sirens, along with a couple of idiots jumping off the bridge."

Her comment was met with a pause at the other end of the line.

Allison Culbertson smiled to herself as she doodled on her notepad. She barely knew Harry Sullinger. She had met him briefly when she represented his fifth wife in an uncontested divorce from the workaholic detective. He was the tough-guy investigator at the prosecutor's office, with an ego as big as his weightlifter physique. Half the women in town were his ex-wives. There was something seriously flawed about a man who had been divorced five times by his mid-thirties. It amused her to listen to his silence as he pondered a response.

"Yeah, well, the jumper has lawyered-up. He won't talk to us without chatting with you first."

A jolt of excitement shot through Allison's gut. She had handled dozens of criminal cases so far in her short legal career, but most had been run-of-the-mill things like driving while intoxicated, domestic assault, or shoplifting. This could be her first chance to represent a high-profile criminal defendant.

"What's the guy's name?" she asked. "The news report didn't give it. They said his name wouldn't be released until he's charged."

"Red Horse. Joey Red Horse. Believe it or not, that's his real name. He's twenty-four years old. Some kind of Indian activist, looking to make a name for himself by stealing a Mound Builder relic from the museum."

"*Allegedly* stealing," she corrected him.

"Oh, that's right, *allegedly*. I suppose I just *allegedly* saw it in his hands right before he *allegedly* threw it in the river right under my nose."

"Why me? Why are you calling *me*, Detective Sullinger? As far as I know, I don't know any Joey Red Horse. Never even heard of him. He's certainly not one of my clients."

"He wants to be. He specifically asked for you. Told me your phone number off the top of his head. Didn't even need to let his fingers do the perp walk through the Yellow Pages."

Allison was intrigued. She stood up, still holding the phone to her ear. She faced the long east window of her office. It provided a panoramic view of the Mississippi River from her second-story law firm in downtown Cape Girardeau.

"Did he say *why* he picked me?"

"Maybe it's your looks."

Allison studied her reflection in the glass of her office window. What she saw pleased her. The young woman holding the phone to her ear was both attractive and professional. She was blonde, with her hair pulled into a tight bun like the ballerina she had been in her childhood. She was also pretty, with big eyes and an oval face with a strong jawline. But her navy-blue wool gabardine suit and her white shirt, open just the right amount at the collar, proclaimed to the world that she was a lawyer, not the Mizzou Golden Girl dancer she had been during her undergraduate years at the University of Missouri.

"*Must* be your looks," Sullinger was saying. "Couldn't be your experience. How long you been a lawyer now, one year? Two?"

She ignored the jab. She supposed she had asked for it with the quip about the idiots jumping off the bridge. "So, he didn't say why he's asking for *me*?"

"Nope. Just said he wouldn't say another word to the cops until he spoke with his lawyer, Allison Culbertson. He wants you to come down to the station."

Allison worked to keep the building excitement out of her voice. She willed herself to sound unenthusiastic. "You know, he hasn't hired me yet. I haven't been paid."

"Give the guy a break. He hasn't exactly had time to get to the bank. He's been sitting in jail since we fished him out of the water. Looked like a drowned rat when we brought him in. I could tell him you said to go take a flying leap. But, of course, he's already done that once today."

"I'll be there in fifteen minutes," she said.

Joey Red Horse was sitting on the edge of a shiny metal bunk in a police holding-cell when Allison Culbertson saw him for the first time. His elbows rested on his knees. He was staring at the floor.

"Here she is, Joey," Harry Sullinger said. "Your lawyer, in the flesh. We aim to please around here. After you visit with her, I'd like to ask you again about who else was involved in your little heist."

Joey Red Horse rose to his feet. He was handsome, slender, and smooth-faced, with damp, shoulder-length black hair pulled behind his ears. His brown eyes were deep and penetrating. He wore an orange jail jumpsuit. Traces of paint still remained on his face, some black and some yellow.

"Hi," he said, holding out a hand. "I'm Joey Red Horse. I want to hire you."

Allison Culbertson shook hands with her potential client. Harry Sullinger was watching with unconcealed interest from his position near the cell's open door.

She turned to the big detective. "May we have some privacy here?"

"Sure. If you want, I can move you two to an interview room upstairs. It would be more private and more comfortable."

Allison looked around. The holding-cell would provide little or no privacy for a conversation. Its front wall consisted solely of iron bars. It faced a small room crammed with a Breathalyzer machine and fingerprinting and photography equipment. The room was a busy place. A middle-aged suspect with an Afro the size of a basketball was in the process of having his mug shot taken. He was smiling for the camera as if he were posing for a Christmas-card photo. From the difficulty he was having holding up the placard bearing his name, Allison assumed he was drunk.

"A change of scenery would be nice," she said.

"No problem, Counselor." Sullinger handcuffed Joey Red Horse for the walk to the interview room.

"Is that really necessary?" she asked, pointing to the handcuffs.

"Standard policy," he said apologetically. "A guy who jumps off the Mississippi River bridge has to be considered a flight risk."

"In more ways than one," Joey Red Horse said. He was smiling. "It's okay. I understand, Harry."

"What about you, Detective Sullinger?" Allison Culbertson asked. "You jumped, too, didn't you? Maybe a person has other reasons to jump off a bridge besides trying to escape from the long arm of the law. Maybe problems with an ex-wife, or two or three or four or five."

Sullinger winced.

"*Touché*," he said. "You're every bit as funny as that ex-wife of mine you represented. I guess she thoroughly poisoned your mind against me."

"As a detective," she said, "you must know that ex-wives are a fertile source of incredibly detailed and defamatory information." She was mostly bluffing. Since his divorce had been uncontested, it had not been necessary for her to dig up any dirt on Sullinger, and she was not a gossip by nature. In fact, the only scandalous thing she remembered from her half-dozen conversations with Sullinger's ex-wife was a lurid account of a midnight lovemaking session on a golf-course putting green during their courtship. The woman had been wistfully nostalgic as she described it. Allison vividly recalled her shock at the notion of doing something like *that* outside.

She walked behind Joey Red Horse as they left the holding-cell and made their way to a second-floor interview room. For some reason, her gaze was drawn to her client's feet. He wore white socks and black slippers with his jail-issue orange outfit.

"Harry's not so bad," Joey Red Horse said. "He saved my life. I was knocked unconscious when I hit the water. I'd be sleeping with the fishes right now if he hadn't jumped off the bridge and pulled me out. Thanks again, Harry. That took courage."

"You're welcome," Sullinger said. "You can show your gratitude by telling me who else was involved."

"Let me talk to Mr. Red Horse in private," Allison Culbertson interrupted. "I'll help him decide whether he wants to give you more information."

"Sure thing," Sullinger said, opening the door to the interview room. "Make yourselves comfortable. I'll be right down the hall. When you're done, just open the door and holler for me."

The room was a tiny rectangle, no more than six feet wide on each side. Its walls and ceiling were covered with a thick shag carpet, a yellowish-green shade Allison thought might be aptly dubbed "Dog-Vomit Green." The room was furnished with a wood-grained Formica-topped table and two chairs bearing fabric that came admirably close to matching the color of the carpet. She and Joey Red Horse sat down as Sullinger left the room. He closed the door behind him.

"So, will you take my case?"

Joey Red Horse was looking at her expectantly. Allison refrained from saying, *Yes, yes, yes!*

"What do the police think you did?"

"I'll tell you exactly what I did."

"No," she interrupted. "Not yet. Don't confess to me. Tell me what the police think you did."

He frowned. "What's the difference?"

"Well, if I later decide to put you on the witness stand in the courtroom, I can't knowingly allow you to give perjured testimony. So if you tell me exactly what you did right now, we're stuck with your story. I can never let you testify to something else in court. It works better if a client just tells his lawyer what the police think he did. It sort of keeps our options open for any trial down the road."

Joey shrugged. "It's not gonna make any difference in my case. I was videotaped on the bridge with Gazing Woman in my hands. I can hardly claim it was somebody else."

He leaned back in his chair. The pride on his face was unmistakable. After a few moments, he chuckled.

"Okay, I'll do it your way. The police have this strange idea that I broke into the Heartland Mound Builder Museum in Cape Girardeau early this morning. They are convinced I'm the one who stole a beautiful piece of American Indian artwork, a sculpture called Gazing Woman. They have this bizarre notion that after I stole her, I dialed 911 and bragged about what I'd done. They think I taunted the police to come to the riverfront. Some of them actually believe they saw me standing on the edge of the bridge, sixty feet above the water, using my cell phone to yak it up with a television reporter, making sure he caught everything on film for posterity. They have the audacity to claim I proudly displayed Gazing Woman for the TV cameras so the world could see her one last time before I threw her into the river and dove off the bridge."

He shook his head. "What imaginations these cops have! Where they get these strange notions, I can't imagine! Needless to say, I was home drinking green tea and leering at Vanna White on *Wheel of Fortune* reruns the entire morning. It must have been someone else."

Allison nodded toward him. "What's with the black and yellow face paint?"

He beamed. "You like it? It's the 'bluff paint' used by the Osages in past centuries when we'd bait an enemy to come out and fight. The Caddos tended to hide in the safety of their palisades. The Osages would paint their faces black and yellow and use sign language to hurl vile insults at the Caddos until they'd finally come out to fight."

Allison raised an eyebrow. "So, you're trying to pick a fight with somebody?"

"You bet."

She leaned back in her chair. "Why did you have the detective call *me*? We've never met, have we?"

"No, but I remember the case you handled a few months ago. The one about the buried gold, the treasure trove? Stories about that case were all over the news. Seems to me you must be an expert on who has the legal right to ancient things buried in the ground."

"I'm afraid the law of treasure trove isn't going to help you much," she said. "It simply holds that a person who finds buried gold or silver gets to keep it against anyone but the true owner or his descendants. I don't see how it could apply to ancient Indian artifacts."

"Gazing Woman is worth a fortune," he said. "She's definitely a treasure."

"That's not the point. The treasure-trove law only applies to gold or silver. Besides, the case against you is going to be a criminal prosecution, not a civil suit. They'll probably charge you with burglary and stealing, maybe resisting arrest. My experience with the civil law of treasure trove isn't going to help you."

With his cuffed hands, he brushed a strand of dark hair from his eyes. "May I tell you what I did and why? My story won't change when we go to court. I promise. The truth is the truth. I won't shade it one way or the other."

"Okay, let's hear it."

"I did everything the cops say I did. I broke into the museum and took Gazing Woman. But I didn't steal her. I liberated her. She was one of the burial items in the grave of the Indian now known as Bootheel Man. An amateur archaeologist dug him up from a burial mound in Cape Girardeau in 1902. His bones and sacred burial items have been on display in a local museum ever since. The ceremonial stone axe used to kill Bootheel Man was firmly embedded in his skull when he was found. That gruesome detail has made this particular skeleton one of the most famous and gawked-at sets of human remains in the world. I broke into the museum planning to take Bootheel Man and everything associated with him, but the only thing I could find was Gazing Woman. I guess the museum was doing restoration work on the other stuff or something. But Gazing Woman was perfect for what I had in mind. She's one of the most exquisitely detailed effigies from the Mississippian era. She's well known in the field of archaeology. She's a world-famous burial object. I knew I could make my point with her."

"Your point being?"

"My point being that whatever good intentions motivated the archaeologist who dug up Bootheel Man and Gazing Woman years ago, it was grave robbery, pure and simple. Bootheel Man isn't just somebody's scientific discovery. He was a human being; a living, breathing man. He died a violent death and was buried with a respectful ceremony. It was wrong and shameful to dig up his bones and put him on display, even in the name of science. I'm calling for his skeleton and the items buried with him to be returned to his grave, or to American Indians for proper reburial. I took the first step today by repatriating Gazing Woman to the depths of the Mississippi River, where she will forever rest in peace. It's the single best thing I've ever done in my life."

He glanced at the handcuffs and shrugged. He was a good-looking guy, face-paint residue notwithstanding. He looked much younger than his twenty-four years.

"You know," Allison said. "I don't know a lot about the law regarding prehistoric Indian bones, but it strikes me that there must have been some civil recourse you could have pursued short of felonious breaking and entering."

"The problem," Joey Red Horse said, "is that the Heartland Mound Builder Museum is a private museum. It gets absolutely no money from the federal government. That means the federal government can't force it to give back the human remains in its possession. There was a law passed back in 1990 called the Native American Graves Protection and Repatriation Act. It forces museums that get federal money to return our ancient ancestors' bones and sacred objects buried with them. But a museum like the Heartland Museum can just thumb its nose at us and keep our ancestors in display cases and cardboard boxes. Nationwide, we're talking about significant numbers. The Smithsonian Institution alone had eighteen-thousand sets of human remains. Experts say there are at least three-hundred-thousand dead Indians in museums across the country, maybe as many as two million."

"How old is Bootheel Man?" Allison asked.

"Scientists believe he was part of the Mississippian era. He would've been alive somewhere around the year 1050 A.D."

"Can you trace your lineage directly to him?"

"Not exactly. But I *am* part Osage, and we Osages are descended from the Indians who lived in this area at that time."

Allison frowned. "If we can't prove you're a blood relative, I'm not sure how any of this is going to help you in a criminal prosecution for burglary and stealing."

26

"I had a *right* to take Gazing Woman!"

"Explain it to me."

"It's simple. The museum doesn't own Bootheel Man and the artifacts from his grave because no one can own the bones of another human being. The museum got these items by looting the grave of a human being. The museum has no better right to these items than I do. Even less, actually, because I'm an Osage and can claim a right to rebury the bones and relics of my ancient ancestor."

Joey Red Horse snorted. "How would you like it if I decided to dig up your grandmother's bones and put them on display to show what the skeleton of an elderly white lady looks like after decades in a coffin? Perhaps we could dig her up out of scientific curiosity to figure out exactly how she died, or to see what sort of clothing and jewelry she was wearing in her grave. Or maybe we want to check the condition of her teeth since she died before modern dentistry. I don't think you'd be reluctant to argue in court that a museum did *not* have the right to dig up your grandmother. What's the difference?"

Allison stroked her chin. She was getting an idea. "You know, there *is* a claim-of-right defense in the Missouri Criminal Code."

"What?"

"Claim of right. It's a defense to stealing. A person is not guilty of the crime of stealing if he was acting with the honest belief he had the right to take the property."

"There you go!" Joey said. "See, I knew you were the lawyer for me!"

"Not so fast," she cautioned. "I'm still thinking out loud here. I'm not sure this defense will fly, and I'm not sure it will help us at all on the burglary count, but it's possible we could convince a judge or jury that whether you were technically correct or not, you were acting with the honest belief you had a right to take the figurine."

"Of course we can prove it! It's true!" he said. "Claim of right. Yeah! I even like the ring of it."

"I can't guarantee we'll win," she said.

"I understand. But what you're telling me is great news. I took Gazing Woman expecting to become a martyr for the cause of repatriation. I was doing it to call for the return of *all* our ancestors' bones, burial objects, and sacred things. Frankly, I expected the jump off the bridge to kill me. That's why I wanted to make sure the TV cameras got good pictures and colorful sound bites. I wanted to do something to put pressure on the Heartland Mound Builder Museum and other private museums like it. I wanted to bring worldwide public attention to this cause. The fact that I lived through the jump has been a pleasant surprise. Your telling me about the claim-of-right defense is more good news. Honestly, though, if you don't win my case, that's okay. I might make a better spokesman for the cause if I have to serve some jail time over this. Still, if you can get me off completely, I'll just have to make do with an acquittal."

"*Make do* with an acquittal?"

"I'm kidding, of course. It would be wonderful if you got me off."

"Well, there's one other important preliminary detail," Allison said.

"What's that?"

"I don't work for free. There will be the little matter of a contract and a fee." She quoted him her standard hourly rate.

He smiled. "Someone will come by your office in a couple of days to discuss your fee. His nickname is Bear."

"Was Bear in on this?"

He grinned. "What about your policy of not wanting confessions from your client? Let's go with the story that Bear is not finding out about this until after the fact. But he is an Osage Indian. He'll be happy about what I've done. He'll loan me the money for my defense. Once you get it, draw up your contract. I'll sign it. Put whatever you want in it. As you know, you whites can really take advantage of us Indians when it comes to business deals. But don't get your hopes up; Bear and I aren't gonna sell you any land."

He laughed. Allison found the sound infectious. When the moment was over, she asked him one last question. "What do you want me to tell Detective Sullinger about further interviews? He wants to know who else was involved, you know."

Joey Red Horse grinned. "Thank him again for saving my life. Tell him I told you I acted alone. Tell him I wanted to talk to him some more, but *you* wouldn't let me. Tell him I am just following your advice."

"The last part happens to be true," Allison said. "My advice *is* to keep your mouth shut. Don't let him coax anything else out of you after I leave."

She rose and went to the door.

"One other thing?" Joey said.

She turned to face him.

"If you can do it, would you mind recording the news for me? I'd love to watch my jump. It's my first leading role, you know."

Chapter 3

"There's some sort of biker here to see you. Says his name is Bear." Allison's secretary was talking in a hushed voice. Allison could tell she was frightened.

"Send him in, Rita."

"He's got a young woman with him."

"It's up to him whether she comes in or stays in the waiting room."

Moments later, a huge, bearded man clad in black leather and metal chains filled the doorway. His shoulders, arms, and legs were massive. His pot belly draped heavily over his belt. His brown eyes glittered. "I'm Bear."

"So I guessed," Allison said. She walked around her desk to shake his hand. "Allison Culbertson. Joey told me you'd be paying me a visit."

Bear's beard was thick and curly. Black whiskers were dappled with streaks of gray. His long black hair was pulled into a braided ponytail. It hung down his back like a whip, ending somewhere between his leather-clad shoulder blades. His cheekbones were wide. His face was rough and weathered. He carried a black Nazi-style helmet, with a large red and white feather painted on each side.

"Got a last name, Bear?"

"Smith. Normal spelling."

Allison Culbertson raised an eyebrow.

"Smith? That doesn't sound Native American."

"Somewhere along the line, somebody wanted to fit in. I'm Osage, though. Full-blood."

A young woman entered the room behind him. She wore tight blue jeans and a bright yellow t-shirt with the big red words CUSTER DIED FOR YOUR SINS emblazoned across her chest. Her deeply tanned face was oval and rather plain, framed by straight black hair. Her body made up for anything her face lacked. Her curves would turn any man's head, and she moved with the athletic grace of a gymnast. She also carried a motorcycle helmet.

It was a monstrosity even an astronaut might have rejected as being too large and cumbersome.

"This is my daughter, Lolita," Bear said. "She'll be a senior at Cape Central High School in the fall."

"Lolita," Allison repeated. "Beautiful. Family name?"

"I don't think so," Lolita said.

"It's not," Bear said. "I'm a Vladimir Nabokov fan. Light of my life, fire of my loins, all that."

Allison beckoned them to the chairs in front of her desk. She pictured this heavily bearded, rough-looking, gravel-voiced biker sitting by some campfire reading the Russian novelist's masterpiece about a nerdy protagonist who falls in love with an underage girl. She banished the incongruous thought from her mind.

"I'm here to put up the money for Joey," Bear said. "I want to bond him out of jail and I want to pay you to represent him. Let's work up a bond assignment. You can take your fee out of the bond when the case is over."

Allison was surprised. Most clients had no idea how a bond assignment worked. Bear obviously had a bit of experience with criminal law.

"He's got a high bond for a first-offense burglary and stealing case," Allison said. "Judge Sterns set it at fifty thousand."

"So I heard." Bear reached into two of the many pockets of his shiny leather jacket. His chains jingled as he withdrew five bundles of paper money, each held together by a thick rubber band. "Here's fifty thousand in hundreds. How about we post it with the court? You keep your hourly tab running. When the case is over, you can take your fee out of this fifty grand, and I'll get back what's left. If it looks like it's going over fifty thousand, let me know. I can get more if I have to."

He was carrying fifty-thousand dollars in cash! Allison opened her mouth to suggest that lugging around such a large sum of money was not a good idea. On the other hand, a mugger would have to be crazy to try to rob this massive man. She kept the suggestion to herself.

Instead, Allison said, "You understand, even though you're paying my fee, I'm Joey's lawyer, not yours?"

"Sure," Bear said. "I've been around the block a few times. I know how it works. Attorney-client privilege and all that. I'm here to help Joey. He'll pay me back some day."

The girl was less patient than her father. "How soon can you get him out of jail?" Lolita asked. "He's been locked up for two whole days. It must be awful for him!"

"We can get him out today. It won't take long to draw up the contract for him to sign. We can do the paperwork right now."

Allison quickly located the bond assignment form on her computer and began typing in the relevant information. "So, what's your occupation, Mr. Smith?"

"Call me Bear. I'm self-employed. In salvage. I own a junkyard."

Allison typed his name, occupation, and home and business addresses into the form.

"There's a spot here to indicate race," she said. "I'm assuming I should put an I for Indian?"

"Whatever. Most white people don't realize that being an Indian is more than being a different race."

"How so?"

"We're a different nation, too. Our people entered into treaties with the United States. Those treaties are still good, with obligations on both sides. There's a whole government agency that still exists to handle matters from those treaties, like annual payments and health care. It's called the Bureau of Indian Affairs. You don't see a Bureau of Irish-American Affairs, or a Bureau of Italian-American Affairs, or even a Bureau of African-American Affairs. That's because our situation is not like any other race's. We're the only people who were here *first*. The government made treaties with us as they took away our land."

"I never thought of it that way," Allison said.

"Surprise, surprise."

Allison glanced up. Had he meant to insult her? His face was inscrutable.

When the routine questions were finished, she leaned back in her chair. "So, what's your connection to Joey?"

Bear stared at her for several moments with an unflinching gaze. The intensity in his dark brown eyes made her uncomfortable.

32

"He's a friend."

"He's an Osage, like us," Lolita said.

"Not exactly like us," Bear corrected. "He's not full-blood. Technically, until the new Osage Constitution was passed in 2006, he didn't have enough Osage blood to even be an official voting member of the tribe. He's a good guy, though. He's a full Osage in his heart."

Allison leaned forward. "Joey and I talked briefly about trying to mount a claim-of-right defense, arguing that Joey should be acquitted because he honestly felt he had the right to take Gazing Woman out of the museum. What do you think?"

Bear scowled. "Personally, I think Joey would have done more for the cause by just capping the dude's sorry ass." The big man cast a quick glance at his daughter. She rolled her eyes at the ceiling.

"Capping?"

"Capping his ass. Shooting him. He should've just shot that arrogant museum director, what's his name, Faulkner."

"Faulkner would be the sorry-assed dude?"

"Right."

"Dad, don't talk that way," Lolita said. "Joey's no killer, and neither are you. It's great what Joey did. What better way to show that the museum doesn't really have a right to these burial artifacts than to steal one and prove you have a better claim to it than they do? Joey's brilliant!"

"What's your beef with Faulkner?" Allison asked Bear.

"He's a vulture. The Heartland Mound Builder Museum makes tons of money showing off the bones of Bootheel Man and all the other sacred Indian artifacts they've collected over the past century. Faulkner's written a book about Bootheel Man that's made him a bunch of money, too. Our tribe has contacted him many times, demanding the return of Bootheel Man. We want to rebury him. Faulkner just ignores us. Makes me sick to my stomach, the way Faulkner makes money on the bones of my ancestors. We've put up with it for way too long."

"We?"

"American Indians. Archaeologists have been collecting our bones for two centuries, supposedly in the name of science. I won't be satisfied until every single bone and sacred burial relic snatched up by these ghouls has been returned."

Lolita interrupted her father. "Ms. Culbertson, have you heard about the Sand Creek Massacre in 1864? A regiment of Colorado Volunteers led by Major John Chivington, a Methodist minister and Civil War veteran, attacked the unsuspecting Cheyenne villages of Black Kettle and White Antelope. The soldiers slaughtered hundreds of Cheyenne people, mostly women and children. Did you know the soldiers scalped and mutilated the bodies of the dead? Some even wore bloody female parts as hatbands. Did you know that one soldier cut off White Antelope's scrotum? He bragged he would use it for a tobacco pouch. Did you know that after the corpses were beheaded, the flesh was removed from many of the skulls and bones, and they were immediately crated up and shipped East. Can you imagine that? The bones of these people were sent off without even bothering to pretend to give them a decent burial? How would people today like it if America's recent enemies in Vietnam, Korea, and Iraq had kept the bodies of American soldiers for dissection and display? It's just creepy. It's like we're second-class citizens."

"You're very articulate," Allison said softly.

"Thanks. I wrote my junior paper on the Sand Creek Massacre."

"When Faulkner takes the witness stand," Bear said, "ask him how the museum got the bones of Bootheel Man. He'll have to admit they were taken from a grave. Get a copy of his book and read it. He wrote all about how the founder of the museum, that Dennison guy, went from place to place, digging up graves. Hell, it's not a book; it's a confession. They should have read the guy his *Miranda* rights before they published it."

"Well, Mr. Smith . . . Bear," Allison said, pointing to a bookshelf, "I did pick up a copy of Clive Faulkner's book yesterday. I read it cover-to-cover last night. Those bones were all unearthed more than a century ago. The statute of limitations for prosecuting any stealing offense has run. Besides, Alfred Dennison found Bootheel Man on his own property. He got permission from all property owners everywhere else he dug. It's an exaggeration to claim anybody at the museum could be prosecuted for stealing those things."

"Maybe so. But you asked what I think of a claim-of-right defense for Joey? I'm telling you it's the best way to go. You're on the right track."

"At some point," Allison said, "I'll probably need someone from the Osage tribe to be an expert witness in court, to talk about the history of the Osages, to connect them to this area at the time Bootheel Man would have been alive. Is that something you could do?"

Bear shook his head. His face darkened. "I'm no expert. I'm not exactly in good standing with the tribal elders, either." He glanced uncomfortably at his daughter. "You don't want to put me on the stand, anyway. I've got a criminal record. My temper sometimes gets me in trouble, and I drink too much. But I can ask around. I can find you an expert."

"Great," said Allison. "Put that on your list of things to do. Right now, let's go get Joey Red Horse out of jail."

Allison Culbertson glanced into her rearview mirror as she pulled her Jeep Cherokee onto the parking lot at the Sheriff's Department. Bear was still following her on his rumbling Harley Davidson motorcycle. His daughter rode next to him on her smaller Harley. Allison parked in one of the empty spaces and met up with them near the parked motorcycles.

Bear gestured toward Allison's sport-utility vehicle.

"Ever wonder whether the Jeep company got permission from the Cherokee Nation to use their name on one of its vehicles?"

"The thought never occurred to me. Did they?"

"Hell, no. But the U.S. government at least *asked* the Apaches before using *their* name on the famous military helicopters." He grinned. "The Apaches gave their permission real quick. They wanted the most bad-ass fighting helicopters in the world named after them."

"How soon do we get to see Joey?" Lolita asked, taking off her helmet and shaking her black hair.

"It won't be long. We've got some more forms to fill out first."

As Allison stood with Bear and Lolita by the two motorcycles, the glass doors of the Sheriff's Department burst open and Harry Sullinger emerged. He was walking with a trim man wearing khaki slacks and a gray polo shirt bearing the emblem of the Missouri State Water Patrol.

Sullinger's eyes widened. He gestured to the motorcycles. "Allison Culbertson, you didn't ride here on one of those things, did you?"

"I might've."

He glanced around the parking lot.

"Nah, that's your Jeep over there." He smiled. "I'm a detective, you know. We notice little details."

"Well," she said. "I'm a lawyer. We notice details, too. What are you doing hanging out with the Missouri Water Patrol?"

"Sorry," he said. "I should've introduced you. This is Jim Taggett. He's with the Water Patrol's dive team. He's in charge of the hunt for Gazing Woman. We're going to see if we can fish her out of the Mississippi."

"What!" Bear's loud voice sounded over Allison's shoulder.

"Why, hello, Bear Smith," Sullinger said. "Haven't seen you for a while. How you been?"

"What do you mean you're going to fish Gazing Woman out of the Mississippi?" Bear asked.

"Well, I don't know if we'll be successful or not, but we're going to give it a try."

"You'll never find her," Bear said. "The river's too deep, the water's too muddy, and the riverbed is too full of valleys and underwater rocks. The current's so treacherous you'll probably kill yourselves. Harry Sullinger, drowned like a rat. What a loss to society."

"Thanks for your kind words," Sullinger said. "All the same, we'll give it our best shot. The Water Patrol's got all sorts of new bells and whistles. Their fancy gizmos find everything from drowning victims to murder weapons. The museum really wants that statue back. Frankly, it might help Joey Red Horse if we do recover it. It would sure cut down on the restitution he'll have to pay."

"Let me know if you find it," Allison said. "I'm officially representing Joey Red Horse now."

Sullinger glanced from her to Bear Smith.

"Yeah," he said. "I sort of figured that out. I guess somebody showed you the money."

Sullinger and Taggett walked across the parking lot and climbed into an F-450 four-wheel-drive dive van emblazoned with the seal of the Missouri State Water Patrol. As it roared off the parking lot, Bear scowled, "I never liked that guy."

"How do you know him?"

"He's the one got me my first felony conviction."

This struck Allison as a conversation stopper.

"I don't know," Lolita said, after a long pause. "He sure is handsome. He's built like Arnold Schwarzenegger, but better looking."

"Put your eyes back in your head," Bear said. "He's too old for you. Just like Joey Red Horse is too old for you. You're still in high school, remember?"

"How could I forget, Dad? You remind me every day."

After the bond paperwork was completed, Allison, Bear, and Lolita waited on hard plastic chairs in the second-floor foyer at the Sheriff's Department for Joey Red Horse to emerge from the depths of the jail. Finally, the heavy remote-controlled doors rumbled noisily open and Joey came out, wearing the jeans and t-shirt Bear had brought for him.

A jailer bid him a friendly farewell and stepped back behind the door as it clanked closed.

They were alone in the foyer.

"Thanks, man," Joey said to Bear. They shook hands.

"You earned it," Bear said. "Your ancestors would be proud."

"The ones on the Osage side, anyway," Joey said.

Joey grinned at Lolita. "Hey, Good-Looking," he said. He studied her CUSTER DIED FOR YOUR SINS t-shirt, obviously appreciating both its message and its strategic presentation on Lolita's attractive body. "Nice shirt! Very cool."

Lolita laughed and hugged him. He kissed her cheek.

"I am so proud of you, Joey," she said. "You'll be as famous as the protestors at Wounded Knee."

Joey Red Horse disengaged from her. The smile left his handsome face. "Time will tell."

He extended his hand to Allison Culbertson. "So, Counselor. You're here. I guess that means you're taking my case?"

"I am."

"Thank you very much," he said.

Allison felt a surge of excitement at the prospect of a looming courtroom battle. "We've got a lot to do to get ready," she said. "I want to learn everything there is to know about Gazing Woman, Bootheel Man, and the Heartland Mound Builder Museum. I want to become an expert on the legal rights of Native Americans in regard to museums, human remains, and burial artifacts."

Joey gripped her hand tightly as he shook it a second time. His eyes glowed with the passion of an evangelical preacher exhorting a congregation of well-heeled sinners.

"I've said it before and I'll say it again. I knew you were the right lawyer for me. Welcome aboard. It is a righteous cause we're fighting! I'm going to make you famous!"

"I'll settle for a nice quiet acquittal," she said.

Chapter 4

Allison Culbertson pulled her Jeep Cherokee onto the parking lot of the Heartland Mound Builder Museum. It had been two days since Joey Red Horse bonded out of jail. The prosecutor's office had not yet given her a copy of the police reports, but she knew Museum Director Clive Faulkner was certain to be a key witness for the prosecution. She had called him and asked permission to come by the museum for a talk. To her surprise, he agreed.

She noticed her reflection on the glittering glass museum door as she walked up the sidewalk: navy-blue J. Crew swishtail skirt, matching lightweight gabardine jacket, pale-blue shirt, open at the collar, and smartly coiffed hair. Well, she looked the part of an experienced lawyer even if she *was* only two years out of law school.

It was a weekday afternoon. She had expected the museum to be practically empty. She was surprised to find dozens of people inside, milling around from exhibit to exhibit. Most appeared to be parents on vacation with their children.

She was early for her meeting with Clive Faulkner, so she decided to browse around the museum alone for a few minutes. She paid the entry fee at the front desk and accepted a map of the museum from the helpful girl behind the counter.

As she walked slowly through the museum, she had to admit that whoever designed it had done a nice job. It was clean and spacious, with great lighting and colorful and fascinating exhibits. She paused a moment in front of a glass case containing a frog-effigy pipe. Made of reddish flint clay, the pipe was six inches long and five inches high. The frog was positioned in the typical frog posture of a pre-jump crouch. Its smooth snout and bulging eyes were incredibly realistic. An attractive oil painting of a Native American man working with flint clay was part of the exhibit, along with a storyboard describing how this particular pipe was created in 1050 to 1200 A.D. and discovered in a mound near Cape Girardeau.

Allison next moved to a glass case exhibiting a chunkey-player effigy pipe. Also made of flint clay, this figurine was nine inches high. It depicted a man getting ready to roll a chunkey stone. He reminded Allison of a bowler. An eye-catching diagram explained that chunkey was a popular game among Native Americans throughout North America, and that the most skillful players often earned tremendous prestige among their peers from their skill at the game, much like modern football, basketball, or baseball stars. The game was played on flat fields created and maintained specifically for that purpose. The fields were usually placed in the center of the village and were often one-hundred feet long and twelve feet wide, made of clay rendered hard and flat by sanding and constant use. The chunkey stone was the size of a small tricycle wheel. The athlete held a long pole in his throwing hand. Although the rules of the game varied from place to place, a chunkey match was usually a contest between two players. One would roll the chunkey stone and both would sprint after it, their eight-foot-long poles poised for the throw. Once they reached a certain spot on the field, each player hurled his spear. A direct hit on the chunkey stone was worth two points. If neither hit it, the player whose stick came to rest closest to the spot where the chunkey stone stopped earned one point. Although the prehistoric people who built the mounds along the Mississippi in the years 900 to 1200 A.D. did not leave written records of their chunkey exploits, explorers who came into contact with Native Americans in 1698 found the native people still enthralled by the game, often betting huge sums on its outcome. Chunkey stones had been found at Mound Builder sites up and down the Mississippi and other inland rivers.

The biggest crowd at the museum gathered in front of the large display case containing Bootheel Man. Spotlights from the top of the exhibit illuminated him like a rock star on a stage as he stood alone in his glass cage. His disarticulated bones had been reassembled and braced so he stood upright. His head was thrown back and his mouth gaped open in a silent scream. At the back of his head, a stone axe the size of a Boy Scout hatchet had punched cleanly through his skull. It was still firmly wedged in the bone.

Allison read the exhibit's storyboard describing how Alfred Dennison, a Cape Girardeau farmer and real-estate developer, had discovered Bootheel Man in 1902 and had thereafter devoted his life to archaeology. A voice behind her spoke.

"Fascinating, isn't it?"

She turned. Clive Faulkner was standing beside her, an amused expression on his face.

"I've written an entire book about that man, but I don't even know the first thing about him as a person," he said. "All I really know is that he walked this earth around 1050 to 1200 A.D., that he was killed by a blow to the head, and that someone liked him enough to bury him with a couple of really exquisite chunkey stones and the beautiful statue we now call Gazing Woman. What's more, I know that by motivating Alfred Dennison to become one of Missouri's greatest archaeologists, this prehistoric man did more than any of his contemporaries to teach our current generation about his era."

He held out his hand. "I'm Clive Faulkner."

She shook his hand. "I know who you are. I'm Allison Culbertson. I'm a bit early for our appointment."

"The early bird gets the client," he said.

She smiled. "I've already got my client. Joey Red Horse."

"So I heard. I forgive you."

He was quite different from what Allison had expected. For one thing, the photograph on the dust jacket of his book didn't do him justice. With the wire-rim glasses and bow tie, the picture made him look like a bookworm. In person, he looked rugged and strikingly handsome. The glasses and bow tie were still there, along with his tweed sport coat, but with his deep tan, his piercing blue eyes, his fit physique, and his powerful jaw, he looked anything but bookwormish.

As he guided her to his private office, he stopped now and then to point out something special about an exhibit.

"President Taft wrote Dennison a note about that one," he said, as they passed another effigy pipe of an athlete rolling a chunkey stone. "Dennison showed it to the President when Taft stopped in Cape Girardeau in 1909. Taft later wrote Dennison, wanting to know if he'd donate it to the government. Taft wanted to present it to Jim Thorpe when Thorpe, a Sac and Fox Indian from Oklahoma Territory, won a bunch of gold medals at the 1912 Olympics. Dennison turned him down. Dennison was nothing if not gutsy. Imagine turning down a request from the President of the United States."

"I would think it might depend upon the president, and upon the request," Allison said, thinking of alleged oval-office trysts.

"Another amusing thing about that story," Faulkner continued, opening his office door for her, "is that when Thorpe won all those gold medals for the United States, he wasn't even an American citizen. Another dozen years passed before American Indians were granted U.S. citizenship. So we had an American hero who wasn't even a citizen of his country. Most people don't know that."

Faulkner's private office presented a sharp contrast to the immaculate orderliness of the rest of the museum. It was strewn with piles of books and boxes of artifacts. A foot-tall stack of *American Antiquity* journals perched precariously on one corner of his desk. An enlarged photograph of Clive Faulkner at an excavation site covered the wall behind him. One shelf of his bookcase was devoted to copies of his own book: *Alfred Dennison and the Bootheel Man*. A small, framed photograph of an attractive blonde sat on the credenza behind his desk.

"I hope you're not allergic to clutter," he said.

"If I were, I'd be dead by now. Self-inflicted."

When they were seated, he spoke somewhat nervously. "When you called, I wasn't sure I *should* meet with you. If you're representing Joey Red Horse, you're in the enemy camp."

She crossed her legs.

"You and I aren't necessarily enemies," she said. "We simply have different outlooks on what we'd like to see happen to Joey Red Horse."

"I want justice from the court system," Clive Faulkner said. "I get aggravated sometimes when I read how serious cases get plea-bargained down to nothing but a slap on the wrist. Something's got to happen to this guy so other people don't get the idea to break into my museum. Once is enough."

He pointed to an oil painting on the wall. It depicted a middle-aged man in a safari hat and a short-sleeved khaki shirt.

"I think the place to start is for me to tell you about the museum's founder, Alfred Dennison. Care to hear more about him?"

"Certainly."

Faulkner stood up and moved to the oil painting.

"He was one of the greatest philanthropists and amateur archaeologists who ever lived. He had a brilliant mind, always curious, always wanting to learn. He devoured a new subject like an intellectual feast. He inherited a big family farm and made a ton of money as a farmer, but he amassed an even bigger fortune as a real-estate developer. Suddenly, in midlife, he got the urge to dig up an Indian mound on a piece of his property in Cape Girardeau, just to see what was there. He found Bootheel Man, and the rest is history."

Allison couldn't help but be moved by the passion in Clive Faulkner's voice. He clearly idolized Dennison.

"A lot of men," Faulkner continued, "would have sold those bones and relics to collectors, but not him. He consulted the leading archaeologists of his era and learned how to go about excavating the site in the most scientific way. His goal was to create a museum that would tell the people of today what life must have been like for the Mound Builders. The artifacts he uncovered on his own property were enough to make his museum one of the most important Mound Builder teaching centers in the country, but he didn't stop with the ones he found in Cape Girardeau. He sold his real-estate business and took up archaeology full time. He bought a boat he named *The Relentless Digger*, and went up and down the Mississippi River, locating and excavating mounds created by these ancient people. When he died, he left every penny he owned to a trust to keep the museum going. I'm its second director since his death."

"He sounds like quite a guy."

"He was quite a guy. The Mississippian Period covers those people who lived in the valley of the Mississippi River and in the southeastern states from about 600 A.D. To 1500 A.D., when the Europeans arrived. Alfred Dennison's work taught us more than any other person's about these people. People flock to this museum from all over the country, all over the world, in fact. We have interns from the local college working here year-round, plus students from summer archaeological programs nationwide. The quality of our exhibits is outstanding. We're not just some tiny little sideshow running on a shoestring budget. We're a first-class operation."

"You have a right to be proud. The museum's impressive," Allison said. "May I ask you a few questions, though?"

"I assume that's why you're here."

"First of all, how did the thief get in? Was there forced entry?"

"You might call it that. Your client threw a concrete block through our front door. Not exactly subtle. We replaced it the next day."

"Did he set off any sort of burglar alarm?"

"As a matter of fact, he did. We've got the windows and doors wired, plus a motion detector. The alarm went crazy when he broke the glass door."

"Why didn't the police catch him inside?"

"That's a good question. You'll have to ask them. I know I did. More than once."

"What time did the break-in occur?"

"About four in the morning. It was still dark. Your client would have gotten away with it if he hadn't called the police at noon that same day, bragging about it and telling them to meet him at the bridge. He called me, too, but the police advised me not to meet him. They weren't sure what he had in mind, whether he was a terrorist or a kook planning to assassinate me."

"Why would anybody want to assassinate *you*?"

"Well, there's lots of crazy people in the world. Among Native Americans, feelings can run pretty high these days against museums still displaying Native American skeletons."

A knock sounded at the door, and a visitor burst in without waiting for an invitation from Faulkner.

She was an attractive blonde, mid-thirties, wearing jeans and a cutoff red Southeast Missouri State University Redhawks t-shirt speckled with multicolored spots of paint.

"Oh," she said, looking flustered when she saw Allison. "I didn't know you had company."

"That's okay, Diedra," he said, rising to his feet. "Let me introduce you to Allison Culbertson."

As Faulkner made the introductions, Allison noticed that Diedra Binzinger was the same woman in the photo on Faulkner's credenza.

"Diedra's an artist," Faulkner said. "She has a studio in downtown Cape. She helps me out with the preparation of some of our exhibits." He beckoned for Diedra to sit down.

"I can't stay," Diedra said. "We can talk later."

"Ms. Culbertson's the lawyer for the Indian who stole Gazing Woman," Faulkner said.

Diedra Binzinger turned sharply to Allison. "*Why* did he do it? *Why* did he throw such a valuable piece of artwork into the river?"

Allison shrugged. "I guess you probably heard his remarks on TV. He did it because he doesn't think Native American bones and funereal objects should be put on display in museums. I don't think I'm divulging any attorney-client secrets by repeating what he publicly said right before he jumped. His televised confession has already run coast-to-coast."

Diedra Binzinger still didn't sit down. "Is it true the police are trying to find the statue in the river?"

"That's what I hear," Allison said. "Seems to me they're looking for a needle in a haystack."

"My thoughts precisely," Faulkner said, "although I certainly appreciate their efforts. I'd love to get our exhibit back."

Diedra Binzinger moved to the door. "I'm sorry to have interrupted you, Ms. Culbertson. Clive, are we still on for dinner tonight?"

"Certainly."

"See you then," she said, closing the door as she left.

"She seems nice," Allison said. "Where's her studio?"

"It's in the one-hundred block of Main Street. She's really talented, in all sorts of mediums, from oils to watercolors to ceramics. You should check out her gallery sometime."

"I will," Allison said. "She's right down the street from my office. I'm embarrassed to admit I've never bothered to peek inside. I guess I'm a bit culturally challenged."

"Well, where were we?" Clive Faulkner asked.

"I was about to ask you why you haven't removed the American Indian bones and burial objects from your museum. Lots of other museums have done so."

"Bootheel Man and the other skeletons and burial artifacts are the heart and soul of my museum. Giving away our skeletons and burial artifacts would basically empty us out. Without them, we'd have little reason to exist. Other museums cover several aspects of local history, like steamboating and the Civil War. We focus solely on the Mound Builders. We're just lucky we never accepted any federal money. Otherwise the Native American Graves Protection and Repatriation Act would apply to us, and we'd be suffering devastating modern-day Indian raids, if you'll pardon the pun."

Allison did not smile. "Doesn't it bother you that American Indians find it hurtful to have their ancestors laid out on display?"

He sighed heavily. "Let me assure you, I've given the matter a great deal of thought. First of all, a real question exists as to *which* current Native Americans are really related to the Mound Builders of the Mississippian Period, if any. Nobody has yet established a 100-percent-certain link through DNA testing or anything like that. We know which tribes were in this area during historic times, but we don't really know which ones were here during the specific times the mounds were built. There are currently about 570 federally recognized Indian tribes in the United States. Who's going to say which tribe would get Bootheel Man if the museum would decide to give him back? Which tribe would determine where he was to be buried, or whether he should be kept on display in one of their own museums or even a casino? It's not as simple as people like your client make it sound."

Allison bristled. "Your crack about casinos is an insult to my client, very disrespectful. No tribe would *ever* consider putting Bootheel Man or other burial objects on display in a casino or anywhere else. Joey just wants him to get a decent burial."

"I understand that, but it's not his choice."

Allison changed the subject. She had come for information, not an argument. "When did you first hear about the break-in?"

"The alarm company called right after they notified the police. It was 4:04 A.M. when I got the call. I've still got it on my caller ID."

"Did you go right down to the museum?"

"Sure did."

"Was anything besides Gazing Woman missing?"

"No, and I did a complete inventory."

"How much is Gazing Woman worth? It can make a difference on the level of the charge. The prosecutor has charged a Class B felony, meaning he has to prove she's worth at least twenty-five-thousand dollars."

"Oh, she's worth far more than that. She's a one-of-a-kind piece of art. One-thousand years old. There's no doubt her fair market value would be at least one-hundred-thousand dollars."

"Who buys something like that?"

"Legally? Other museums. Illegally? Collectors. Worldwide, I'm sure there are far more pieces in private collections than in museums. That's where the real money is made on these things."

"Where do these collectors come from?"

"I'm told there's a big demand for black-market Native American artwork in Japan, China, Indonesia, Colombia, and other South American countries."

"What do South Americans want with our relics? Don't they have the Mayan stuff?"

"That's exactly what I thought," he said, smiling. "Turns out lots of rich collectors in South America want to add *North* American relics to their private collections. They'll pay big money, too."

"What would you think about probation, if my client were to plead guilty?"

"Probation? No way! I don't like it. First of all, it doesn't send much of a message to the public. This museum can't afford to be losing its exhibits. These are public treasures, irreplaceable. This has got to be a case where if you do the crime, you do the time."

Allison uncrossed her legs, aware that he was looking at them. "Well, I think I've covered everything," she said. "Can you think of anything else I should know to do an adequate job for my client?"

"Is *adequate* all you aspire to be?" His eyes twinkled. "You should always strive for excellence."

He walked over to a bookshelf and pulled out a copy of his book *Alfred Dennison and the Bootheel Man*.

"Here, I want you to have this."

Allison decided not to tell him she had already bought and read a copy. She would let him go on underestimating her.

He returned to his desk, opened the cover of the book, and quickly scribbled an inscription.

When he passed it across the desktop she read what he had written: "To Allison Culbertson, the most breathtaking lawyer I have ever met. Never settle for mere adequacy! May you be the next Clarence Darrow, but prettier! Best Wishes, Clive Faulkner."

"Thanks," she said, standing up. "Let's hope you still feel the same way about me when this case is over."

Chapter 5

Allison Culbertson yelled at Harry Sullinger, trying to get his attention. "Hey, Sullinger! Over here! Come here for a second!"

The Cape Girardeau Police Department had temporarily blocked eastbound travel over the Mississippi River bridge. Allison had walked to the bridge from her nearby office and was standing at the barricade. The uniformed officer, although polite, had refused to let her past his position.

Harry Sullinger was wearing a black t-shirt and black multi-pocketed tactical pants. He was standing with a uniformed Missouri State Water Patrol officer in the area where Joey Red Horse had jumped from the bridge. Beneath the bridge, two 18-foot Water Patrol boats crammed full of officers and scuba divers lingered like crocodiles waiting for Captain Hook to fall into the water.

Sullinger noticed Allison and sauntered over to the barricade.

"Spying on me?" he asked. "Or just hanging around to see if you'll catch a glimpse of a good-looking guy in a swimsuit?"

She snorted; she hoped with derision. "Actually, I heard about all the boats down here. I figured it must have something to do with my client."

"Well, Sherlock, as a matter of fact, we *are* here because of your client. Been here all day. We're looking for that darn statue. We're going to find it, eventually. Got a surefire plan. Just takes time."

"May I watch?" she asked.

"Be my guest. Get some popcorn and make yourself comfortable over there on the waterfront."

"I mean on your side of the barricade."

He pursed his lips. "Well, that wouldn't exactly be standard procedure, having the defense lawyer help recover evidence for the prosecution." He gave her a sly glance. "Promise not to touch anything?"

She eyed his muscular biceps. "I think I can resist."

"I'll bet you can." He shrugged. "Well, why not? We'd eventually have to give you a copy of our police reports, anyway. This way you won't have to bother reading them, because you'll already know what they say."

He helped her step over the sawhorse barricade, holding her elbow as she scissored her legs over the wooden barrier. She was glad she had worn slacks.

"You have a nice kick," he said.

"Like a mule. Don't mess with me."

The big Missouri Water Patrol dive van was parked on the bridge, next to Joey's jumping-off spot. Its cargo doors were open. Sullinger led her to it. They were joined by the Water Patrol officer, Jim Taggett. He wore a black Water Patrol baseball cap above his gray polo shirt and khaki pants.

A small television and video-recording unit was set up in the back of the van. Sullinger hit the play button.

"Here's a copy of the KFVS tape of Joey's big adventure. There he is, standing on the ledge at the side of the bridge. Okay, there goes his cell phone. Plunk. Now, watch closely. Using this tape, we can pinpoint exactly where Gazing Woman went into the river."

"I suppose that's where you've been looking?" Allison said.

"Right," Sullinger said, "but the water's so muddy, the divers can't see a thing underwater. Plus, the current's so powerful they can't stay in one place for any length of time. They're in constant danger of being banged against some hidden hazard like a boulder or sunken tree. The bottom of that river is not some pristine, sandy ocean-bottom, but a muddy and uneven valley. It's treacherous. Before we give up, though, we're going to look at every inch of that river-bottom within one-hundred yards of the bridge, using under-water sonar."

"Underwater sonar? How does that work?"

"Tell her, Taggett," Sullinger said. "It's your toy."

The veteran Water Patrol officer pointed to one of the boats under the bridge. "See that yellow torpedo-shaped thing the boat's pulling? It's shooting sonar rays to the bottom of the river. A computer in the boat gives us a picture of that part of the river-bottom. It's not as clear as a regular photograph, but we can spot all sorts of things, like bicycles, tires, cars, and dead bodies."

"Can it spot something as small as a twelve-inch-tall statue?" Allison asked.

"We've found handguns and concrete blocks this way. Unless it's already buried in the muck, I don't see any reason why we won't be able to find it. The good news is that the water under the bridge is not as deep as you'd think."

"I thought the Mississippi was really deep," Allison said.

"It is, some places," Taggett said. "Up by Cape Rock, the channel's about ninety feet deep. Lots of murder weapons stay hidden forever in the mud down there. But under the bridge, the deepest part of the channel is only about seventeen feet deep. Over by the riverbank, it's only seven feet."

"What do you do if you spot something that looks like it might be Gazing Woman?" Allison said.

"We mark it and swim to it."

"Sounds dangerous." She looked at Taggett and nodded toward Sullinger. "Has the big guy been in the water?"

Taggett smirked. "We've been trying to get him wet. So far, he's just stayed in the boat. He's not near as tough as he looks."

Sullinger grinned. "You're the outfit with the word 'water' in the name of your organization. I'm staying dry unless it's a life or death situation."

"Seems like you're spending a lot of time, trouble, and risk just to recover one piece of evidence," Allison said.

"We're here to serve and protect," Sullinger sighed. "Besides, the Heartland Mound Builder Museum is important to Cape Girardeau. Brings tourists from all over. We're doing a significant community service by recovering one of its most important and irreplaceable exhibits."

"If you find it, you're sort of raining on Joey's parade," she said.

"Exactly, but that's merely a fringe benefit."

"May I ride along in one of the boats?"

Taggett shrugged. "That's up to Sullinger."

"Please, Harry?" she asked, batting her eyelashes at him.

Allison felt like a dog hanging out of a car window as the breeze whipped her hair around her face. She enjoyed the feel of warm summer air beating on her cheeks. She was sitting next to Harry Sullinger at the front of the Water Patrol's eighteen-foot-long aluminum johnboat, facing backwards. A redheaded Water Patrol officer manned the controls at the rear of the boat, steering as they made their way slowly upriver. Jim Taggett sat next to the redhead, staring at the color monitor of the yellow plastic-encased, splash-proof computer. A cable led from the computer to the bright yellow torpedo-shaped tube they were pulling. The tube was about a yard long and had a fin at its tail end.

Another boat filled with divers followed them. It was similar to their boat, except for its platform for the divers. Both boats bore the seal of the Missouri State Water Patrol in the middle of each side.

The boats were a surprisingly far distance north of the Bill Emerson Memorial Bridge.

"I don't think Joey threw it this far," Allison said.

Sullinger disagreed. "You look at the television newscast, he did."

"Hey, there's another tire," Taggett interrupted, pointing to the computer screen. He turned it around so Allison could see it.

Allison stared at the monitor. Sure enough, in the middle of the brown-tinted screen, she saw the shadowy but unmistakable image of a tire. "I see it," she said. "What's that thing moving right next to it?"

Taggett swiveled the computer screen to face him. "Looks like a big old catfish," he said. "That sucker's got to be three feet long."

"Say, this thing would be handy for fishing," Sullinger mused.

"You're not the first person who ever thought of that," Taggett said.

Allison watched Taggett as he studied the computer monitor. He held a photograph of Gazing Woman in one hand and occasionally compared it to the images on his computer screen.

"Most of these things are just rocks," he said. "I'm looking at them real close today. We might have passed over it yesterday without realizing what we were seeing. One thing we know for sure, it's down there somewhere. It didn't swim away. Hey, look at this!"

He turned the computer screen so Allison could see it again. She spotted an unusual geometric image on the screen.

"What is it?" she asked.

"Looks like a boat trailer," Taggett said. "I imagine there's an interesting story how that thing ended up on the bottom of the river." Taggett turned the computer monitor back to face him and squinted at the screen.

"How often does your dive team get called out?" Allison asked.

"Around forty times a year," he said, without looking up. "I think we logged eighteen-hundred hours in dive operations last year, mostly looking for dead bodies or murder weapons. I'd much rather be looking for a stolen statue, like today. It'll be a whole lot nicer touching a little statue in the blackness down below instead of a cold corpse."

Allison scrunched up her face.

"I suppose so." She took a deep breath, liking the smell of the river. "How many members of the dive team *are* there?"

"Eleven, statewide. We're scattered all over. We're not all here today. This job didn't require everybody."

Allison glanced at Harry Sullinger. "This reminds me of waiting for a jury verdict," she said. "You wait around, knowing something exciting will happen any minute, but there's nothing you can do to speed things up."

They made several trips up and down the river, back and forth underneath the bridge. Finally, Taggett tapped the computer screen excitedly. "That could be it!"

The boat slowed to a standstill and all three of them stared at the monitor. Taggett glanced at his photograph and looked back at the screen. "Yeah, this looks promising. That could be it, if it's standing straight up. Let's mark it."

Taggett used the digital global positioning system feature of the computer network to note the exact location of the unknown object. Afterward, he and Sullinger lifted a fifty-gallon plastic trash can and lowered it carefully into the water.

"What are you doing?" Allison asked.

"We've got an anchor fastened inside this trash can," Sullinger explained. "We also attached a buoy to it to float above it. More importantly, we've got a line fastened to it for the divers to use to swim directly to it underwater."

Once the trash can was on the river-bottom, Allison spotted it on the computer screen.

"According to the global positioning system, the trash can is fifteen feet upriver from the bump we think might be the statue," Taggett said. "Time to send in the divers."

Both boats started upriver, toward the Missouri shore.

"Why don't they just jump into the water from the boats?" Allison asked. "They were right above it."

"Current's too strong," Taggett explained. "If they start from the shoreline, they can get to the bottom right away. They'll be underneath the worst part of the current as they swim out to the spot. Two divers follow the cable all the way from the shoreline to the underwater trash can. Once there, they use it as a reference point. One diver stays near the trash can. The other makes slow U-shaped sweeps, feeling every inch of the river-bottom. We intentionally dropped the trash can north of the spot we want to check. The diver starts near the trash can and gradually works his way south, gliding with the current, not against it."

Sullinger handed the line to the two divers on shore. Both wore black wetsuits, yellow flippers, yellow masks, and yellow scuba tanks. Moments later, they disappeared into the water. A third diver sat on the shoreline, near the anchored cable.

"Why isn't he going along?" Allison asked.

"He's the safety diver," Taggett said. "If the others get in trouble, he'll go out to help them. Like me, he'll be listening to the divers with headphones. We'll hear everything they say."

Taggett ordered the boat to return to the spot where the buoy marked the place they wanted the divers to search. The second boat followed them, ready to take the divers aboard at the end of the dive.

Fascinated, Allison watched as one of the divers, swinging like a pendulum, moved slowly back and forth across the computer screen.

"Remember," Taggett said, "he can't see a thing down there. He's going strictly by feel."

"Try moving to your right, Wayne," Taggett said into his microphone. "Whatever I'm looking at is still a bit to your right."

"This is exciting!" Allison said. "Reminds me of pin-the-tail-on-the-donkey."

Sullinger grinned. "I hope you're not billing your client for the time you're out here having fun. What do you charge, a hundred dollars an hour?"

Allison scowled at him. "More than that. But it hadn't even occurred to me to bill Joey for riding in a boat and watching the great Harry Sullinger in action," she said. "I *am* having fun, actually. I won't be sending Joey a bill for today."

Suddenly, the diver ceased his crablike crawl and remained stationary, his hands and arms out of sight beneath him.

"What's he doing now?" Allison asked.

"He's found something," Taggett said, excitement creeping into his voice. "I can't tell what it is."

The diver began swimming for the surface. The strong current pulled him downriver from the boat. When he broke the surface, he thrust Gazing Woman high above his head as if he were holding an Olympic torch. "I found her!"

The cops and water patrol officers on both boats broke into cheers.

"Congratulations," Allison said. "I never thought you'd find it."

"I'm sure nobody did," Sullinger said, "especially not your client."

Still perched in the boat, Allison was fifty feet from the diver who held Gazing Woman aloft. The effigy of the beautiful girl appeared to be in tact. At least, from this distance she could spot no damage. What a history this statue was acquiring! From being buried with a dead body for one-thousand years, to being stolen, to being thrown to the bottom of the Mississippi River, to being recovered from its muddy depths by modern underwater sonar equipment, this lovely piece of art was building quite a resume. She felt a connection to Gazing Woman. She was part of its history. It was a beautiful moment, one she knew she was unlikely to forget.

Like the others on the boat, Allison stood up and moved to the port side, facing the diver. Once everyone gathered on the same side, gravity took over and the aluminum boat lurched precariously toward the water.

"Look out!" someone yelled.

As the men threw themselves backward to avoid capsizing, Allison found herself being catapulted into the water, face-first. Her initial sensation was panic, but she reminded herself that she was a good swimmer and that professional divers in both boats were nearby. She struggled to the surface, bothered by the fact that her feet were encased in shoes.

She was amazed by how quickly the current caught her.

When she looked around, she was already a good forty feet from the nearest boat. She kicked off her shoes, reflecting sadly that they were Prada pumps that cost several billable hours. She called for help.

At the back of the boat, she spotted Harry Sullinger. He was facing her. At least someone knew she had gone overboard.

But he was laughing.

The other men on the boats were busy welcoming Gazing Woman aboard the johnboat. If they had noticed her departure, they didn't seem to care.

Great, she thought, spitting river water from her mouth, *the Missouri State Water Patrol is saving a rock statue while a real-life person is drowning right under their noses!*

Not Harry Sullinger, though. He was ignoring the commotion over the prehistoric statue. He was focused on her.

Well, this is going to be ironic, she thought. *He saved my client from drowning in the Mississippi, and now he's going to save his client's lawyer.*

She pictured Harry Sullinger wrapping his big arms around her and pulling her to safety. He did have the most muscular arms she'd ever seen.

This might be fun, she told herself, surprised by her unbidden thought.

"Help!" she called out again. She watched Harry Sullinger, waiting for him to dive into the water. Heck, he leaped off the Bill Emerson Memorial Bridge and plummeted sixty feet to the water. Jumping from the boat should be nothing to him.

She wondered if he would take off his shirt. She wouldn't mind one bit if he did. She recalled from representing his ex-wife that he'd won several bodybuilding competitions. Was he still in buff condition? She would soon find out.

He bent down. She supposed he was stripping to his swim trunks. This was going to be interesting.

What was taking so long? If he didn't hurry, she really would need saving.

When he rose, he was holding a big white life preserver on a rope. He hurled it like a supersized Frisbee. It landed behind her with a whap.

"Grab it!" he yelled.

Dutifully, she caught the rope with her hand. Moments later, she was clutching the life preserver and he was pulling her toward the boat like a hooked fish.

As she neared the side of the johnboat, she saw that Gazing Woman had been momentarily forgotten. Every man on both boats was doubled up with laughter.

When she had been reeled to the side of the boat, Sullinger grasped each of her wrists and effortlessly lifted her out of the water. As he lowered her feet to the deck, the two of them stood pressed together for a moment, belly to belly. She was dripping wet. Her hair clung to her head. Water dripped from her nose.

"You should be more careful," he said.

She stepped away from him.

"Does anybody have a towel?"

One of the Water Patrol officers tossed her one.

She was keenly aware that her wet blouse had been a bit too flimsy to get soaked and leave her any modesty. The officers on both boats were suddenly becoming extremely solicitous of her welfare. The second boat had pulled alongside, and men in each johnboat were giving her their full attention, in spite of the fact that Jim Taggett was at the front of her boat, holding Gazing Woman. Apparently, trembling flesh and blood was more fascinating than stone-cold flint clay.

"Here," Sullinger said, handing her a life vest. "I guess you should've put this on a bit sooner."

"Right," she said, thankful for the coverage it provided as she strapped the big orange life vest over her wet shirt.

The attention of the officers immediately switched back to Gazing Woman. Allison and Sullinger were left alone at the front of the boat.

"You *could* have jumped into the water to save me," she said as she toweled her hair.

He snorted. "In lifesaving, it's standard practice to throw an object to someone in distress before going in yourself. You only go in the water as a last resort."

"Well, heaven forbid you should get wet on my account."

He handed her another towel. "Allison Culbertson, as much as I would enjoy grabbing you and dragging you through the water, frankly, I've swallowed enough river water for one week." He chuckled. "Hey, guys," he called out to the other officers. "What do you call one lawyer sinking to the bottom of the Mississippi River?"

"A good start!" three of them chorused in unison, guffawing loudly.

"It's an old joke," he apologized.

When he smiled, deep dimples formed in each of his cheeks. He really was a handsome man. It was a shame those five divorces loomed like shipwrecks warning other boats to pick a different channel.

Chapter 6

Allison Culbertson put down the article from the *American Indian Law Review* and rubbed her eyes. She was sitting at her office desk, the only light in the room coming from her desk lamp. She had not yet closed the curtains of the panoramic window overlooking the Mississippi River. The long sheet of glass shone like black obsidian. At its south end, the lights of the Bill Emerson Memorial Bridge were visible in the distance, glowing like an enormous carnival ride. She recalled hearing that the $100-million bridge was bedecked with hundreds of decorative lights, each paid for by private donors. All were ablaze tonight.

She rubbed her eyes again. She'd been reading for four hours straight, ever since sharing the pepperoni pizza with Joey Red Horse and Lolita Smith in her law library.

Something made her think of Clive Faulkner's comment about Alfred Dennison devouring a new subject *like an intellectual feast*. Allison related to Dennison because she felt the same drive in herself. When something piqued her intellectual curiosity, particularly a new area of the law, she threw herself into mastering it. That was why she had been so successful in her scholastic career: valedictorian in high school, Honors College as an undergraduate, Law Review and National Appellate Advocacy finalist in law school. She had a knack for enforcing tunnel vision upon herself. But "enforcing" wasn't the right word; she embraced it, relished it.

Since hiring on as Joey Red Horse's lawyer, her tunnel vision had focused on the legal conflict between museums and American Indians over what should be done with the skeletons and burial relics housed in the museums. How was it she had never heard a word about this fascinating subject before meeting Joey Red Horse? The whole topic was captivating. She had been particularly entertained by some of the terrific titles in the scholarly publications. The authors displayed unusual creativity for academic works. She had just finished reading a law-review article by Michelle Hibbert bearing the catchy title "Galileos or Grave Robbers? Science, the Native American Graves Protection and Repatriation Act, and the First Amendment." Another excellent one was the book *Skull Wars: Kennewick Man, Archaeology, and the Battle For Native American Identity* by David Hurst Thomas. Her favorite title, though, belonged to the book by Kathleen S. Fine-Dare. The witty anthropology professor had encapsulated the entire subject matter with just two words: *Grave Injustice*.

Allison Culbertson had devoured a stack of books, law-review articles, and appellate cases, hoping to find something that might help her defend Joey. It was a scary and weighty responsibility, having someone's freedom depending upon your skill at legal research and trial advocacy.

The claim-of-right defense offered her client his best hope. Somehow, when the case came to trial, she had to make jurors feel the grave injustice inflicted on American Indians by museums placing the bones of their ancestors on display. She hoped the trial judge would give her some leeway on admitting evidence about the way these bones had been collected. If she could somehow get before the jury the story of the Sand Creek Massacre and how the skulls of those women and children ended up at the Army Medical Museum in Washington DC, it would be a huge boost to the defense.

"Grave robbers or Galileos?" she doodled on her legal pad. Grave robbery would need to play a big part in her trial strategy and closing argument.

She put down her pen.

Her best defense in this case would be to brand Alfred Dennison a grave robber. She had read Clive Faulkner's book on Dennison. Twice. She admired Dennison tremendously. This selfless man had used his entire fortune in his effort to learn more about prehistoric civilization along the Mississippi River. He'd devoted both his life and his money to creating a museum that still brought pleasure and knowledge to men, women, and children many years after his death. Her job would be to belittle him as a grave robber, looter, and defiler of sacred burial grounds. Her mission was to convince a jury that since Dennison had stolen the bones and artifacts from graves in the first place, her client was justified in believing he had a right to take them back.

60

She *would* brand Alfred Dennison a grave robber, but it would be somewhat painful for her to do so because she and he were kindred souls.

Yes, kindred souls. She, too, liked a good intellectual feast, and perhaps that characteristic had cost her much happiness in her life. *You choose your paths*, she realized. *You could never know where the untrod path might have taken you. If you had gone out for beer and pizza every now and then, instead of studying those extra hours at the law library, would you have met that one special guy? Would you now be married, with children? Or would you merely have failed to make law review?* Life never provided the answers. The roads not traveled were shrouded in impenetrable mist.

She could not help but notice that Dennison had never married and that he had died leaving no heirs. It was somewhat ironic. Here was a man tremendously engrossed in history and in lost peoples, yet he had let his own family tree die off with himself. Was it because of his need for the thrill of an intellectual feast? Had he simply never made time for courtship or friendship or interaction with others? Was this need for an intellectual feast an addiction for some people? For her? Did it prevent and obstruct other human emotions and relationships? Was it a roadblock to love?

Again, she saw parallels to her own life. She was now twenty-seven years old. Except for a brief and embarrassing fling during her second year of college, she'd never had a serious relationship. She was always focused on the next goal, the next achievement, the current intellectual feast. If she were a client needing a lawyer, she definitely was the attorney she would choose. Nobody could ever research a topic better or harder. The realization made her glow with pride. But what if she were a child needing a mother or a man needing a wife? She would not pick herself. It was sad but true.

She heard laughter coming from her law library. Joey Red Horse and Lolita Smith were evidently still there.

Joey had proved to be one of the most helpful clients in the history of the attorney-client relationship. From day one he had provided her with a reading list on American Indian history and issues, starting with *Bury My Heart at Wounded Knee* by Dee Brown, *Repatriation Reader: Who Owns American Indian Remains?* by Devon A. Mihesuah, and *Custer Died For Your Sins* by Vine Deloria Jr. When she ran across additional references to the Mound Builders or to the Native American Graves Protection and Repatriation Act or to Alfred Dennison or to the Heartland Mound Builder Museum, she simply let Joey know the titles of the books or periodicals she needed and he hunted them down for her. He was better than any intern or research assistant because he knew that his freedom hung on the outcome of her work. Talk about diligence! Joey and Lolita were in the law library now, reading articles she had assembled, highlighting things they thought were potentially important. They were a huge help to her.

She sighed and stood up. It was probably time to call it a night. Her intellectual feasting was over for this particular evening. Still, she felt satisfied that she had been exposed to lots of new ideas and information.

When she opened the door to the law library, she received an additional bit of exposure. Joey Red Horse and Lolita Smith were entwined on top of her conference table, locked in a loving embrace. Since many key clothing items had been removed, she got a completely new and revealing view of Indian affairs.

"Joey!" she exclaimed. "Get off of her!"

To their credit, her client and his research partner were just as embarrassed as she, if not more so. They hurriedly buttoned and zipped.

"I can't believe you would behave this way at my office!" Allison said. "This is a law office, not a Motel 6!"

"Sorry," Joey said. "We didn't plan it. It just happened."

"Joey, you should be ashamed of yourself! She's only seventeen!"

"It was my idea," Lolita said. "We're in love."

"She's legal," Joey offered. "She's old enough."

"Well, what would her father think, Joey? After he put up your bond? Is this the way you thank him?"

Joey hung his head. "You're not going to tell him, are you?"

"I'm not going to tell anybody. But next time the two of you do research at my office, both of you keep your feet on the floor and the library door open."

As Joey and Lolita headed out, the girl paused and apologized. "I'm sorry, Ms. Culbertson. It really *was* all my fault. Joey tried to say no, but he couldn't resist." She smiled sweetly, a touch of pride in her brown eyes. "I promise you it won't happen again, at least not at your office."

As they left, Allison plopped down onto one of her library chairs. She was feeling old and tired.

Her thoughts went involuntarily to Clive Faulkner and Harry Sullinger. She wondered what each of them was doing right at that moment. Were they enjoying something better than an intellectual feast?

It was ironic that the two most interesting men she had met in a very long time were both going to be witnesses for the prosecution in one of her cases. Her job would be to attack them.

"Just my luck," she said aloud. "You never make a friend with a good cross-examination of him."

When the case was over, if she did her job well and managed to get Joey Red Horse acquitted, both men would probably hate her guts.

Chapter 7

Allison Culbertson rose to her feet as Associate Circuit Judge Wallace Portell took the bench to preside over the preliminary hearing in Joey's case. The judge was sporting a recent haircut, perhaps because he had granted the requests of both the *Southeast Missourian* newspaper and KFVS-12 TV to allow cameras in the courtroom.

"The court calls the case of *State of Missouri v. Joseph Michael Red Horse*. The defendant appears in person and by counsel, Allison Culbertson. The State appears by Prosecuting Attorney John Marshall Plimpton," Judge Portell announced, glancing at Allison. His face remained inscrutable but they shared a silent communication marking the significance of actually seeing the elected prosecutor in court. John Marshall Plimpton was more of a politician than a prosecutor. He normally delegated the trial work of his office to his assistants. The standing joke was that the only way to lure him to a courtroom was to give him a case that was both ironclad and dripping with media coverage. Allison was not surprised to see the prosecutor personally handling Joey's prosecution. It certainly passed the two-part test. He was not even letting any of his assistant prosecutors share the counsel table with him.

"Any pretrial matters on behalf of the State?" the judge asked.

"No, Your Honor."

"What about you, Ms. Culbertson? Any preliminary matters?"

"The defense invokes the rule on witnesses."

"Very well," the judge said. "Anyone subpoenaed as a witness in this case is ordered to leave the courtroom. The witnesses will appear and testify one at a time. Mr. Plimpton, you may call your first witness."

"The State calls Clive Faulkner."

Allison glanced at her client. Joey Red Horse was sitting next to her. She still had not completely recovered from her shock at his wardrobe selection. He was wearing a long-sleeved, bright blue shirt, mid-thigh length. Around his waist, he wore a five-inch wide beaded belt, adorned with a colorful pattern of stripes and geometric shapes. Matching beaded armbands encircled his arms, just above his elbows. Although it probably appeared to the judge that Joey was wearing pants, he was actually wearing a breechcloth and leggings. The soft deer-hide breechcloth went between his legs, with its aprons hanging down in front and back. Fringed leather leggings covered each leg from thigh to ankle. They were tan, with a green stripe down each outer side, large stars embroidered onto the stripes. He wore beaded moccasins on his feet. His chest was covered by a breastplate made of rows of horizontal white bones, each a quarter-inch to a half-inch in diameter. He wore a matching choker on his neck, consisting of four rows of bones running horizontally around his neck, with a circular freshwater mussel shell in the middle of the choker, directly under his chin. His outfit had been entirely his own idea. He had not bothered to alert her to his plan to wear traditional tribal dress to court. She would probably have tried to talk him out of it. Judge Portell was a stickler for proper attire in the courtroom. His posted sign, however, only expressly forbid shorts. It said nothing about breechcloths.

What he doesn't know won't hurt him, Allison thought to herself, thankful that Joey's shirt was so long.

Allison was decked out in a brand-new Diane von Furstenberg Mittise jacket and matching Dali skirt. The tailored cotton jacquard knit suit had cost a fortune, but Allison had figured she could probably count on one hand the number of times her courtroom appearances would ever be televised, so she splurged for the occasion.

Joey was glaring at Clive Faulkner as the museum director made his way to the witness stand.

A court reporter sat near the witness box. Allison had hired her. A preliminary hearing is not a full-blown trial but merely a probable-cause hearing. The prosecution need only call enough witnesses to prove the elements of the crime by probable cause, not by proof beyond a reasonable doubt. Joey was charged with burglary, stealing, and resisting arrest. The state could undoubtedly show probable cause by merely presenting the testimony of Clive Faulkner and Harry Sullinger. By having the court reporter record their testimony, the hearing would give Allison a chance to pin down the testimony of two key witnesses, so they couldn't change their stories later.

After he was sworn in, Clive Faulkner waited expectantly for the first question from the prosecutor.

Allison was struck again by the good looks of the museum director. Had he chosen a Hollywood career instead of academia, he would have been leading-man material. He even managed to make a bow tie look sexy.

"State your name, please," boomed John Marshall Plimpton.

"Clive Faulkner."

"What is your occupation?"

"I am an archaeologist, an author, and the Director of the Heartland Mound Builder Museum in Cape Girardeau, Missouri."

Under the methodical questioning of the prosecutor, Faulkner described his educational background, his long list of scholarly publications, his field experience as an archaeologist, and his employment history. None of it was news to Allison.

"Tell us about the Heartland Mound Builder Museum, Mr. Faulkner."

"It was established by Alfred Dennison in 1905, three years after he found Bootheel Man. It's a private museum, funded completely by a trust he set up. The trust is managed by a Board of Trustees. They meet monthly. As the Director of the museum, I work for them. Every item in the museum is one-hundred percent owned by the museum. We don't exhibit items loaned to us by other sources. We don't accept any sort of federal money or financial aid. We don't apply for federal grants."

"What sort of exhibits do you display at the museum?"

"Well, it's like Henry Ford said about the color of his Model-T cars. He always bragged that you could have any color you want, as long as it's black. As far as our museum goes, you can learn about any topic you want, as long as it's Mound Builders."

He glanced at Allison, obviously pleased with himself. She gave him no response. She was listening intently to his answers, alert for objectionable statements.

"What do you mean by Mound Builders?" the prosecutor continued.

"By the phrase Mound Builders, I am referring to those prehistoric people who lived in the Midwest, who built earthen mounds, usually along rivers. These mounds were built before our recorded history. The most famous are at Cahokia, Illinois, right across the river from St. Louis, at the junction of the Mississippi and Missouri Rivers. The largest mound at that site, known as Monk's Mound, is 100 feet tall and covers 13.8 acres. It contains about 814,000 cubic yards of soil. This man-made mound has a larger base circumference than the Great Pyramid of Khufu in Egypt or the Pyramid of the Sun at Teotihuacan, Mexico. Experts believe its construction began around 950 A.D. and that it was essentially completed by 1050 A.D. At one time, probably around the years 1050 to 1100, the six-mile area around this mound reached its zenith as a metropolitan center boasting a population of 10,000 to 30,000 people, depending on whose estimate you accept. Yet by the time Lewis and Clark came through in 1804, nothing remained but barren mounds amid empty forests."

"So, the Heartland Museum is about the Mound Builders of Cahokia?"

"Not exactly. We have the words Mound Builder in our title, because that's the wording Alfred Dennison used, but it is really more accepted these days to call these people Mississippians. This Mississippian culture began around 1050 A.D. Its early period lasted until about 1200 A.D. Its late period then lasted until about 1600 A.D. The forming of Cahokia was synonymous with the beginning of the early period. Cahokia was undoubtedly the cultural and political center for a region of smaller communities scattered along the inland rivers, especially between St. Louis and Memphis. But our museum is really about all Mississippians, not just those at Cahokia. We focus primarily on those who lived in Southeast Missouri, especially those whose remains were found in and around Cape Girardeau."

"Is one of your exhibits called Bootheel Man?"

"Yes. Bootheel Man is a nickname bestowed by Alfred Dennison on a skeleton he unearthed on his property in Cape Girardeau in 1902. It was the first archaeological find Dennison made. It triggered his subsequent lifelong interest in archaeology. Bootheel Man is the skeleton of a man who lived sometime between the years 1050 and 1200 A.D. He died, quite obviously, from a blow to the back of the head from a stone hand axe. In fact, the axe was driven into his skull with such force, it remains embedded in the bone to this day. Whoever buried him in the mound in Cape Girardeau, placed with his body two very high-quality chunkey stones and a beautiful flint-clay figurine of a young woman. Dennison nicknamed the figurine Gazing Woman, because her eyes were lifted toward the sky in an unblinking gaze."

"Unblinking?" Joey whispered into Allison's ear. "What? They think a statue is going to blink?"

Allison scrawled a quick note: DON'T TALK!

"You mentioned chunkey stones. What is a chunkey stone?"

"Across the North American continent, our prehistoric predecessors loved to play a game called 'chunkey.' We know this from the artifacts we've found. We also know it from Native Americans who were still playing the game with the same sort of equipment when Europeans first encountered them during the late part of the Mississippian era. This game involved a cylindrical stone shaped like a small wheel, often about five inches in diameter."

"What about Gazing Woman? Describe this piece of art in a little more detail, please."

"It's a statue or figurine of a young woman. It's about twelve inches tall. It's made of red flint clay, fired hard as stone. The remarkable thing about Gazing Woman is the detail. The artist who created her was incredibly talented. Flint clay is a hard medium to work with in regard to detail, but this artist created a beautiful face, a lovely and anatomically correct female body, and a pose that evokes pathos and reverence in virtually everyone who looks at her. She's been compared, favorably, to the *Venus de Milo*."

"Did Gazing Woman disappear from your museum on August 11 of this year?"

"Yes."

"Tell us about it."

Clive Faulkner related his story about the figurine disappearing from the museum, complete with the details of the concrete block being thrown through the front door, the burglar alarm going off, and the thief getting away before the police arrived.

"Sir, as the Director of the museum that owns Gazing Woman, do you have an opinion as to the fair market value of this particular piece of art?"

Allison rose to her feet. "I object, Your Honor. The question calls for an opinion."

The Prosecutor acted as if his feelings were hurt. "The owner of stolen property is permitted to give an opinion as to its value, Your Honor. Furthermore, this witness, by his experience and training, qualifies as an expert to give his opinions on matters pertaining to the Mississippian culture and period."

"Objection overruled. You may answer the question, Mr. Faulkner."

"In my opinion, Gazing Woman is worth at least one-hundred-thousand dollars."

"Did you or any member of the museum's Board of Directors give Joey Red Horse permission to take Gazing Woman from the museum?"

"No."

"Did you or the museum's Board give him permission to even be on the property of the museum after business hours?"

"No."

"Did you give him permission to throw Gazing Woman into the Mississippi River?"

"Of course not."

John Marshall Plimpton retrieved a cardboard box from the floor behind the counsel table. He made a show of placing an exhibit sticker on it, then opened it and removed the lovely figurine from the box.

Even though Allison had seen it just days earlier when it was recovered by the Missouri Water Patrol, she was struck once again by its beauty.

Plimpton placed the figurine on the table in front of Clive Faulkner. "Sir, would you identify State's Exhibit 1 for us, please?"

"Identify?" Faulkner said.

"Yes. Identify this exhibit for the record. Is State's Exhibit 1 the statue you call Gazing Woman?"

Clive Faulkner turned his gaze to Allison Culbertson. His eyes seemed to challenge her.

"State's Exhibit 1 is indeed the statue stolen from the Heartland Mound Builder Museum."

"Thank you, Mr. Faulkner. No further questions."

"Cross-examination, Ms. Culbertson?" asked the Judge.

Allison rose to her feet. Although lawyers were not required to stand up to question witnesses at preliminary hearings, and although the courtroom was small and cramped, she never liked to cross-examine while sitting down.

"Mr. Faulkner, what makes *you* qualified to give an opinion as to the value of this statue?"

"I'm a trained archaeologist and the Director of a museum devoted to artifacts of this specific time period and type. I read and keep abreast of the major periodicals in the field. I have bought items of this type from other museums and collectors for our inventory. I wrote a book about this particular artifact and the items found with it. The book is considered an authoritative work in its field. I've given lectures for various archaeological associations worldwide."

Allison clasped her hands in front of her.

"Are you the *only* person in the country qualified to give an opinion about the value of Gazing Woman?"

"Certainly not. Dozens of qualified experts could do so."

"Can you give me the names of three or four?"

He quickly listed nationally renowned archaeologists from the Smithsonian Institution, the Peabody Museum at Harvard, and the Field Museum in Chicago.

"So, it should be possible for me to contact these experts about doing an appraisal of Gazing Woman to verify that your estimation of her value is correct?"

"That's right," he said. "In fact, you may find that I have been too conservative in my estimate."

A red flush was creeping up his neck. Although his answers were cool and collected, he was obviously not enjoying this part of his time on the witness stand.

"Are you familiar with the Native American Graves Protection and Repatriation Act?" she asked, changing topics.

"I am."

She picked up a copy of the law from her counsel table and handed it to him. "Would you agree with me that this is a copy of that particular federal law?"

"Yes."

"It is sometimes known by its initials, NAGPRA?"

"Yes."

"Isn't it true that NAGPRA, passed in 1990, reads in part: 'Each museum which has possession or control over holdings or collections of Native American human remains and associated funerary objects shall compile an inventory of such items and the inventory shall be filed with the Secretary of the Interior and published in the Federal Register'?"

"That's what it says."

"Your museum has never filed such an inventory with the Secretary of the Interior, has it?"

"No. We weren't required to."

"You're a museum, aren't you?"

"Yes, but when you look at the definition of museum in the fine print of NAGPRA, they limit it to museums that receive federal funds. It doesn't apply to private museums like us."

She frowned, acting a bit surprised. "The fact your museum didn't meet the definition of museum would not be immediately clear to a person without reading the definitions section of the law very closely, would it?"

"Objection, calls for speculation and opinion!" said the Prosecutor.

Allison responded hotly, "Mr. Plimpton is the one who offered this witness as an expert in the field, Your Honor."

"Overruled. Answer the question."

"Well, NAGPRA, like most federal laws, is long and detailed. Without reading the definitions section carefully, a person would probably assume it applied to my museum. But it doesn't."

"Now," Allison continued, "another section of this federal law specifically points out *who* owns Native American human remains and funerary objects, doesn't it?"

"In some cases."

"Well, I refer you to Section Three of NAGPRA. Does it not specifically say that in the case of Native American human remains and associated funerary objects, ownership or control is in the lineal descendants of the Native Americans, or, in a case where such lineal descendants cannot be ascertained, then in the Indian tribe recognized as aboriginally occupying the area in which the objects were discovered?"

"That's what the section says in part, but it also says some other pretty important things, too."

"Isn't it true, Mr. Faulkner, that the Osage Indians would be considered a tribe that aboriginally occupied the Cape Girardeau area?"

"Yes, the Osages were one of the tribes there in prehistoric times."

"Now, by funerary object, we're talking about objects that as a part of a death rite or ceremony of a culture are reasonably believed to have been buried with the individual human remains either at the time of death or later, right?"

"That's the gist of the definition, yes."

"Now, Gazing Woman is clearly a funerary object under this definition, isn't she?"

"Yes."

Allison moved to Plimpton's counsel table and pointed to the figurine. "It is clear, isn't it, that this figurine was placed in the grave with the body of Bootheel Man as part of a ceremony connected with his death."

Faulkner nodded. "I agree that Gazing Woman is a funerary object."

"Don't you also agree with me, sir, that it is *reasonable* that my client, as a layperson untrained in the law, and as an Osage Indian, could read the NAGPRA statute and believe that, since he is a member of a tribe that aboriginally occupied the Cape Girardeau area, he had an *ownership* right in Gazing Woman?"

"Objection! That calls for speculation and opinion. It also contains facts not in evidence. There's been no proof offered that the defendant is an Osage Indian."

"Overruled. I'll let him answer the question."

"Could you repeat the question?" Faulkner asked.

"Certainly. Don't you agree that it's *reasonable* that my client, as a layperson untrained in the law, and as an Osage Indian, could read the NAGPRA statute and believe that, since he is a member of a tribe that aboriginally occupied the Cape Girardeau area, he had an ownership right in Gazing Woman?"

72

Faulkner crossed his arms over his chest. He leaned back in the witness chair and looked hard at Joey Red Horse. "I can see where your *client* might have believed he had a right to Gazing Woman. But I don't see how any *intelligent* and *reasonable* person could have believed it."

"So he's just a dumb Indian?" Allison said.

"Objection!" Plimpton thundered.

"Sustained."

Allison took a step toward Clive Faulkner, fixing him with her gaze. "Mr. Faulkner, exactly how many human skulls are currently in the possession of your museum?"

"Objection!" Plimpton said. "Irrelevant."

"Overruled. You may answer the question."

"Thirty-seven."

"They are not all on display, are they?"

"No."

"When they're not on display, they're kept in storage, in some back room in a box or storage bin?"

"That's right."

"All thirty-seven are Native American skulls, aren't they?"

"Yes."

"And you can tell that how?"

"From their shape and their teeth."

"All were dug up by Alfred Dennison or an employee of your museum, weren't they?"

"Yes."

"Your museum did not get permission from any American Indian tribe to dig up its ancestors, did you?"

"We weren't required to do so at the time. It was all done legally. We got permission from the property owners."

"So, you view it pretty much as finders keepers?"

He stared at her coldly. "You might say that."

Allison had a few other questions planned, but she always liked to end a cross-examination on a high note, and this seemed to qualify.

"No further questions of this witness."

Allison sat down. Faulkner shot her a hurt look as he left the courtroom. *Well*, she thought, *so much for the future of that relationship.*

Allison's heart was still pumping hard as the prosecution called Harry Sullinger as its last witness. Cross-examination was always difficult and exciting, because you were trying to get a witness to say something that he or she didn't want to say. More often than not, the witness made a fool of the lawyer. Nationally renowned law professor Irving Younger had quipped that a good cross-examination was usually short, a commando raid as opposed to the Normandy Invasion. Allison thought she had scored some points questioning Faulkner. If nothing else, she had probably earned her client more sympathy in the court of public opinion.

She focused her attention on Harry Sullinger. The big man was in the witness box relating his experience as a law-enforcement officer. He'd started out with the Cape Girardeau Police Department and had risen to the rank of sergeant. After several years, he switched to the County Prosecutor's office and became its investigator. Under Plimpton's questioning, he told about the standoff with Joey Red Horse on the bridge. He described how Joey threw Gazing Woman into the water before jumping himself. He was especially careful to note that Joey had been told he was under arrest before he jumped, thereby establishing a necessary mental element of resisting arrest by fleeing.

The Prosecutor's last question was meant to be dramatic: "Detective Sullinger, do you see in the courtroom today the man on the bridge, the man you personally saw holding Gazing Woman in his hands on the very same day it was stolen from the museum?"

Joey made the moment even more dramatic than the Prosecutor had expected. He proudly raised his hand, the bones on his breastplate rattling.

"He's right there," Sullinger testified, "the one with the beads and bones, the guy holding his hand in the air. That's Joey Red Horse."

It was all Allison could do to keep from burying her face in her hands. She definitely needed to talk some more with her client about courtroom demeanor.

"Cross-examination, Ms. Culbertson?" the Judge asked.

"Thank you, Your Honor." Allison stood. "I just have one question for you, Detective Sullinger."

He looked a bit relieved.

"It's important, so take your time in answering."

He nodded.

"What were my client's last words before he jumped off the bridge?"

Harry Sullinger scrunched up his face and stroked his chin.

"His last words? If I recall correctly, he said: 'The men who dug up the bones of my people weren't scientists! They were grave robbers!'"

Allison sat down. "No further questions."

Minutes later, the State rested. As expected, Judge Portell ruled that the State had shown sufficient probable cause to bind over Joey Red Horse for arraignment. But Allison was pleased with the way the preliminary hearing had gone. She had planted the seeds for her claim-of-right defense, she had forced Faulkner to vouch for the credibility of at least three potential expert witnesses who might challenge his estimate of the value of Gazing Woman, and she had fired the first salvo toward labeling Alfred Dennison a grave robber.

As they left the courtroom, Joey Red Horse was ecstatic. It was all she could do to herd him past the television cameras. The last thing she wanted was for him to give an interview to the media. She instructed him that both of them would have no comment whatsoever. She was sure, though, that footage of the handsome young man in the flashy American Indian regalia walking down the courthouse steps next to his lawyer in her brand-new Diane von Furstenberg suit would play on newscasts throughout the country.

She smiled inwardly as she walked past John Marshall Plimpton being questioned by reporters on the courthouse steps. He was uncomfortably addressing the issue of grave robbery. This particular prosecutor had never really accepted the notion that Supreme Court rules required cases to be tried in the courtroom and not in the media. He was taking his best shot at explaining why Alfred Dennison should not be considered a grave robber. The reporters were asking him aggressive questions. He was sputtering and scowling as he gave his answers. She looked forward to watching his lame performance on the evening news.

Chapter 8

Allison Culbertson was generally pleased with the way the local media presented the story about Joey Red Horse's preliminary hearing. The television station ran the case as its top story, with the tease: SCIENCE OR GRAVE ROBBERY: STORY AT 10:00. The newspaper's front-page headline blared: MUSEUM SAYS FINDERS KEEPERS. Both news outlets focused more on how the museum had acquired the items than on Joey's taking of them.

So far, so good.

Allison was in the middle of her early morning treadmill run when her phone rang. She paused the treadmill and answered the call.

"Allison Culbertson?"

"Yes."

"This is Marge Tappinger. I'm the President of the Heartland Mound Builder Museum Board of Directors."

Oh, brother, thought Allison, *here it comes.* Marge Tappinger was a pillar of the community. The wife of a bank president, and a retired teacher herself, she was involved in a prodigious amount of charitable work, everything from the Girl Scouts to the American Cancer Society. Allison had never met her personally, but it was impossible for anyone who read the local paper not to have heard of Marge Tappinger. As the President of the museum's Board of Directors, she certainly would not have enjoyed the morning's news.

"I need to talk to you," Tappinger said, her voice far from friendly.

"I'm listening."

"No, I mean in person. In private."

"I can see you first thing this morning at my office, say 8:00?"

"I'll be there."

The line went dead.

Allison got back on the treadmill. If she were going to take a butt-chewing she might as well have a presentable butt.

Marge Tappinger looked exactly like her newspaper photos. She was a cross between a battle-axe and a Playboy bunny. Around forty-five years old, she was an aging trophy wife at the precarious cusp between sexpot and matron. After a teaching career not much longer than a sneeze, she had married Rex Tappinger, a prominent local banker old enough to be her father. Their age difference did not challenge the gold standard set by Anna Nicole Smith and J. Howard Marshall, but it had been enough to raise eyebrows when the wedding bells rang twenty years earlier. Marge Tappinger quickly put the tongue-wagging behind her as she successfully spearheaded one community project after another.

Marge Tappinger did not say a word as Allison greeted her by Rita's desk near the front door of the law firm. She remained silent as Allison escorted her back to her private office. When the important lady seated herself in one of the chairs in front of Allison's desk, she sat quietly for several moments, staring at Allison.

At least a desk separates us, Allison thought. *This is not going to be pretty.*

Finally, Marge Tappinger spoke. In a voice much softer than Allison had expected, she asked, "How's Joey?"

"What?"

"How's Joey handling all of this? Did they treat him well in jail? Is he holding up emotionally?" A pleading look danced in her eyes. "Has he said anything about me?"

Allison was not sure she was successfully hiding her shock. "You're not here to chew me out for representing Joey?"

"Oh, no, no," Marge Tappinger said. "I'm *glad* you're representing him."

"I'm not sure I understand why you're here," Allison said.

"I'm here because I love Joey." The eyes of the pillar of the community moistened. "Joey and I, well, it's been a long time since I've been head-over-heels in love with a man."

Allison said nothing. What was there to say? Why was this woman telling her these secrets?

"Since his arrest, I haven't been able to get him out of my mind. Night and day, all that matters is him. When I wake up, he's the first thing I think about. I lie awake at night imagining our next conversation. I've been waiting for him to call me, to let me know how he's doing. Tell me, Miss Culbertson, how is he?"

Allison recalled the image of Joey on top of Lolita on the conference table in her law library. "I think he's holding up remarkably well, under the circumstances."

"Has he told you about *us*?"

"You mean, you and him? As a couple?"

"Yes. Our affair."

"No. I guess he's not one to kiss and tell."

"I knew it," she said. She took a handkerchief from her purse and dabbed at her eyes. "He's too noble to drag me into it. I can help him, though. I can help his case."

"How?"

"I gave him a key to the museum. I told him the alarm code."

"You helped plan a theft from your own museum?"

"No, no. I didn't know he was going to *steal* anything. He had the key and the alarm code for our secret meetings, our rendezvous, our love trysts. We would often meet in the Board room at night."

"Why are you telling me this?"

"I saw in the paper that he's charged with burglary, for being on the premises of the museum without permission. I thought it might be useful for you to know that I'm willing to testify that I had given him permission to be at the museum after hours."

"When you *weren't* there?"

"Well, no, I never intended for him to be there unless I was there, too. But still, if it will help him, I'm willing to be a witness for the defense. No matter what happens."

"Does your husband know about this?"

"No."

"What about Clive Faulkner?"

"Nobody knows. Joey and I were discreet. In fact, I'm dying to see him now, if you could make it happen."

Allison raised both hands as if warding off a blow.

"Oh, no. Absolutely not. I think it would be better for Joey to stay completely away from the museum and its Board members for the time being. But I'll certainly tell him you're anxious to help."

"I know it will be personally embarrassing," Marge Tappinger said, with a little more drama than necessary. "All those hateful gossips who criticized my marriage to Rex will be crowing *I-told-you-so*, but it's so wonderful to be in love again, to feel passion. He makes me feel alive. I haven't felt this way for years. I'm willing to give up everything I have for Joey."

"That may not be necessary," Allison said. "I'm not sure at this point that your testimony would be helpful. But I'll definitely think about it and let you know."

"Tell him to call me. Please!"

"It would be better for the two of you to curb your passion for now, at least until this case is over. Let me figure out Joey's absolute best defense, and I'll get back to you."

"Give him this, will you?"

Marge Tappinger pulled a sealed pink envelope, the size of a greeting card, from her purse and placed it on the corner of Allison's desk. Allison could smell its heavy dose of perfume from where she sat.

Later that day, Joey was sitting in the same chair vacated by Marge Tappinger. He was wearing his American Indian attire again, just in case any news reporters were lurking outside Allison's office, seeking to snap a picture of the dashing defendant visiting his mouthpiece.

Allison waved off his explanation of his garb. "Why didn't you tell me about your affair with Marge Tappinger!"

He winced. "Hey, you're the one who delivered the big speech about not telling you the whole story so you'd be free to put me on the stand."

"Well, it's rather important that the President of the museum's Board of Directors gave you a key to the building and the alarm code and is prepared to testify that you had her permission to be there. It could really hurt the prosecution's burglary count."

Joey grinned. "If Marge knocks out the burglary count, and you knock out the stealing count with my claim-of-right defense, then that just leaves the resisting-arrest charge, doesn't it? If I'm found not guilty of burglary and stealing, does that automatically make the resisting-arrest charge go away, too?"

"No," Allison said. "It's still a crime to resist arrest, even when you didn't commit the underlying crime. The theory is that a citizen, even when innocent, should always submit to an arrest and then litigate his case in court, rather than fighting with the officer making the arrest or running away from him."

"I didn't fight and I didn't run."

"Of course not. You just jumped sixty feet off a bridge. That's flight, Joey."

"Dove," he corrected. "I dove. Sullinger jumped. It's a lot harder to dive."

Allison slid the envelope from Marge Tappinger across the table. "Your lover left this for you."

Joey took the pink envelope and slipped it behind his beaded belt.

"Aren't you even going to read it?" Allison asked.

"With you gawking at me? No thanks. I'll read it later."

"Joey, that woman loves you. What are your feelings toward her?"

"She's okay. We had some good times. But I'm ready to move on. I'm spreading my wings. I don't have time for a serious relationship with any woman right now. This case is going to put me on the map."

"It might put you in jail, Joey. Think about it for a minute. The burglary charge carries up to seven years in prison. The stealing charge could tack on another fifteen. The resisting-arrest charge could add another four. That's twenty-six years."

"I can count," Joey said. "But I've got the best damn lawyer in Cape Girardeau. You're gonna get me off. I know it."

Allison sighed. "So, tell me how you went about using Marge Tappinger's key."

"That's how I got in and out so fast without getting caught. I turned off the security alarm, went inside with the key, snatched Gazing Woman, went back outside, locked the door, reactivated the alarm, and then threw the concrete block through the window. Smart, huh? I was long gone by the time the cops got there."

"Why go to all that trouble if you just planned to jump off the bridge and become a martyr to the cause, anyway?" she asked.

"Scene selection."

80

"What?"

"Indian gets caught red-handed in the museum? That's not nearly as dramatic as Indian successfully steals Gazing Woman, gets completely away with his crime, then summons the police to the Bill Emerson Memorial Bridge where he throws the sacred figurine into the water and leaps himself. The world is a stage, but somebody has to do the directing. We're all playing bit parts in a never-ending drama."

Joey examined the bones on his breastplate and seemed to find them satisfactory. "The only thing that's gone wrong so far," he said, "was Harry Sullinger and those Water Patrol cowboys finding Gazing Woman. Who would've thought anybody would find her at the bottom of that river? I wanted the distinction of being the one who returned her to a peaceful resting place. Now she's sitting in some evidence locker at the police department, probably next to some stolen TV or a bag of dope. She's in a bad neighborhood right now, thanks to me."

He stood and walked to the picture window overlooking the Mississippi. "We'll still return her where she belongs, Ms. Culbertson, by shaming the museum into repatriating Bootheel Man and every single bone and burial object taken out of all those mounds by Alfred Dennison. I really believe we're going to get it done."

Joey put his hand over his heart. "When my life is over, I want to have made a difference. When somebody writes the history of Indians in this country, I won't merit a full chapter like Sitting Bull, Geronimo, or Crazy Horse, but I'm shooting to be at least a footnote. A guy who helped pressure a bunch of private museums into turning over their ancient Indian remains and sacred objects for reburial, that's what I'm aiming for."

Allison rolled her eyes. "Joey, *you* are living dangerously. Rex Tappinger is a powerful man. You've been committing adultery with his wife. She's so in love with you she gave you a key to the museum. You apparently intend to break her heart and cuckold her husband publicly. Are there other things about your case you haven't told me?"

"Lots," he said. "But I'm keeping my secrets to myself, Counselor, because I intend to take the witness stand at my trial and what you don't know won't hurt you."

Chapter 9

The sign read: "Welcome. Pawhuska City Limits. Population 3,825. Please Drive Carefully."

"We're here," Allison Culbertson said, as she drove the Jeep Cherokee into the small town nestled amid the rolling hills and prairies of Northeast Oklahoma, about forty miles north of Tulsa.

"How long a drive was it from Cape Girardeau?" Lolita asked.

Allison checked her odometer. "Four-hundred and ninety-four miles from my office door."

"I used to come here with my dad when I was a little girl," Lolita said. "Grandma was still alive then. This is where he grew up, Osage County. I haven't been back since Grandma died. But my dad comes here every May and September for the biker rallies." She lowered the sun visor and checked her appearance in its mirror. "He won't let me come. Says the rallies at Pawhuska sometimes get pretty wild. He only lets me tag along to the *tamer* ones."

Allison pictured herself making a trip to a biker rally in the company of the huge be-grizzled and potentially violent Bear Smith. She could think of few things she would less want to do. She had brought his daughter along on this fact-finding trip because the girl wanted to come and Allison figured she could use the company on the long drive. It was okay with Bear Smith, as long as Joey Red Horse wasn't accompanying them. Bear was concerned about overnight accommodations and doubted Allison's ability to successfully chaperone the couple had Joey and Lolita made the trip together. Allison figured he didn't know the half of it. She had not shared with him her eyewitness observations about the accuracy of his instincts.

"Dad says I can't go to the Biker Days rally in Pawhuska until I'm twenty-one! Can you believe that? What a hypocrite! I found snapshots he brought back from those bashes. He's one to talk!"

"You like biker rallies?" Allison asked Lolita.

Lolita adjusted a strand of her dark hair, still peering into the mirror. "Well, sure. You get to see the coolest bikes in the world and meet some pretty interesting people. You've got to have a certain amount of courage to get on a motorcycle. It's fun to hang out with gutsy men. I think it puts a crimp in my dad's style to take me along, though. When I'm around, he feels obligated to be a parent. It's a chore for him."

"Keep an eye out for Mathews Avenue," Allison said. "We're staying at the Black Gold Motel tonight. Our meeting with Joe Black Dog is first thing tomorrow morning at the Osage Tribal Museum. The museum's on Grandview Avenue. Keep an eye out for it."

"Man, there's lots of old buildings in this town," Lolita said.

"I read somewhere that eighty-six of the ninety-eight buildings in downtown Pawhuska are listed on the National Register of Historic Places," Allison said. "That's impressive."

"I'm more interested in the present," Lolita said. "You think your meeting with Joe Black Dog will help you get Joey off? I know Joey wants to be a martyr and all, but I sure don't want him to go to prison."

"Well, Joe Black Dog is an elder with the Osage Nation. He's one of the tribe's historians. If he'll do it, he'd make an excellent expert witness for us. He could help prove the point that the Osages occupied the Cape Girardeau area long before the white men came. It could really help us win the argument that Joey, being an Osage, reasonably believed he had more of a right to Gazing Woman than did the museum. Really, all we have to do is convince one juror. The prosecution has to get a unanimous verdict to get a conviction. All we need is one strong vote, willing to hold out to the bitter end."

"May I sit in on the interview?"

"Sure. Unless he objects."

"How did you find out about Joe Black Dog?"

"I got his name from an anthropologist at the University of Missouri. She said Joe Black Dog knows more about Osage Indians than just about anyone in the country. I called him, and we set up this meeting at the museum."

"Does he work there?"

"No, but he picked the place for our little powwow."

Lolita took a swig of Dr. Pepper from her McDonald's cup, spilled some on her CUSTER DIED FOR YOUR SINS t-shirt, and dabbed at the wet spot with a napkin.

"You know, Miss Culbertson, I really admire Joey for what he's done and what he's doing. His passion is one of the things I love most about him." She sighed. "But if he goes to prison for a long time, it'll really be hard for me. He and I will miss some of the best years of our lives together."

Allison debated whether to say what she was thinking. Complete candor on her part could make for a long trip home tomorrow, if the conversation between Allison and this love-struck teenager veered down an unpleasant path. Did she really want to broach the subject of Lolita's relationship with Joey? Did she want to crush this girl's dreams by letting her know that Joey did not appear to have monogamy in his long-range plans? Candor eventually won out over delicacy.

"Lolita, I think maybe you should try to cool down things between you and Joey."

"What do you mean?"

"Well, you need to be careful about having a relationship with him. You're only seventeen. He's twenty-four. That's a pretty big difference at your age, especially since you're still in high school and your father doesn't seem to approve."

"Will being in love with me *hurt* Joey's case?"

Allison thought about her meeting with Marge Tappinger. Marge's enthusiasm for helping Joey might wane if she found out about Lolita. Allison certainly couldn't tell Lolita about Marge, at least not unless and until she decided to call Marge Tappinger as a witness. Then the whole world would find out about Joey's philandering. Letting the jury know that Marge had given Joey the key and *why* was definitely a two-edged sword. She hadn't decided whether they would use Marge's testimony or not.

"If no one knows about Joey's relationship with you, it won't hurt his case. But what if your father finds out? Will he still be so keen on paying Joey's attorney fee? Will he still want to keep Joey out of jail? You and Joey are playing with fire. It would be best to put your love affair on hold."

84

Lolita crossed her arms over her chest. She was silent for more than a minute.

"Miss Culbertson," she finally said, in a calm tone, "may I ask *you* a couple of questions?"

"I suppose so."

"How old are you?"

"Twenty-seven."

"Are you married?"

"No."

"Have you ever been married?"

"No."

"Do you have a steady boyfriend?"

"No."

"Have you ever loved somebody so much that you would do *anything* for him, I mean absolutely anything? No matter what it cost you?"

Allison didn't need to think twice about it. "No. I can't say that I have."

The soon-to-be high-school senior rummaged through her purse and found a nail file. She began working on one of her nails. With exasperation, Allison realized that she had just driven through the intersection with Grandview Avenue. So much for finding the museum. At some point she would need to turn around.

"You know," Lolita continued, "I'm sure you're crammed full of knowledge about the law and are a great lawyer and all that, but I'm not really convinced you're the best person to be giving me advice about my love life. Thanks for being concerned about my welfare, though. Really. I appreciate what you're doing for Joey."

Allison cringed. The girl had a point. Allison was a decade older than Lolita, but her experience lay in areas other than romance. She glanced at Lolita. She and this attractive girl were very different women who had led very different lives.

Well, Allison thought, *I tried.*

"Hey," Lolita said. "There's Mathews Avenue, and there's the Black Gold Motel right around the corner."

Sometimes cars just had a way of finding the destination.

"Let's check in now and find the museum later," Allison said, glad for the change of subject.

It turned out that the Osage Tribal Museum was just a couple of blocks from the motel. The one-story building boasted walls made of sandstone brick. A white cupola perched atop it like a pilothouse on a steamboat.

Joe Black Dog was waiting for them the next morning underneath the green canopied entrance to the building. Allison studied her potential expert witness as she and Lolita walked up the sidewalk toward him. *Yes, he just might do.*

He was a tall man, several inches over six feet in height. His age was indecipherable. He was somewhere between fifty and seventy. He was a slender man, wearing jeans and a plaid shirt. His skin was weathered and bronzed by the sun. His jet-black hair was pulled back in a short ponytail.

"You're early," he said, introducing himself.

"Not early enough to beat you here," she said. "I'm Allison Culbertson and this is Lolita Smith. She's a friend of my client's. She made the trip with me."

Lolita had left her CUSTER shirt at the motel, and was instead wearing a modest white blouse.

"Pleased to meet you," Lolita told him. "My father is Osage. Bear Smith, of the Buffalo Bull clan. My grandmother was Pauline Smith."

"I am pleased to meet you both," Joe Black Dog said. "I knew your grandmother. She was a fine woman. You have her eyes."

They all shook hands. After some small talk, he led them through the gift shop at the entrance of the museum to a table in a brightly lit, high-ceilinged room in the heart of the museum. Every wall of the room was covered with paintings of former Osage chiefs and tribal leaders, all posing in traditional Osage attire, most bedecked with blankets and many with headdresses and feathers. The one exception was the oil painting of Major General Clarence L. Tinker of the Army Air Corps, a modern-day warrior, shot down while leading a bombing mission against the Japanese at Wake Island in 1942. Posing next to a model airplane, a cigarette in his hand and a playful expression on his rugged face, he did not evoke the same aura of solemnity generated by the other paintings. Allison felt as if generations of Osage dignitaries were watching her as she took a seat at the table across from Joe Black Dog. The big man smiled at her.

"The Director is a friend of mine. She said we could meet here. I thought this would be the best place to answer your questions about the Osages. This museum was opened in 1938. At that time, it was the only museum in the world owned by an Indian tribe. What would you like to know?"

Allison pulled a legal pad from her briefcase. "I've been reading up on Osage Indians," she said. "I have big gaps in my knowledge, though. I think it would be best if you would assume I know absolutely nothing and just start with what you would tell a totally ignorant person about the history of the Osages."

"A totally ignorant person?" He smiled. "You don't look totally ignorant."

"She's not," Lolita said. "She's really smart. But she's right about the gaps in her knowledge. There's some things she knows absolutely nothing about."

Allison and Lolita exchanged a knowing glance.

"Well, you knew enough to come to the right place," he said. He made a wide, circular gesture with his finger, pointing to the room around them. "You are currently sitting in Pawhuska, Oklahoma, the county seat of Osage County. But this particular county is not just a normal Oklahoma county. The entire county is also the Osage Nation Reservation. Geographically, it's the largest county in Oklahoma, consisting of 1,475,000 acres or 2,251 square miles. It is larger than the states of Delaware and Rhode Island. As big as it is, though, it's a tiny fraction of the land that once belonged to the Osages."

He used a map of the United States to make his point. "We are right here, in the northeast part of Oklahoma. Before the white man came to this continent, the Osage lands stretched from where we sit all the way east to the Mississippi River, all the way north to the Missouri River and all the way south to the Arkansas River. The Osages were known as the 'Children of the Middle Waters' because those three rivers were our borders. As you can see, the

Osage land included the bottom half of Missouri, the top half of Arkansas, the upper northeast part of Oklahoma and the lower southeast part of Kansas. It was well over a hundred-million acres."

He spoke slowly, in complete sentences, never rushing himself nor fumbling for the right word.

"The white men speak of the *discovery* of the New World by Europeans such as Columbus and De Soto. They refer to the time before the arrival of the Europeans as *prehistoric* times, simply because they, the Europeans, had no written history of it. We Osages don't call the pre-European times prehistoric times. We call them *pre-contact* times. We have our oral history. It goes back to the time when *Wah'Kon-Tah*, the Great Spirit, brought the People of the Sky together with the People of the Land to form one tribe, the Children of the Middle Waters. The tribe was further divided into clans, which were family groups related through the father's side. The word 'Osage' evolved through mispronunciation and atrocious spelling on the part of the Europeans. The true name of the tribe was 'Wa-shah-she.' The French settlers called us 'Wa-sa-gee,' and using the letters 'ou' to give the sound of 'w,' they wrote it 'Ouasages.' The English later pronounced this word 'Osages' and the name stuck. It has been adopted by the American Bureau of Ethnology and by the Indian Bureau. Of course, this isn't the most well-known example of Europeans botching Indian names. Columbus called all of us Indians, thinking he had reached the Indies. Many times our ancestors asked, 'Why do you call us Indians?' It took many years before we understood the confusion came about because of the poor navigational skills of a white man named Christopher Columbus. By then, though, we were used to being called Indians."

He folded his hands on the tabletop. Allison was picturing him on the witness stand and liked what she was seeing. His voice, too, was perfect. Deep and resonant, it was similar to the wonderful voice of the actor James Earl Jones. She hoped this articulate man would be willing to be a witness for the defense.

"The first white man to mention the Osages in writing was Father Marquette, of Marquette and Joilet fame. He wrote about our tribe on a map he made in 1673. Of course, we had been here long before Father Marquette came down the Mississippi River."

Joe Black Dog pointed to the map of the United States. "By the time of Marquette and Joliet, the Osages no longer lived on mounds like those at Cahokia. Those mounds were already abandoned and in ruin. Our people no longer lived in a big city. Rather, we lived in smaller villages, scattered throughout our land. Our lifestyle was based upon both hunting and farming. The tribe would make three long hunts per year, in the spring, summer, and fall. The hunts were primarily for deer, buffalo, elk, and bear. Men would kill the animals and women would butcher them and smoke or dry the meat. Women would also prepare the hides. Before leaving on the summer hunt, though, women would plant crops of corn, beans, squash, and pumpkins. When the Osages returned from the summer hunt, they would harvest the crops."

Allison leaned forward as she asked a key question. "Do you believe the people who built the mounds at Cahokia and along the Missouri, Mississippi, and Arkansas rivers were the Osages?"

He nodded. "Our traditions say we were the first people in our land; no one came before us. We existed on the land for thousands of years before the arrival of the Europeans. The Mound Builders most likely splintered into several different smaller tribes, including the Osage, Kansa, Omaha, Quapaw, and many others. But the Osages became the masters of the hills and plains between the three rivers, constantly warring on neighboring tribes and beheading trespassers who ventured into our territory. Our warriors often put their victims' heads on stakes to warn intruders to stay away. It worked better than a no-trespassing sign."

He was not smiling, so Allison was not sure if she was expected to laugh. She plowed ahead with her next question. "So the land in Cape Girardeau was formerly Osage land?"

"Absolutely. It was part of the one-hundred-million acres sold to the United States in the treaty signed on November 10, 1808. You can read the treaty yourself. You can use a copy as an exhibit in court. Would you care to guess what the Osages got for the one-hundred-million acres?"

"I give up," Allison said.

"Twelve-hundred dollars in cash, fifteen-hundred dollars in merchandise, some hunting rights, protection from encroachment by other Indians, promises to pay the debts the Indians owed settlers for previous thefts and property damage, and promises that Fort Clark would be kept available to them for blacksmith work and trading."

Allison did some quick math. "That's less than a penny per acre! Lands sells for a tad more than that in Cape now."

"What else would you like to know?" he asked.

"How did the Osages end up on this reservation in Oklahoma?"

He placed his fingertips together, forming a steeple. "The treaty of 1808 was followed by other treaties. Bit by bit, the Osages were forced out of Missouri and Arkansas. For fifty years, part of the Osages lived in Kansas and part lived in Oklahoma. Those in Kansas were eventually forced to move here. Since 1872, the reservation for all Osages has been this 1,475,000 acres in Oklahoma. This was part of our land before the United States of America existed, and it is still our land today by treaty."

"Lolita's father was telling me that an argument can be made that Joey does not have enough Osage blood to be considered a true Osage. How does that work?"

"It varies from tribe to tribe. It has recently changed with the Osages. In 1906, the United States Congress officially recognized Osage tribal control in the oil-rich mineral rights beneath the soil of our reservation, even if the land on top was sold to someone else. A record was made of every member of our tribe at the time, called the allottees, and they were each given a share of royalties from the oil, known as headrights.

"The names of the 2,229 original allottees were specifically listed. Until recently, an Osage could not have a full vote in tribal matters unless he or she had inherited a headright from one of those specifically listed allottees. As a result, our tribe only numbered about 4,300 voting members. President Bush signed a new bill into law in 2005, giving the Osages the right to change their method of recognizing membership in the tribe. The ownership rights in the minerals and the income therefrom were left unchanged, but in 2006 we adopted a new method of determining citizenship. Now anyone who can show direct descent from one of the original 2,229 allottees of 1906 has a full vote, even if his or her percentage of blood is far less than fifty percent, and even if he does not have even a partial ownership interest in a headright. By the outcome of one election, our voting population increased to over 16,000. Of course, they don't all live on the reservation. Most, like Lolita and her father, live elsewhere. The degree to which they have kept their Osage ways varies tremendously."

"So, you could testify in court that as long as Joey Red Horse has *some* Osage blood, he could consider himself an Osage?"

"Yes, he could. More importantly, the tribe would recognize him as an Osage and give him voting rights on matters affecting the tribe."

Allison found herself growing excited by the prospect of a trial in Joey's case. It would be exhilarating and sensational! Of course, unlike her client, she would not be the one going to jail if she lost. That was the biggest drawback to being the client rather than the lawyer.

"Let me ask you a personal question," she said. "You know what Joey Red Horse is accused of doing, don't you? What do you think about it?"

"I understand that he removed the Gazing Woman figurine from the Heartland Mound Builder Museum. It is a very serious allegation. Gazing Woman is a priceless burial object. All things considered, I believe he deserves a medal."

"So do I!" Lolita exclaimed.

Joe Black Dog smiled grimly. "Most of our people believe it is wicked and dangerous to remove skeletons and burial objects from graves. The spirit of one who has died is going through different levels in the next world. When his bones are unearthed, it interferes with his progress through those levels, and he may try to take revenge on those who have tampered with his grave. Both the people who took the bones and burial objects from the grave and those who continue to work with them in museums are put in serious danger from the ill will of the spirits. What many don't realize is that we are not just concerned with the rights of the departed when we seek to return bones to graves. We are also concerned with the well-being of the people who are handling those bones. We believe these people are in great danger until the repatriation occurs."

"Based on Osage oral history, was Joey's belief that he had a claim of right to Gazing Woman reasonable?"

Joe Black Dog spread his hands slowly.

"Absolutely. Alfred Dennison, like so many other archaeologists, was well-intentioned. He thought he was doing a good thing by digging up the remains of men, women, and children who died on Osage lands so many years ago. But, when all is said and done, he was looting the graves of human beings. He disrupted the journeys of many souls through the afterlife, and put into danger the souls of many more still on this earth, including himself. Joey Red Horse, as an Osage, even a mixed-blood Osage, has a better claim of right to Gazing Woman than did Alfred Dennison or his museum. In my opinion, Joey's belief was not only reasonable, it was correct."

"Mr. Black Dog," Allison said. "I'd like to hire you as an expert witness for Joey Red Horse. As you may be aware, an expert witness is a person who by experience or training has expertise that the members of the jury don't have. An expert is allowed to give opinions in his field of expertise to help the jury fully understand the evidence in the case and its significance. I'm sure the judge would consider you an expert on the Osage Indians and would allow you to say the same things in court that you've told me today. How about it? May I hire you?"

"No."

Allison was shocked. Things had seemed to be going so well. "Why not?"

Joe Black Dog rose from his chair and stood proudly in the small room of the Osage Tribal Museum. Portraits of his ancestors in traditional Indian dress stared at him from the museum walls.

"You may not hire me because I am willing to testify for free."

The Osage historian smiled. The weathered skin around his eyes crinkled with laugh wrinkles. Allison took his hands in hers.

"No wonder you Osages sold the Cape Girardeau land for less than a penny an acre," she said. "You're way too nice!"

Chapter 10

Allison Culbertson took the call from Joey Red Horse.

"How did the meeting with Joe Black Dog go?"

"Wonderful. He'll make a terrific witness. He agreed to do it. He's not even going to charge an expert-witness fee."

"Great! When are you and Lolita coming back?"

"Tomorrow. Our meeting with Joe Black Dog lasted until noon. We went to lunch and came back and toured the museum. It's fascinating. I figure the more I know about the Osages, the better job I can do for you in court. We plan to spend another night at the motel and come back tomorrow morning when we're good and fresh. It's a long drive."

"Well, be sure to watch the *CBS Evening News* tonight."

"What?"

"You'll both want to watch the *CBS Evening News* tonight."

"Why?"

"They're running a story about my case."

"Joey, did you talk to them? I told you to hold off on the interviews until after the trial is over. We don't want the judge to think we're litigating this case in the media."

"Hey, *they* called me. They had already talked to the prosecutor. I'm not letting that scalp-hunter give his side of the story unchallenged. I was careful what I said."

"You've already given the interview? Without even telling me?"

"That's what I'm saying. I'm telling you right now. It's going to be on the *CBS Evening News* tonight. You might want to watch it."

After the phone call, Allison brooded for a few minutes. Joey Red Horse was proving to be a difficult client. She hoped he didn't do anything to torpedo his case. At some point, she and he would need to have a long talk.

Allison and Lolita ended up watching the *CBS Evening News* at a truck stop near Springfield, Missouri. After Joey's phone call, they decided to forgo another night in the motel and drive back to Cape Girardeau immediately, even though they wouldn't get home until after midnight. They stopped at a truck stop boasting a room where truckers could relax for a few minutes, grab a bite to eat, and watch television. Allison and Lolita had already fended off advances from three truckers during the fifteen minutes they'd been waiting for the six o'clock news to begin.

After they'd broken the hearts of two more truckers, Joey's segment finally ran.

"Our next story comes to us from Cape Girardeau, Missouri, a town on the banks of the Mississippi River, halfway between St. Louis and Memphis, near the Missouri Bootheel. It's a criminal case that's being called one of most dramatic acts of American Indian activism since the Wounded Knee occupation in 1973. Here's CBS reporter Cory Blaze in Cape Girardeau to tell us more about this fascinating case."

Allison couldn't help smiling. *Cory Blaze must be in hog heaven*, she thought. *One of his local stories is going national.*

"I'm standing here in front of the Heartland Mound Builder Museum, a place where people have come for decades to learn more about the ancient people who lived along the banks of the Mississippi River before recorded time. These people, who vanished centuries ago, have been studied extensively by archaeologists, who don't always agree about who they were."

Clive Faulkner's face filled the screen from a prerecorded interview.

"Historians formerly thought the mounds were built by people other than the Indians who lived here when Europeans arrived. Maybe people from China or the Ten Lost Tribes of Israel or even people from the long-lost continent of Atlantis. Most of us now believe the mounds were built by American Indians, who for some unknown reason changed their lifestyle from living in bigger communities to living a more seminomadic existence."

Cory Blaze appeared again, standing in front of the museum.

"For over a century, archaeologists across the Midwest have been excavating these mounds, looking for clues as to who the Mound Builders really were, and what happened to them. Many of the mounds contained skeletons, several of which have been put

94

on display in museums across the country, like this one in Cape Girardeau."

A full shot of Bootheel Man filled the screen. The stone axe protruding from his skull was prominently featured. The voice of Clive Faulkner provided background information.

"Bootheel Man lived some time around the years 1050 to 1200 A.D. He was killed by a blow to the head from a ceremonial axe, which was still embedded in his skull when archaeologist Alfred Dennison found him in 1902. Dennison spent the rest of his life creating the Heartland Mound Builder Museum and tracking down exhibits for it. Everything he did, and everything we have done since, has been in the name of science."

The screen flashed back to Cory Blaze.

"Alfred Dennison found most of his exhibits in the typical way of archeologists—he dug them up from the ground. Specifically, from the mounds dotting the hillsides along inland rivers."

Joey Red Horse's face filled the screen. "It's nothing but grave robbery! These archaeologists are the thieves, not me! They are the ones who should be prosecuted!"

Lolita gushed. "Oh, he looks so handsome! You go, Joe!"

The newscast showed a clip from the KFVS-12 files of Joey Red Horse standing on the Mississippi River bridge, tossing Gazing Woman into the river. As the tape played, Cory Blaze explained what the viewers were seeing.

"Joey Red Horse is an Osage Indian. Earlier this summer, he allegedly broke into the Heartland Mound Builder Museum, stole a burial relic that had been buried with Bootheel Man, and threw it into the Mississippi River."

Joey's face returned to the screen.

"I was repatriating this burial item to the earth. The grave robbers took it from my ancestors. I was merely returning it to the grave."

Cory Blaze was back on screen. "Not everybody sees it that way, especially the man who charged Joey Red Horse with three felonies, County Prosecutor John Marshall Plimpton."

Plimpton was sitting at his office desk for the interview, shelves of law books lining the wall behind him.

"There are *legal* ways to do things," Plimpton was saying. "What Joey Red Horse did was illegal, and I've charged him with burglary, stealing, and resisting arrest. He faces up to twenty-six years in prison. Maybe he should've written the museum a protest letter instead of breaking and entering. Maybe he should've picketed them."

The screen filled next with a clip from the preliminary hearing. Allison saw herself questioning Clive Faulkner. For a moment, the voice of Cory Blaze provided the only sound.

"At a preliminary hearing earlier this month, Joey Red Horse's lawyer, Allison Culbertson, dug up some choice questions for the museum director."

Allison, sitting in the truck stop, suddenly found herself listening to her own voice.

"Don't you agree that it's reasonable that my client, as a layperson untrained in the law, and as an Osage Indian, could read the NAGPRA statute and believe that, since he is a member of a tribe that aboriginally occupied the Cape Girardeau area, he had an ownership right in Gazing Woman?"

At the truck stop, Allison cringed at the Southeast Missouri twang in her voice. She needed to work on that.

On screen, Faulkner was crossing his hands over his chest and leaning back in the witness chair. "I can see where your *client* might have believed he had a right to Gazing Woman. But I don't see how any *intelligent* and *reasonable* person could have believed it."

"So he's just a dumb Indian?"

Parts of the clip had been edited, and Allison watched herself taking a step toward Clive Faulkner on the witness stand. She watched with a critical eye. *Do I look mean enough to be a trial lawyer?*

"Mr. Faulkner, exactly how many human skulls are currently in the possession of your museum?"

"Thirty-seven."

"All thirty-seven are Native American skulls, aren't they?"

"Yes."

"All were dug up by Alfred Dennison or an employee of your museum, weren't they?"

"Yes."

96

"Your museum did not get permission from any Indian tribe to dig up its ancestors, did you?"

"We weren't required to do so at the time. It was all done legally. We got permission from the property owners."

"So, you view it pretty much as finders keepers?"

His expression looked unfriendly, even on national television. "You might say that."

The news story jumped back to Cory Blaze standing in front of the Heartland Mound Builder Museum. "The case is not expected to go to trial until midwinter. But the defendant says it will definitely be tried to a jury."

Once again, Joey's face filled the screen. "I will not plead guilty to anything because I am not guilty of anything. I had a right to take Gazing Woman from the people who stole her. I believed it then and I believe it now."

The screen switched to a person Allison didn't recognize. Cory Blaze's voice gave an introduction before the man's words became audible. "Mark Windfoot is the head of ARROW, the activist organization called Angry Reformers Resisting Oppressive Whites, headquartered in Washington DC. He is rooting for Joey."

"We here at ARROW wish Joey Red Horse success in the courtroom. In 1990, Congress required museums receiving federal money to begin the process of returning Native American bones, sacred objects, objects of cultural patrimony, and burial objects to the appropriate tribes, but the federal law does not apply to private museums. It's a loophole that needs to be closed. We applaud Joey Red Horse for bringing this important issue to the attention of the American public."

Cory Blaze reappeared to close the segment.

"Some people say this case could change the way people view archaeologists. Others say it's a case about a thief getting what he deserves for breaking into a museum. Either way, it is a matter of grave justice."

As the news broke for a commercial, Allison saw a potbellied man in denim jacket and jeans approaching her. A red bandana was tied pirate-like over his head. In a moment, he was towering over her chair.

"Say, little lady," he said. "That was you on TV, wasn't it? Could I have your autograph?"

"Joey *said* he was going to make you famous," Lolita whispered. "See, he already has!"

When they arrived in Cape Girardeau shortly after midnight, Allison dropped Lolita off outside Joey's apartment. Lolita had insisted. Allison took the precaution of calling Bear Smith, who said it was okay as long as Joey brought Lolita home immediately. Allison waited until Lolita unlocked Joey's door and disappeared inside. She then drove home herself.

An hour later, she got a frantic call from Joey.

"Miss Culbertson. Something terrible has happened! Can you meet me at your office? Hurry!"

Chapter 11

Joey Red Horse was waiting for Allison at the front door of her law office. He stood in the purplish glow of the streetlights. Blood dripped from scratches on his face, dotting his white t-shirt and blue jeans.

"Let's go inside," Allison said, concerned that Joey's bloody appearance might draw unwanted attention or even a 911 call.

He followed her up the narrow, enclosed stairway from the ground-floor door to her second-floor law office. At the top of the stairs, she unlocked the door to her waiting room and ushered him inside. She locked both doors behind them.

"What happened?" she asked, turning from the door.

"I screwed up," he said. "Screwed up really, really bad. I need your help."

She gave him Kleenex to dab at the blood on his face. He shook his head with self-disgust as he pressed the tissues to his cheek.

"What happened?" she asked again.

"You said you weren't coming home until tomorrow," he said. His voice sounded almost plaintive.

"So?"

"So, Marge Tappinger came by tonight. I was trying to break things off with her, but I was trying to do it nicely. I still wanted her cooperation as a witness, you know. She was crying and carrying on. I felt so sorry for her. I tried to comfort her. One thing led to another." He paused, frowning. "To make a long story short, Lolita came into my apartment after you dropped her off and sort of caught us in a compromising position."

Allison rolled her eyes, remembering her own experience at catching Joey in a compromising position on her conference room table. "I thought it was over with Marge Tappinger."

"It was. This was sort of a farewell thing. I was breaking up with her."

"Oh, for God's sake!" Allison said. "Why couldn't you keep your pants on!"

"You weren't there," he said. "I wanted to, but Marge is a beautiful woman. You don't know how hard it was."

Allison stared at him, feeling little sympathy, but resisting the temptation to sting him with the obvious pun.

"Which of your squeezes put the scratches on your face?"

"Lolita. She went sort of crazy. She was like a cat climbing a tree. She did this to my face and broke just about every piece of glass in my apartment. She and Marge screamed at each other. They both screamed at me. Marge ran out, crying. Who knows what she's told her husband, if anything. I tried to calm Lolita down. I talked with her for a long time. It was more like talking *at* her, though. She wouldn't respond to anything I said. She was still sitting on my living room floor when I left. I asked her to wait there and talk with *you* before she did anything else."

"Pardon me?"

"Yeah, I thought maybe you'd talk to her for me?"

"I am supposed to talk to your girlfriend for you? I'm your lawyer, Joey, not your social secretary. What exactly am I supposed to tell her? Do you expect me to set up your next date? To mediate her dispute with Marge Tappinger over property rights to your body?"

He shook his head. "No, no. But she needs to calm down before she goes home. In her frame of mind right now, Bear will know something's wrong. Oh, man, I'm so stupid!"

"I'll say!" Allison said. "Marge Tappinger's testimony might have been very helpful to your case and Lolita's father is paying your attorney fee. You may have just alienated the two most important people in your life!"

"I know, I know," he said, sinking onto a chair. He looked like a whipped puppy. She felt her irritation with him softening.

"Well, okay," Allison said. "Let's go over to your place. You can wait in your car while I talk to her. I have no idea what I'm going to say, but I'll do some groveling on your behalf, and we'll see what happens next. I guess things can't get any worse."

They went outside. Joey's Honda Civic was parked across the street from Allison's Jeep Cherokee.

"I'll follow you to your place," Allison said, using the button on her key fob to unlock her doors.

Allison settled into her seat and pulled her driver's door closed. As she was reaching for her seat belt, she heard popping sounds.

Puzzled, she looked toward Joey, who was still in the street. He was jerking and lurching, performing some bizarre break-dance. *Why is he dancing in the middle of the street?* Allison thought. *And the noise? What's that noise?*

She caught sight of a man standing at the back of Joey's car, twenty feet from Joey. The dark shadow was pointing a gun at Joey, firing it over and over. The staccato pops flashed in the night as Joey sank to his knees.

"Stop it!" Allison screamed without thinking.

The man, swathed in darkness and clothed in black, turned his gun in her direction. Instinctively, Allison threw herself to the right, landing hard on her console. She pressed her face to the passenger seat and covered her head with her arms. She heard glass breaking as gunshots thwacked into the windows of her Jeep. A spray of bits of broken glass rained on her hands as she pressed them to the back of her head. All she could think about was that the man in black was probably walking toward her car and soon would be pointing the gun at the back of her head. She was certain he would shoot her if she raised up even an inch. She realized with profound sadness that he would probably shoot her anyway when he reached the side of her Jeep. She squeezed her eyes tightly shut, waiting for the bullet to penetrate the back of her skull. Absurdly, she pictured Bootheel Man and the stone axe embedded in his skull. Had it been like this for him? Had time stood still as he awaited the killing blow? She could not will herself to look up to see what was coming. She was frozen in her prone position across her front seats, a lamb waiting for the slaughter.

Suddenly, the passenger-side front door of her Jeep jerked open. *God*, she thought. *I didn't even think to lock the doors!*

She pressed her face to the slick vinyl of her passenger seat, but opened her eyes a crack. The shooter was standing right next to her. She could see him from the knees down: the black pants, the black Nike shoes. His shadow was thrown onto the sidewalk by an overhead streetlight. The shadow's arm was pointing a gun downward at her. Once again, she squeezed her eyes closed. *This is it. The end of everything. What a lot of education and training I went through for a two-year legal career. All that school, all that study, just to end like this!* She braced herself for the bullet.

The door slammed shut.

She listened, but heard nothing, not even the sound of footsteps walking away. Was he standing right outside the door, waiting for her to look up? She pictured herself staring down a gun barrel if she were bold enough to raise her face. Maybe he wanted to look into her eyes as he shot her. Maybe he got his kicks out of seeing his victim's eyes widen with fear.

No way! She kept her nose pressed to the car seat. *I won't give him that!*

What was he doing? Why hadn't he killed her? She pictured a cat toying with a baby bird, sharp claws ready to take a life at any moment, but the thrill of the hunt keeping the bird alive. Was she the bird? Was this man just playing with her before he finished her off? Allison had no idea how much time was passing.

She heard someone crying. Was it a witness? Had someone seen what happened? With shock, she realized that the sobs were coming from her own mouth. She made herself stop.

Then she heard groans. Were those hers, too? No. It was Joey. The groans came from Joey. She remembered his ghostlike deathdance in the middle of the street. Could he still be alive?

How long had she been lying across her front seat, hiding her face? Time had lost its meaning for her. Cautiously, expecting at any moment to feel the impact of a bullet, she raised her head and looked around.

Her side window was pocked and spiderwebbed from bullet holes. More holes dotted her front windshield. But through the shattered shards of glass she saw Joey Red Horse lying in the street.

She pulled herself erect, opened her driver-side door and spilled out of the Jeep. She landed on her hands and knees.

Half-running, half-crawling, she made her way to Joey's body.

The chest of his white t-shirt was soaked red with his blood. It was a second skin, stuck to him, molded to the contours of his body, like a snake's skin ready to slough off. Already, a large pool of blood was underneath him, spreading into an ever-widening circle on the pavement, as if his very soul were in the act of fleeing his crumpled body.

His left leg twisted underneath him at an odd angle. *That must be uncomfortable*, Allison thought, instantly realizing the absurdity of her observation. A crumpled leg was the least of Joey's problems.

"Miss Culbertson," Joey whispered. He was looking at her.

She scooted closer to him, pulling his head onto her lap. "Joey," she said. "Oh, Joey."

"They're grave robbers," he said, his voice so soft she could hardly hear him. "Don't let them get away with it. Please don't. Keep up my fight. Please."

It occurred to her that she should try to find his worst wounds and apply pressure to them, but before she could pull up his shirt, Joey heaved a rattling gasp, and his head fell limply and lifelessly against her knee. His eyes were still open, but Allison knew he was gone.

In the distance she heard sirens.

A voice from the darkness told her, "Lady, it's okay. The police are on the way. I called the police."

Everything was blindingly bright. It was as if she were an actress on stage, holding the hero's head in her lap, with brilliant theater lights illuminating the tragic couple for the audience. It gradually dawned upon her that cars had stopped on Main Street to avoid hitting her and Joey. The combined beams from many pairs of headlights bathed them in eerie brightness.

She felt wet. She looked down. The pool of Joey's blood was expanding beneath her knees. She was sitting right in the middle of it. Her pants were as blood-soaked as Joey's shirt.

She wished the unseen woman nearby would stop screaming. She needed to think. She needed to understand what had just happened. That woman's screaming was unnerving. She couldn't concentrate. She couldn't think.

"Shut up!" she yelled. "Shut up!"

The next thing she knew, she was lying on her back on the pavement, being examined by paramedics. Harry Sullinger was looking over their shoulders, an anxious expression on his face.

Chapter 12

Harry Sullinger stood near the doorway of Joey Red Horse's apartment. He held a search warrant in one hand, his Beretta pistol in the other. After a quick walk-through of the apartment to make sure no one was hiding inside, he positioned himself near the front door and tried to stay out of the way as two experienced evidence-technicians examined every inch of Joey's home, photographing and studying every nook and cranny. Occasionally they paused to let him know where he could walk.

The Major Case Squad had been activated within minutes of the killing of Joey Red Horse, the moment it became apparent that the shooter had gotten away. Sullinger's first lead assignment had been to obtain a search warrant for Joey Red Horse's home. It had taken less than two hours to get the paperwork prepared and presented to a judge. The judge issuing the warrant agreed that Joey's status as a murder victim provided a fair probability that evidence pertaining to his murder might be found in his home. Sullinger hoped to find a clue about the identity of Joey's killer.

Sullinger was careful about what he touched as he moved through the apartment. He followed the evidence technicians as if they were minesweepers. Carter and Brewer, both well-trained specialists, were checking for fingerprints and swabbing for DNA. At this point, Sullinger was more interested in spotting obvious clues.

Joey Red Horse's small apartment was a physical wreck. Lamps were broken. Ashtrays were smashed. Broken plates and drinking glasses littered the floor. Framed pictures lay on the carpet, their glass cracked.

"There was either one hell of a ruckus in this apartment or somebody was looking for something," Carter said.

"Or both," Sullinger said, studying the spines of the books stacked on an end table by a couch in the living room: *Mound Builders of Ancient America* by Robert Silverberg, *The Moundbuilders: Ancient Peoples of Eastern North America* by George R. Milner, *Ancient Cahokia and the Mississippians* by Timothy R. Pauketat,

Cahokia: The Great Native American Metropolis by Biloine Whiting Young and Melvin L. Fowler, *The Archaeology of Missouri* by Carl Chapman, and *Alfred Dennison and the Bootheel Man* by Clive Faulkner.

"Don't walk over here," Brewer said, kneeling near the couch. "I think I've found a couple drops of blood."

"I won't go anywhere without your permission," Sullinger promised.

In the kitchen, Sullinger noticed nothing out of the ordinary except broken dishes and glassware and some cactus plants growing in clay flowerpots on the windowsill over the kitchen sink. The refrigerator was stocked with the usual items. He noted that Joey Red Horse's beer of choice was Crazy Horse Malt Liquor.

"That's a surprise," he said.

"What?" asked Carter.

"Our Indian activist was drinking a brand of beer made by a company featured prominently on the Indians' boycott list. You know, like the Washington Redskins football team? The name itself just irritates them. You wouldn't think Joey Red Horse would want to give that company his business. In fact, the beer must be really old, because I seem to remember that the brewing company quit making it years ago and apologized after the estate of Crazy Horse sued them."

"Maybe we'd better analyze it," Brewer said, "and make sure he wasn't poisoning the stuff to put back on some liquor-store shelf to hassle the company. Remember the cyanide in Tylenol packages back in 1982? We'd better check every cabinet for potential poisons."

"Good idea," Sullinger said.

In the bedroom, Sullinger was the first to spot a used condom lying on the carpet next to the bed.

"Make sure that's checked for DNA," he said.

"Gee, thanks, Harry. DNA in a condom! I never would have thought of that all by myself." Carter knelt to take a photograph. "We're so lucky you're here."

Sullinger glanced around the small bedroom. He moved to a desk in a corner of the room. The stack of books on Joey's desk included *Grave Injustice: The American Indian Repatriation Movement and NAGPRA* by Kathleen S. Fine-Dare, and *Peyote: The Divine Cactus* by Edward F. Anderson. An electronic weighing scale of the sort preferred by drug dealers was also on the desk.

Sullinger took his pen and used it to pull open a desk drawer.

Inside, he spotted two shoeboxes full of baggies packed with brown pieces of plant material about the size of acorns.

"Looks like we've got some kind of drug here," Sullinger said. "Be sure to photograph it before we take it out of the drawer. I'm not sure what it is."

After Carter snapped photographs of the desktop, Sullinger picked up the book about peyote and thumbed through it.

"I would say the stuff in the baggies is something called 'peyote buttons' or 'mescal buttons,' pieces of dried cactus."

"It's a controlled substance," Carter said. "Peyote has mescaline in it. We used to see a lot of it, but not so much anymore. It was used by the same hippies and baby boomers who fancied LSD."

"Joey, Joey, Joey," Sullinger sighed, looking around the bedroom. "What other secrets did you hide?"

When the evidence technicians finished photographing and collecting Joey's drug stash, Sullinger opened another desk drawer. This one contained Joey's correspondence. Slipping on surgeon's gloves, so he would not contaminate the paper with his own fingerprints, Sullinger glanced at the envelopes. Two letters were from Joey's lawyer, Allison Culbertson. They bore the return address of her office. The letters, though, proved to be nothing more than routine legal correspondence. The next notes were more interesting. They bore the return address of Marge Tappinger. They proved to be rather steamy.

Sullinger smiled faintly. His third wife had once written him indiscreet letters like this when he was off for sixteen weeks for special training at the FBI Academy at Quantico, Virginia. Of course, that was before she met that rich oral surgeon with the terrific bedside manner.

"Be sure to fingerprint these," Sullinger said.

Sullinger's cell phone rang and he answered it. He listened a few moments and flipped it shut. "Sorry, guys," he said. "You'll have to do the rest of the search without me. Think you can handle it?"

"I don't know, Harry," Carter said. "How will we know what to fingerprint or check for DNA without you right here looking over our shoulders? What's the big rush, anyway?"

Harry couldn't help smiling. "The Squad Commander has a witness he wants me to interview. He picked me because I've talked with this particular individual before. He thinks I might have a rapport with her."

"Who is it?"

"Oh, some lawyer named Allison Culbertson."

Allison Culbertson huddled on an examination table in the hospital emergency room, clad in a standard-issue light-colored hospital gown. Harry Sullinger poked his head around the curtain.

"Hi, Counselor," he said. "The doctor says I can see you now."

She glanced up at him. In spite of her general irritation with the police department for swabbing her fingernails and collecting her clothing as evidence, she was pleased to see Harry Sullinger. Her pleasure surprised her. She had a vague memory of glimpsing his face right before she passed out.

"Come in," she said. "Pardon me if I don't stand up." She nodded to the IV attached to her arm. "Apparently I was in shock when they brought me in. They're still dosing me with drugs. Legal ones, of course."

"Last time I saw you, you didn't look so hot," Harry said. "Or, I should say, hot, maybe, healthy, no. Do you feel well enough to talk to me?"

"Yes." Allison shuddered, remembering Joey's jerky dance of death, and the terror she experienced when the man with the gun fired at her and opened her car door.

Allison squeezed her hands tightly together, trying to forget the awful images. She glanced at the laminated, hospital name-bracelet on her wrist. Her gaze moved to her hands. A question rose to her lips. "Why did the police swab my fingernails?"

Harry shrugged, conveying by the movement his impression that the act had little or no significance. "Joey had scratches on his face. It's standard police procedure to swab the fingernails of people he's been around. For DNA transfer, you know."

"Well, that will be a real helpful test. My hands were covered with his blood from holding his head in my lap. Of course I have his DNA on my hands!" She felt a sob catch in her throat. "What about my clothes? The nurse said you guys took them as evidence?"

"Standard procedure. Your pants and shirt were covered with blood."

"They even took my underwear!"

"Again, the crime lab will be checking for DNA transfer. It's all routine."

Allison blushed. "You will *not* find Joey Red Horse's DNA in my underwear."

"I am glad to hear that."

"I guess they'll tell you. I wet my pants." She looked down.

"That's a pretty normal reaction," Sullinger said. "Studies show that twenty-four percent of soldiers in combat in World War II lost bladder control. It's physiological, the old fight-or-flight thing. Your body is sending its reserves to your arms and legs, including the sentries who were formerly stationed at your bladder."

Allison glanced up sharply. Sullinger was smiling at her gently.

"See, you're normal," he said. "If you feel well enough to talk about it, I need to know what happened tonight. The sooner we know the facts, the sooner we catch the killer. The officer who swabbed your hands said you told him the shooting was done by one man dressed in black. The doctors were still checking you out, though, and asked him to leave the room. I'd like to get a more detailed statement from you. Is that okay?"

"Yes."

"Why don't you start at the beginning? Tell me what happened."

Allison described the trip to Oklahoma with Lolita Smith. She told him about dropping Lolita off at Joey's apartment when they got back to Cape Girardeau. She described getting the frantic phone call from Joey and meeting him at her office. She told how Joey had been fooling around with both Marge Tappinger and Lolita Smith, and how Lolita had caught him with Marge.

"He wanted me to go back to his apartment with him, to talk to Lolita."

"Lolita was still there?"

108

"That's what he said."

"Had you ever been to his apartment?"

"No."

"Why did he want you to talk to Lolita?"

"Her father, Bear Smith, posted Joey's bond. Joey was afraid Lolita would tell her father about their affair and Bear might ask the court to return his money and put Joey back in jail."

"Was Joey also afraid that Bear Smith might kick his ass for messing around with his daughter?"

"Maybe. Bear Smith is a scary guy. I don't remember Joey saying specifically that he was afraid of him, though. They were friends."

"So, what happened when you left to go to Joey's apartment?"

Allison described the shooting outside her office. As she spoke, she vividly remembered her shock and surprise at hearing the sound of the shots. She told him about her bewilderment when she first saw Joey jerk and flinch.

"I didn't realize he was being shot for the longest time," she said. "It must have lasted just a few seconds, but it seemed to take forever before it registered in my brain that someone was shooting him. Then I looked over near his car and saw a man standing there pointing a gun at him. I could see fire coming from the end of the gun."

"What did the man look like?"

"I don't know," Allison shook her head with frustration. "I was focusing on the gun and the dawning realization about what was happening. It was dark over by Joey's car. I never got a look at the man except to see that he was dressed all in black, but I can't even say that for sure. Something dark was covering his face, but I don't know if it was a ski mask or what. I have no idea how big he was. I can't even say for sure it was a man, it all happened so fast. And then . . . " She shuddered.

"What?" Harry added softly.

"Then the shooter turned the gun toward me and pointed it right at me."

Allison hung her head. In spite of her determination not to, she began crying.

"I was too afraid to keep looking. I threw myself across my front seat. I could hear the gunshots hitting my car. I thought for sure I was being killed. It seemed to last forever, all the gunshots and all the glass breaking, but suddenly it was quiet, completely quiet. I thought about raising my head to look around, but I pictured him shooting me, so I just kept lying there. I was so afraid."

Allison shuddered again, reliving the awful moment.

"Then the door right by my head opened, the passenger door. I knew the man was pointing the gun down at me. I knew my life was ending. I waited for the bullet to hit me. But finally he closed the door and left. I eventually heard Joey groaning, and I got out of the car and went to him. He was still alive when I reached him. I sat next to him. I remember holding his head in my lap. He died while I cradled his head in my lap."

"Did you ever get a good look at the shooter?"

"No."

"Not even when he came to the car?"

"No. I know it was cowardly. I'm ashamed to admit it, but I just kept my head down. I was positive he was going to shoot me. I didn't want to watch."

He asked her more questions about Marge Tappinger, and she told him everything she knew about the affair. He asked her more questions about Bear Smith and Lolita Smith, and she told what she knew. It felt strange, telling a police officer her client's secrets, but Joey was dead and the police were trying to catch his murderer. She was sure Joey would not have minded.

"What about Joey's drug use?" Sullinger asked. "What can you tell me about that?"

Allison was surprised by the question. "Drugs? As far as I know, Joey wasn't involved in drugs."

"Cocaine?" Sullinger asked.

"No."

"Meth?"

"No."

"Peyote?"

"I read somewhere that many Osages used peyote in religious practices years ago, but Joey never told me anything about using it himself," Allison said. "I can tell you that he never seemed to be under the influence of *any* sort of drug or alcohol during the times I was around him. Not ever."

"Did Joey have any enemies?" Sullinger asked.

"Enemies?" Allison wrapped the flimsy hospital gown around herself more tightly as she pondered the question. "I know he considered archaeologists and museums to be his adversaries, but enemies might be too strong a word. His goal was to make them repatriate the bones and burial relics of *all* Native Americans. I don't know that the museums and archaeologists considered *him* to be an enemy, though. Joey was actually a very likeable guy."

"He certainly would not have been on Clive Faulkner's list of favorite people," Sullinger suggested.

"No, but Joey never spoke of getting any sort of threats from Faulkner or any other archaeologist types. In fact, the big goal of his life was to convince these private museums to voluntarily repatriate the bones of his ancestors."

"Rex Tappinger had a reason not to like him," Harry said.

"True, but I don't think he ever met Rex Tappinger. I suppose it would depend upon what Marge told her husband, and when."

"Lolita was so mad at him she scratched his face and tore up his apartment," Sullinger said. "She was gone by the time we got to his place with the search warrant two hours later. She had motive and opportunity."

"She's just a girl, a young girl," Allison said. "She loved Joey. Murder was the last thing on her mind."

"They don't call jealousy the green monster for nothing," Sullinger said. "What about her father? Would finding out about the affair make him mad enough to kill?"

"You're asking the wrong person," Allison said. "I can't imagine being mad enough at anyone to commit murder." She recalled the terror of lying facedown on the car seat, awaiting her execution. She remembered the paralysis of her fear. "I don't ever want to be so helpless again," she whispered.

"What?" Sullinger asked. "I couldn't hear that last part."

Allison felt tears welling in her eyes as she looked at the big, muscular detective. This man would not have sprawled facedown on his car seat, waiting spinelessly to be shot in the back of the head.

"I don't ever want to feel so helpless again," she repeated. She took a deep breath, and exhaled slowly. Her eyes met Sullinger's. "Joey didn't deserve this."

"No, he didn't. They seldom do."

"I want you to find his killer."

"We'll find the person who did it. I promise."

Part II

Grave Danger

Most modern Americans think of the Indians who occupied the United States before them as nothing more than nomadic savages, primitive people hunting and fishing for food, pitching their rude wigwams wherever game was plentiful. That these aborigines could build a great metropolis, and from it operate a huge trading network, would seem incredible. Yet that is exactly what the Indians did. Four centuries before Columbus arrived, an extraordinary city—30,000 inhabitants, 10-story-high structures, streets, docks, and warehouses—covered some six and a half square miles just east of what is now St. Louis.

> —John E. Pfeiffer, "Indian City on the Mississippi"
> *Nature/Science Annual*, 1974

Cahokia was North America's Rome, the center to which awe-struck pilgrims traveled miles to worship at the sacred eternal fires burning on the hilltops of the gods.

* * *

It is now known that at the time the Saxons were first settling into Bristol, when Leif Eriksson was blown off course from Greenland and encountered the Western Hemisphere, and when England's King Ethelred II was demanding that merchants in London pay their taxes in peppercorns, the Indians of Cahokia were constructing a city near the banks of the Mississippi—the first expression of urbanism in North America. For more than three hundred years that mighty city influenced life over half of the continent. Yet when the first Europeans came down the river, Cahokia did not exist in a single living memory. America's first metropolis had truly been forgotten.

> —*Cahokia: The Great Native American Metropolis*,
> Biloine Whiting Young and Melvin L. Fowler (2000)

Chapter 13

The deafening roar of the crowd reverberated in Thunder Runner's ears as his spear struck the rolling chunkey stone a direct hit, sending both spear and disc flying across the hard-packed clay surface of the playing field. As usual, his powerful sprint and forceful toss had vanquished an opponent. Naked from the waist up, wearing only a deerskin breechcloth, he raised a muscular arm, acknowledging the cheers of the crowd as he trotted back to the starting point.

Out of the corner of his eye, he noticed the Grand Chief, the great Triumphant Falcon, applauding. It thrilled him. Here he was, barely old enough to be considered a man, and even Triumphant Falcon, the world's greatest ruler, a man chosen to lead his people by the will of the Great Spirit, the all-powerful mystery force *Wah'Kon-Tah*, not only knew of Thunder Runner's existence, but was actually cheering for him. It felt good.

Life was good. He closed his eyes and turned his head toward the sky. The late summer sun beat soothingly on his eyelids, its heat an orange glow. He savored the praise from the crowd.

Thunder Runner kept his face stoic as he rejoined his teammates to watch the next man from their village go up against an opponent from Cahokia. The crowd noise made it hard to hear the game crier announce the score.

The chunkey tournament was taking place at Cahokia, the thriving community at the juncture of the big rivers. Cahokia was both the home of the Grand Chief and the pulsing heart of his empire. Thunder Runner and his team from the Village of Gray Wolf were visitors. The contest was being played on the great plaza of the breathtakingly large village. Thousands of boisterous fans filled the flat plaza surrounding the chunkey field. More people covered the terraced slopes of the mounds above it.

Triumphant Falcon stood at the top of the steps leading up the huge Temple Mound. He was silhouetted against the sun as he presided over the tournament being held in his honor on the chunkey field below him. The sun was bright. The delicious smells of popping corn and sizzling deer meat filled the air. Thunder Runner breathed deeply and thanked *Wah'Kon-Tah* for blessing him with the speed of a mountain lion, the strength of a bear, and the throwing accuracy of the great warrior in the heavens who hurled lightning bolts from the sky.

Maybe I will have that lightning-bolt-throwing job someday. Perhaps the Grand Chief will put in a good word for me. Thunder Runner smiled at his bold and sacrilegious thoughts. Modesty sometimes came hard for him.

Thunder Runner had been the most gifted athlete in his age group for almost as long as he could remember. Over the past year, he had emerged as the best chunkey player of his generation. Born with blazing speed and a powerful throwing arm, he had stalked squirrels and birds living near the Village of Gray Wolf since he was old enough to throw rocks. His uncle had given him a chunkey stone and throwing spear when he was a small boy. He had fallen in love with the game. It had fascinated him ever since. It was the first thing he thought of when he awoke in the morning, and the last thing in his mind before drifting off to sleep at night.

His right arm held a power not possessed by other men. He could throw farther, harder, and with more accuracy than anyone else. Most of it, he knew, was simply a gift. Some men were blessed with handsome faces, others with a great talent for storytelling, and others with deep and rich singing voices. He had *the arm*. He could throw. Much of his skill, though, came from diligent practice. Long after others became physically tired or mentally distracted, Thunder Runner found in himself not only a willingness, but an irresistible urge to remain alone on the chunkey field or to make solitary excursions into the woods, repeatedly throwing his poles and spears at targets, some standing and some moving. He was positive no man on earth had ever spent more time throwing a spear than he. Repetition had honed the skill he was born with to the highest level humanly possible. That was why it was sometimes hard to stay humble.

He joined those around him in uttering a loud groan as a Cahokia man scored another point against one of Thunder Runner's clansmen. Both players had missed the chunkey stone. The Cahokia player's pole landed closest to the disc, earning the Cahokia village yet another point.

"It is not fair," Red Hawk muttered. "Their village is so much larger than ours. How can we hope to challenge them?"

"It is simple," Thunder Runner told his best friend. "I will keep beating my opponent and you keep beating yours. We will defeat them one man at a time, one contest at a time. Concentrate. Run like the wind. Throw accurately. See the chunkey stone. Hit the chunkey stone. That is all there is to it."

"Easy for you, maybe," Red Hawk said. "I cannot remember the last time you lost an individual match."

Thunder Runner recalled the day vividly. It was many seasons ago. The embarrassment of losing still galled him. But he said nothing. He did not wish to boast. To talk about how long it had been since he had lost a chunkey match would sound like bragging. No, it *would* be bragging. He would resist the temptation. He had been wrestling with his vanity ever since the comment from that pretty girl in the woods.

"Come on!" he yelled to Holes in His Wings, the teammate poised at the starting line. "You can do it!"

Thinking of the girl, he took a moment to casually scan the crowd, looking for her. Her name was Dawn Breaks. She was the daughter of Night Owl, one of the tenders of the fire at the Village of Gray Wolf. She and her family had made the trip to Cahokia for the chunkey tournament and the Green Corn Festival. He had seen them in a canoe on the way upriver. But he had not spotted her yet among the crowd at the chunkey tournament. Surely she was watching.

It surprised him that he was looking for her. In the first place, it did not speak well for his mental preparedness. Normally, before a chunkey match, he developed tunnel vision, an ability to block out everything else and concentrate completely upon the task at hand: hitting that incredibly fast rolling stone with a powerful throw of his eight-foot-long blunt-tipped spear. He would take his turn, win his individual contest, and then watch and cheer for his clansmen as

116

they competed against their opponents. He always knew the score. He always knew the game situation. He always knew precisely what he personally needed to accomplish in order for his village to win.

So what was he doing, thinking about this girl?

He never would have guessed she could have such an effect on him. Dawn Breaks was a slender reed of a girl. Growing up in the same village, several seasons apart in age, he had barely noticed her until recently. She had been one of the many children of the village, one more little thing beneath his notice. More voluptuous girls had been throwing themselves at him since he had reached puberty, some his age and many older. Once he became a highly regarded chunkey player, even adult women, sophisticated and sensuous women, many already the wives of powerful men in the tribe, had shown interest in him. Dawn Breaks had barely reached woman-hood. Willowy as a cattail, she had been invisible to him until that moment in the woods a few days ago.

He had been on one of his throwing excursions when he met her. He had taken a sharp-tipped spear into the woods to hurl at wild critters. He was the bane of their existence. In fact, he was the only man in the village who could routinely hit a bird with a spear. Most simply could not do it. Thunder Runner, on the other hand, virtually never sojourned into the forest without returning home with a collection of birds, rabbits, and squirrels to add to the village's stew pots. He was, he had to admit, already something of a legend.

It was fun being a legend. But it did tend to swell one's head.

On that memorable occasion when he first noticed Dawn Breaks, he had thrown his spear at a particularly obnoxious squirrel sitting on a tree limb in a tall oak. He missed the chattering target and his spear soared out of sight over a hill. He heard a dog yelp and a girl scream. He sprinted through the woods and found Dawn Breaks in a clearing next to a brook, kneeling beside a fuzzy little wolf-like puppy.

Dawn Breaks was very pretty, big-eyed and smooth-faced, with straight, black hair hanging long and loose in front of her ears. Like all women in the village during the hot summer season, she wore only a skirt. As she knelt next to her whimpering puppy, the skirt hiked up, exposing nicely shaped and muscular legs. He noticed.

She was examining her quivering dog's paw. Thunder Runner's spear lay on the ground nearby.

"I am Thunder Runner," he announced, slowing to a walk as he came close. "Let me help you."

He expected her to beg him to tend to her wounded dog. He did not know much about caring for injured dog feet, but he was sure he knew more than some young girl. He would wait for an appropriate amount of thanks for his noble generosity, and then he would magnanimously agree to help.

His offer was barely out of his mouth before she jerked her face toward him, eyes flashing.

"I know who you are! Help? Haven't you done enough already! You did this!"

He was startled, both by the tone of her voice and her disrespectful words. Most girls his age swooned over him. This one was two or three winters younger than he. He would have expected a great deal of swooning. Instead, her voice was filled with venom.

"What happened to the dog?" he asked.

"What happened! You almost killed my puppy!" She caressed the pup's bloody paw, feeling for broken bones. "Your spear came out of nowhere. It bounced across the ground and hit my dog's foot! You should be more careful! You could kill someone with your carelessness!"

Blushing, he strode to his spear and picked it up. He was irritated. He thought hard for a retort. After all, he had his honor and reputation to maintain. "If you know who I am, then you also know how well I throw. My accuracy is unmatched. If I wanted to kill your dog, I would have killed her. She would be dead right now."

The girl stood up, her dog in her arms. She held it out so its belly and underside faced him.

"It is a he," she said. "See!"

"What difference does it make? You know what I mean."

The dog began urinating. The yellow stream arced through the air and rained upon Thunder Runner's moccasins.

"There is one difference," she said.

"Hey! Look out!" He backed away from her.

Still not smiling, she cradled the puppy in her arms. Her eyes met his. "Do you mean to say that you aimed at my dog's foot?"

Thunder Runner shook his head with exasperation. "Of course not. It was an accident. I was throwing at a squirrel."

"So, you missed the squirrel and hit my dog? What does that say about the accuracy you speak of with such pride?"

He forgot about her pretty face and her attractive legs. Who was she to speak this way to *him*, the best chunkey player in the village? Had she intentionally pointed that squirting dog at him? It seemed likely.

"Everyone misses now and then," he said. "I am Thunder Runner. I miss less often than most."

She studied him, her eyes thoughtful. "I told you, I know who you are. Everyone knows who you are, famous chunkey player. But if you were half as important as you think you are, *Wah'Kon-Tah* would have made you Grand Chief at Cahokia, instead of a game-player in the Village of Gray Wolf. You can throw a stick. So what? Forgive me if my dog and I are not impressed."

She turned her back on him and headed back toward the village. "I guess I should be glad you did not hit *me* with one of your wild throws," she added over her shoulder, not even bothering to turn around as she hurled her last insult. "I suppose I should consider myself lucky!"

He admired her shape and her graceful movements as she stalked off. It was hard to stay mad at a girl who looked like that. "Maybe I *should* have hit you!" he yelled. "Somebody needs to teach you some manners."

When she was gone, he thought about her words. *If you were half as important as you think you are,* Wah'Kon-Tah *would have made you Grand Chief at Cahokia, instead of a game-player in the Village of Gray Wolf.* Ouch. Surely he was not so arrogant to deserve such an insult. Yet, he *had* boasted about his throwing accuracy. Perhaps she had a point.

At that precise moment, alone in the woods, he vowed to begin working on the virtue of humility. It was a prized trait among his people, but a rather new concept for him.

He started by visiting her camp that evening to apologize, something he should have done in the first place. Her father and stepmother were flabbergasted when he showed up at the entrance to their lodge. It was apparently the first time a young man had come calling for Dawn Breaks. She accepted his apology politely, and even apologized for her own words, all the while telling him with her eyes that she found his efforts to impress her little more than mildly amusing. He had not seen her since.

Now, at the biggest chunkey contest of the season, the All-Village Tournament at the Green Corn Festival, where people traveled long distances from all across the region to pay tribute to the Grand Chief and to *Wah'Kon-Tah*, to celebrate another good harvest, and where the best chunkey players from each village vied for bragging rights as champions, he was hoping she would be watching him play. He wanted her to be impressed. With him.

The crowd was loud and boisterous. But he was not even sure she was in it. Was it possible she had come all the way to Cahokia from the Village of Gray Wolf and not even shown up at the big game?

Chunkey is more than just throwing a stick, he told himself. *It is more than a game. It is speed, skill, talent, coordination, concentration, patience, stamina, strategy, strength, dexterity, and endurance. It rewards those who work hard to improve themselves, to become the best athletes they can be. When I compete on the highest level, like today, I feel the power of* Wah'Kon-Tah *in me.*

He scanned the crowd for the pretty face of Dawn Breaks. He hoped she was somewhere amid the masses, watching him play, watching him soar to the heights of victory, watching him make a name for himself right under the nose of the powerful Grand Chief.

He took his turn again, this time paired up against Cahokia's best player. Once again, he experienced the thrill of an explosive start, the knee-pumping sprint, the arm-whipping fling of the spear, the anticipation of watching the wooden shaft soar through the air, and the exhilaration of a direct hit. Amid the cheers of the crowd, he trotted back to his team.

Above him, Triumphant Falcon, the Grand Chief, sat watching the proceedings, as if he were *Wah'Kon-Tah* himself. No living man had ever seen *Wah'Kon-Tah*, the invisible, all-pervasive power residing in the air, sky, clouds, stars, sun, moon, and earth, and in all living and moving things. But if *Wah'Kon-Tah* were ever to appear before mortals in the form of a man, Thunder Runner expected him to look much like Triumphant Falcon. The Grand Chief gleamed in the bright sun, tall and handsome, his entire being shining like the inside of a conch shell. He was naked except for a white breechcloth, a breastplate of white shell beads and bones, and a huge robe made of thousands of small white beads. His attendants were fanning him and holding a shade over his head.

A sacrilegious thought struck Thunder Runner. *If the great man's priests can predict the future, as they claim, why does he bother to watch the game? Why not simply ask them who will win?*

Thunder Runner found himself staring at Triumphant Falcon. This man's power had eclipsed that of any man who had ever lived. His vision had greatly expanded and centralized a federation of formerly autocratic villages dotting the inland rivers. This Grand Chief possessed mystical powers. His incomprehensible woodhenge could accurately predict the positions of the stars in the heavens. His favored position in the eyes of *Wah'Kon-Tah* protected the villages under his control from floods and famine. His charisma burned so brightly that even stubbornly independent men yearned to be in his presence, to follow him wherever he might lead, to laugh at his jokes, and benefit from his wisdom. His message that all men are connected had united different peoples and had ignited trade up and down the great Father of Waters. His military genius lay in building an army so strong and awesome that all usurpers feared to attack him. Most frightening of all, he surrounded himself with bizarre and mysterious priests who could always counsel him exactly what he should do next to most please *Wah'Kon-Tah*.

Such a man was Triumphant Falcon, whose attention now focused solely upon Thunder Runner excelling at the game of chunkey.

Time passed quickly. Soon, Thunder Runner was lining up again, matched against yet another Cahokian, one who could throw a long way but whose aim was occasionally poor. The game was tied. This time, Thunder Runner intentionally let his opponent throw first and miss. The chunkey stone continued its trek toward the far end of the field. Letting it roll farther and farther away, he carefully assessed its speed, its angle, the distance involved, and the force of the breeze whipping in from the west. At just the right moment, Thunder Runner hurled his spear. The crowd heaved a collective gasp as it soared high into the air. Underneath, the chunkey stone rolled along like a clueless rabbit loping across a field, oblivious to its impending doom from a hawk gliding through the sky above it. After reaching the apex of its flight, the spear dropped with increasing speed. The space between the chunkey stone and the descending spear grew smaller and smaller until, finally, the chunkey stone rolled to a stop and the spear hit the ground right next to it.

The crowd erupted in a roar. It was probable that not one of them had ever seen a man throw a spear so far, much less have it strike so close to a moving target. Thunder Runner's village had won this round. They would advance in the tournament.

Once again keeping his face stoic, Thunder Runner saluted the crowd and made his way back to his teammates. This time, though, two things increased his already keen sense of pleasure and anticipation. The Grand Chief was waving at him, a respectful and friendly salutation. It was a heady thing to have the great Triumphant Falcon acknowledge one's skill, especially when one is already battling a humility deficit.

But the other thing actually excited him even more.

Dawn Breaks, the lovely if rather insulting girl from the woods, was standing with her father and stepmother among a contingent of spectators from the Village of Gray Wolf. So she *was* watching the game! She was not applauding, but she was smiling. A big smile. Directed right at him. No question about it. He allowed himself to smile back. It was a good day to be alive!

Chapter 14

Thunder Runner dressed slowly as he prepared for his meeting with Grand Chief Triumphant Eagle. He dressed at the visitor's camp just outside the south end of Cahokia. His clean breechcloth, leggings, fringed shirt, and moccasins were all made of buckskin. His shirt was decorated with beads cut from seashells. When he felt ready, he made his way through the crowd toward the huge Temple Mound that towered over the north end of the city.

The visit to Cahokia for the Green Corn Festival at the end of each summer was his favorite seasonal event, and not just because of the chunkey tournament.

The Green Corn Ceremony was an extremely important rite for his people. It took place at the first full moon after the late corn became ripe. It was a time of thanksgiving, renewal, and excitement. Corn was the main foodstuff for the Mississippian people. A failure of the annual crop could trigger a life-threatening famine. The Green Corn Ceremony, held in late summer, was a formal expression of gratitude to *Wah'Kon-Tah* for providing another successful crop. It was the beginning of a new season. It marked a moment when the people, purified by ceremonies conducted during the festival, began their lives anew. It was a time of games, music, dancing, ceremony, marriages, speech-making, bartering, fasting, feasting, and vows of self-improvement. No one was permitted to eat any of this season's late corn until after the Green Corn Ceremony.

Thunder Runner made his way through a busy Cahokia. Both the welcoming feast and the chunkey tournament were over, but much remained to be done before the fasting would begin the next day. Workers were busily refurbishing the public lodges, adding a fresh coat of white clay to the wattle-and-daub walls of the village's most prominent lodges. Women were cleaning their homes and their cooking vessels, and sweeping out and renewing the hearths of the densely packed clusters of lodges.

Thunder Runner nodded to several busy men and women as he made his way toward the huge lodge of the Grand Chief.

Tomorrow at high sun, the men would gather at the plaza to begin their fast. It would last until the second sunrise after its beginning. By then, each man would have purified his body, not just by fasting, but by repeatedly dosing himself with a bitter drink containing button snakeroot, to purge impurities from his body. Women and children would be barred from the plaza during the fast. Sentinels would be posted at the perimeter of the plaza to keep the women away from the men. As they fasted, the men would discuss bad behavior committed during the past year and evaluate the consequences of that behavior. They would attempt to settle offenses if hard feelings lingered.

Early in the morning on the last day of the fast, the women would cook large amounts of food and place it outside the square perimeter of the plaza. They would return to the lodges and camps. The men would bring the food into the restricted area and eat it, always remembering that it was poor etiquette to eat quickly. When ending a fast of such length and gravity, it took much self-control to eat slowly, particularly because the food was always delicious: white-tailed deer cooked slowly over open fires, fish fried in bear oil and breaded in cornmeal, boiled shellfish, roasted duck and swan, boiled squash and beans, ash cakes, corn mush, nuts, and fruits. The only thing missing would be fresh corn, which had to be avoided until the end of the Green Corn Ceremony.

Thunder Runner did not mind the fast. In fact, he enjoyed it. He always felt renewed when it was over. The annual ritual helped purify not only his body but his mind. What's more, no meal the entire year tasted better than the feast following the fast. He was sure this year would be no exception. The Grand Chief and his advisors knew how to throw a feast.

After the men ate, the women would be summoned to the plaza. The Grand Chief and the Head Priest would give rousing proclamations, reminding the warriors of their responsibilities to remain pure and to provide meat and protection for the women and children in their care. They would remind the women of their duties to harvest the corn crop and their personal vegetable gardens, to cook food for their families, to tend to their lodges and children, and to refrain from breaking marital and sexual rules.

At the end of the speeches, the crowd always grew silent as the Head Priest started a new fire. He would take a piece of dry poplar, willow, or white oak, place it between his legs, and use his hands to vigorously spin a short shaft of wood in a hole until the piece of wood began to smoke. He would add chips and splinters of pitch pine and fan the flames with the wing of a white bird. Once the flames burned briskly, he would put the burning wood block into an earthen vessel reserved specifically for that purpose and carry it to a waiting pile of wood in a prominent place in the plaza. Once he ignited the large pile, an old woman would bring a basket of newly ripened corn and vegetables and feed her offering to the hungry fire.

When the fire was roaring, the Head Priest would circle it four times. As pottery drums beat an intoxicating rhythm, he would start his Green Corn Dance, singing the sacred song and stomping his feet. He would soon be joined by five other priests and six prestigious old women, all wearing their finest clothes, anointed with bear oil, and shaking tortoiseshell rattles fastened to their legs. They would circle the fire, stamping their feet with short, quick steps, singing and dancing to the rhythmic pounding of the drums. The dance was always an exhilarating mix of beating drums, shaking rattles, and deep male voices singing and chanting the familiar song, accompanied by shrill, beseeching wails from the women.

Once the priests finished their dance, they would retire, replaced by younger members of the community, both men and women. Forming a double line, the men and women would face each other and dance to rhythmic songs in a shuffle step. Their dance usually lasted three times as long as the dance of the priests.

Most men loved the dance. In fact, for many it was the highlight of the Green Corn Festival. In the past, the dance was always rather anticlimactic for Thunder Runner, whose favorite part of the festival was the chunkey tournament. Now, he found himself looking forward to the dance with great anticipation. Dawn Breaks might be there.

He had no sooner thought about Dawn Breaks than he glimpsed her at the outdoor trade bazaar, standing by a woven mat strewn with pottery. He altered his course and headed right for her.

She was haggling with a heavyset woman over the number of conch-shell beads the woman might part with in exchange for a piece of pottery. Thunder Runner waited patiently for the negotiations to end. The woman eventually refused to trade as many beads as Dawn Breaks sought and moved along to barter with someone else.

"Hello," he said. "How are you?"

"Good morning," she said. "Congratulations on your big game. I saw you score the winning shot. No wonder you find it so difficult to be humble."

He smiled. "It is nothing. I am merely good at throwing a stick. That is what a wise person recently told me."

She smiled. She was beautiful, even prettier than he remembered. On her mat she displayed a large collection of pottery, consisting mostly of bowls and jugs. Behind her, she had placed items she had already received in trade for her pottery. Her acquisitions included furs, skins, salt, seashells, small sheets of flattened copper, and a quiver of arrows. He searched for something to say. He spotted her puppy behind her.

"How is your dog?"

"Improving. He gets around better on three feet than most do on four."

"Well, be careful picking him up," he said. "Some of his behavior could be bad for your business."

He was rewarded with a smile.

"He is a smart dog. He aims to please."

"His aim did not please me too much."

"Maybe not, but I enjoyed it."

They both laughed.

"So, who is the artist in your family?" He gestured at the assortment of pottery.

Her chin rose almost imperceptibly. "I made everything here."

"You did?" He was impressed. The pots were among the best he had ever seen. He picked up one of the bowls. It was shaped like a frog. He could not remember seeing such intricate detail in the work of other artists. He had to admit she was good. "How long have you been doing this?"

"All my life. Probably as long as you have been throwing that stick of yours."

"Very impressive. You are really good."

She raised an eyebrow. "Thank you."

He carefully replaced the bowl on its spot on the woven mat.

"Are you going to the Green Corn Dance?" he asked.

"Most likely."

"Do you have a partner for the dance?"

"Not yet."

"Would you be my partner?"

She chuckled. "I fear I am not important enough for you. Perhaps you should dance with the Grand Chief's wife."

He shrugged. "She is already taken. You have seen the man, tall and scary, with a beaded cape? What's his name? Triumphant Falcon?" He took a deep breath and continued. "I know I was rude to you when we met that day in the woods. I am a better man than you think. Let me prove it to you."

"You do not know what I think," she said, fixing him with her soft brown eyes. "The truth is, I turned down two offers just on the chance you might ask. It appears my gamble paid off."

He could not keep the grin off his face. "Good," he said. "Now I will have something to look forward to during the fast."

He glanced toward the Temple Mound. "I need to go," he said. "But I will see you at the dance."

"Where are you going?"

He hesitated. "I must meet the Grand Chief."

"You are trying too hard to impress me. Tell the truth."

"It is true. Triumphant Falcon saw me play and asked to meet me."

She rolled her eyes.

"Now I lose all hope that you will learn humility. It is a shame, because you were showing real potential." She was smiling as she said the words.

He felt happy as he left her and continued his trip to the lodge at the top of the Temple Mound.

The Temple was an imposing building at the top of the mountainous, four-sided mound. It capped the mound like the point at the end of a spear. The lodge itself was so tall that even if ten men stood on top of each other, the top man would barely touch its highest point. Its length and width were even more impressive. It was by far the largest building Thunder Runner had ever seen, and the prettiest. Its thick walls were made of wattle and daub, consisting of upright poles interlaced with vines and smaller sticks and coated with mud mixed with straw. Its walls were painted white. In the bright sunshine, the majestic building glowed like a giant star. Around it, the city stretched out in all directions. The towering Temple Mound was surrounded by hundreds of smaller mounds, each dotted with clusters of thatch-topped lodges.

As Thunder Runner climbed the many steps toward the top of the great mound, he occasionally allowed himself to marvel at the breathtaking view. The tops of trees were below him, as if he were a bird in the sky. In the distance, the massive, winding river meandered its way south, stretching far off into the distance. All around him, the great community of Cahokia spread out in each direction. This community made his own village seem like an anthill. A feeling of insignificance overwhelmed him.

Guards met Thunder Runner at the front door and led him to a large meeting room where a number of men had gathered. Triumphant Falcon sat in a circle made up of chiefs from each village. Thunder Runner was ushered into their presence. Many of the important men were smoking ceremonial pipes. A blue haze of tobacco smoke hovered above them.

"Here is the great chunkey player," Triumphant Falcon said. "Sit. You are Thunder Runner?"

Thunder Runner nodded as he settled onto a woven mat near the Grand Chief. "Yes. I am Thunder Runner from the Men of Mystery clan, of the Village of Gray Wolf."

He nodded to Gray Wolf, who sat on the other side of the circle. His chief nodded back, obviously pleased that one of his men had been summoned for an audience with the Grand Chief.

"You have many talents," Triumphant Falcon said. "Speed. Endurance. Your arm. I believe you are the best chunkey player I have ever seen, and I have been watching chunkey tournaments for a very long time."

"Thank you."

Triumphant Falcon was even more impressive up close than he had been from a distance. His face was ruddy and handsome, exuding strength and vitality. His arms were muscular and powerful. His forearms were as thick as most men's calves. He was a tall man and sat erect on his mat. In spite of the heat, he wore a white cape made of thousands of tiny beads. His iron-gray hair matched the color of his eyes.

"Tell us about yourself, Thunder Runner." The Grand Chief gestured toward the lesser chiefs sitting nearby. "We have seen you play. Most of us do not know you. We wish to learn more about you."

Thunder Runner remembered his vow of humility. He was determined to resist the opportunity to boast. "My mother was Star Woman of the Puma clan. My father was Comes Roaring of the Men of Mystery clan. Both have already passed to the next world. I live with my uncle and his family. When I am not hunting, I am playing or practicing chunkey. If I am good at what I do, it comes from hard work and countless hours of practice."

"It is true," Gray Wolf said. "He practices more than any four men put together, but still finds time to fulfill his hunting obligations. He is a credit to our people and to your leadership."

"I will trade you four of my players for him," Triumphant Falcon offered.

Thunder Runner was startled. Was he actually being traded like a deerskin?

"He is not for trade," Gray Wolf said, grinning. "We need him so we can beat you again at the next Green Corn Festival. I hope you understand."

Triumphant Falcon laughed and clapped Thunder Runner on the knee. "Do not look so alarmed, young man. I knew Gray Wolf would not trade you. I had to ask, though. I would like to see you playing for Cahokia's team some day, but I do not blame Gray Wolf for not wanting to lose such a productive member of his village."

The Grand Chief reached into a nearby bag and stood up. "Rise, Thunder Runner. I have something for you. Hold out your hand."

Dutifully, Thunder Runner sprang to his feet and extended a hand, palm up.

Triumphant Falcon handed him a necklace. Its pendant was a piece of white flint, carved into the shape of a small falcon.

"I like to recognize excellence," Triumphant Falcon said. "Wear it proudly. Do not forget the day you stood tall above all others, the day you won the tournament for your clan and brought acclaim to the Village of Gray Wolf. You are an example of the high standards I seek in the young men who make up the heart and soul of our people."

The Grand Chief took the necklace from Thunder Runner's hand.

"Lean forward," he said.

Thunder Runner bent his chin toward his chest as the most powerful man in the world fastened the necklace around his neck.

"Wear it with pride. The falcon is the swiftest of all birds. This feathered, keen-eyed warrior flies high. When it spots its prey, it dives down in a blaze of glory. It moves with such speed and force that when it strikes its victim with its feet and talons, the impact alone kills its adversary. This method of attack contrasts with the more usual killing technique of the hawk, which grasps its prey and rips it to pieces with sharp talons. There is great beauty in the death-strike of the falcon."

He turned to face the collection of chiefs watching him.

"Long ago, I chose the falcon as the symbol of our collective power. When we fight an enemy, we hit them with force they cannot survive. Savages roam these woods and rivers. Some are wild animals, but the more dangerous ones are human. These predators want our food, they want our women, and they want our children. We protect what is ours. By joining with me, you have come under the cloak of my protection. You share the power of Triumphant Falcon, the Grand Chief."

He eyed Thunder Runner. "We are having a council of the chiefs. This is a special day for you. You may leave or you may stay. If you remain with us, you may not repeat what you hear."

"I would like to stay, if it pleases Gray Wolf." Thunder Runner glanced at the chief from his village. Gray Wolf nodded, so Thunder Runner lowered himself to a mat. He listened as Triumphant Falcon continued his speech to his assembled chieftains.

"We gather once again for the Green Corn Ceremony, the beginning of a new season. Once again our villages have been blessed with another fine corn crop. Not as good as last year, but adequate for our needs."

He paused, looking from man to man.

"In the past, when we lived in separate small camps, our forefathers were a nomadic people. Circumstances required it. When a tribe lives in the same place for a long time, the humans deplete the land of its game animals. The people must eventually move, following the prey, or they perish. But when *Wah'Kon-Tah* gave us corn, he gave us the ability to stay in one place, to sink our roots into the soil, to build sturdy lodges. He provided us with peace of mind, with the satisfaction of knowing that our people will not starve just because we return from an arduous hunt empty-handed or with too little meat to feed every hungry mouth. *Wah'Kon-Tah*'s gift of corn gave us the opportunity to grow as a people, to spend time doing more with our lives than simply gathering food all day."

The Grand Chief smiled at Thunder Runner. "We would not even have time to play chunkey, if *Wah'Kon-Tah* had not given us corn! Imagine a world without chunkey! Unthinkable!"

Several members of the circle laughed at his joke.

"At the same time, even though corn has made us less dependent upon our hunting skills, it has made us more dependent upon *Wah'Kon-Tah*'s other gifts. We depend upon receiving rain, but not so much that our fields flood. We depend upon a warm growing season, but not so hot that the plants turn brown and shrivel. We depend more than ever upon *Wah'Kon-Tah* to make conditions right for our food plants to grow and thrive."

Triumphant Falcon put his hands behind his back and stared at his audience. He was the tallest man in the room, powerful and dignified. He had the full attention of each lesser chief.

"How many of you felt the earth shake during the past rainy season?"

Every man in the room raised his hand.

The Grand Chief nodded.

"I felt it, too. It was a message. I asked Head Priest Black Moon what it meant. He did not know at the time. But he has since fasted and prayed and sought guidance from the stars and from Grandfather Sun. He received an answer. It is very important. Today I pass it on to you."

Every chief, each one the most powerful man in his village, listened intently. They waited for Triumphant Falcon's next words.

Thunder Runner glanced at Head Priest Black Moon, who lurked nearby in the shadows, not participating in the discussion but observing it closely. The Head Priest was a thin man with stringy black hair. His large nose seemed too big for his face and his eyes burned with intensity. He wore a heavy bearskin mantle even though it was a warm day. Looking at the Head Priest made Thunder Runner uneasy. He quickly looked away.

"The Head Priest was given a vision," Triumphant Falcon continued. "It is disturbing and alarming. He was told that *Wah'Kon-Tah*, the all-powerful spirit, the mystery force that flows throughout all things, is no longer satisfied with the gifts we have traditionally provided at the Green Corn Ceremony. Baskets of corn and vegetables! What are such small things to him! He has grown bored with them. Singing and dancing? Beautiful, perhaps, but where is the suffering required to truly earn something of value? No, the Head Priest had a vision, a terrible vision, but a very reliable one. This time, at the Green Corn Ceremony, for the first time in a very long time, *Wah'Kon-Tah* wants blood. That was the message he was sending when the earth shook."

The chieftains stared at their ruler.

Thunder Runner stole another glance at Head Priest Black Moon. The holy man was smiling grimly.

"Yes," Triumphant Falcon said. "*Wah'Kon-Tah* has been shaking the earth to relay his message to us. He wants blood at the Green Corn Ceremony. He wants human sacrifice."

Several men in the circle murmured disapproval. Triumphant Falcon raised a hand.

Thunder Runner held his breath. He hoped this did not involve him. Surely he was not the intended donation to the heavenly thirst for blood.

132

"Silence!" the Grand Chief shouted. "Listen to me. We have several prisoners from battles with our enemies to the west. The Head Priest says that blood from prisoners will suffice for sacrificial purposes. It must be done. Think of the disaster that would befall us should we lose our corn crop next season. Remember the rumbling you felt under your feet. The mountains themselves were shaking. *Wah'Kon-Tah* is restless. *Wah'Kon-Tah* is dissatisfied. *Wah'Kon-Tah* revealed to the Head Priest his thirst for human blood. Each of us received the message through the trembling of the earth. We felt the message, but did not have the ears to understand it. Now we do. The Head Priest has never been wrong. Not once. He studies the stars. He predicts the coming and going of our seasons. He tells me exactly when certain stars will reappear in the night sky. He has been proven right over and over again. He knows the ways of *Wah'Kon-Tah*. I have faith in him. When he tells me *Wah'Kon-Tah* wants a human sacrifice, I believe him!"

Several of the chiefs murmured, making vague sounds of disagreement.

The Grand Chief was clearly irritated. He raised his hand again. "Do any of you challenge me on this?"

He was met with absolute silence.

After several heartbeats, he gave an elaborate shrug. "What do we lose by complying with the wishes of *Wah'Kon-Tah*? One prisoner? Four prisoners? Is that too much for your queasy stomachs to endure to ensure a successful corn crop?"

Many of the chiefs averted their eyes from his forceful gaze. The silence was broken by one voice of dissent.

"We lose more than that," Gray Wolf said.

Triumphant Falcon narrowed his eyes, obviously not pleased by the interruption. "How so?"

"Once we start killing prisoners of war, we become murderers. We lose righteousness. We lose self-respect."

The Grand Chief frowned. He was silent for several moments, carefully considering Gray Wolf's words.

"I do not agree with you," he said finally. "When *Wah'Kon-Tah* sends word that he wants a human sacrifice, we cannot ignore him. It would be foolish to do so. We must provide the blood he craves. It is not murder to do his will. The welfare of our people is my responsibility. It is a heavy one. But I do not intend to make this decision alone. We must agree to this as the leaders of our people. What do the rest of you say?"

He looked from one to another of the assembled chiefs.

"Each of you felt the earthquake. You heard the warning. You know what *Wah'Kon-Tah* demanded. How many of you want me to follow the advice of the Head Priest and give *Wah'Kon-Tah* the tribute he has requested? Those who agree with me raise your hands."

Triumphant Falcon thrust his own arm high into the air. "Who is with me?"

One by one, hands raised. The chieftains nodded in agreement. In the end, even Gray Wolf, the last holdout, joined the others.

"Good!" the Grand Chief exclaimed. "It is unanimous. The festival will have a new grand finale. Next season's corn crop will be the best ever!"

Thunder Runner glanced again at Head Priest Black Moon, who prowled the back of the room. The Head Priest bore a satisfied smile on his homely face. He obviously looked forward to performing the rite of human sacrifice.

Thunder Runner looked away quickly. The man made his skin crawl.

Chapter 15

Dawn Breaks felt the thrilling beat of the music caressing her soul with its pulsating rhythm. A circle of drummers pounded earthen drums in perfect unison, their flashing hands frenzied blurs as they beat the tightly stretched deerskins. Scores of men added to the power of the song by shaking gourd rattles. Others played haunting melodies on flutes made of cane and deer tibia. Powerful human voices raised in song, the deep chorus of chanting men accompanying the high-pitched voices of the women.

The music gave Dawn Breaks goose bumps. It was her favorite part of the Green Corn Festival. For her, the music alone made the celebration the grandest event of all. Certainly, it was a time of thanksgiving, a marking of the new season, a rekindling of friendships with people from neighboring villages, and a grand ceremony. Nowhere in this world, she was sure, did so many talented drummers and singers make such powerful music.

The season's new sacred fire had been lit by the Head Priest. The older priests and the specially chosen elderly women had finished their dance around the huge ceremonial fire in the center of the Grand Plaza. Double lines of younger dancers formed on all sides of the fire, lines of women facing lines of men. The plaza was crammed with people. The vast plain overflowed with throbbing and vibrant life. Like those around her, Dawn Breaks stamped her feet with short, quick steps. She added her voice to the multitude singing the sacred song.

She scanned the faces of the men lined up across from her, letting her gaze come to rest on the handsome young man directly in front of her. Thunder Runner smiled when their eyes met.

She wore her finest outfit. Her white buckskin skirt, reserved for special occasions, was bright and clingy. Its fringe seemed to dance its own frolic against her stamping thighs. Her best copper pendants dangled from her ears, glittering in the firelight. Several strings of white beads looped around her neck, accentuating her unblemished, tanned skin. Tortoiseshell rattles adorned her ankles, their river pebbles clattering merrily with every step she took. Her hair was pulled back in a long tail. Its sleek blackness was slicked down with shining bear oil, made beautifully fragrant by scent from sassafras and wild cinnamon.

She stole another look at her dance partner. Thunder Runner still focused his attention on her, his eyes twinkling. His muscular torso was bare and gleaming with sweat. His black hair framed the smooth and powerful lines of his face. He bore no ill effects from two nights and a day of fasting. If anything, his handsome features had been sharpened. His face was glowing. He was a beautiful and powerful creature! And he had picked her!

She closed her eyes and let her body move to the potency of the music. She sang along with the beautiful Green Corn Song she knew so well. She felt a glow at the core of her belly. Its sublime rush spread in warm waves, clear to her toes and the tips of her fingers. She had never felt so perfectly in tune with the world around her, so in touch with the universe. As she sang her praise to *Wah'Kon-Tah*, she felt the power of the song's words, and found herself truly thankful to *Wah'Kon-Tah* for granting her people another season of prosperity. And what a season this promised to be for her, with her growing acclaim as a potter and her budding romance with the village's most handsome man.

Oh! It was so wonderful to be alive!

She opened her eyes again. While many male dancers were staring at their feet, intently concentrating upon their own moves, Thunder Runner was focused completely on her, his feet and powerful thighs perfectly mirroring her every movement. She let her gaze travel up his body. The muscles of his hard abdomen rippled like a tightly woven mat. His waist was unbelievably trim, in striking contrast to his huge, muscular shoulders and arms.

He was truly something special. She found it hard to believe he was actually here, dancing with her, this young man who could have his pick of any woman in the village.

Once again, their eyes met. The Green Corn Song was approaching its rousing climax. Their feet were pounding a fast staccato, her every motion matched by an equal movement on his part. She followed the time-honored steps of the traditional dance, careful not to make a misstep. He followed suit, never missing a beat. His dark eyes laughed at her silently. She felt herself blushing, aware of his hot gaze and the primal urge coursing through her body.

He had to be the most graceful two-legged creature in the world. A deer might glide through the woods with his ease, or a hawk might soar through the sky with his gracefulness, but the movements of other men could not compare to those of this man.

She wondered if she could convey her thoughts to him through her eyes. With silent communication, could she reveal to him her passionate feelings while still retaining a certain amount of modesty? Did she dare to allow herself to think frivolous but pleasurable thoughts about this man during such a sacred and ritualistic dance? Yes, she dared! She quit singing and held her eyes to his as the dance reached its crescendo.

I have never been with a man, she thought hard, looking him right in the eye. *I suppose those who were interested were turned away by my indifference. But you, Thunder Runner, I cannot turn my face from you. I long to feel your arms around me, to feel my mouth on yours, to feel your chest pressed against mine! I have always seen myself only as a potter, an artist who works with clay. You make me want to be a woman! I am falling in love with you, Thunder Runner. Can you feel it? Do you know it?*

The dance ended with a dramatic drumroll and a final great rattling of gourds.

Dawn Breaks felt lightheaded. Sighing, she took a deep breath.

Thunder Runner stepped toward her and took her hands in his. Her heart swelled. Obviously, they were meant for each other. He had read her innermost thoughts. The two of them were connected. She looked into his face and willed herself to know his deepest thoughts. After all, he knew hers!

She could not quite tell what he was thinking. He leaned close, his lips near her ear. Her heart pounded as she waited for his words of love.

"Are you in pain?" he whispered. "There at the end of the dance you looked like you were about to be sick. Do you need to sit down?"

The beauty of the moment scampered away like a lizard that had lost its tail.

"I am fine," she said, as brightly as she could manage.

"Good. You are a wonderful dancer."

"So are you." *But not much of a mind reader,* she added to herself.

"Quiet, you two!" a man nearby complained. "The Head Priest is speaking."

Head Priest Black Moon stood on a wooden platform at the top of the Temple Mound. From the plaza, nobody could hear his words. It gradually dawned upon the crowd that he was summoning them to approach him, so they began walking up the steps of the huge mound. There was not room for all of the thousands of people on the plaza to climb to the very top, but Thunder Runner and Dawn Breaks managed to squeeze close enough to hear what was being said and to have a good view.

Bright fires burned on both sides of each level of the great mound. The huge ceremonial fire still roared in the center of the plaza, while other fires dotted its sides. The entire night was ablaze with firelight. The flickering light bounced off the starlit canopy of the midnight sky. The star-filled heavens surrounded the towering mound like a vast ocean around a tiny island.

Dawn Breaks caught her breath, moved to silent tears by the beauty of the moment.

The Head Priest was positioned behind a large, solid stone table, a waist-high slab of rock, his arms upraised. The hook-nosed holy man was dressed in a white buckskin waistcoat, with a white buckskin cape draped over his shoulders. Around his neck he wore a carved gorget made from a conch shell. His head was adorned with a piece of swanskin, doubled and wrapped so that only the white feathers showed. As the crowd finished climbing up the mound, the Grand Chief stepped to the platform and took a position at the side of the Head Priest. The Grand Chief was resplendent in his long, white beaded cape. He had pulled up the hood. It was shaped like the head of a huge falcon. His handsome face peered out beneath its beak.

Black Moon stood frozen, reaching for the sky, his ugliness bathed in glowing moonlight, his fierce appearance made more terrible by the flickering firelight. As the Head Priest stood motionless, Triumphant Falcon's powerful voice filled the night, ringing loud as thunderclaps.

"My people," he called out. "*Wah'Kon-Tah* is listening and is pleased with you. Thank you for the devotion you have shown to him and to me these past days. Friends, we hope we have treated you well!"

The crowd roared. Triumphant Falcon moved his hands to his hips and faced his people, a satisfied smile on his chiseled face. His white falcon cape flowed from shoulders to ankles, its individually carved white beads glistening. His falcon headdress was larger than life, its feathers flowing out in a majestic spray around his head. His chest was naked, a shining copper falcon glistening from its dangling position over his heart.

"This season we begin a new tradition to end our Green Corn Ceremony," he announced when the crowd quieted. "We start this new practice because of a message our Head Priest received directly from *Wah'Kon-Tah* himself."

A light murmur rippled through the masses, none of whom had ever personally received a message directly from *Wah'Kon-Tah*. In fact, such a thing was unprecedented.

"How many of you felt the earth shake earlier this year?"

Many people responded with shouts.

"Did you feel the power?"

The crowd responded loudly.

"Did you know what it meant?"

His question was met with silence. He continued. "I felt it, too. The shaking of the ground was a message from *Wah'Kon-Tah*. He was warning us that our enemies in this world and the evil spirits in the underworld seek to harm us. They yearn to destroy us. We prosper only through *Wah'Kon-Tah*'s intervention and protection."

The crowd remained absolutely silent. This was serious. Frivolity was over. It became so quiet Dawn Breaks could hear wood popping and hissing in a nearby fire.

"*Wah'Kon-Tah* has spoken to our Head Priest. Through him *Wah'Kon-Tah*'s will was revealed to me, your Grand Chief, Triumphant Falcon of Cahokia. Listen closely and hear my words. *Wah'Kon-Tah* has decreed that he wants more from us than we have recently given. He demands tribute for his protection. For us to continue to prosper, for our fields to be fertile, for our crops to grow, for our water to remain pure, for our forests to be filled with animals, for our rivers to be full of fish, he wants something more from us. He thirsts for blood. Fresh blood! Human blood! He wants it tonight! He demands it tonight! And we are going to give it to him! Now!"

From the nearby Temple, Triumphant Falcon's priests dragged four struggling prisoners to the platform. The first man, bound hand and foot, was carried up the steps by eight burly priests. As he writhed violently, they threw him onto the stone table and unbound his hands and feet. With two men gripping each arm and two men pulling each leg, they spread him over the rock, rendering him helpless, exposed and vulnerable.

Dawn Breaks watched in horror as the howling prisoner was forcibly stretched across the sacrificial stone. He was flat on his back, flopping ineffectually as the priests pulled his body in opposite directions. He struggled, but his situation was hopeless. He was pinned to the knifing stone. The Head Priest stood over him, arms outstretched.

A sharp flint knife suddenly appeared in the right hand of Head Priest Black Moon. Dawn Breaks had not seen him pull it.

"Oh, *Wah'Kon-Tah*," called out the Head Priest, tilting his head toward the heavens, "you who keep Grandfather Sun on course so your children may have nourishment and life, you who prevent the evil spirits of the underworld from shattering our lives with shuddering ground, windstorm, and famine, you who give us water and life and fire, we ask you now to accept from us our humble offering of lifeblood. Accept it to quench your thirst for the hot heartbeat of life you have provided us. Take our offering and smile upon us, *Wah'Kon-Tah*, knowing that we give you this gift to honor you and praise you. We adore you, oh great *Wah'Kon-Tah*!"

The Head Priest raised his arm even higher into the air. The blade of the flint knife glistened in the flickering light. It seemed to hover over the spread-eagled victim for a lifetime. Indeed, at least one life would be measured by the amount of time it took for the knife to descend.

Dawn Breaks could not tear her gaze from the face of the Head Priest. Black Moon's dark eyes were cold. His big nose looked like a hawk's beak. His jaw clenched and he grimaced as he stretched the knife high above his head.

"To you who gave us life, we return life!" he shouted as he drove the knife straight into the chest of the struggling man.

140

The man's scream died in a bubbling gurgle.

In less than five heartbeats, the Head Priest had cut the man's heart from his chest and was brandishing the red meaty organ in the air above the stricken captive. The heart squirmed spasmodically in Black Moon's gory fingers. Blood ran in torrents down his wrist and arm.

How had the Head Priest removed the heart so quickly? There had been no sawing of bone, no careful feeling nor searching. His movements had been swift, violent, and precise. One moment the heart had been beating in the chest of a living man. The next moment it was quivering wildly in the cool night air, tightly clutched in the hand of the Head Priest.

Dawn Breaks felt a wave of sickness deep inside her chest tug at the base of her throat. She could hear gagging sounds. People around her were vomiting.

She closed her eyes as the next prisoner was dragged to the stone. Although she did not watch the second sacrifice, she heard the sharp knife slice into the body just under the rib cage and the sucking sounds of the beating heart being torn from living tissue.

Someone squeezed her hand. It was Thunder Runner. She had forgotten all about him. He was holding her hand, squeezing tightly.

From that point, everything was a blur. Two more prisoners screaming and crying, a bloody knife held high in the night sky, arterial spurts splattering the robes of the Head Priest, the smell of fresh blood commingling with the sickly odor of vomit, lesser priests grunting from the exertion of holding down doomed men fighting for their lives, the singsong chanting of the priests, the exhortations of the Grand Chief, and the vibrating noise of the crowd, when, upon Triumphant Falcon's urging, his people broke into a powerful rendition of the Green Corn Song, it was all a nightmarish dream. Over and over the people sang the stirring words proclaiming their praise for *Wah'Kon-Tah* and their need for his protection.

The last thing Dawn Breaks remembered was collapsing against Thunder Runner, too insensible to enjoy the very thing for which she had been wishing—his strong arms around her shoulders.

Chapter 16

Dawn Breaks could not forget the sight of the gory heart in the hand of the Head Priest. The image was burned into her mind. She saw its bloody pulp every time she closed her eyes. It danced on the backs of her eyelids. She shuddered and let her hand dip into the cool water of the Mississippi River. If only she could forget.

Seated next to her stepmother, she rode quietly on one of the middle planks of the enormous dugout canoe. The flat-bottomed vessel shot through the water, propelled by twenty-five paddlers on each side. With thirty additional riders, the huge dugout carried eighty members of the Village of Gray Wolf. Going downriver, they were traveling at the speed of a running deer. They would make the trip from Cahokia to their home within just one day. Shorter canoes, with six to ten paddlers per side, dotted the river behind them, as the five hundred travelers from the Village of Gray Wolf returned home from the Green Corn Festival.

Night Owl, her father, sat directly in front of her. His crippled leg, frozen straight and sticking out in front of him, did not prevent him from being one of the paddlers. The muscles of his shoulders rippled as he repeatedly dipped his oar into the water and pulled. Sweat poured over the tattoo of the sun in the middle of his back. She remembered his stoicism as she had given him the tattoo years earlier, punching his skin thousands of times with a sharp needle dipped in red cinnabar. The circular tattoo with its halo of flames extended from the base of his neck to the small of his back. He and the other oarsmen were singing a rhythmic song as they paddled. Normally, the sensation of flying over the river would have made Dawn Breaks happy. Now, all she could think of was that quivering heart. She could swear it had still been beating when the Head Priest held it up. Was it her imagination or was it really possible?

"You are awfully quiet." The voice of Whispering Wind, her stepmother, intruded upon her thoughts.

"Yes, Mother," she said. Whispering Wind was as close to her as any real mother could possibly be. Her natural mother had died from childbirth complications on the day Dawn Breaks was born. Whispering Wind was her mother's younger sister. Night Owl had married her just a month after the death of his wife. Normally, social rules would have required a widower to wait four Green Corn Ceremonies before remarrying, but a man could circumvent the rule by marrying a woman of his deceased wife's lineage. Dawn Breaks had never known any other mother than Whispering Wind. She was glad her father had remarried.

"You should not have gotten so close to the ceremony," Whispering Wind said. "You should have stayed farther back, as I did."

"I did not know what was going to happen. I expected merely talk. I wanted to be close enough to hear. I did not plan to see a man's heart ripped from his chest."

"You wanted to be close to that young chunkey player, is what you wanted."

Dawn Breaks glanced around to see who might be listening. The paddlers closest to them were busy singing the rowing song. She glanced at the canoes following them. In one, Thunder Runner would be paddling. She could not tell from where she sat which one bore him.

"I saw your eyes when you were dancing with him. My daughter, who has never before been interested in boys or games, seems smitten now. I predict you will soon be attending many chunkey matches. Perhaps we will be adding a new man to our fireplace."

"Mother, I do not know this man."

"It was good that he carried you to us after you fainted during the ceremony. You might have been trampled by the crowd but for him."

There it was again. The ceremony. Human sacrifice. Four men killed right before her eyes. The memories were terrible. Yet, it was curious how little the blood and gore seemed to bother most other people from the Village of Gray Wolf. The vast majority took the viewpoint that if the Grand Chief claimed that *Wah'Kon-Tah* wanted a sacrifice, then a sacrifice must be given. They were people with strong faith.

Maybe she would have been less traumatized had she not enjoyed such a close view of the horrible spectacle. Remembering the sight of the pulsating heart and the odor of the flowing blood, she leaned over the side of the canoe and vomited into the river. Perhaps she should not have eaten those sunflower seeds on an empty stomach.

The oarsman behind her groaned loudly.

Embarrassed, she dipped her fingers in the water and dabbed her lips.

"I cannot stop thinking about that heart," she whispered.

"You have always been a tender child," her stepmother said softly. "It is your mother's Gentle Sky clan blood in you."

"I really do not know if it makes a difference to *Wah'Kon-Tah* whether or not we killed those men," Dawn Breaks said, still whispering. "Why does *Wah'Kon-Tah* want anyone killed? Are we not all his creations? The idea of human sacrifice is bad! I do not understand it."

Whispering Wind shushed her. "Do not say those words aloud again! It is blasphemy. We do not question the Grand Chief or the priests. You know this."

"I know. I am sorry. I will not speak these thoughts."

Whispering Wind sighed. "It is hard for a young person like you to imagine what it was like in the days before we had a Grand Chief at Cahokia. Back then, everyone lived in isolated tribes, unconnected, disorganized, always foraging for food, always on the brink of starvation, often reduced to eating snakes, lizards, frogs, snails, and insects. The tribes constantly fought each other. You were not safe in your own lodge. Raiding parties would attack in the middle of the night, killing men and carrying off women and children. The Grand Chief's grandfather brought us peace. He organized the tribes and set up a system of trade and mutual protection. He and his priests taught our people about *Wah'Kon-Tah*. They made many prophecies that have come true. The next Grand Chief improved upon what his father had done. Triumphant Falcon is the third Grand Chief, the greatest yet. He is brilliant. The size of Cahokia has tripled under his leadership. Under him our people have enjoyed peace and prosperity. We get copper from the Great Lakes and beautiful shells from the ocean. We are so powerful, no one dares attack us. When they foolishly do so, they are swiftly caught and punished. But always, despite the progress, we remain just one severe drought away from famine. We depend

144

upon *Wah'Kon-Tah* to give us a nourishing crop each season. I trust Triumphant Falcon's judgment and you should, too. He knows best."

"I hear your words, Mother, but you did not see the face of that first man as he was being led to the stone. You did not see the terror in his eyes."

"No, I did not. I regret that you did. Next time, do not stand so close."

They rode in silence for a while before Whispering Wind spoke again. "In my mind I have counted the number of different recipes we make from corn. It is a large number. Do you know?"

"No."

"How many? Guess."

"I do not know."

"Forty-two!"

Dawn Breaks rolled her eyes, careful not to let her stepmother notice. She knew what was coming. She would now get a full run-down of everything from roasted green corn, to hominy made from late corn, to baked corn bread, to fried corn bread, to corn soups, to cold cornmeal grits, to popped corn. Well, at least the conversation would keep her mind off that pulsating heart.

Dawn Breaks listened politely as Whispering Wind recited the recipes. Her stepmother was an extraordinarily good cook. Dawn Breaks knew it would do her good to memorize everything her stepmother was saying. Someday she might be in charge of a hearth of her own, might have a family. Coming up with different ways to cook the same food always made meals more interesting.

"For good corn fritters," her stepmother was saying, "you have to fry them in hot bear grease. Always make sure your bear grease jar is full. Do not let it run out. Bear grease is the best cooking oil. I have heard that your Thunder Runner is not merely a good chunkey player, but quite a hunter, too. He might prove to be a good source of bear oil."

"Mother!"

"His father's clan is Men of Mystery. That is one of the Sky People clans. Since *your* father is from the Mottled Eagle clan, the young man is an eligible suitor for you. As you know, as a person from one of the Earth People clans, you must marry someone from one of the Sky People clans."

"Mother, it is too soon to talk of marriage. I hardly know him."

"That is what you said. Yet, I saw you dancing with him. I saw what I saw."

Dawn Breaks glanced again at the men around her. They were still paddling and singing.

"My favorite corn recipe," Whispering Wind continued, "is chestnut bread. You start out with regular corn batter but add chopped chestnuts. You can bake it, fry it, or boil it, but I like baked the best. It is my favorite food, next to strawberries. I think I will make a batch when we get home. Does that sound good to you?"

"Yes, Mother."

Whispering Wind paused, the subject of corn dishes pretty much exhausted.

Dawn Breaks watched a hawk circling in the sky over the shoreline. How wonderful it would be to be able to fly. She imagined herself gliding high above the trees, looking down at the world below, traveling from one point to another in a straight line, never worrying about crossing creeks, rivers, mountains, ravines, or dense forests. She would love to be a bird, if she ever came back to earth in a different form.

"What pottery pieces are you working on now?" Whispering Wind asked.

Dawn Breaks considered her works in progress, all stored at the lodge of her mentor, Tall Oaks.

"I am making another one of those turtle bowls. I recently made one shaped like a frog. I had a lot of fun with the bulging eyes. I think my next will be a running fox. I would use red flint clay for that, of course."

"You should make a chunkey player. A chunkey-player bowl would bring quite a bit at barter. Everybody likes chunkey. Lots of players. Lots of fans. There would be a big market for it. Or you could give it as a gift to one special person. Perhaps a certain chunkey player?"

"Mother!"

"Just a suggestion."

146

Dawn Breaks let her mind wander to thoughts of Thunder Runner. He had been watching her anxiously when she awoke after fainting. Her stepmother was dabbing her cheek with water. Her father was encouraging her to sip hot sassafras tea. But when she opened her eyes, the first person she glimpsed had been Thunder Runner, standing over her as her parents knelt next to her. When he saw her looking at him, he smiled and put his fist over his heart.

She had not had a chance to talk to him since. She had not even seen him. Her parents had taken her back to their camp. After a night's sleep, they had arisen at daybreak to begin the trip down-river. Gray Wolf wanted his villagers to leave early so they would get home before sundown. Everything had moved so quickly she had not had time to look for Thunder Runner.

She was surprised by how anxious she was to talk to him. She wondered what he thought about the human sacrifice. He, too, had seen it up close. But he was a man, a tough man, full of courage. She was curious to know his reaction.

She wondered, too, how his meeting with the Grand Chief had gone. They had not had a chance to talk about it during the dance. She wanted to hear every detail.

When would she get a chance to talk to him again? It was hard to say. The men of the village usually had little contact with the women during the day. The men went hunting or fishing or worked on the lodges in the village. The woman tended the gardens and did the cooking. At planting time everyone worked together to plant the large cornfields, and at harvest time the entire village helped carry in the crop in large pack baskets; but at this point in the season, the weeding and watering were women's work. Where might her path next cross his? He lived with his kinsmen in a large lodge on the other side of the village. His family's lodge was not exactly on the route to anywhere she would have reason to be going. She did not want to be following him.

"He is a handsome young man," Whispering Wind said.

Dawn Breaks considered scolding her stepmother again. In-stead, she said, "Yes, he is."

She glanced at Whispering Wind with affection. She realized what she had been up to. By all her chatter, her loving stepmother had managed to get her mind off the terrible sights and sounds of the night before.

She reached over and squeezed her hand. "Thank you, Mother."

"For what?"

"For everything."

Time sped by for the rest of the trip as the two women talked about everything except human sacrifice and violent death.

Before long, the towering bluff marking their village became visible in the distance. The huge outcropping of rock jutted into the west side of the river, a wall of rock thrusting itself from the hills and looming out into the water like a chewed-off peninsula. At its top edge, bare white rock gleamed in the summer sun. Grass and trees covered the sides of the landmark with a green robe of foliage. In its shadows nestled a cove, providing natural protection for the canoes and lodges of the Village of Gray Wolf. Most of the village was scattered over nearby hills and mounds. Wooden lodges with thatched roofs dotted the ridges, mounds, and bluffs above the river's flood level. Even from the distance, tall corn could be seen growing in the fields covering the rich bottomland along the river.

At the top of the towering white bluff, the Temple Mound of the Village of Gray Wolf presided over the community from its preeminent perch. Inside the depths of the tall building, the priests conducted their elaborate ceremonies and plotted the future of the community's spiritual life. Midway down the back of the eminence, significantly lower than the Temple Mound, lay the residence of Chief Gray Wolf, where he lived with his extended family.

Like Cahokia, the Village of Gray Wolf featured a flat plaza for large meetings, events, and chunkey games. It was much smaller than Cahokia's grand plaza, but big enough to accommodate any event hosted by a village of six hundred.

Dawn Breaks stared at the riverside village where she had grown up. It was clean. It was pretty. It was familiar and comfortable.

"Oh, it is good to be home," she said. "I do not think I ever want to go to another Green Corn Festival at Cahokia. I have seen enough blood to last a lifetime."

Chapter 17

Thunder Runner visited Dawn Breaks several times during the weeks following the Green Corn Festival. Each visit left him more and more captivated. She was not only beautiful, but intelligent, funny, and clever. He was positive she was the woman he wanted to marry. He spoke to his aunt about making the proposal for him.

There was nothing peculiar about sending a woman on such a mission. Marriage in these hard times was as much a relationship between kin groups as between individuals. According to tradition, a young man interested in a girl was not to speak directly to her or her parents about a possible match. Instead, he was to send his mother's sister to broach the subject with the girl's mother's sister. After a discussion between the women, the girl's mother's sister would convene with other members of the girl's family to further deliberate the advantages and disadvantages of the marriage. The girl might or might not be consulted. Consulted or not, she would never be forced into a match she did not want. Finally, when the matter was all talked out, the girl's family would deliver word to the suitor's relatives as to whether or not the marriage was a real possibility.

A month after the Green Corn Festival, Thunder Runner sent his aunt Wet Moccasins to be his messenger. He had lived with her, her husband, her six children, and his own two little brothers since his parents had died two years earlier. She was clearly delighted with the assignment. He thought she might be glad because of the opportunity it presented to get him out of her lodge. It was pretty crowded. Whatever her motive, he appreciated her help.

She departed for the all-important visit with Whispering Wind right after supper. Impatiently awaiting her return, Thunder Runner left the family fireside and met up with his best friend, Red Hawk, for a bit of night fishing.

They paddled a small dugout canoe upriver to their favorite fishing hole in a creek feeding into the river just north of the village. After reaching the creek, they came to a cove where the current was practically nonexistent and the water only twelve feet deep. The still water was filled with a tangle of dead trees, brush, and limbs. They seldom failed to find catfish lurking in its depths. It was not uncommon for some of the big cats to weigh more than one-hundred pounds.

As usual, they were fully equipped for the task at hand.

Red Hawk's job was to tend a fire built in a clay basin in the middle of the canoe. The basin was elevated so the fire burned a few inches above the sides of the canoe, throwing its light across the surface of the water, attracting and illuminating the curious fish. Red Hawk always brought pine as their firewood because it burned so brightly.

Thunder Runner's job was to man the fish harpoon, a long spear tipped with a sharp flint point, edged with hooks made from deer bones. When a fish came too close to the surface, Thunder Runner would stab the spear straight into the meaty body of the fish, impaling it. Most of the time, he could hoist the fish into the boat. For a huge cat, he sometimes released his hold on the spear, knowing its buoyancy would eventually tire the stricken fish and float it to the surface. He also carried a bow with special arrows fixed with lines attached to wooden floats. Sometimes, instead of using the spear, he would shoot a fish with one of the arrows. When he hit a fish, it was doomed. Even if it fled, the float would eventually exhaust it, and they would find it by following the bobbing float.

Red Hawk spent most of the evening talking excitedly about the Green Corn Ceremony, especially the sacrifice of the four prisoners.

"You were closer than I was," Red Hawk said. "How did the Head Priest get the hearts out of those men so fast?"

Thunder Runner frowned as he watched the dark water for the telltale glow of an approaching fish. "It looked like he cut them under the bottom rib and went right up underneath the breastbone, directly to the heart."

"I wonder who he practiced on," Red Hawk said. "He must have practiced to get so fast."

"Probably on wild animals," Thunder Runner speculated.

"Right. Just keep telling yourself those were his first human victims. I am telling you, he practiced on people. He has done it before. You are not that good your first time."

"What of it?"

"What of it! Cahokia is a spooky place. It frightens me!"

"Do not be afraid of the Grand Chief and his priests. They are our brothers. It is good to have their protection."

"Perhaps. But I would not want them sneaking up on me some dark night. What I want to know is, if we still get a drought and the corn crop fails, does that mean the sacrifice did not work because it is wrong to kill, or does it mean we should have offered more lives instead of just four?"

"It will work," Thunder Runner said. "Triumphant Falcon would not have allowed it otherwise. He is a great man."

He felt a jolt of excitement as he saw the light shape of a big fish sliding into the illuminated water next to the canoe. He raised his spear into the throwing position.

"Yes, a great man," Red Hawk said. "You and the Grand Chief are great brothers now. Next he will be giving you the hand of one of his daughters in marriage! Will you be too important to go fishing with me then?"

Thunder Runner smiled to himself. He was tempted to tell Red Hawk about his aunt's matchmaking mission, but his fear of rejection and humiliation made him remain silent. The fewer people who knew, the better.

The big catfish glided near the canoe. From his kneeling position, Thunder Runner drove the spear down hard, sticking it deep into the fish's back. He felt the strength of the impaled fish as it tried to lurch away. He twisted the spear, embedding its hooks in the fish's guts. It tried to jerk away, but the hooks held.

Meanwhile, having learned from bitter experience, Red Hawk moved to the opposite side of the boat, leaning away from Thunder Runner to prevent the boat from tilting so far to one side that they'd capsize or lose their fire.

Thunder Runner braced the spear against his right thigh. Anchoring the base of the spear with his right arm, he began raising the spear out of the water with his left. He curled his arm upward. In moments, the impaled blue catfish was out of the water, its frenzied, whiskered face glaring at him.

"That is a big one!" Red Hawk yelled.

Grunting, Thunder Runner jerked the spear sharply, tossing the catfish to the bottom of the canoe.

Red Hawk scampered away from its spikes. He grabbed a war club and whacked the big fish on its head. It quit thrashing.

"Oh, we are going to be popular when we get home!" Red Hawk crowed. "Fried catfish! I can taste it now! Let us see if we can get another. The night is still young!"

It was late when they returned to the village. Red Hawk volunteered to take the fish home and clean them. Thunder Runner was glad to let him do it.

Wet Moccasins was still awake when he got back to the lodge. She was sitting at the fire in front of the lodge. He could not tell from his aunt's expression whether her report would be good or bad. He was glad she was not inside the lodge. He preferred to have his conversation with her outside the presence of an audience of curious family members.

"Did she accept?"

"Who?"

"Who! We both know where you went tonight, and why."

She sniffed. "I prefer to tell you what happened in my own way."

He sighed and sat down next to her. "I am listening."

"Whispering Wind, her stepmother, is also her aunt, her mother's sister."

"Yes, I know that."

"Good family," she continued. "Her father is one of the tenders of the ceremonial fire. He is crippled, so he cannot hunt. The chief provides him with a share of corn in return for being one of the three men who tend the communal fire to keep it eternally burning."

Thunder Runner nodded. There was no point in trying to rush her.

"Dawn Breaks is a very special girl. I never realized it, but she is the star pupil of Tall Oaks, the master sculptor. She spends most of her time making pottery with him. She has made many of the most beautiful pieces in the village. The turtle bowl recently given as a gift by Gray Wolf to the Grand Chief, for instance, was one of hers. I never dreamed it was made by one so young. Such artistry! Did you know she was so talented?"

"Yes. I have seen her work. What did her aunt say? Is she interested in me?"

His aunt was not to be hurried. "At first glance it would seem that you and she have nothing in common. She is probably the only girl in the village who has never cared for chunkey or the men who play it. While others spend a good deal of time watching you boys compete, this girl is usually with Tall Oaks, working on her pottery."

"That explains why I have not noticed her before," he said.

He searched his aunt's face. Was the answer going to be good or bad? It was impossible to tell from looking at the chubby woman's inscrutable expression. He hoped she was enjoying making him miserable.

"Her mother died in childbirth, you know. I remember her. She had a lovely singing voice. A very pretty woman. After she died, the widower took her sister as his second wife. Whispering Wind is devoted to Dawn Breaks. She loves her like her own daughter. That is a good sign."

Thunder Runner nodded. "Yes."

"If you were to marry Dawn Breaks, you would have Whispering Wind as your mother-in-law. It is to your benefit that I consider this."

"Yes. Thank you."

"Dawn Breaks is extremely close to her father. Do you know what happened to his leg?"

"No."

"He was hunting bear with other members of the tribe. They found a hollowed-out old tree where a bear was hibernating inside. They built a fire and forced it out. When it emerged, they shot arrows at it and fled when it chased them. They all ran to saplings too small for the bear to follow and climbed them. Night Owl was safely up his tree when one of the other hunters fell, and the bear was heading right for the man. Night Owl dropped from his tree and diverted the bear away from his friend. The bear got Night Owl, though. It mauled him severely, ruining his leg. Sadly, it was his last hunt. This happened when Dawn Breaks was very young. She nursed her father back to health, young as she was. They are tremendously close to each other. That, too, is a good sign."

"I agree," Thunder Runner said. "It is good."

"Now, unlike you, Thunder Runner, this girl is quiet. You have always been the center of attention with your pack of boys. This girl is friendly to everyone, to be sure, but she is not the type to sit around giggling and gossiping with other women. She does her chores quickly and efficiently and hurries off to work on her pottery. You and she would appear to be quite different in that respect. It causes me a bit of concern."

"I spend lots of time alone, too, when I am practicing my throws."

"Yes, I know. That is why I said you and she *appeared* to have little in common. After hearing more about her, I came to realize that you and she both share a drive for excellence. Hers happens to be pottery. Yours is the game of chunkey. Both of you are exceptional people and very hard workers."

"Is it to be a match, then?"

"Thunder Runner, your impatience is bordering on rudeness."

"I am sorry."

"You are going to need to be patient, because a proper courtship takes time."

He nodded.

"You have passed the first step," Wet Moccasins said. "Her family has no objection to your courtship of this young woman."

Thunder Runner wanted to whoop with pleasure, but restrained himself. "What about *her*? What does *she* think?"

"I did not speak directly to her, but if she had objections, her family never would have given you permission to pursue her. Do you know what this means?"

"I can lay with her?"

"Men! I was not speaking of that! What I mean to say is that now that her family does not object, we must put together a col-

154

lection of gifts. You must deliver them personally. You must build a lodge for her and begin raising a crop for her. You must also go into the woods and kill a deer or bear for her, proving you can provide meat. Only after you have done all these things may the marriage ceremony be performed. This will interfere with your chunkey practice. Perhaps you should let your gambling brothers know that your performance may begin to suffer and they should bet on someone else."

"I thought tending a corn crop was women's work."

"It is, eventually. But a groom must grow the first crop for his bride. It is tradition."

"With all of this building lodges, growing crops, and killing animals, when exactly do she and I become man and wife?"

"Even after her family has accepted your collection of gifts, she will continue living in her parents' lodge, but the two of you will be considered engaged, and you can lay with her then, if you can find any privacy. Once you have built her lodge and presented her with the crop and the meat, she will give you corn she has personally cooked. You will then exchange beanpoles bearing vines full of beans. After this, the lodge becomes her property and the two of you move in together as a married couple. You remain married until the next Green Corn Ceremony. At that time, if the marriage has proven unsatisfactory, it can be dissolved, and you would move back with us and she could keep the lodge."

He reached over and hugged his aunt. "Thank you," he said. "You have made me very happy. Let us get to work on those presents. What do you suggest?"

She chuckled. "We will discuss it tomorrow. It is late. I need to get some sleep."

He watched his aunt gather her feathered matchcoat around her shoulders and shuffle into the lodge. He felt tremendous gratitude to her. She had done well for him.

Thunder Runner clasped his hands behind his head and leaned back, gazing at the stars. Was it possible Dawn Breaks was as excited as he this very moment? He hoped so.

It was a very long time before he calmed down enough to fall asleep.

Chapter 18

Dawn Breaks sat on the ground outside the lodge of Tall Oaks, the master craftsman who had been her teacher and mentor for as long as she could remember. She sat cross-legged, with a flat board on her lap. On the board she was kneading fresh blue clay, tempered with powder made from crushed freshwater shells. She formed the clay into coils and skillfully worked it into a tall water jug. The coils miraculously disappeared, replaced by a perfectly proportioned jar with walls the thickness of her finger. As she smoothed the vessel inside and out, she occasionally moistened her fingertips in a nearby bowl of water. When she was finished, it would be a perfect mate to the one she had made earlier in the morning. The first sat next to her, on its own flat board.

She looked up and caught Tall Oaks staring at her.

The elderly artist was a lover of all things beautiful. She knew his interests included the female body. She did not mind that he occasionally stole glimpses of her. He never touched. *Wah'Kon-Tah* had made her body with the same care she used when creating her art. Beauty was meant to be appreciated.

"Nice job," he said.

"Thank you."

Dawn Breaks picked up a sharp reed and began incising the side of the water jug with an intricate sketch of a warrior with a human body and a bird's beak. She drew him with outstretched arms, the human appendages transformed into wings by the addition of seven long falcon feathers draping down from each arm. She gave him a breechcloth, a necklace, ear-pendants, and a headdress.

When she glanced up, Tall Oaks was standing in front of her, critically examining her work. She held her breath as the old sculptor peered at her design. His eyes looked rather birdlike themselves.

Tall Oaks sniffed air sharply into his lungs through his nose, making a faint whistling sound, before exhaling loudly.

She squirmed nervously. His critical comments sometimes made his apprentices break into tears. It had been quite awhile since he had made an unfavorable remark about one of her pieces. Perhaps the good times were about to end.

She glanced at his two other apprentices, both younger than she. The girls were on the other side of the fire, busy with their own pottery, paying no attention to the interaction between their mentor and his oldest pupil.

"These are among your best yet," he finally said, nodding at the water jars. "I like the detail. I like the proportioning. I like the way the designs match exactly. You get better every day, Dawn Breaks. Better every day."

Her spirits soared. Tall Oaks was not merely the best sculptor in her village. He was the best in all of the extended villages controlled by the Grand Chief. The old potter was notoriously frugal with compliments. She glowed inside. "Thank you."

"Do not thank me, girl, for recognizing talent when I see it. I did not give you the talent. You were born with it. *Wah'Kon-Tah* gave it to you. I have merely nurtured it during the years you have been apprenticed to me."

Dawn Breaks lowered her head, a smile playing at the corner of her mouth. Now he was pretending to be irritable. She knew he just wanted to talk. "Everything I know I learned from you," she said.

"Well, I am glad you realize it." He chuckled, his round head bobbing on his long neck, reminding her of a baby bird. The bronze skin of his ruddy face and bald head was leathery from years of exposure to the sun. White hair, hand-length, encircled his head and covered his ears. His arms and legs were thin and bony. His upper torso was covered with intricate tattoos. His breechcloth seemed a bit too big for him.

She felt tenderness for the old man, which surprised her, since she usually felt only awe. She felt an urge to say something that would please him.

"If I could accomplish a fraction of what you have done, Tall Oaks, I would be forever grateful to *Wah'Kon-Tah*."

He waved a thin hand dismissively. "You've already accomplished much. Your frog-shaped bowl is one of the best pieces of art I have ever seen. It does what art is meant to do—it breathes with life. You are on the brink of a truly promising career, Dawn Breaks. I predict that you will not only equal my work, but surpass it."

Dawn Breaks could not believe her ears. "Oh, no. I could never!"

"Oh, but you will," he said, his smile punctuated by gaps mourning missing teeth. "You are the best student I have ever taught, and I have taught plenty."

Dawn Breaks smiled, amazed and delighted by his flattery.

"I will tell you something else," he continued. "Having your pretty face nearby has been a joy to me these past years. You are a burst of sunlight on an otherwise dull winter evening. If I were not such an old man, I would send my mother's sister to talk to your mother's sister about the possibility of marriage."

A bolt of apprehension shot through Dawn Breaks. She admired the old man and loved him as a teacher, but had no desire to be his wife. She did not want to hurt his feelings, but just last night her stepmother had conducted a very eventful meeting with the aunt of Thunder Runner. She hoped Tall Oaks would not say anything that would embarrass them both.

"Of course, it would be hard to send my mother's sister," he said, "because she has been dead for twenty winters."

He chuckled again. "Do you know how old I am?"

"No."

"I am quite likely the oldest man in the village. I am seventy-seven winters old. Most men do not live past forty!"

"Your art keeps you young."

"There is truth to that," he agreed. "It keeps me excited about living. Also, molding clay and chipping chert is a bit safer than chasing deer and bear through the woods. Most of our men live hard and die young. I create art from the materials *Wah'Kon-Tah* provides us."

She saw a chance to divert the conversation from eventually culminating in a marriage proposal.

"A young man's aunt came to visit my stepmother last night," she said.

"Oh?"

"Yes. Wet Moccasins, the aunt of Thunder Runner."

"The chunkey player?"

"Yes."

"Well, he would make an excellent match for you. Tall, powerful, handsome! What fine children the two of you could produce."

Dawn Breaks blushed. The thought had crossed her mind more than once.

158

"Did your family approve of the idea of having a star chunkey player in the family?"

"They seem to like the notion."

The old man stroked his chin and regarded her thoughtfully. "Promise me one thing," he said.

"Yes?"

"When you become a wife, do not give up your art. It would be too great a loss to our community."

"I would never give it up!"

"Good." He sat down next to her, groaning as he did so. "I had a dream last night. In the dream, I fell off the rock cliff behind the Temple Mound. I have had the falling dream before. Usually I awake before I hit. This time, though, I was killed. My soul rose from my mangled body and hovered over our village."

"Oh! No wonder you have been talking about death and dying today."

"Exactly. The worst part was that the priests gathered together all of the pottery I had made over the years and smashed it to pieces. Nothing I created was left in this world. It made me realize how much it means to me for my work to live on after my death. I hated the destruction of my art more than I hated death itself. It was a horrible nightmare. The sadness has stayed with me all day. I suppose I am feeling my age."

She patted his bony shoulder. "Your pottery is scattered through-out villages all along the Father of Waters. The priests could never find it all, much less destroy it. The task would be impossible, even if they wanted to do it. You've got nothing to worry about."

"I suppose that is true."

"Of course it is true."

Suddenly, a piercing wail cut through the afternoon air.

"What is that?" Dawn Breaks jumped up.

Moments later, another wail sounded, and deep voices joined in a mournful song. The lamentations came from the Temple Mound at the highest point of the village.

People stopped what they were doing and faced the Temple Mound. The singsong chant of the priests floated eerily over the entire village.

"What is happening?" Dawn Breaks asked.

Tall Oaks used his cane to pull himself to his feet. At first, his face bore a confused expression. Eventually, he nodded with recognition.

"I have heard this song before," he said. "It is one of the few advantages of being old. You have seen it all before."

"What does it mean?" Dawn Breaks asked. "I have never known the priests to break into a lament like this in the middle of the day."

"It is the death song for a Grand Chief," Tall Oaks said. "It means Triumphant Falcon has died."

"But I just saw him. He did not look sick."

"You never know when your time is coming," Tall Oaks said. "That lack of forewarning is both a blessing and a curse."

The song continued for a long time. The two younger apprentices ran home to be with their mothers. Dawn Breaks stayed with Tall Oaks, staring at the Temple Mound as the voices of the priests mourned the passing of Triumphant Falcon of Cahokia, the Grand Chief, the greatest leader their people had ever known.

"Who will take his place?" Dawn Breaks asked.

"His oldest son. I believe he is about your age."

"What about his wife? Can't she rule us?"

"A woman chief? Do not be absurd. She will probably be going with him."

"What? Going where?"

"It has been many years since we lost a Grand Chief. The last time was long before you were born. But according to custom, his wife will accompany him into the afterworld. Some of his servants will go along, too."

"You mean they will be killed?"

"That is right."

"What if they do not want to go?"

"Oh, they will go. It is an honor to be chosen."

"Some honor!" she said. "I think I would rather stay around and serve the new Grand Chief."

Dawn Breaks peered toward the Temple Mound. The voices of the priests had stopped wailing. The entire village was weirdly silent.

"How do you think they learned about his death?" she asked.

160

"I am sure Cahokia sent out runners the moment he died, notifying every village in his domain. This will mean another trip to Cahokia. The funeral of a Grand Chief is a big event."

"I am not going," Dawn Breaks said. "I saw the four prisoners cut to pieces at the Green Corn Ceremony. I vowed that was my last trip to Cahokia."

Dawn Breaks glimpsed movement at the front of the Temple Mound. The priests had come outside and were walking in single file down the path to the heart of the village.

Dawn Breaks shuddered. Like everyone else in the village, she feared the priests. They dealt with the supernatural. They spoke with spirits. They received and interpreted messages from the stars and from *Wah'Kon-Tah*.

They were not normal men.

These peculiar and frightening beings lived a separate life from the rest of the village. Secluded in their tall lodge at the top of the Temple Mound, they never married and took vows of celibacy. They seldom, if ever, bathed. Instead of the breechcloths worn by the rest of the men of the village during the warmer months, the priests wore heavy robes of fur or feathers, even on the hottest days of the year. They greeted the sun each morning at dawn with an eerie chant. They smoked copious amounts of tobacco and other mysterious plants. They ate herbs forbidden to other villagers. Their yelling and screaming often kept the rest of the village awake long into the night. Although the priests were members of the village and subjects of Chief Gray Wolf, their spiritual role made their dictates supreme. The chief always followed their advice.

Dawn Breaks was glad women could not be priests. What a dirty and unpleasant life!

When the priests reached the bottom of the Temple Mound, they marched their strange processional through the middle of the village.

"I wonder what they are doing now," Dawn Breaks said.

"Who knows?" Tall Oaks frowned. "They seem to be coming our way."

"Maybe they want you to make a gift for the new Grand Chief, or something to be used in the ceremony," she suggested.

"Perhaps." The old man adjusted his breechcloth and brushed dust from it.

Sure enough, when the priests reached the bottom of Tall Oaks' mound, they began climbing the steps to the lodge of the famous sculptor.

Dawn Breaks held her breath. Her mentor had dreamed of his death. She prayed it had not been an omen. She was worried for him. What did the priests have in mind? Chances were it was not good. She glanced at Tall Oaks. He stood as rigidly as his bad back would allow, preparing to face unpleasantness.

The five priests stopped in front of Tall Oaks and Dawn Breaks. Body odor emanated from the depths of their fur robes. They reeked of fire smoke. Why did they not bathe like other villagers? They were just plain disgusting. But frightening, too.

Makes Afraid, the Head Priest of the Village of Gray Wolf did the talking. "Greetings, Tall Oaks."

Beads of perspiration ran down the Head Priest's neck and disappeared into his bearskin robe. Copper bracelets adorned his wrists and copper pendants dangled from his ears. A dozen strands of pearl beads coiled around his neck.

Dawn Breaks admired the beads in spite of her uneasiness. They were the prettiest pearls she had ever seen. They must have come from the great ocean to the south. Still, the exquisite jewelry was not enough to make her want to be a priest.

"Good day, Makes Afraid," said Tall Oaks. "What can I do for you?"

Dawn Breaks swallowed hard. This was the moment they would find out what the priests wanted. *Please*, she thought desperately, *let it merely be a request for some special piece of work. Do not let them take him away!* She felt a tingly chill shoot down her back. She was now certain that Tall Oaks's dream had been a premonition of his death. She was going to lose her teacher and mentor.

"Actually," Makes Afraid said, bowing his head respectfully to the elderly sculptor, "we have not come for you."

He pointed to Dawn Breaks.

"We have come for her."

162

Chapter 19

Dawn Breaks stared with disbelief at Makes Afraid. They had come for *her*! What did *that* mean? She had often watched the priests from afar as they performed their religious ceremonies and secret rites, but she had seldom met them in person. She never thought they even knew she existed. She gaped at Makes Afraid in astonishment.

"I do not understand," she said. "What do you mean?"

"Dawn Breaks, this is the most important day of your life. Give thanks to *Wah'Kon-Tah*. You have been chosen." Bright red blood vessels crisscrossed the whites of the eyes of the Head Priest like footprints of tiny birds. His expression was a combination of ecstasy and suppressed frenzy.

"Chosen?" she asked.

"That is correct. We received word from Cahokia this afternoon. The Grand Chief has died."

"Then it is true," she murmured, feeling white-hot jolts of fear shooting from her spine down her arms and legs. But why were they coming for her? This could not be good. It absolutely could not be good.

"I do not understand," she repeated. "What does the death of the Grand Chief have to do with me?"

"You have been chosen," Makes Afraid repeated, reaching out and touching her cheek. His fingers were gnarly and rough.

"Chosen for what?"

"To accompany Triumphant Falcon into the afterworld. Each village under his rule chooses its most worthy maiden to make the journey with our fallen leader. You have been selected for that honor. You will be the representative from the Village of Gray Wolf!"

Dawn Breaks involuntarily sucked in her breath.

"This afternoon," Makes Afraid continued, "when the runner brought us word of the Grand Chief's death, we met to perform a very important function. We were charged with the duty of selecting a young woman to travel with Triumphant Falcon into the next world. You will pass through the Milky Way at his side and journey through the upper world with him. This selection is the highest honor that could ever come your way. I wish you the most sincere congratulations."

Dawn Breaks felt her legs weakening as Makes Afraid spoke. "There must be some mistake," she whispered. "I do not even know Triumphant Falcon. I have never met him."

"There is no mistake. We selected you because you are the most worthy. Our orders were to choose the most outstanding young woman in the village. We have heard many good things about you." Makes Afraid smiled. "There is no need to thank us. We are just doing our duty."

Thanking them was the last thing on her mind.

She glanced at Tall Oaks. The blood had drained from his face, leaving his cheekbones with a gray, sickly tint. His eyes brimmed with tears.

"Most revered Priest," she stammered, "I am flattered to be chosen, but I must tell you . . ."

I do not want to die! her mind screamed.

"I am not worthy of this honor."

I want to live!

"I am sure the Grand Chief would find my company extremely boring. I am just an ignorant village girl."

Makes Afraid caressed her cheek again. "You are too modest, Dawn Breaks. You were chosen for your beauty, your talent, and your chastity. The Grand Chief will find you to be delightful company. Think of your future! You will know the Grand Chief intimately and personally! You will share his life in the next world. How many people can say that? You will be the envy of every young woman in your village."

She remembered the beating heart being yanked from the body of the human sacrifice. Was losing her heart to be her fate?

Makes Afraid was still talking. "Accompanying Triumphant Falcon to the afterworld is the greatest honor a young woman can receive. Your family will be extremely proud of you. I am sure your father, who tends the sacred flame, will be especially pleased you were selected."

Dawn Breaks seriously doubted it. She knew her father well. He would be aghast. She was struck by inspiration.

"Speaking of my father," she said. "He is crippled. He relies on me to tend to his needs in our lodge. I am an essential part of my family. Perhaps it would be better to give this honor to another deserving girl, one from a larger family, one with a father who is not lame. Really, as much as I am honored, I am willing to forgo this opportunity."

Tall Oaks spoke up. "It would be a great waste of talent to send Dawn Breaks out of this world at such a young age. She is capable of producing many great works of art. Her talent is exceptional. Choose someone else. Take me. I am old. I do not have long to live, anyway."

The youngest priest sneered at the elderly sculptor. "Look at you, old man. What would the Grand Chief want with you when he could have her?" He turned his attention to Dawn Breaks and narrowed his eyes, his greasy black hair dangling over his shiny forehead. "Dawn Breaks was chosen. It is done." His shrewd eyes studied her face. "I take this opportunity to tell you, in case you do not know, that if you refuse this honor or flee the village, your entire family will be executed and die in terrible dishonor. Surely you would not want that to happen."

"Bloody Nose!" interrupted Makes Afraid. "No need for such harsh words. A young woman of her high character would never dream of shaming her family and our village in such a manner."

Makes Afraid gripped Dawn Breaks by the hands. She was tempted to pull away, but overcame the urge.

"I apologize for Bloody Nose's bluntness. This is his first time as a messenger to the chosen. He is a very able young priest. I am sure he will learn more tact in the future. Nevertheless, what he said is completely true. This is an honor you cannot refuse. You have been chosen. *Wah'Kon-Tah* guided us in our choice."

Bloody Nose said nothing more, but the triumphant expression on his face could not be missed. He clearly read her mind. He understood her horror. Makes Afraid either did not or pretended he did not.

Makes Afraid turned his face upward and peered briefly at the sun, directly overhead. "It is high sun. You may either come to the

Temple to pray with us until it is time to leave for Cahokia, or you may meet us at the waterfront at dawn tomorrow. Either way, we will leave for Cahokia at daybreak."

"I would rather not go with you right this moment," Dawn Breaks whispered, her voice catching in her throat. *I would rather not go with you ever*, a frantic voice screamed inside her head.

"Very well," Makes Afraid said. "We will see you in the morning."

"Do not forget my warning," Bloody Nose hissed. "Do not do anything stupid."

Chapter 20

"Mother, what am I to do?"

Dawn Breaks and Whispering Wind were alone in their family's lodge. She had just told her stepmother the awful news.

Whispering Wind's face filled with anguish. "I am so proud of you," she stammered. "It is such an honor to be chosen. Only the most beautiful, pure, wonderful . . ." Her voice broke off.

"Oh, Mother! Why me?"

Both women dissolved into tears and hugged each other. The two young stepsisters of Dawn Breaks, who had been playing outside, came running into the lodge and joined the wailing, without knowing the reason for the tears.

Several minutes passed before Dawn Breaks was able to speak. "Where is Father?"

"He is visiting Chief Gray Wolf. He should be back soon."

"Does he know?"

"Not when he left his morning. I do not know if he has heard since then. He has been with Chief Gray Wolf." Whispering Winds' lips quivered. "This will break your father's heart."

Dawn Breaks felt her throat ache. She and her stepmother embraced again. Whispering Wind caressed the younger woman's face.

They were still hugging when Thunder Runner charged through the door.

"This cannot be true!"

Dawn Breaks pulled apart from her stepmother and faced her suitor, the man she had expected to spend the rest of her life with.

Thunder Runner was covered with sweat. There was no telling how far he had run, or how fast. His eyes pleaded with her for reassurance. "Say it is not true!"

Dawn Breaks again felt the ache in her throat.

"It is true. I have been chosen. The Grand Chief died. I am to accompany him to the afterworld. Of course, the drawback to this honor is that one must die to make the trip."

"No!" Thunder Runner yelled. "You are to marry me. It has already been decided. I have been gathering presents. They cannot take you away from me!"

Dawn Breaks spoke softly. "They chose me. There is nothing I can do. Tall Oaks tried to take my place, but they would not let him." Her voice broke off.

Thunder Runner threw his hands in the air and began pacing the room. "Come with me," he said. "Right now. Come with me. We will get far away from this village and those stinking priests. I can take care of you. You will be safe with me."

Dawn Breaks saw the power in her young man. She knew he could provide for her, even in the wilderness. Was it possible? Was this something they could do?

"No," Whispering Wind said. "She cannot go with you. By law, if a chosen one flees, her entire family is put to death. Not only that, but the entire village would feel the wrath of *Wah'Kon-Tah* through famine and earthquake. She cannot go."

"Rubbish! I do not believe in *Wah'Kon-Tah*. As for the Grand Chief, I met him. He was nothing more than a mortal man. He is a corpse now. He does not need other corpses to accompany him to the afterworld. He is beyond caring. He will not even know those girls have been killed. What a waste! The world will continue whether or not Dawn Breaks dies. This is madness!"

"Silence!" Whispering Wind said. "You speak blasphemy. You could be struck dead just for saying such things. Dawn Breaks cannot run away with you."

"Then we should all leave," Thunder Runner said. "Come with me, all of you. We will find a safe place. I can paddle a canoe fast. They will never catch us."

"No, we must stay. Dawn Breaks must stay." Whispering Wind's voice softened. "I understand your grief, Thunder Runner. Sorrow has hold of your tongue and your mind. You have said things you do not mean. This is a sad time for all of us. But it is a proud time, too. It truly is an honor for Dawn Breaks to be chosen."

Thunder Runner crossed his arms and faced the woman he had expected to have as his mother-in-law.

"I meant every word I said. I want Dawn Breaks to come with me."

He turned his attention to Dawn Breaks. The strength of his willpower filled the emptiness in her soul. "Come with me, Dawn Breaks."

He held out his arms. She ran to him, burying her face upon his bare shoulder, smashing her tears into his bronze skin. He held her as she shuddered. He caressed her back.

"She will *not* go with you!"

The voice was her father's. She heard him before she even realized he had come home. He was standing by the door to the lodge.

"Dawn Breaks is my daughter. She was taught right from wrong. She will do her duty. It is selfish for you to ask her to do anything less." Night Owl limped into the room, using his cane for support. "For reasons unknown to us, *Wah'Kon-Tah* has chosen her for this special honor. She is obligated to do *Wah'Kon-Tah*'s will."

Thunder Runner hugged her even harder.

"All I want is for her to be my wife! If it means running away, we will do it. Please, let your entire family come with me."

"No!" Night Owl moved closer to them. "The trickster is influencing your thoughts. My family will not be cursed for eternity because Dawn Breaks resisted *Wah'Kon-Tah*'s will. I would trade my life for hers. In fact, I tried to do so when the priests came to tell me the news. But they do not want me. They want her. We must accept *Wah'Kon-Tah*'s will."

Thunder Runner released Dawn Breaks and faced her father.

"Did *Wah'Kon-Tah* personally tell you anything?" Thunder Runner shouted. "Did the Great Spirit communicate directly to Dawn Breaks? No! It is those priests, those filthy priests. If *Wah'Kon-Tah* wants Dawn Breaks to die with the Grand Chief, let *Wah'Kon-Tah* tell her personally."

"Blasphemy," wailed Whispering Wind. "*Wah'Kon-Tah* never speaks directly to any mortal, except the priests. Do not talk that way in this lodge."

Night Owl looked from Thunder Runner to Dawn Breaks. His gaze softened when it landed on her. Although his voice was strong, his hands were shaking. "What about it? Are you going to run off with Thunder Runner? Are you going to put the lives of your family in jeopardy?"

"Of course not, Father."

The answer had been automatic. Without thought. As soon as the words left her lips she regretted them. Now it seemed so certain, so final. She would be dead by the end of Triumphant Falcon's funeral.

Her father limped over to her and gently pulled her head to his shoulder.

"Dawn Breaks, you have been the joy of my life. I do not know what I will do without you. But you are making the right decision."

Night Owl turned to Thunder Runner. "The priests will take her to Cahokia tomorrow. A large contingent from our village will be going to the Grand Chief's funeral. Our biggest canoes will be taken. You are welcome to ride with us, Thunder Runner, as a member of our family."

Thunder Runner closed his eyes and looked down.

Dawn Breaks saw terrible pain in her father's eyes. Everything was so hopeless. She felt so helpless.

She remembered Tall Oaks's dream about the smashing of his life's work. At least she would be leaving *some* pieces of sculpture by which she might be remembered.

She pictured her father after she was gone, sitting by a fire, staring into it, trying to remember her face. She wished she had taken the time to make a self-portrait. If only there were time now.

Perhaps there was.

"Father," she said softly. "If you would like, I will make you a statue of me. It would be something you could always remember me by."

Even as the words left her mouth she realized the difficulty of the task. Could she make something so important in such a short amount of time? Could she even begin to create something worthy of such an event? Could she get it done in just one afternoon?

"I would be honored," Night Owl said. "I would treasure it."

From the look in her father's eyes, she knew she would try to make it the best thing she had ever created.

She could not bring herself to meet the eyes of Thunder Runner. In them she had seen the despair she felt in her heart.

Chapter 21

"I have come to you one last time," Dawn Breaks said to Tall Oaks. "I want to make a gift for my family, something they can remember me by. I would like to make a figurine of myself, a self-portrait."

The old sculptor frowned. "It is bad luck to make self-portraits."

Her laugh sounded more like a grunt. "Could my luck be any worse?"

"Forgive me." He sighed. "You have a point."

She was surprised by the calmness she was feeling. "Obviously, I must finish it today, but I want it to be perfect. That is the problem."

"You can do it," he said. "Make it this afternoon. Leave it with me. I will fire it and paint it for you. I will give it to your father when he returns from Cahokia. You can count on me."

"Thank you."

Moments later, she was sitting on the ground, one of her flat boards in her lap, her fingers immersed in wet red flint clay, tempered with extremely fine blue sand. She kneaded and worked the clay. When it was ready, she began molding it to the proper shape for her figurine.

Her mentor sat by her side, watching her, silent tears wetting his wrinkled cheeks.

She glanced at him and offered a slight smile. "I will miss you."

"Not as much as I will miss you."

He wiped a tear from the corner of an eye.

"May I ask you something?" she asked

"Of course."

"Would my family *really* be executed if I were to run away?"

Tall Oaks shifted uncomfortably. He was silent for a long time.

"I am an old man," he said, eventually. "I have lived through the deaths of two Grand Chiefs. I attended their funerals at Cahokia. Each time, the wives and servants of the Grand Chief voluntarily went to their deaths with the great man. Each time, certain young women from villages throughout the land also accompanied the Grand Chief on his journey. During my lifetime, none of the chosen has ever fled."

Dawn Breaks was not looking at Tall Oaks, but she listened intently as she worked on the shoulders and arms of her figurine.

"So, we really do not know what would happen?" she asked.

"Before my time," he continued, "I heard of a young girl who disappeared from the village when chosen to accompany a dead chief. People who were old when I was young told me that the girl fled during the night before the funeral. She ran off with a lover. Of course, the funeral went on without her. The wife and servants were sacrificed in the normal way. Then the chosen women met their fate, all except the girl who had run. Finally, the family of the runaway girl was brought forward. Her parents, grandparents, brothers, and sisters were all killed. Their names were stricken from our oral histories, never to be repeated aloud again. The girl and her lover never returned. What was left to come home to, anyway? Nothing but death and shame."

Dawn Breaks felt hot tears flowing down her cheeks as she shaped her figurine. She would portray herself kneeling, with her face turned toward the heavens.

"Yes, Dawn Breaks. The priests would execute your family if you fled. I am sure of it. You heard Bloody Nose."

"You are right, of course. Please do not hate me for asking the question."

"I do not blame you for considering your options. You are so young. I fully understand. I am sorry for you. I wish they would have taken me instead."

"Thank you for your offer. It was very brave of you."

"Brave!" He snorted. "Not at all."

She worked silently on her figurine. Her spirits lightened as she lost herself in the work and the statuette began to take shape. She created a smooth, rounded face. The work was easier than she had expected. She had seen the same face reflected in pools of water many times. She angled the head so the face tilted toward the sky, as if looking at the Morning Star. She placed a smile on the face of the chosen girl, as if she were happy to be giving her life to

Wah'Kon-Tah and to her Grand Chief. What was a little lie at this point in her life?

"How do you think they will kill me?" It was a question she had been contemplating, but had been afraid to voice. Perhaps because she dreaded the answer.

As she waited for a response from Tall Oaks, she added a tiny tear to the cheek of her figurine. It wandered down the girl's face, a lonely talisman for the lover and family left behind.

Tall Oaks cleared his throat. "I am not sure I have the strength to tell you," he said.

"Tell the truth."

"I am not sure you want to hear it."

"I do, trust me."

He sighed. "When I attended the funerals of the two prior Grand Chiefs, the family, servants, and young women were lined up in rows. Priests in front gave them a potion to drink. Priests behind slipped cords around their necks and strangled them."

Dawn Breaks's hands froze.

"It all happened very quickly," Tall Oaks added. "I believe the potion put them to sleep. I am not sure the, um, the chosen, felt any pain at all."

Dawn Breaks closed her eyes.

"They did not cut the hearts from their chests?"

"No."

"Well, at least that is a relief," she muttered. "I did not want to be heartless."

She positioned the girl's arms so they folded in submission in front of her. The hands clasped together right under the girl's breasts.

"Thunder Runner wants me to run away with him."

Tall Oaks did not reply.

"It is impossible, really," she continued. "I could not live with myself if I knew my family had been put to death because of my selfishness. But it hurts to see the pain in Thunder Runner's eyes. I wish I could take that pain away." She sighed. "I so much wanted to be his wife."

She was making her self-portrait completely naked. The girl would be helpless before *Wah'Kon-Tah* and as naked leaving the world as she had been when entering it. Breasts, rib cage, abdomen, thighs, and buttocks were all easy to duplicate. After all, she had studied this particular body every day of her life. She shaped the thighs, knees, and ankles so they pressed tightly together. It was simpler and more modest. She made the breasts a bit larger than real life. Another small lie. Well, why not?

She used a sharp reed to add detail to the face, shaping the nose, eyes, and lips. All in all, the work was going faster than she had expected.

"Wonderful job!" Tall Oaks said. "Your work with human faces is unmatched. It is a remarkable likeness."

She added fine lines to the long hair flowing from the tilted head and hanging halfway down the naked back. She rounded the buttocks into a perfect likeness of her own.

When she was finished, she held out the board for Tall Oaks. On it balanced her foot-tall self-portrait.

"What do you think?"

"Beautiful! You captured your own spirit. It is a perfect image of you. I have never seen a better piece of work. Not by any student. Not by myself. It's as if *Wah'Kon-Tah* entered your hands today to recreate the dazzling beauty he had already created once before."

She stared at the red clay figurine on the flat board. It was just mud, sand, dirt, and water. Yet, it did indeed look like her. This represented a girl of sixteen winters, somewhat past the time most girls have married, who had recently fallen in love, only to learn that *Wah'Kon-Tah* had chosen her to travel with the Grand Chief into the next world, leaving behind all she knew and cherished. This girl was looking to *Wah'Kon-Tah* for guidance about the right way to act, for help in finding the strength to accept her situation, and for compassion for her family and friends. This girl was putting her faith in *Wah'Kon-Tah* and submitting to the wisdom of the priests of her village.

Was that really how she felt?

Not exactly.

She pictured herself fleeing downriver with Thunder Runner. How exhilarating it would be! That is what she truly wanted to do. But how short-lived the excitement would be, knowing her reckless act would doom her family.

174

She closed her eyes tightly.

"I just do not know what to do," she whispered.

Tall Oaks put a hand on hers.

"You are in an awful position. You are young. You are passionate. You have everything to live for. You have a brave young man willing to take you to the end of the world to save you. But think carefully before you act."

His hand rose and touched her cheek. She opened her eyes.

"Everyone must die eventually," he said. "We are all dying every single day from the moment we are born. It is a chilling rite of passage when a child reaches the age where the concept of personal mortality is fully understood. As children, we believe we will live forever. We flit from activity to activity like a butterfly, never once thinking that a time will come when we will depart this world. It is a sobering moment when we learn that our stay on this earth is temporary. From that point forward, time rushes by with increasing speed."

His old eyes were unwavering. They seemed to peer into the depths of her soul. "Everyone must die, but most of us never know our time or place in advance. We go about our lives, oblivious to our fate. Take the people in our village. We number about six hundred. The average man lives perhaps forty winters. You have already lived more than a third of that time. Of the six-hundred people in the village, each will die in his or her own appointed way. Most will succumb to illnesses or old age. Others will drown in the river. Many will die in hunting accidents or be killed by wild panthers or bears or snakes. Others will freeze or die of starvation. Some will perish in warfare or in quarrels with others."

He raised her hand to his lips and kissed it.

"Consider this, Dawn Breaks. Not *one* of those deaths will be so noble as the sacrifice you are making for the Grand Chief and for *Wah'Kon-Tah*. Not one of those deaths is so honorable as accompanying Triumphant Falcon into the afterworld. You have the chance to have lived a life worth living, to have died a death worth dying. Your life will have had real meaning. What if it is true that *Wah'Kon-Tah* will be pleased that you are accompanying the Grand Chief? What if he rewards your village with good weather and good fortune because of you? In that case, your death would have made the world a better place for others. How many people can say that?"

He squeezed her hand. "You thought I was being brave when I offered to replace you." He chuckled softly. "The truth is, I would rather die a noble death in front of thousands of people than fade away alone in my lodge. I was not being brave. I was being selfish. I *wanted* to take your place. But you can keep thinking I am brave if you wish."

She smiled and patted his hand.

"As always, Tall Oaks, I have learned something from you. Thank you. You have made me feel better. Thank you for everything you have done for me."

He studied her self-portrait again. "You know," he said. "This is so beautiful I may keep it myself."

She wagged a finger at him. "It is for my father," she said. "If you do not give it to him as you promised, I will come back and haunt you with a vengeance."

She would not have believed it possible, but she was actually laughing. When the moment passed, she closed her eyes, wondering if that instant had been the last time she would ever laugh in this world.

Chapter 22

When Dawn Breaks returned home, she smelled the hickory-nut cornbread even before she reached her family's lodge. While she had been making her figurine, Whispering Wind had been preparing many of her favorite foods.

"I hope you are hungry," her stepmother said. "I have prepared venison, sweet potatoes, corn soup, hickory-nut cornbread, persimmon fritters, and grapes."

At the sight of the food, Dawn Breaks found she did have an appetite.

"Thank you, Mother," she said, getting a bowl and serving herself.

Her dog danced between her legs, a jumping and cavorting fur ball, greeting her as if she had been gone for a full moon. The frenzied welcome at a return home was one of the nicest things about having a dog. A jolt of sadness shot through her. *He will never know what happened to me. I wonder how long he will wait for my return before giving up on me?*

"Did you finish your sculpture?" her father asked.

"Yes. Tall Oaks will add the final touches and bring it to you when you get back from Cahokia."

"Did it turn out well?"

"You will like it, Father. It is rather good, if I say so myself."

She sat down on a woven mat next to Night Owl. Her young stepsisters hurried to sit next to her. They were barely past being toddlers. She wondered how well they would remember her, if at all.

Her father sat with his good leg underneath him. His crippled leg stretched out to the side. He smiled at her. "You look so much like your mother."

She glanced at her father's eyes. He seldom talked about his first wife, especially in front of Whispering Wind.

"Tell me more about her, Father."

He lowered his plate to his lap and gazed through the mists of time.

"She was the most beautiful girl in the village. Everyone recognized it. She stood out even as a child. She had talent, too. She could play a reed flute so sweetly you would think you were listening to a joyful bird just learning the thrill of singing." He smiled. "I was one of the village's best young hunters in those days. I had my eye on her since we were children, but you do not talk about that sort of thing when you are growing up, of course. Eventually, when we were both fifteen, my aunt paid a little visit to her aunt. Later that summer I killed my first bear and delivered part of it to her lodge. We were married at the next Green Corn Ceremony."

"Where was our Mother?" one of Dawn Breaks' younger sisters asked.

"She was just a little girl then," Night Owl said. "Too young to be noticed by a big, successful hunter like me."

Whispering Wind snorted. "I am only three winters younger than my sister. You make it sound like I was a baby."

He smiled. "I will tell the story my way. You can tell it your way. But wait your turn."

The little girls ran to Whispering Wind and climbed into her lap. "We love you, Mother!" they chorused.

"I know," Whispering Wind said softly.

Night Owl nodded, delving back into his memories.

"Your mother and I made a wonderful life together for two winters. I would hunt for the most part of each day, and play as much chunkey as time permitted. She fixed our food and tended our garden." He sighed. "Your mother had a gift for laughter. She saw the bright side of everything. She brought much happiness to those around her. She was very like you."

He took a deep breath.

"When we discovered she was pregnant with you, it was one of the happiest days of my life. I cannot do justice to my feelings with mere words. I had loved your mother for so long, so deeply, that it was overwhelming to realize that I was going to have a child by her. It felt like a miracle."

He stared into the fire.

"When she began having her birthing pains, we were excited. Your mother and I had spent much time preparing our lodge for your arrival. We had tentatively picked your name, subject to an official naming ceremony, of course. But as the hours dragged on, and the midwives became more and more alarmed, I began to realize that something was wrong. We both knew. I came to her side. I held her hand. She did her best to hang on, to be there for you, to live to be your mother, but it was not meant to be. *Wah'Kon-Tah* called her to him that night. I watched as the light went out of her eyes, even as you were uttering your first cry of life."

Night Owl looked down at his hands.

"I was devastated. What was I to do with a baby? I could barely care for myself. Your grandmother was a great help." He glanced up at Whispering Wind. "Your stepmother was also a great help, right from the start. Such a wonderful, generous girl. She was your mother on this earth from the day you were born. She could not have loved you more had you come from her body."

"That is true," Whispering Wind said.

"I married Whispering Wind at the next Green Corn Ceremony. It was permitted since she was your mother's sister."

Night Owl's eyes glistened.

"You need to know, Dawn Breaks," he said, "that your mother would be very proud of you. You are everything a good daughter should be: loving, kind, thoughtful, helpful, courteous, cheerful. She would have loved you so much."

"I am sure she does love her," Whispering Wind said, "wherever she is."

"Yes," Night Owl echoed. "Wherever she is."

They sat in silence for a long time.

"Thunder Runner is going to come by later this evening," Dawn Breaks eventually said. "May I take a walk with him?"

"Of course," her father answered. He glanced at Whispering Wind. "Would you take the little ones outside? I would like a moment alone with Dawn Breaks."

"Yes." Whispering Wind corralled the children and the dog and took them outside, closing the door behind her.

The fire in the hearth at the center of the lodge popped, sending a small cloud of orange gnats circling toward the hole at the top of the hut. They burned out within a few feet of the flames.

"I know it sounded like I was forbidding you to leave with Thunder Runner," he said quietly.

She nodded.

"I am not forbidding you from doing so. It must be your decision. I know what I would do, but my faith in *Wah'Kon-Tah* is strong. You must make your own choice. You are an adult and it is your life."

"Father," she said. "I . . ."

He put a finger to his lips, shushing her. "You have been the best daughter a man could ever have. You are an exceptional young woman in every way. I have seen your mother in you every day of your life. It has brought me tremendous joy to watch you blossom into a young woman. I will love you nonetheless, no matter what you do. I want you to know that."

She moved to him and hugged him hard. "I love you," she whispered.

Chapter 23

The moon was high in the night sky when Thunder Runner came for Dawn Breaks. He spoke briefly and respectfully with her father before they left for their walk. The evening air was cool. She wore a wrap over her shoulders. She held his arm as they made their way through the village. In the bright moonlight, her face close to his, she was the most beautiful thing he had ever seen.

They walked to the riverfront, where Thunder Runner held her hand as they talked. He had been rehearsing what he wanted to say. He was hoping to be persuasive. He considered it the most important conversation of his life.

"I have a canoe packed. We can leave tonight. We can be so far away by morning that the priests will be forced to leave without you. I love you, Dawn Breaks. I have spent many hours planning our life together. I can no longer imagine a life apart from you. I do not care about anything else in this world. I want to be with you. I want us to live and flourish. I want us to have children. I want us to grow old together. For the past month, I have lived the major part of each day eagerly anticipating our marriage. When I am awake, I think of you. When I am asleep, I dream of you. Please, Dawn Breaks. Come away with me."

"No. I cannot," she said. "Have you forgotten what would happen to my family if I ran off with you?"

He grunted in derision. "Big talk! I do not believe a word of it. *Wah'Kon-Tah* would not kill a girl's family just because she chose life over death. The priests are bluffing to keep you from running. They are liars and charlatans."

"I wish they *were* bluffing," she said.

"I have never heard of anyone's entire family being put to death, even a murderer's," he said. "They are just trying to scare you. Nothing would happen if we ran off."

"Tall Oaks says it is no bluff. A girl's family was really killed."

She knotted her hands into small fists.

"I could not live with myself if something happened to my family because of me. As much as I love you, I would not be worth having if I had my family's blood on my conscience. Surely you understand."

He released her hands and turned toward the river. "I knew that is what you would say."

Tears welled in his eyes. He picked up a small rock and skipped it across the surface of the moonlit river. Emotions swirled throughout his body. He still could not believe this girl was going to be leaving him, that all of his plans and fantasies were falling apart.

"We only have a few more hours alone together," he said.

"I know."

"We should make the most of them."

"I agree."

"I know a spot where we can have some privacy, where I can hold you in my arms and tell you all the dreams I had for us."

"I would like that very much."

He led her to a cornfield just south of town, in the lowlands next to the river. It was the most fertile ground in the village. The corn was tall, providing a natural curtain of privacy. Two guards tended the edges of the field, assigned to drive away raccoons and other corn thieves. They would not intrude upon the intimate moments of a young couple venturing deep into the field, though. Neither would dare risk the wrath of Thunder Runner.

Like all cornfields of the time, the corn was not planted in rows, but in individual circular groups on little mounds. Each tall corn stalk served as a stake for beans to climb. Squash plants covered the ground at the foot of the corn and beans. The plants were called the "three sisters" since it was so common for all three to be planted in the same fields.

Thunder Runner led her to a place deep in the cornfield, just the right size for them to lie on their backs and gaze at the stars. He brought along a soft bearskin. He spread it carefully on the ground.

She nestled against him. Together they looked up at the Milky Way.

"According to the priests, the path to the next world runs through the Milky Way," he said. "Supposedly you will encounter some challenges along the route. I wish I were going with you."

"Sounds like I will have plenty of company. If they really are selecting a girl from each village, there will be dozens of us. Not to mention the Grand Chief's servants."

"I want you to have this." He pressed something into her hand.

She held it up in the moonlight. It was the falcon necklace the Grand Chief had given him.

"Thank you. It is beautiful."

"Put it on," he urged. "I am hoping it will give you strength. Perhaps you can take it with you, to remind you of me. Maybe it will remind others that you belong to someone else. Maybe it will help me find you one day."

She smiled. "I will never take it off. I will be yours forever."

He put the necklace around her neck. When she looked up at him, he kissed her. Her lips were soft and yielding at first, hesitating and uncertain, but then he felt an urgency in her embrace that cried out for reaffirmation that she was alive, that she could feel, that she was flesh and blood, and that at least for one more night she could still soar to heights of physical ecstasy. With their mouths joined, their bodies pressed together, fumbling at first, but finally in perfect unison. Her breath was hot on his mouth as every part of his body ached to become one with hers. In the ripe corn-field, the midnight breeze caressed the tall stalks, pushing them gently to and fro, as the young lovers came together, their passion intensified by the bittersweet knowledge of the briefness of this exquisite moment in time.

Afterward, they lay for hours under the moonlit sky, wrapped in each other's arms. At times, her tears dripped into his open eyes as she lay on top of him, his arms pulling her chest close to his. He imagined her tears becoming part of his body, coursing though his system, leaving traces of her life force embedded in his soul forever.

Likewise, part of him was coursing through her. The knowledge eased the pain he was feeling. They were truly man and wife now, no matter what. Nobody could take that away from him. She had given herself to him, wholly and completely. He would cherish this night forever. If only they could have more time together.

They were lying quietly next to each other, fingers entwined, her thigh resting on top of his, when Dawn Breaks broke the peaceful silence.

"Tall Oaks told me something that made me feel a bit better."

"Better than you feel with me?"

"No. Nothing could be better than how I feel with you. I mean, he helped me understand the importance of what is happening to me."

She told him what Tall Oaks had said about the different ways to die and the nobility of giving one's life for one's community.

Thunder Runner grunted. "As deaths go, yours will indeed be glorious. With my luck, I will probably suffer some embarrassing end, like tripping and hitting my head on a urine pot."

She chuckled. "At least people would talk about that for a long time. There lies Thunder Runner. He died in a puddle of glory."

He hugged her again.

"Do you know how I would like to die?" he asked. "If I had my choice?"

"How?"

"Playing chunkey. I would be in the championship game. The score would be tied. I would be coming up for the tie-breaking point. Thunderclouds would be rolling in, but the game would continue. The chunkey stone would be rolling. It would be streaking across the field. My opponent and I would hurl our spears. Suddenly, a bolt of lightning would come crashing from the sky and strike me dead while my spear was still in the air. I would fall to the ground, lifeless, but my spear would continue flying through the sky and would hit the chunkey stone after my death. I would win the match after I died. That is the way I want to go!"

She patted his shoulder. "I will see if I can arrange it. It looks like I will be spending time with some important individuals in the next world. Keep playing chunkey and I will see what can be arranged."

"Well," he said. "Just save a place for me. I will find you, wherever you go. I promise you. If there is another life, I will find you."

"I will count on it. There is life after death. I truly believe it."

Thunder Runner drew her hand to his mouth and kissed her fingers. "I will never love another woman."

"Of course you will. You will find someone else. Look at my father. He found Whispering Wind after my mother died. Life will go on."

He pressed her hand to his chest. She could feel his heart beating beneath his rippling muscles.

"I mean it. I will never love another woman. I promise."

She touched a hand to his cheek. "I do not want you to make that promise. I want you to be happy, not a bitter old man."

He engulfed her in his arms again.

"I would do anything for you," he whispered. "Anything! I just do not know what I could do that would make things better. I wish I were wiser."

Thunder Runner had never felt so helpless. He wanted to save her, but every avenue of escape was blocked, thoroughly and completely.

"There is one thing you could do for me," she said softly.

"Anything!"

"You could make love to me again."

It was quite late when he returned her to her family's lodge. He did not go inside. Her parents were waiting up. He knew they would talk all night. He did not want to intrude. Nor did he feel he could bear it.

As he walked home, it occurred to him that there was a better way to die than being struck by lightning. There was something important he could do with his life. As he turned his face to the stars, his destiny was revealed to him with chilling clarity. If he could just pull it off.

Chapter 24

Dawn Breaks felt prickles of apprehension shoot down her back as the city of Cahokia came into view. She rode in the middle of one of the long dugout canoes making the trip upriver for the funeral of the Grand Chief. Over half of the six-hundred inhabitants of her village were attending the funeral. For many, it would be a once-in-a-lifetime event.

That certainly appeared to be the case for her.

The canoes veered off the Father of Waters and traveled up a smaller stream toward Cahokia. In the distance, the immense Temple Mound loomed over the city like a tremendous mountain. At the top of the four-sided pyramid a large lodge gleamed in the sunshine—the Temple itself, amazingly tall and coated with white plaster.

The mammoth mound overlooked the huge, flat plaza. Dozens upon dozens of smaller mounds surrounded the grand plaza. They were covered with lodges of varying sizes.

Thousands of people filled the street. The huge population of Cahokia had been supplemented by visitors from all over the empire, arriving for the funeral. More people would attend this monumental event than even the largest Green Corn Festival.

Night Owl was sitting next to her as their canoe glided closer to Cahokia. Whispering Wind and her stepsisters rode behind them. Thunder Runner had chosen to ride in a different canoe, saying that being with her during the ride would be too painful for them both. He was right. It hurt to be near him, to see the anguish in his eyes. He was one of the oarsmen in a canoe behind them.

"It is hard to believe the Temple Mound was made by human hands," her father said. "I am struck with awe every time I see it."

Smoke from hundreds of cooking fires lingered in the air above the city like a fine haze. Sunlight danced through the smoke, creating a shimmering and visible pattern of heat over the expanse of buildings.

"What will happen when we arrive?" Dawn Breaks asked.

"I do not know," Night Owl said. "We will find out soon enough."

As the canoe glided closer to the crowded bank, Dawn Breaks was surprised by how little fear she felt. Rather, she found herself marveling at the immensity of Cahokia. A huge village in the middle of a wilderness, Cahokia was the center of a vast spiderweb of enterprise. Copper from the great lakes to the North, seashells from the huge ocean to the South, chert and obsidian from the West, sheet mica from the East, salt from nearby flats less than a day's journey away, grain from the vast fertile fields planted in the bottomland surrounding the city—all these things passed through the hands of the barterers on the waterfront in the great village of the Grand Chief. If all of this could spring out of nothing, maybe the priests at Cahokia knew what they were talking about. Maybe *Wah'Kon-Tah* really did reveal his wishes to them. Maybe her death would truly benefit the entire empire.

When her canoe reached the sandy bank, her village's Head Priest, Makes Afraid, and a cluster of other priests from the Village of Gray Wolf, awaited her.

"Bid your family farewell," Makes Afraid said as he helped her from the canoe. "We must take you to the place where the chosen ones are being prepared for the ceremony. We know you are going to represent our community well."

Dawn Breaks was startled. This was so sudden. She had expected to have time alone with her family and with Thunder Runner. This was so abrupt.

"Could I not have a few moments with my family?" she asked Makes Afraid.

"No!" Bloody Nose answered for the Head Priest. "We are already late because we have come so far. The funeral is at high sun today. The morning is half gone. You need to be prepared for your part in the ceremony. We have no time to waste."

"Waste? Saying goodbye to my family is a waste?"

Makes Afraid gently patted her shoulder. "You have time to say goodbye, but Bloody Nose makes a good point. We must hurry."

Dawn Breaks rushed to her father and gripped his hands. "I love you," she said. "I will make you proud. I promise."

The tendons in Night Owl's neck bulged as he fought to maintain his composure.

"You already make me proud. Go with the Grand Chief. Travel to the next level in the Upper World. I will follow you someday."

"Do not forget the statue I made for you."

"No matter how beautiful it is, it will never compare to the real thing," he said hoarsely, hugging her tightly.

She knelt and said her goodbyes to her tiny stepsisters. It pained her that they were so young they did not seem to realize she would not be going home with them. They were more interested in a lizard perched on a nearby pile of firewood.

She turned to her stepmother. They embraced. "Take care of Father," she whispered. "And take care of yourself. You will need each other."

"I will pray for you every day," Whispering Wind said softly. "You will not be forgotten."

Thunder Runner's canoe had arrived during her farewells with her family. He stood nearby, erect and tall, his expression stoic.

She moved to him and put her hands on his face.

"I love you," she said.

He wrapped his arms around her and hugged her.

"We are man and wife," he whispered. "Be brave, my love. Whatever happens. As you said, there are a thousand ways to die, and you have chosen a noble one."

She sighed. "I did not exactly choose it. It chose me."

As the embrace ended, they continued holding hands as she backed slowly away from him. When their hands no longer touched, she moved her right hand to her neck and held up the necklace he had given her, showing him she was wearing it.

"Good bye," she said.

His grim face stared at her, betraying none of the deep emotion she knew must be raging inside his soul.

The priests took her by the arms and guided her toward the Temple Mound. She was vaguely aware of her surroundings as she stumbled along with them. She kept thinking of Thunder Runner and of the life they might have enjoyed. She looked back over her shoulder for one last glimpse of him. He still stood motionless in the spot where she had last embraced him.

They guided her along a processional route past scores of large lodges, arranged more or less in rows. They crossed the central plaza, filled shoulder-to-shoulder with people. Ahead of them, the giant pyramid loomed over the rest of the town like a mountain trail to the heavens.

For her, she supposed, that was exactly what it was.

People were pointing at her as the priests guided her toward the Temple Mound. Look! There goes one of the chosen. Look at her now. You might not get a good look later. Get a glimpse of her now, while she is still alive!

When they reached the bottom of the Temple Mound, Dawn Breaks stared upward. The terraced levels rose toward the sky. The steps stretched endlessly toward the sun.

"What's it like, knowing you will soon be learning exactly what happens after death?" The voice belonged to Bloody Nose, the greasy, young priest from the Village of Gray Wolf. He was at her side, gripping one of her arms.

Her mouth was dry. She did not answer. She quietly followed the other priests as they began the climb up the hundreds of steps.

"The Temple Mound is one-hundred feet high," Bloody Nose was saying. "It takes you very close to Grandfather Sun. It has four levels. Except on holy days like today, workers seek to improve it every day, carrying baskets of earth from nearby pits, adding to the mound. It is meant to produce awe. It works. You feel it, do you not? You feel its power?"

Dawn Breaks nodded.

Bloody Nose pointed to the different levels of the mound. "The crowd will be permitted on the first three levels, but only priests and those departing will be allowed at the very top level. You are extremely lucky."

She kept her thoughts to herself. She was not sure her voice would work, anyway.

The first terrace, forty feet high, occupied a fourth of the surface area of the Temple Mound. It was already jammed with people. Early risers, she supposed. Those who wanted a good view. She wondered how long they had been waiting.

She and her escorts climbed the steps to the next level. Ahead of them, she spotted priests from other villages, also accompanied by young women. For the first time, she began to consider the other girls sharing her fate. Who were they? How many would there be? Where had they come from? What were their stories? How had they been selected?

She slipped and barked a shin on a wooden corner of one of the steps. She welcomed the minor pain. It proved to her she was still alive.

"Be careful," Bloody Nose said. "We would not want anything to happen to you today."

What a fool! Did he realize what he had said? She glanced at him sharply. His face was inscrutable.

The second terrace was sixty-two feet high. It was also crowded with spectators. By dress and ornamentation, they appeared to be more wealthy and elite than those on the lower level.

When they reached the third level, they were almost at the top of the pyramid. Priests and chiefs from many villages packed this area.

"My family," Dawn Breaks asked. "Where will they be?"

"On this third level with the chiefs," Bloody Nose said. "It is an honor they will enjoy because of you."

Dawn Breaks seriously doubted her family would be *enjoying* any part of this grisly day.

At the far end of the mound's top terrace, the Temple crowned the pyramid like the heavy point at the tip of a spear.

"That's where you will be prepared for the ceremony," Bloody Nose whispered in her ear. "At the proper time, you will be brought back out for the important role you will play."

Head Priest Makes Afraid took her by the hand. "You were chosen to represent our village," he said. "Make us proud. Represent us well. You are to be commended for the calm demeanor you have displayed so far. You are doing well." He gave her hand a squeeze and nodded toward an approaching woman. "Go with this woman. She will take you to the proper place. Goodbye, Dawn Breaks."

She followed a nondescript female attendant into the Temple of the Grand Chief. She noticed as she entered that the walls were three feet thick. Smooth clay floors were cool and comfortable underfoot. Thick wooden posts a foot in diameter supported the huge lodge.

The guide took her to a large room filled with people. The room was abuzz with activity. Priests in robes were painting young women with white paint. Some girls were completely naked as paint was being dabbed onto their bodies. Others, paint already dry, were wearing white skirts, adorned with lovely beadwork. The long black hair of each girl was being braided into two tails, one behind each ear. Bright sunlight flooded the room from open windows in the roof. The clay walls and floor of the room were also painted white. Altogether, it was the most dazzling spectacle Dawn Breaks had ever seen.

"Over here," an elderly priest called.

She crossed the room. The old man smiled at her, sunlight reflecting off his snow white head.

"You are a lovely girl. The Grand Chief and *Wah'Kon-Tah* will undoubtedly be pleased with you. Where are you from?"

"The Village of Gray Wolf."

"Ah, Makes Afraid must have picked you. He has good taste. I am Dust Maker. I'm in charge of preparing the chosen for the funeral ceremony. Welcome. What's your name?"

"Dawn Breaks."

"A pretty name, too. Wonderful."

He nodded to the attendant and told her she was free to leave, then turned his attention back to Dawn Breaks.

"Although you may not have realized it yet," he said, "your selection as the representative of your community is the best thing that ever happened to you. You have been assured of immortality. You have been assured of long-lasting fame in your village. You are very lucky."

Dust Maker spoke with such sincerity it was impossible not to feel somewhat comforted by his words.

"As you can see," he continued, "we are painting the bodies of you charming girls completely white. That is our way of making you closer to the brightness of *Wah'Kon-Tah*. We will paint your lips bright red, clothe you in a dazzling white skirt, and braid your hair in matching braids. When the fifty-three of you leave this room you will be the most pleasing sight any mortals have ever seen."

"Fifty-three?" murmured Dawn Breaks.

"Yes. This is the largest sacrifice ever made to *Wah'Kon-Tah*. You can rest assured the Great Spirit will be happy and satisfied. The Grand Chief, too, will be tremendously pleased to have your companionship in the afterworld."

A girl much like Dawn Breaks approached the priest. Her face and body were already painted white. Her lips were bright red. She wore one of the white deerskin skirts. She was exquisitely pretty.

"Dust Maker," she said, glancing hesitant at Dawn Breaks. "A girl just told me the priests sometimes use knives. I told her you promised we would get a poison and that it would be painless. There are no knives, are there?"

"No, Slender Leaf. I assure you. You and the other girls will drink a specially made potion. You will feel no pain. The knives are only used upon prisoners of war who are being sacrificed. Not you."

The delicate girl was obviously relieved. She looked at Dawn Breaks with interest. "I am Slender Leaf from the Village of Big Eagle."

"I am Dawn Breaks from the Village of Gray Wolf."

"I am happy to meet you, Dawn Breaks. This is my day to please *Wah'Kon-Tah* and accompany the Grand Chief on his journey through the Milky Way. I am glad to do it in such beautiful company."

Dawn Breaks studied the eyes of the comely girl. Was she drunk? She detected no signs of it. The girl was truly glad to be here. In a way, Dawn Breaks envied her. If only she herself had more faith.

"May I help Dawn Breaks prepare?"

"Certainly," Dust Maker told Slender Leaf. "Others seem to need my counsel more than the two of you."

The dark-robed priest shuffled to the other side of the room, where several girls were crying, making their white paint run.

That is the group I should be with, Dawn Breaks thought. *The less-than-enthusiastic clan. That is how I feel. Exactly.*

"I have been here for two days," Slender Leaf was saying. "I was one of the first to arrive. I was so lucky to get here early. I had the opportunity to benefit from a long talk with Dust Maker. He helped me appreciate my good fortune in being one of the chosen. Only a few in any generation are given such an honor."

Dawn Breaks looked around the room. She was apparently one of the last to arrive. Most of the other girls were almost finished with their preparations.

"If you will take off your clothes, I'll help you get ready," Slender Leaf offered.

Feeling as if she were in a trance, Dawn Breaks unfastened her skirt. It dropped to the floor at her feet, looking dirty next to the brightness of the room.

"I have been fascinated by the different reactions of the girls," Slender Leaf said. "Some are happy and calm. Others are hysterical. Dust Maker has a drink you can take to ease your nerves if you need it. I did not."

Dawn Breaks detected pride in the girl's voice. "How have you stayed so calm? It must have been awful, being in this place for two full days, knowing you are going to die when you leave this room, knowing that each girl you meet does not have long to live."

She felt icy footsteps flitter across her spine as she said the word "die."

"It is all about faith," Slender Leaf said. "I have faith in the priests. I have faith in the Grand Chief. I have faith in *Wah'Kon-Tah*. I know I am not going to die and turn into dust. My soul is going to a new place, a better place in the Upper World. I am going with the Grand Chief into the next world, a higher level, a whole new experience. I am truly excited."

A priest joined them and began dabbing white paint on Dawn Breaks's shoulder blades. Dawn Breaks stared into the calm face of the girl in front of her.

"I wish I had your faith, Slender Leaf."

The girl smiled. "Just open your heart to *Wah'Kon-Tah*. Ask him for peace. Ask him to uplift you, to let you feel his greatness and power. Let him take control and lead you into the future. That's what Dust Maker told me."

"I suppose that is the right attitude," Dawn Breaks said.

Slender Leaf leaned forward and whispered loudly, "Even if I am wrong and there is just nothingness when we die, at least our families will be happy and comforted by thinking we are enjoying everlasting life with the Grand Chief. Either way, worse things could happen."

The priest applying the paint to Dawn Breaks gave Slender Leaf a sharp look.

"Oh, be calm," she said. "I have plenty of faith, as much as anybody, I imagine. I am merely saying that it is an honor to be chosen." Slender Leaf gave a sly grin. "You know what I am going to do when I drink that poison? I am going to look right into the sun and stare at it long and hard to see if I can see *Wah'Kon-Tah*. I have always wanted to stare at the sun, but my mother told me I would go blind."

Dawn Breaks closed her eyes as the priest applied paint to her breasts. A question occurred to her. Perhaps Slender Leaf knew the answer.

"Did any of the chosen refuse to come?"

"Refuse?" Slender Leaf repeated, sounding surprised. "Why, no, not that I have heard."

The priest now knelt behind her, applying white paint to her buttocks with his gentle fingers. Bloody Nose would have liked that job, she imagined. She was glad the young priest from her village had not drawn the assignment.

"My parents were devastated when I was chosen," Slender Leaf continued, "and so was my betrothed. But who can argue with *Wah'Kon-Tah*'s will? Who wants to risk *Wah'Kon-Tah*'s wrath?"

Slender Leaf began braiding Dawn Breaks's hair as the priest smeared the paint onto her face with soothing caresses.

"What about you, Dawn Breaks? How do you feel about being one of the chosen?"

Dawn Breaks considered her answer. The truth? It was an honor she did not seek and did not want. She had difficulty believing that her death would please *Wah'Kon-Tah*. She had doubts whether the Great Spirit would even take notice. She felt despair rather than rapture. Her faith was not strong enough to be happy about the way her life on this earth was ending.

Before she could voice an answer, a strikingly handsome middle-aged woman with an unpainted face, who was dressed in a white skirt, entered the room. She was a bit stout, but carried herself with pride and dignity.

"That's the wife of the Grand Chief," whispered Slender Leaf. "That's Good Eagle Woman."

The conversation in the room gradually died as the great lady crossed the room and stopped at a spot directly underneath one of the windows in the ceiling. The bright sun engulfed her and bathed her in its rays.

"I am Good Eagle Woman, wife of Triumphant Falcon."

The attractive woman glanced around the room. Dawn Breaks felt their eyes connect when the formidable woman looked at her.

"My husband, your Grand Chief, died four days ago. In a very short time I shall be following him into the afterworld. You fifty-three girls have been carefully chosen to accompany us."

She spoke calmly and with a strong voice. She seemed absolutely devoid of fear.

"I will be accepting my death proudly and with dignity. I fully recognize, as should each of you, that we are part of a long line of people who have occupied this land since the beginning of time. Thousands have come before us, and thousands will follow. Only by sacrifices made by our ancestors has *Wah'Kon-Tah* allowed our people and our villages to prosper. Only by our sacrifices today will our loved ones be allowed to survive and multiply and flourish in this hard and difficult world."

Good Eagle Woman seemed to be looking directly at Dawn Breaks, but perhaps every girl in the room felt the same connection to the impressive woman.

"I want each of you to remember what a privilege it is to be chosen to represent your village. Only one girl in thousands is selected. You were chosen because of your beauty, talent, and temperament. Each of you has the inner strength to do your duty in front of the multitude assembled here today, to willingly give your life to *Wah'Kon-Tah*. If you did not have this strength, you would not have been chosen. *Wah'Kon-Tah* himself guided the priests in making their choices. *Wah'Kon-Tah* has chosen you. Praise be to *Wah'Kon-Tah*!"

Good Eagle Woman's eyes glistened with tears.

"Death frees the soul from the physical body. It allows us to begin our journey in the next life. I shall go to my death before each of you, little ones. We will drink from the same cup. My fate is your fate and yours is mine. I shall set an example for the rest of you to follow. Each of us must be worthy. It would be embarrassing for you to lose your nerve in front of family, friends, and the assembled clans. It would be humiliating for you and your village. Hold your heads high! Be proud and thankful you were selected!"

She glided out of room, gone as quickly as she had appeared.

Dust Maker, the elderly priest, brought a white skirt to Dawn Breaks.

"Put this on," he said. "It is almost time."

She slipped into it, marveling at the whiteness of her entire body. It seemed like she was evolving into something fantastic and unearthly.

The priest with the paint leaned toward her face and carefully dabbed red paint to her lips with his forefinger.

She closed her eyes and asked *Wah'Kon-Tah* for the strength to live her last moments in this world with dignity and grace.

Chapter 25

Thunder Runner dabbed a spot of charcoal onto his forehead, rubbed another onto his cheek, and added a third to his chin. When a warrior wore charcoal over his entire face, it meant he was heading for a fight where he would show no quarter to his enemy, a fight to the death. Normally, his face should have been completely covered with the black charcoal, but Thunder Runner did not want to draw attention. The element of surprise would be extremely important. A few smudges might be passed off as simply dirt on the face of a traveler. He did not want anyone to suspect his real intentions until the very end.

Glancing around, satisfying himself that nobody had seen him apply the charcoal, he began making his way to the Temple Mound. As he strode across the flat plaza, he passed the chunkey field, the scene of his memorable exploits at the Green Corn Festival. How his fortunes had changed since then.

He was glad the fall day was cool. It gave him a reason to wear a matchcoat with his breechcloth. The coat was made of deerskin, with red, yellow, and black designs painted on it. It draped over both shoulders and extended down his back to his knees, concealing two sharp knives he carried at the small of his back. They were encased in sheaths fastened to the belt of his breechcloth.

He carried his spear openly. The empire's star chunkey player might be expected to be carrying his pole. He had placed a leather pouch over one end, covering the extremely sharp and heavy point. It was not the normal spear used for chunkey. It was a warrior's spear, meant for killing.

He had fasted during the entire trip up from the Village of Gray Wolf, drinking only water and emptying his bladder and bowels every chance he got. His body had become a weapon, purged and lean and ready for a fight. He gripped the spear tightly, liking its heavy weight in his hand. He was ready.

He would not be able to save Dawn Breaks. He had accepted that fact. She would be positioned at the top of the pyramid, surrounded by thousands of people, with armed guards assigned to make sure everything went smoothly. He did not delude himself. He could not prevent her death. Only a miracle could save her. But he could choose the way he wanted to die, and he could select at least a few to take with him.

When he had made the decision during the awful walk home after his last moments alone with Dawn Breaks, the weight of the world had lifted from his shoulders. He was going with her on her journey through the afterworld. He would accompany her. He was choosing the exact moment, manner, and place of his death. He would show the priests that they were not the only ones who could make choices. He would show them that life was full of surprises and that not all men were content to let fraudulent holy men make all the rules.

At the bottom of the Temple Mound, he was challenged by a guard.

"You will not need the spear. Leave it with me."

"I am Thunder Runner," he said, allowing his voice to ring with arrogance, "the great chunkey player from the Village of Gray Wolf. I do not go anywhere without it."

The stern look left the guard's face. "Thunder Runner! I watched you win the last point at the Green Corn Festival. You were impressive!"

"Thank you."

"That was the longest throw I ever saw!"

"My spear stays with me." Thunder Runner brushed past the man.

Tall Oaks was right. We all must die. Some deaths are nobler than others. Few of us, if any, get to choose our deaths. I am one of the lucky ones. I am dying a warrior's death. It is a good day to die.

Twice more, he was challenged by guards concerned about the spear. Each time, his status as a famous chunkey player won them over. Everyone thought it natural for a star chunkey player to be so vain that he would carry his pole to a Grand Chief's funeral. One even told Thunder Runner where he lived and asked him to come by to meet his son after the funeral. The boy was an avid chunkey player and a fervent admirer.

"I would be glad to meet your son," he said. "I will come if I can."

He smiled grimly as he walked away from the man and continued up the steps toward the blazing sun. He climbed higher and higher, feeling calm and alert. To gain entry to the third level, he had to claim that he was part of the family of one of the chosen. He was aided by Chief Gray Wolf, who spotted him and vouched for him. He hoped the kind act would not cost his chief later. But he had made up his mind. Nothing could stop him now.

He inched as close to the front as he could get, carefully noting the positions of the armed guards. They carried knives, war clubs, spears, and bows and arrows. The priests, too, were armed. Each bore a sharp knife. Once he made his move, he would be tremendously outnumbered. He would need to act quickly.

All of the priests from villages throughout the Grand Chief's domain were assembled at the top of the Temple Mound. They were taking their assigned positions for the ceremony. They formed a semicircle facing the crowd, much like a choir. Thunder Runner's face remained stoic, but he smiled inside. *These charlatans are in for a big surprise.*

When the sun reached a point in the sky directly overhead, Head Priest Black Moon emerged from the Temple. Next to him walked Triumphant Falcon's son, the heir to the position of Grand Chief. The boy, perhaps fourteen winters old, was ushered to a seat of honor. The Head Priest moved to a position at the front of the top level of the Temple Mound, his fellow priests forming a backdrop behind him.

"We gather today to mourn the loss of the greatest ruler of our time," the Head Priest intoned, "Triumphant Falcon, the Grand Chief, Great Falcon of Cahokia."

His voice carried down the levels of the great pyramid and across the vast, flat plaza. It was easy to hear him. Even those far away would have no problem making out his words.

"Many of you came from villages far away," the priest continued. "Thank you for honoring our fallen leader by your attendance here today. I speak for all of us at Cahokia when I tell you we thank you for coming and we welcome you. We expect you to join us for a great feast at the conclusion of the ceremonies."

The Head Priest raised his arms. He was bare-chested, but he wore a feathered robe over his shoulders. It flowed down his back, reminding Thunder Runner of a great bird. No doubt the effect was intentional.

"Our Grand Chief is departing on a long journey, one that will take him across the path of the Milky Way, to the Upper World, to adventures we cannot foresee. Join me in a prayer for his safety on this arduous trip."

The Head Priest led the crowd in the Song of Safe Journey. Thousands of voices joined in unison, chanting the familiar words. Thunder Runner, in spite of his skepticism, was moved by the huge volume of sound.

While the crowd sang the mournful dirge, the body of the Grand Chief was carried from the Temple on a litter. The pall-bearers bore it down the long steps of the mound as thousands of mourners joined the singsong chant wishing him a safe journey.

The Grand Chief's corpse was dressed in his glittering white robe, bedecked with thousands of white beads carved from seashells. The top of the robe was shaped like the head of a falcon. The white robe shone in the noonday sun as the litter was carried down the steps.

"Triumphant Falcon will be buried with his forefathers in the royal family's Holy Burial Mound," the Head Priest continued. "His corporeal body will join those of his forefathers in the tomb while his soul begins its journey to meet his ancestors in the next world. Please join me in singing the Song of Our Forefathers."

The crowd added its voices to the well-known song, singing the praises of the former leaders of Cahokia, who had successfully forged the scattered and disparate villages of the empire into one vast network, providing trade and protection to each other. The collective voices rose in song, rolling across the assembled masses.

When the song ended, Head Priest Black Moon launched into a spirited eulogy of Triumphant Falcon, correctly pointing out that he was the greatest yet of the Grand Chiefs, and that the empire had grown both in size and strength during his long tenure. Thunder Runner listened respectfully. He had no quarrel with Triumphant Falcon. His enemies were the priests, especially Black Moon. He hated them, with their sanctimonious gibberish. They were the ones responsible for taking away the love of his life.

After the eulogy, Black Moon exhorted the crowd to join him in singing the Song of Praise, extolling the generosity of *Wah'Kon-Tah* for providing them with sustenance and prosperity. Since this song was always sung at the Green Corn Ceremony, everyone in the audience knew it well. The volume rose even higher than during the previous songs. Thunder Runner closed his eyes. The entire mound was vibrating.

As the last notes faded away, the Head Priest raised his arms again, calling out loudly to the mourners: "The journey our Grand Chief embarks upon is both long and lonesome. It is made easier by the company of others. As you know, he is not making this journey alone."

The crowd was deathly silent, listening to every word.

"First, I call forward Dark Eyes, the noble warrior who served as the bodyguard of our Grand Chief for more than a decade. His role now is to accompany his leader into the next world, performing the same important function."

A tall, muscular warrior strode forward, wearing his everyday deerskin breechcloth and mantle of furs. He knelt proudly in front of the Head Priest.

Two other priests came forward. One put a black cup to Dark Eyes's lips. The big man drank from it. Moments later, he swooned to his side. At the same time, the second priest whipped a cord around his neck and strangled him from behind.

Painless? Thunder Runner was not so sure.

As the bodyguard's lifeless corpse was lifted and placed on yet another litter, the Head Priest again addressed the crowd. "Dark Eyes will have the tremendous honor of being buried directly underneath the body of his Grand Chief, face down, guarding his ruler's back from approaching demons from the Underworld. Join me in singing again the Song of Safe Journey for this loyal and brave warrior."

Once again, the voices of the crowd joined in song. To Thunder Runner, nothing on earth sounded so powerful as thousands of human voices singing in unison. He felt chills shooting up and down his spine.

At the end of the song, the Head Priest summoned twenty-four of the Grand Chief's servants from the Temple Hut. They wore their normal work clothes: the plain, everyday breechcloths they had worn when doting on Triumphant Falcon during his life. They would wear the same attire while attending to his needs in the afterworld.

As the Head Priest explained what was happening, the servants assembled in a long row facing the crowd. Behind each trembling servant stood a priest, clad in black fur robes. When the servants knelt, the priests drew choking cords from the depths of their robes and held them above their heads. Another priest went from servant to servant, administering the drink from the black cup. For the first time, Thunder Runner noticed that the priest providing the drink was Bloody Nose, from the Village of Gray Wolf. Thunder Runner gritted his teeth. It must have been quite an honor for Bloody Nose to be placed in charge of the cup of death. The young priest was undoubtedly quite pleased with himself.

Well, Thunder Runner thought. *Time will tell how much you like your honor by the end of the day.*

One by one, the servants drank from the cup, swooned, and succumbed to strangulation from the priests behind them.

You put on quite a show, Thunder Runner thought, staring hard at Head Priest Black Moon. *But I can stage a show, too, and I am growing impatient!*

Thunder Runner took a deep breath and held it. He had learned to control his heartbeat by managing his breathing. He could always keep himself calm, even in the most stressful chunkey game or even when hunting the most dangerous animals. A man whose heart was beating wildly made mistakes. Thunder Runner intended to make no mistakes on this important day, the last day of his life.

As the bodies of the servants were piled on litters and carried down the long steps, the Head Priest faced the crowd. Following his cue, the masses joined him in another rendition of the Song of Safe Journey. They repeated the verses many times, since it took quite awhile for all twenty-four bodies to make the journey down the steps. Each corpse eventually made it safely to the bottom of the Temple Mound.

At the end of the song, the Head Priest gestured for absolute silence from his audience. His eyes sparkled as he gazed at the crowd. He was truly enjoying himself, Thunder Runner realized.

"Now we present for you the young and lovely members of the journey," Head Priest Black Moon proclaimed, pointing toward the front door of the Temple Hut, "the widow of Triumphant Falcon and the chosen maidens from your villages."

A murmur arose from the crowd as Good Eagle Woman, painted in white, strode from the Temple Hut, followed by the fifty-three girls. Every one of the beautiful girls shone brightly in the midday sun. Exquisite faces, exquisite bodies, they were a dazzling sight. The murmur that began when they first emerged rippled through the crowd, gathering intensity as people from each village strained to catch a glimpse of their own lovely representative.

Thunder Runner immediately spotted Dawn Breaks. She was the thirty-fourth girl to emerge from the Temple. The young women formed a crescent facing the crowd, with Good Eagle Woman positioned at the center point in front of them. Behind them loomed the black-robed priests, like wolves encircling a fire. Their hands were empty, their choking cords not yet pulled.

Thunder Runner breathed deeply and flexed his muscles. It was almost time. He felt ready. Whatever happened next, it would be spectacular. It would be violent. It would never be forgotten.

Chapter 26

Thunder Runner casually removed the deerskin covering from the sharp head of his spear. No one was watching. All eyes were fastened upon the Grand Chief's widow.

Good Eagle Woman stood proud and dignified in front of the semicircle of beautiful young women. At the encouragement of the Head Priest, the crowd had begun singing the Song of Our Forefathers. Bloody Nose relinquished the black cup to the Head Priest, and Black Moon was advancing toward Good Eagle Woman. He personally would hold the cup to her lips.

Good Eagle Woman was a beautiful sight. Tall and statuesque, regal and breathtaking, she was the center of attention. Her face was perfectly shaped, her legs were long and attractive, and her breasts displayed the fullness of a much younger woman. Gleaming white with painted skin and white skirt, she was a vision of loveliness, every bit as beautiful as the girls behind her. Her red-painted lips were moving as she sang along with the song.

What is going through her mind? Thunder Runner wondered. *Is she even the least bit sad to be departing her world of comfort and power? Or is she anxious to be joining her departed husband?* Who could know what was really in her mind? She certainly did not look sad. Her face was radiant.

Thunder Runner glanced at the widow's son, Soaring Falcon, the new Grand Chief. Now there was a young man who did not look radiant. He had lost his father four days ago. Now his mother was about to be killed before his eyes. The young ruler bore a forlorn expression, but was not crying. *Welcome to the most powerful position in the world, boy. The Grand Chief is dead. Long live the Grand Chief! What other madness will your priests thrust upon you during your tenure as supreme ruler? Be wise enough to break away from their superstitions before it is too late!*

Good Eagle Woman knelt in front of Head Priest Black Moon. She drank deeply from the cup of death. When she finished, she wiped a drop of dark liquid from her lips with the back of her hand, leaving a black smudge on the white paint. As Thunder

Runner watched from his position in the front row, her eyes rolled up in her head, revealing only ghastly white, and she slumped to one side. Behind her, a priest looped a cord around her neck and yanked it so hard the cord disappeared into the skin of her neck. Thunder Runner was pretty sure the proud woman felt nothing. The drink had done its work quickly.

Led by the Head Priest, thousands of voices joined in an eerie crooning wail as they sang the Song of Safe Journey while the body of Good Eagle Woman, wife of Triumphant Falcon, was placed onto a litter and borne down the lengthy steps of the great mound.

The new Grand Chief watched silently as his mother was carried away from him. Whatever emotions he was feeling, he did not display even a quiver of a lip.

It took awhile for her body to reach the bottom of the steps. The sun had moved slightly to the west by the time the Head Priest motioned for the fifty-three young women to come forward.

As Black Moon chanted and sang, the lesser priests showed the girls where to stand. Several stumbled as they moved forward. Many tottered upon wobbling legs. How could they not be terrified?

Thunder Runner watched Dawn Breaks. She walked gracefully, with strength and purpose. She looked good, all painted in white. She was a perfectly proportioned woman. It was no wonder she had been selected. She was absolutely beautiful. She was watching the priest closest to her for guidance. He was forming the girls into one long line, having them kneel, positioning a dark-robed priest behind each girl.

Once they were lined up, Head Priest Black Moon moved toward a girl at one end of the line. He carried the cup of death in his hands.

It was time.

Thunder Runner let the matchcoat drop from his shoulders and leaped forward. Four quick bounds took him from the third level of the Temple Mound to its top. Before anyone realized what was happening, he was within a spear's length of the Head Priest.

"Stop!" he yelled. His voice carried down the temple mound and across the plaza, every bit as loud as Black Moon's.

The Head Priest whirled and faced him.

"Get back!" Black Moon hissed.

"*Wah'Kon-Tah* demands that you stop!" Thunder Runner yelled, even louder than before.

The crowd gasped, hearing every word.

"Fool! What do *you* know of *Wah'Kon-Tah*'s wishes?" Black Moon sneered. "Who are *you*?"

"I am Thunder Runner, hunter, warrior, and chunkey player from the Village of Gray Wolf. *Wah'Kon-Tah* spoke to me this morning. He came to me in a vision. He told me he does *not* want these women to die. He wants them to live! He does not want us to kill our own people, even in his name!"

Many people in the crowd began murmuring.

"Blasphemy!" Black Moon shouted. "*Wah'Kon-Tah* does not talk to anyone but the priests. This man is a liar!"

Thunder Runner held his spear high in the air. "*You* are the liar! If I speak untruth, let *Wah'Kon-Tah* strike me down with lightning!"

The priests and guards inching toward him stopped abruptly.

A hush filled the air. For several seconds, no one uttered a sound.

"Blasphemy!" Black Moon repeated. "*Wah'Kon-Tah* would never answer a challenge from a lowly hunter! Foolish boy! Your stupidity has put our entire civilization in jeopardy! Seize him!"

With speed acquired from countless hours of practice, Thunder Runner flipped his spear to the throwing position and hurled it at the Head Priest. The sharp flint tip struck the holy man in the center of his bare chest. The spear drove deep into the cavity beneath his sternum. Behind him, the bloody point emerged through his feathered cape. The cup of death went flying as Black Moon gripped the shaft of the spear impaling him and tugged at it helplessly. His mouth gaped open like a gigged frog's as he slumped to his knees, blood pouring out of his mouth and down his chin. His dark eyes met Thunder Runner's. They burned with hatred until their light went out and he pitched forward on his face.

Shocked, everyone else froze for several moments, giving Thunder Runner time to yank his two knives from their sheathes and lunge for Bloody Nose, who was bending over to retrieve the cup of death.

In two quick strides he overtook the young priest and drove a knife into Bloody Nose's gut. The long blade sliced into him all the way to its handle. The ugly priest from the Village of Gray Wolf screamed in pain. Thunder Runner felt hot blood spurting onto the back of his hand as he twisted the knife inside the body of the squirming young holy man.

Thunder Runner yanked the blade from Bloody Nose's abdomen and whipped it savagely across the neck of another priest, who was charging him. Blood from the priest's ripped-open throat sprayed a circle in the air as the stricken attacker dropped his knife and spun to the ground. Lunging to his left, Thunder Runner drove his other knife into the chest of a priest who was coming at him with an upraised blade. As the fourth priest's body fell to the ground, Thunder Runner pulled his knife free and snarled at the guards and priests encircling him.

As the circle closed, Thunder Runner lunged and hacked. He was the center of a ring of death and mayhem. The priests and guards closest to him jabbed at him with their weapons, trying desperately to keep out of his reach. Pressure from those behind forced the circle tighter. With a knife in each hand, Thunder Runner wheeled and cut and stabbed and thrust, producing screams and howls from disemboweled priests and guards closest to him. Every time one went down, another pressed forward. Thunder Runner knew it was only a matter of time before it would end. But he was taking a lot of them with him. If *Wah'Kon-Tah* really wanted sacrificial blood, the Mysterious Great Spirit was getting a river of it today, much of it from priests.

Eventually, one of his attackers clung heavily to Thunder Runner's right arm while another latched onto his left. Try as he might, he could not wrench free. He strained to lift his attackers off the ground as the circle around him tightened. Over his shoulder, he glimpsed a stone axe being raised. He was pulling with all his might to yank his arms free when something hit the back of his head, and everything exploded in a flash of blinding light.

Dawn Breaks watched the melee with conflicting emotions. She was thrilled to see Thunder Runner when he leaped from the crowd, but quickly became horrified when she realized what he was doing. When he claimed to have spoken to *Wah'Kon-Tah*, she knew he was trying to bluff the priests into setting her and the other girls free. Even as he said the words, she knew it would never work. She knew he was a dead man. It pained her, because she had taken comfort in imagining him going on with his life, finding happiness without her. She was astounded when he quickly and effortlessly killed Head Priest Black Moon. She watched with shock and disbelief as he killed at least ten other priests and guards. She screamed an ineffectual warning when the priest behind him drove the ceremonial axe deep into Thunder Runner's skull.

When he went down, the surviving priests stood motionless. Many knelt in shock and exhaustion. For good or bad, Thunder Runner had certainly disrupted the funeral. For a time, Dawn Breaks became hopeful that her lover might have saved her life. With all of the confusion, it looked like the sacrifice of the fifty-three girls might be cancelled or postponed. The scattered bodies of dead and dying priests temporarily overwhelmed their colleagues and clearly took much of the enjoyment out of the ritualized killing of attractive young women. But eventually, Makes Afraid, the Head Priest from her own village, took charge. He ordered the bodies of the dead priests dragged to one side. He forced many seriously wounded priests, whose shrieks and cries were disconcerting to their brethren, to drink from the black cup to shut them up. Other wounded priests benefited from watching him deal with the others and thereafter bore their injuries with improved stoicism. He reassembled the girls in their long line of death and positioned a healthy priest behind each one. He spoke calming words to the crowd about the importance of keeping *Wah'Kon-Tah* happy. He reminded everyone of the distress the late Grand Chief would feel if these chosen girls did not accompany him on his long journey. Finally, Makes Afraid marched to the first girl in line and forced her to drink from the cup of death.

He worked his way quickly down the line, giving the next girl a drink even before the preceding girl had fallen. Clearly, he was anxious to finish the ceremony. One or two did not take big enough drinks. Dawn Breaks heard them gag when the cords were yanked tightly around their necks. She must remember to take a big gulp, she told herself.

She counted twenty-nine girls between herself and the black cup. How long would it be before it got to her? How long did she have to live?

A strange peacefulness was calming her heart. She did not mind that she had only moments left of life in this world. Thunder Runner had already flown this earthly existence. He was waiting for her on the next level, unless the Grand Chief was so angry with him that he was being punished in some way. She tried not to think about that possibility. Watching these girls sip, swoon, and fall was all Dawn Breaks had left of life. It was not something she wanted to witness. She was ready to go. The waiting was the worst part.

Slender Leaf, the girl with the tremendous faith, was right next to Dawn Breaks. Before long, her new friend was kneeling and Makes Afraid was putting the black cup to the sweet girl's lips. Slender Leaf drank deeply. When she finished, she tilted her head back and stared straight into the sun, a smile spreading across her face.

"May the Grand Chief welcome you with open arms," Makes Afraid said softly to Slender Leaf.

Dawn Breaks closed her eyes. She heard Slender Leaf fall to the ground, and noticed a slight rustling noise as the priest with the rope made sure she was dead.

When Dawn Breaks opened her eyes, Head Priest Makes Afraid from the Village of Gray Wolf was standing directly in front of her.

His eyes were hard and mirthless. "Did you know he was going to do that?"

She shook her head.

"I did not think you did."

She wondered if he blamed her for the actions of Thunder Runner. Surprisingly, she did not care. The more she thought about it, the less she minded the ruckus her lover had caused. He had certainly delivered a profound statement against the practice of human sacrifice. He had chosen the way he would die. At the same time, by forcing them to kill him, he had arranged for the two of them to depart the world on the same day, within moments of each other. It was possible that in a very short time they would be reunited. Somewhere. Some place. In some form. Upon whatever path lay before them.

"It is your time," Makes Afraid said.

She knelt. Time stood still as the priest's sweaty hands moved the black cup toward her lips. She saw the detailed artwork on its sides. The potter who made it had been very talented. Although the bowl was painted completely black, detailed scenes of human sacrifice were etched on its sides. Still, she thought, as its cool edge touched her lips, she could have done better. The priest in the picture on her side of the bowl was rather out of proportion.

She steadied the cup with her own hands and helped Makes Afraid tilt it. Inside, a deadly black liquid, thick as the yolk of a bird's egg, flowed snakelike toward her mouth. She took a big drink. It was bitter, terribly bitter. She took another drink, already feeling lightheaded. The sour smell filled her nostrils as the bitter taste numbed her tongue.

"May the Grand Chief welcome you with open arms," Makes Afraid intoned.

The Grand Chief? She was more interested in the open arms of Thunder Runner.

Weak, she slumped back on her heels. Her right leg had gone to sleep. Both legs, it seemed. Feeling tired and sick, she closed her eyes.

She was light-headed, floating, drifting toward a light. She felt incredible peacefulness. Somewhere, Thunder Runner was calling her name. She tried to answer, but her tongue was thick. She glided swiftly toward an incredible brightness. It glowed brighter than anything she had ever seen, yet the blazing light did not hurt her eyes. Was it Grandfather Sun? Was it the Mysterious Great Spirit? Was it *Wah'Kon-Tah*? Within moments, she would know.

Chapter 27

Concealed by midnight darkness, Night Owl dug through the soft earth of the fresh grave in the garbage pit. Kneeling in the reopened hole, he ignored the stench of rotting fish bones, animal entrails, and excrement as he set aside his tools and clawed through the moist earth with his bare fingers. He carefully felt for the corpse, sifting dirt and refuse with his fingertips. When he would finally find it, he wanted to touch the corpse with his hands, not with one of the sharp flint shovels.

He had dug quietly. Not a soul knew he was in the great garbage pit outside Cahokia. He was not sure what would happen if they caught him, but he did not want to risk finding out.

As he scooped handfuls of dirt and refuse, he thought again about why he was doing it, why he was digging through rotting garbage for a corpse in the middle of the night. He was doing it because Thunder Runner, even if misguided, had tried to save his daughter's life. He was doing it because his daughter had loved this man and because he had obviously loved her back. He was doing it because this brave, young warrior deserved better than to be buried for eternity in the midst of stinking garbage.

Night Owl shook his head in amazement as he recalled the tumult Thunder Runner had caused at the Grand Chief's funeral. The final count showed that Thunder Runner had killed nine priests and four guards. For one exhilarating moment, when everything dissolved into chaos, Night Owl had let himself hope that perhaps Dawn Breaks would be spared. But Makes Afraid had stepped forward to take over the proceedings, and the ceremony had continued. Ambitious and sly Makes Afraid, always ready to take charge, always knowing the correct things to say and do. Dawn Breaks and the other girls had been sacrificed almost on schedule. Like the others, her body had been borne down the long steps and carried across the plaza to the royal burial mound. She had been wrapped in a mat and buried in a mass grave with the other fifty-two beautiful young women. Once the girls were dead, Makes Afraid had culminated the bloodbath by sacrificing four prisoners of war, whose hands and heads were chopped off to prevent them from performing mischief in the next world. By the end of the ceremony, even the most thirsty lust for blood would have been quenched.

Some of the priests wanted to hack the body of Thunder Runner into tiny bits, but the holy men eventually decided he would simply be buried ignominiously in the refuse pit. No place in the royal burial mound for him! He would lie forever amid the garbage. As for the dead priests, they would be buried in their own burial mound with their own special funeral rites. Their funeral services were always conducted in secret.

The idea of retrieving Thunder Runner's body and taking it home to the Village of Gray Wolf occurred to Night Owl the moment he heard that his daughter's lover was going to be thrown out with the garbage. He never would have considered such a thing had Thunder Runner been entombed with the others in the royal burial mound. But being buried in the muck of a great village's refuse—the nastiness of it struck Night Owl as intolerable.

Thunder Runner had committed a terrible act by killing the priests and the guards. Murder was murder, after all. But the priests had been armed, and they had been performing killings themselves when Thunder Runner attacked them. They were taking lives. One of the sweet, young lives they were in the process of taking had been his wonderful and beautiful daughter, Dawn Breaks. Night Owl was not sure he might not have done the same thing himself had he not been lame, had he not been so unquestioning of the priests, had he not had a wife and two young daughters still dependent upon him for their own existence, and had he thought of it.

But Thunder Runner's actions had made him question his own beliefs. Could a society based upon human sacrifice last? Could a government bent on killing its best and brightest young citizens every time a ruler died maintain the trust and confidence of its people? Could a religion embracing mass murder retain its moral high ground? For the first time in his life, Night Owl himself was questioning the core beliefs of his religion.

Well, he thought, *if it is wrong to dig up the body of a young man who tried to save my daughter's life, then I am committing a wrongful act. So be it!*

The hard part was going to be getting Thunder Runner's corpse back to his family's burial mound at the Village of Gray Wolf. Night Owl, a lame man, would be forced to carry the body all by himself from the garbage pit to the riverfront, where he had a small canoe waiting. But Night Owl knew he could do it. He was a strong man with unusually powerful shoulders and arms. His good leg was strong. He could wrap Thunder Runner in the deerskin blanket he had brought and throw him over his shoulder. Using his cane, he could carry him to the canoe, bad leg and all. The trip downriver would be easy. Once home, he would decide who would be told what he had done. Surely Thunder Runner's family would want to be involved in the reburial of their loved one. But those he told must be sworn to secrecy. They would all face the wrath of the powers at Cahokia should the deed ever be discovered. He would ponder the question at greater length during the trip downriver.

Another notion that gave him satisfaction as he dug for the corpse was the thought that he would retrieve from Tall Oaks the figurine Dawn Breaks had made of herself and bury it with Thunder Runner. These two young people had loved each other. They had planned to spend their lives together. Night Owl did not need a flint-clay sculpture, no matter how beautiful, to remember his daughter. He could never forget her, not ever. His memories, forged by a lifetime of love, were indestructible. But this boy deserved something special. For his brave and foolish act of trying to save her life, Thunder Runner had earned the right to rest forever next to a handmade image of the young woman he had loved so fiercely. The young couple was joined in their hearts and in their souls, no matter what the priests said. It was fitting that Thunder Runner's bones would share a grave with her painstakingly made figurine. Perhaps the boy's family would add a couple of chunkey stones, too.

Night Owl knew that he personally would go on tending the sacred fire for the priests of the Village of Gray Wolf, diligently rotating with the other fire-tenders to maintain a constant vigil, making sure the eternal fire in the Temple never went out. But for Night Owl, a fire had gone out. The honor of constantly being in the temple, of living in such close day-to-day contact with the priests, of working with them side by side, would never be the same. A fissure in his faith had opened up, and it presented a grave danger of evolving into a devastating quake that would shatter his entire belief system.

His fingers touched cold flesh.

Night Owl paused.

He gingerly brushed the earth away from the moist skin, slowly and respectfully. Gradually, Thunder Runner's chest came into view, then his neck, then his chin, and finally his handsome face. His eyes were closed.

The stone ceremonial axe came into view, still lodged deep inside Thunder Runner's head. Night Owl gave it a tug, but it was firmly embedded in the bone of the skull.

Well, what did it matter? Thunder Runner could not feel anything now. The young man had truly died a warrior's death, and this was proof of it. Proof that would last forever.

"Do not worry, my son," Night Owl whispered to the corpse of the young warrior who had almost become his son-in-law. "You are going to rest in peace in a place of honor. I am going to take you home."

Part III

Grave Consequences

Are those archeologists who disinter skeletal remains like modern Galileos, irrationally persecuted because of their scientific method, or are they simply 'grave robbers'?
—Michelle Hibbert, "Galileos or Grave Robbers?"
23 *American Indian Law Review*: 425 (1999)

When human remains are displayed in museums or historical societies, it is never the bones of white soldiers or the first European settlers that came to this continent that are lying in glass cases. It is Indian remains. The message that this sends to the rest of the world is that Indians are culturally and physically different from and inferior to non-Indians. This is racism.
—Senator Daniel Inouye, *Congressional Record* (October 26, 1990)

How could anything that my studies did with the bones of these ancient people harm any living person? The condemnation seems extreme for a 'crime' that is merely a failure to invite mythical descendants to control my research and destroy museum collections held in the public interest.
—Clement W. Meighan, "Some Scholars' Views on Reburial," 57.4 *American Antiquity*: 704 (1992)

Chapter 28

Allison Culbertson was discharged from the hospital shortly before dawn. It was still dark outside, but the eastern skyline was beginning to lighten with the reddish tint of sunrise.

"I think my Jeep Cherokee is still in the police evidence garage, being poked and prodded, much like I was," Allison told Rita Rhodes, as she got into her secretary's car. "Thanks for coming to get me. I'm sorry to call you out in the middle of the night."

"No bother at all. I'm glad to do it. You're the best boss I ever had. I'd carry you home on my back if I had to. I'm just glad you weren't seriously hurt."

When they drove by police headquarters on Sprigg Street, Allison saw cars parked all around the station, from various agencies including the Missouri State Highway Patrol, the Jackson Police Department, the Cape Girardeau Police Department, the Cape Girardeau County Sheriff's Department, the Southeast Missouri State University Department of Public Safety, and the Bollinger County Sheriff's Department. Every light in the large rectangular building was burning brightly.

"A lot of police officers went without sleep tonight," she said. "Harry Sullinger told me the Squad works around the clock as long as they have leads to pursue. I sure hope they find Joey's killer."

"Must have been awful, seeing it happen," Rita said.

"It was." Allison was glad Rita did not press her for details. She didn't feel like telling the whole story again.

When Allison finished showering, it was close to the time she normally got up to go to work. She thought about taking a day off. It was tempting to just call in sick and let her nerves settle down, but she had an appellate brief to write in one of her civil cases. Not only that, she was a sole practitioner. Unless she was putting in billable hours, her law firm wasn't generating income. She called Rita and hitched a ride to work.

When Rita dropped her at the front door of her office, Allison tried not to look at the spot on the street where Joey Red Horse had fallen, but she couldn't keep her eyes from darting in that direction. A chill shot down her back when she saw remnants of the bloodstain still marking the death scene on the pavement. Someone had tried to hose it off but had not gotten it all.

Once in her office, she called the police station and asked for Harry Sullinger.

"He works for the prosecutor's office, not the police department," a dispatcher said.

"I know, but the Major Case Squad has been called out. I think he's wherever their temporary headquarters is."

"Oh, that's right," the dispatcher said. "Just a moment. I'll connect you to the training room."

Seconds later she was talking to Sullinger. "Have you solved it yet?" she asked.

"Not yet. But we're working on it."

"I'm actually calling about my car."

"What about it?"

"When do I get it back?"

"Evidence techs are processing it right now, checking gunshot angles, looking for fingerprints, that sort of thing. You should be able to pick it up tomorrow."

"What am I supposed to do for a car in the meantime?"

"Does your phone book have Yellow Pages?"

"Yes."

"I'd suggest looking under 'A' for automobile renting."

"That's very helpful. Thank you."

"I'd be glad to chauffer you around myself, but I'll be on duty until the Squad disbands."

"Well, happy hunting," she said, feeling anything but happy.

An unsummoned vision of Joey Red Horse dancing and jerking amid the fusillade of gunshots filled her mind. She clenched her eyes, put her hands to her face, and let the memory come. She examined it like a tangible object, looking at it from all angles, trying to see more details about the shooter, but it was no use. She had not seen a face. It was not in her memory bank. All she saw was the figure in black, shooting over and over. All she saw was Joey Red Horse twisting in pain as the bullets hit him.

She opened her eyes, forcing the memory away, and resolved to get something productive accomplished. She called her insurance company and confirmed that her car insurance would cover the damage to the Jeep as well as pay for a rental car. She then immersed herself in work on her appellate brief, a rather boring lawsuit stemming from a landlord-tenant squabble between a building owner and the tenant who operated a bar out of the building. The bar had closed; and the tenant left barstools, tables, and mirrors in the building after his lease expired. The building owner claimed they were legally abandoned and sold them. The tenant wanted the proceeds of the sale. Allison was representing the landlord. She had won the case at the trial level and was now defending the victory on appeal.

The next thing Allison knew, it was nearly noon and Rita was standing in her office.

"I hate to bother you when you're writing a brief," she said, "but I think you'll want this interruption. Bear Smith is here. He wants to see you."

Allison followed Rita to the waiting room, wondering what to expect from Joey Red Horse's burly friend.

Bear Smith stood by Rita's desk, his face inscrutable. "I heard what happened to Joey," he said.

"I'm sorry for your loss," she said. "I know he was a friend of yours."

"I'm thinking we need to go over to the courthouse and get the bond money back," Bear said. "Under the bond assignment, you're the only person who can pick it up. I want my fifty-thousand dollars returned to me today, less your fee for whatever you did for Joey."

"I haven't calculated his final bill yet."

"I can wait." Bear Smith moved to a chair. It creaked when he sat down.

Allison returned to the inner sanctum of her office and worked up her final bill in *State v. Joey Red Horse*. She didn't charge Joey for the time spent riding on the Water Patrol boat with Harry Sullinger, searching the river for Gazing Woman. Those were not really hours spent doing necessary work on Joey's case, especially the minutes spent falling into the river. Nor did she charge for the time it took to watch Joey being shot to death, nor for her time at the hospital being treated by the staff and being interviewed

218

by Harry Sullinger as a witness to Joey's murder. She figured her work on Joey's burglary and stealing case had officially ended the moment the first bullet hit him. From that point forward, she was merely a witness to a murder, not an attorney for her client. After adding the last mileage expenses and the motel bill from Pawhuska, Oklahoma, she printed off Joey's final bill.

Bear Smith stood up when she entered the waiting room.

He accepted the bill and examined it. "Looks fair to me."

He put it into one of the many pockets of his black leather jacket.

"You want to ride over to the courthouse together? Once they turn the money over to you, you can take out your part and give me the rest."

"My car is still at the police station," she said, "and I don't do motorcycles."

"Well, good thing for us I'm driving my pickup truck today."

Allison did not want to spend a forty-minute roundtrip to the County Courthouse in Jackson in the same vehicle with Bear Smith. The big man made her uncomfortable. But now that the case was over, he was entitled to get his bail money back. She had been too afraid to look up while the killer was walking toward her Jeep Cherokee. Was she now too cowardly to even ride to the courthouse and back with a biker who simply wanted to pay her attorney fee and get his money returned?

"All right," she said. "Let's go."

What if she went with Bear Smith and ended up disappearing off the face of the earth? What if he was involved in Joey's killing and was wanting to find out how much she knew? The thought seemed to be a real stretch, but still. . . .

She turned to Rita and said, primarily for the benefit of Bear Smith, "If Harry Sullinger calls, tell him Mr. Smith and I are just running to the courthouse and back. He can call me on my cell phone. He said he might have other questions, and I've been waiting for his call."

Bear Smith's pickup truck was at least twenty-five years old. When she climbed in, Allison noticed she could see the pavement through a hole in the floorboard on the passenger side. *God, don't let us drive over the bloodstain!*

219

"Now you see why I usually ride the Harley," Bear said.

Allison wondered why a man who could afford to post a $50,000 cash bond would be driving such a dilapidated truck, but decided the question would not be well received. She was dying to ask him how Lolita was doing, but that, too, seemed like a rather thorny thicket at the moment.

Bear was silent during the ride to the courthouse. Allison decided that if he was not going to start a conversation, neither was she.

Once she collected the bail money at the courthouse, they stopped by the bank to get smaller bills to divide the money between her fee and Bear's remainder. He then drove her back to her office.

When they were within a few blocks of the riverfront, he stopped at a red light and stared at her.

"I guess you lost yourself a high-profile client."

"I suppose so."

"Too bad."

"Yeah, too bad."

"Would you have been able to get him off?"

"We'll never know now. I was beginning to think I would."

"Did you know he was having sex with my daughter?"

Whoops, there it was. Allison pursed her lips.

"Did *you*?" she asked.

"I asked you first."

"Well," she said carefully. "The police are investigating Joey's death right now. You and I are both potential witnesses. I think it would be better if we didn't talk about it until the investigation is over. I'll be glad to discuss it with you to your heart's content once the killer is put away in prison and the case is over."

"Did you tell the cops about Joey and his peyote?" Bear asked.

"I didn't know anything about Joey and any peyote."

"Well, somebody told them, they asked me all about it."

"Maybe they found something at his apartment or in his car. Like I said, it would be better if you and I don't talk about it. We don't want it to look like we're trying to get our stories straight, know what I mean? The less said, the better."

Bear pulled up in front of Allison's office and stopped the pickup truck in the middle of the street, not far from the place where Allison knew the faded bloodstain loomed, lying in wait to make her miserable. She willed herself not to look at the spot as she opened the passenger-side door.

"You don't care who killed Joey," Bear Smith said.

"What?"

"You don't care who killed Joey."

"I most certainly do."

She got out of the truck and closed its door, but kept looking at him through the open passenger-side window.

"You white people only care about money," he said. "Now that you've been paid and the meter has quit running, your interest in Native American bones and artifacts is over. You're like all those superintendents of Indian Affairs who completely forgot about the Indians once their stints as superintendent ended. You're a lawyer. You'll move on to work for other paying clients. You were probably already working on something else this morning. Joey is a dead file for you, somebody else's problem."

Allison started to protest, but remembered how easily she had settled in to work on the appellate brief that morning. She had certainly not spent much time grieving for Joey Red Horse. But, she told herself, she had intentionally been trying to forget the horror of the experience. Work had been therapeutic for her. It wasn't that she was coldhearted. She wasn't. Really!

Bear Smith was looking at her coldly. "You *don't* care who killed Joey," he said again.

It struck Allison that he was threatening her.

With a loud roar of the engine, he pulled away and sped down Main Street, leaving a cloud of nasty-smelling exhaust dissipating in the air behind the decrepit truck.

Was he threatening me? she wondered as the truck disappeared around a corner. What did he say exactly? "You don't care who killed Joey." Was that an accusation, or merely a statement of fact? Or was he telling her in so many words, "You'd better not care who killed Joey because if you try to find out who did it, something bad might happen to you!"

Shaken, Allison turned and made her way to the front door of her office. She told herself that she was imagining things. After all, it had been thirty-six hours since she'd had any sleep. In the meantime she'd seen a man get shot to death, had held him in her arms as he died, had been thoroughly examined, stuck with needles and dosed with drugs at the hospital, had been questioned by the police, and had written the major part of a complicated legal brief. Not to mention riding back and forth to the courthouse with the physically intimidating Bear Smith.

Involuntarily, she glanced at the ghostly bloodstain on the street as she opened the door to her office. Joey's blood refused to quit marking the place where he fell. Where was the spirit of Joey Red Horse right now, she wondered? Had be begun his progress through the afterworld? Was he on his journey through the Milky Way? Was he beginning another stage of life? Or was all that was left of him the bit of blood on the street and the body lying in the morgue?

Chapter 29

The next day, after a fitful night's sleep, Allison Culbertson was back at her office, sitting at her big desk as if it were the console of the Starship *Enterprise*. Ensconced in her oversized, high-backed leather chair like a starship commander hurtling through space to fight Klingons, she was surrounded by her solid oak desk, her matching oak credenza, her computer, her fancy telephone packed with the latest high-tech gizmos, her all-important Rolodex, and her law library. She was ready to rack up billable hours. No court appearances were scheduled for that morning, so normally she would have immersed herself in the process of knocking off items from her long list of things to do. She had two wills waiting to be written, an answer to file in a divorce petition, interrogatories to draft in a slip-and-fall case, and calls to make to find an expert witness to challenge the accuracy of a breathalyzer reading in a DWI case.

Yet she found it hard to focus on the normal flow of her law practice. She kept glancing at the stack of books and law-review articles piled on her credenza. They dealt with Mound Builders, Osage Indians, archaeology, and the legal conflict between museums and American Indians. All of these materials were now rather moot.

The newspaper containing Joey's obituary lay folded next to the stack of books. His funeral was scheduled to take place at a church in Pawhuska, Oklahoma, on the day after tomorrow. The body was going to be laid out for four days prior to the funeral at a place called the Indian Camp Family Ground. The only living relative listed in the paper was Joey's mother, Louise Red Horse. Allison wondered whether she should attend the funeral.

In a way, Bear Smith had been right. It was over for her. Her case had ended. The meter had stopped running. There was no reason for her to finish reading those books. Before Joey's death, she had been studying each volume carefully, searching for nuggets to pull for her closing argument and strategies to employ in her overall presentation of the case to a jury. She had been trolling for ammunition to persuade a jury that her client reasonably believed he had a claim of right to Gazing Woman, that beautiful and haunting piece of prehistoric art. Before the bullets hit Joey, it was her job to read the material, and she was being paid for it. Like all lawyers, she had overhead to pay: rent and utilities for the building; bills for law books and computerized legal research; Rita's salary and benefits; and monthly invoices for office supplies and equipment, particularly the computer and its never-ending and increasingly costly upgrades.

As Abraham Lincoln, one of America's greatest trial lawyers, had said in a quotation she had framed and placed prominently on her wall, "a lawyer's only stock in trade is his time and advice." The minutes in her day were the only inventory she could sell to generate her law firm's income. Sitting at her desk, brooding over what might have been, hurting over what she had seen and heard, was not going to pay those bills. She needed to do something productive. But every time she started to draft Mrs. Wortman's will, she thought about the bones of Bootheel Man on display at the Heartland Mound Builder Museum, especially his mouth stretched open in that silent scream and the ancient stone axe embedded so firmly in the back of his skull. She vividly remembered Joey Red Horse's passionate desire to return that prehistoric man's bones to the Osage people. Who could concentrate on drafting some boring will when your favorite client had just been murdered right before your eyes?

Thinking of Joey's case reminded her of Joe Black Dog. It had been only two days since she had met with him, but so much had changed. Her meeting with the expert witness in Pawhuska seemed so long ago. She ought to let him know what happened to Joey, she realized, although he had probably heard about it from Joey's mother or some mutual friend. She found Joe Black Dog's phone number and dialed it.

When his deep voice came on the line, she found it easy to talk to him. After very few preliminaries, she got right to the point. "We won't need you as an expert witness, after all. Joey was murdered early yesterday morning."

"So I heard. Were you there? What happened?"

"He was shot to death on the street in front of my office. So far, it hasn't been solved."

"I am very sorry for your loss, Miss Culbertson. He was doing a good thing, a worthwhile thing. You both were. I was excited about the prospect of testifying for you. I was looking forward to it."

"I'm thinking about coming to his funeral," Allison said. "Do you think it would be painful for his mother to see me? She may associate me with his case and with his death."

"It would be good for his mother to meet you. I am sure she would be grateful if you made the trip."

"I should have taken the time to visit her when I was in Pawhuska before," Allison said.

"Life is full of should-haves," Joe Black Dog said. "The goal is to live your life so you end up with as few as possible."

"You know," she said, "I don't think I ever asked you this, because I never really thought it would happen, but exactly what would the Osage people do with the bones of Bootheel Man if the Heartland Mound Builder Museum were to turn them over?"

"I cannot speak with absolute certainty for our tribal elders and our government, but in the past, when we recovered bones of our ancestors from various museums, we conducted funeral ceremonies for the souls of the departed and returned their bones to proper graves. I am sure we would do the same for your Bootheel Man. As I told you when you were here, we believe the soul of a human being is not at rest as long as his bones are being tampered with and publicly displayed. We also believe the people who handle those bones and burial relics are in physical danger from the wrath of his spirit. We think the repatriation of those bones is a very important thing for both the dead and the living. For those reasons, we conduct the funeral services and provide the land for the burial at our own expense."

Allison Culbertson did not consider herself a superstitious person, but at that moment she was glad she had not physically handled Gazing Woman during the preliminary hearing. She had merely pointed at it. On the other hand, the prosecutor, John Marshall Plimpton, had his hands all over it when he put the exhibit sticker on it, plus he was working hard to return it to the museum for public display. She'd keep her eye on the news. If the sanctimonious prosecutor got hit by a truck, she'd know there was something to the curse.

"I am glad you called me, Miss Culbertson," Joe Black Dog was saying. "I will add Joey Red Horse to my prayers, and I will tell his mother that you may be coming to his funeral."

After the phone call, Allison once again tried to work on Mrs. Wortman's will, but the stack of books on her credenza kept catching her eye. Eventually, she pulled Clive Faulkner's book about Alfred Dennison and reread the last chapter. Dennison had been killed in a car wreck on Snake Hill in Cape Girardeau when he was in his seventies. That particular stretch of Cape Rock Drive got its name from its snakelike curves. It was a one-car accident. His car left the roadway and hit a tree. Had Bootheel Man's spirit gotten him? Allison snapped the book shut. She couldn't believe she would even consider such a ridiculous thought. She placed *Alfred Dennison and the Bootheel Man* back on the stack of books.

Mrs. Wortman, Mrs. Wortman, she thought, reopening the file on her desk containing her notes from her meeting with the blue-haired lady who lived in the historic home on Bellevue Street. The nice old client was the mother of a man in her fitness class. *I've got to get your will written before you die!* Drafting Mrs. Wortman's will would not be complicated. She wanted to leave her jewelry to her daughter in St. Louis, and she wanted the remainder of her estate split between that same daughter and Mrs. Wortman's two sons. The only complication was that she wanted a trust set up to pay someone to care for her Miniature Schnauzer until its natural death. The whole idea of the dog trust struck Allison as a bit silly. Most people simply made informal arrangements with family or friends to take care of their dogs upon their death, but Allison wasn't going to argue with Mrs. Wortman about it. The widow apparently didn't trust any of her children to adequately care for her precious Darby. Who was Allison to prevent Mrs. Wortman from requesting extra legal work that would more than double the fee normally charged for a will?

Allison's phone rang. It was Rita.

"You have a visitor who wants to see you. He doesn't have an appointment, but he hopes you'll work him in. It's Rex Tappinger."

Mrs. Wortman and her lucky dog were instantly forgotten. Rex Tappinger—millionaire, banker, and cuckolded husband of his trophy wife—was at her door. This could prove to be uncomfortable for both of them. She steeled herself for the meeting and headed for the front office.

Rex Tappinger was a tall, slender man with slightly stooped shoulders. His face was square. His white hair, neatly cropped short, appeared to have the texture of Brillo pads. He wore a sharply tailored, tan summer-weight suit. His skin was deeply bronzed from a cheap tanning booth or an expensive Caribbean vacation.

"I want to hire you," he said, almost the moment she greeted him in the waiting room. His good-man-well-met voice was the personification of a self-confident, glad-handing banker. His perfect teeth were undoubtedly capped.

"Come back to my office and we'll talk about it."

She led him to her lair and he settled into one of her chairs. As Allison seated herself behind her desk, he leaned back in his chair and studied her. She noticed his eyes lingering chest high upon two of her more attractive features. She was also studying him, wondering about the real purpose of his visit and wondering if this powerful man had anything to do with the murder of Joey Red Horse.

"Miss Culbertson," he said, "I've been a fan of yours ever since you handled that treasure-trove case. Fascinating stuff. Made quite a name for yourself, especially for a young lawyer."

Allison recalled Joey Red Horse saying similar words, and she felt a pang. A vision of Joey being shot to death flickered through her mind like an old reel-to-reel movie.

Rex Tappinger was gesturing expansively with his long, bird-like hands.

"You're probably aware of my job as bank President, but you may not know that I also own several large apartment complexes in Cape Girardeau. I'd like to hire you to completely rework all of my standard lease agreements. I'm using forms drafted twenty years ago. I want you to redo everything. Make sure each document is state-of-the-art. I'll put you on retainer so I can call you to send eviction letters and file rent and possession lawsuits and all that sort of thing when needed."

"Well, I'm flattered. . . ," Allison began.

"Don't be, don't be. I always want to hire the best. The retainer will be two-thousand dollars per month. You can bill your hourly fee to that retainer. I've been having trouble getting deadbeat tenants out of my units. Having a good lawyer streamlining the process and troubleshooting the whole operation will be cost-effective in the long run."

Allison pictured getting a two-thousand dollar check each month, guaranteed. It would go a long way toward paying her overhead. But what a coincidence that Rex Tappinger was coming to her now! He had something else up that elegant sleeve. Allison searched for exactly the right words.

"Mr. Tappinger," she began.

"Call me Rex."

She paused, but could not bring herself to use his first name. "As a successful banker and landlord, you must have all sorts of lawyers at your beck and call. Don't you think one of them would be delighted to do this work for you?"

"Of course they would," Rex Tappinger said. "I've never met a lawyer who didn't want to take somebody's money! But I want *you*, young lady. Like I said, I always want the best, and I'm willing to pay for it."

In her mind, Allison sorted through the conflict-of-interest rules applicable to attorneys. She considered what she knew about Marge Tappinger's affair with Joey. *Joey* had been her client, not Marge. Allison wasn't bound to keep any of Marge's secrets. A lawyer couldn't represent a client if the representation would be directly adverse to the interests of another client. A lawyer couldn't use information from one client to the disadvantage of another client. Those rules would not bar her from accepting Rex Tappinger as a client. Unless, of course, either Marge or Rex Tappinger had murdered Joey, in which case Joey's interest would be having his murder solved, and that interest would certainly conflict with the killer's interest in getting away with murder. At this point, no one knew who killed Joey, but each Tappinger was certainly on the short list of people having a potential motive.

Allison chose her words carefully. "I'm honored you've come to me, Mr. Tappinger, but I don't think the timing is right."

228

Rex Tappinger stared at her, dumbfounded. "Are you turning me down?"

"I'm afraid so. It's not the right time for me to take you on as a client."

"I suppose the retainer was a bit too low," he said. "It's been a while since I've hired a new lawyer. Let's make it three-thousand dollars per month."

"No, it's not the size of the retainer. I'm sure the amount is more than adequate for the work." She picked up the copy of Clive Faulkner's book. "As you may have heard, one of my clients was murdered this week, Joey Red Horse. He took something from the Heartland Mound Builder Museum. Your wife is on its Board of Directors. So, in a sense, he stole from her. I just don't feel right taking you on as a client right now."

"That makes absolutely no sense to me," he said. He crossed one long leg over another. His black socks were emblazoned with a pattern of gold dollar signs. "I know about your client being killed. I am sure it was an unpleasant experience for you and I offer my condolences, but I can't see why that incident should cause you to turn down my business. Your client is dead. How does his theft from the Heartland Mound Builder Museum have anything to do with me or my wife? It doesn't! At least not anymore."

"I'd rather not go into the details," Allison said. "The police are investigating the matter, obviously. Until the murder is solved, I need to limit my contact with certain people."

"What does that mean? Certainly you don't consider me a suspect in your client's murder!"

"I didn't mean to imply any such thing," she said. "I'd rather not discuss it, really."

He uncrossed his legs and leaned forward. "Look," he said. "The police questioned me about my wife's whereabouts on the night your client was murdered. Apparently your client was shot shortly after midnight and apparently my wife met with him earlier in the evening. Whatever happened before midnight, by the time of the shooting, my wife was home with me. I'm her alibi and she's mine. I don't see where *you* have a conflict of interest in handling my landlord-tenant business."

"Technically, I may *not* have a conflict," Allison said. "But an ounce of prevention is worth a pound of cure. I just don't feel comfortable taking you on as a client right now." Allison wondered how much, if anything, Marge Tappinger had told her husband about her affair with Joey. Had Marge told him about meeting with Allison, about offering to be a witness for the defense? How much had Marge Tappinger admitted to the police? Had the cops told Rex about the affair, if Marge hadn't?

Rex Tappinger rose to his feet. "I would think a young lawyer just starting a law practice might not want to be so choosy about turning down paying clients," he said. "Frankly, I'm a bit insulted. People usually try their best not to insult me."

Allison stood up.

"One reason I don't want to represent you," she said, "is that every time I'd meet with you I'd be wondering when, exactly, you found out about Joey's affair with your wife."

His eyes narrowed. She detected no surprise on his face.

"Who told you I found out about it at all?"

"When *did* you find out about it?"

"That's none of your business."

"So you did know about it?"

"That's none of your business."

"What did Marge tell you when she got home from Joey's?"

"You'd better stop asking questions, little lady."

"Or what? I thought you *wanted* to give me your business."

"Go to hell!"

He left her office. Moments later she heard the front door near Rita's desk slam shut.

Allison was still standing behind her desk when Rita poked her head through the door a few minutes later. "I guess we didn't get that client?"

"No. He'll be taking his business and his nice, fat retainer elsewhere. That's bad news for *you* because it would have gone a long way toward paying your salary."

When Allison calmed down, she picked up the phone and called Harry Sullinger. "Have you solved it yet?" she asked.

"Not yet."

"When do I get my car back?"

230

"Actually, it's ready for you to pick up. Did you ever get the rental?"

"No."

"Why don't I come pick you up in my van, transport you in luxury to your shot-up Jeep, then follow you to wherever you're getting it fixed? Last but not least, I'll run you by the car-rental place. All the while, I'll interrogate you mercilessly so I can tell my bosses it's all part of my job."

She smiled into the telephone. "How soon can you get here?"

"I'm on my way right now. I'll be there before you have time to change your mind."

Chapter 30

There was something disconcerting about driving a car riddled with bullet holes. It was like having a horrible tear in your nylon stocking, multiplied a thousandfold. With the hole in the stocking, you just *imagined* everyone was noticing it. With your windshield and side windows pocked full of bullet holes, you could actually see people pointing at you and nudging their companions.

The drive from the police station to the Jeep dealership would have been unpleasant merely from the unwanted attention. To make matters worse, the bullet holes reminded her of watching Joey being shot to death and of huddling helplessly in her car. She was in a bad mood by the time she reached the dealership.

Harry Sullinger waited in his government-issued van while she made the arrangements to get her Jeep Cherokee fixed.

"Looks like this Cherokee didn't make it back to the reservation in one piece after the Little Big Horn," joked the man writing up her ticket.

"It was mostly Sioux at the Little Big Horn, not Cherokees," she said, not smiling, "and the white guys lost that one. It wasn't even close."

By the time she climbed into the passenger seat of Harry Sullinger's van, she was feeling a bit better.

"Thanks for doing this," she said.

"Think nothing of it. I enjoyed following you and watching you cringe every time someone gawked at the bullet holes."

"I guess it's understandable people would stare," she said. "Every bullet-riddled windshield must have an interesting story behind it."

Harry Sullinger pulled the van into the midday traffic.

"How are you holding up?" he asked.

"Fine," she said, automatically.

She felt far from fine, though. The night before, for the first time in her life, she had been afraid in her own home. She had checked the doors and windows three times before going to bed. She kept thinking that the man who killed Joey might come after her. This terrifying notion kept returning, despite the logical rebuttal from the other side of her brain that if the man really wanted to kill her, he would have done so while she lay sprawled facedown on her car seat.

"That surprises me," Sullinger was saying, "because usually when people are involved in a shooting, even as witnesses, they aren't *fine* for a long time."

"Really?" Allison said.

"Yeah, it's a traumatic thing, seeing someone killed. It's even worse when the killer robs you of your pride and self-respect by making you feel helpless. Victims of violent crime usually take quite awhile to get back to normal."

"I guess I'm not fine," Allison admitted.

She glanced at Sullinger. He was wearing a dress shirt and tie, but even spiffed up he looked powerful. It was hard to imagine him being afraid of anything.

"Have you ever been shot at?" she asked.

"Where'd that come from?"

"Just wondering."

"As a matter of fact, yes. I have been shot at."

"Have you ever shot anybody?"

"Yes." Sullinger used his blinker as he changed lanes. He was looking straight ahead. "The Crime Victim Advocate at our office can hook you up with a good counselor. You should give her a call."

"I don't need a counselor. I need a gun."

Her words surprised her. She had never in her life considered owning a gun. Not once. The thought had never occurred to her until the moment she voiced the possibility to Harry Sullinger.

"Well," he said, "our Crime Victim Advocate can't help you with weapons, but I know a thing or two about firearms. What do you have in mind?"

"Something that will let me feel safe again. Last night when I was home alone I realized that if someone broke into my house, he could kill me long before help would ever arrive."

"Well," Sullinger said, "for home protection you'd probably be best off with a shotgun. Don't need a particularly good aim with a shotgun. Nasty kick, though."

Allison was staring at her hands in her lap. She spoke softly.

"And when I walk from my office to my car at night, I'd like to maybe have something in my purse."

"Well, a shotgun won't fit in your purse. Sounds like we're going to need to equip you with an entire arsenal."

Allison recalled the terror of watching Joey's killer turn and point his gun toward her as she froze behind the steering wheel of her car. If she'd had a gun, she could have at least fought back. Maybe she'd have some pride left.

"I never want to feel so helpless again," she said.

"Tell you what," he said. "You give the matter more thought. If you decide you really want a gun, I'll help you get the permit from the Sheriff's Department, I'll help you pick out just the right one, and I'll personally teach you how to shoot it. How's that for an offer you can't refuse?"

She smiled.

"I suppose that's how you courted your five ex-wives? At the firing range?"

"Just wife number two," he said. "The others were already plenty dangerous when I met them."

They rode in silence to the next stoplight before Allison finished debating in her mind the pros and cons of asking Harry Sullinger a delicate question. She didn't want him to get the impression she was flirting with him, but she was very curious about the answer. "May I ask you a personal question?"

"Sure. I've asked you plenty."

"How is it a man your age has been married and divorced five times?"

He winced. "Good question. I've given the matter much thought myself. I've come to the conclusion that I suffer from Elizabeth Taylor Syndrome."

"Elizabeth Taylor Syndrome?"

"A genetic predisposition to marry anyone you sleep with, no matter how many red flags and warning buzzers are sounding."

"I don't recall reading about that condition in the psychiatric literature."

"No surprise there. I made it up."

"So you ignore red flags and warning buzzers completely?"

"Every time. Just blow right past them."

234

"That would explain it," she said.

"What about you?" he countered. "You're the opposite extreme. Here you are, twenty-something, great-looking and intelligent. Far as I can tell, you not only have never been married, but don't seem to have had too many boyfriends. How is it a good-looker like you hasn't left a trail of broken hearts and shattered lives?"

"How do you know I haven't?"

"Just a hunch. I haven't run across any police reports about ex-suitors skulking around town."

She felt oddly defensive. She started to tell him about her work ethic, her drive to succeed, her long hours preparing herself for her profession, and her passion for her job.

Instead, she shrugged. "I don't know. Unlike you, I don't have a glib answer for all of my personal dysfunctions."

He laughed. "You're really going to be a bad ass, once you start packing heat."

As they neared the rental car lot, Allison asked another question. "Can you tell me anything that's going on with Joey's investigation? I realize it's probably top secret, need-to-know, and all that, but I was his lawyer. I got shot at, too. I'd like to know anything you can tell me. I won't repeat it to anybody."

"Well," Sullinger said, "you might be relieved to know that *you* are not considered a suspect."

"Me! A suspect!"

"Well, sure. Gunshots are heard. People run out of buildings. A bunch of witnesses see you in the street, holding a dying man's head in your lap. He's got scratches on his face. You have blood on your hands. You're crying up a storm and seem a tad, well, hysterical. Think about it."

"I never thought for a second I *was* a suspect."

"*I* never considered you a suspect. Couple of the young street cops did, but not me. Another witness confirmed your account. She was a designated driver. She had just come out of a restaurant up the street to get her car. She heard the first shot and started watching. She saw the shooter kill Joey. She watched him fire into your Jeep and walk over and open the door. Her account matches yours exactly. Like you, she described the shooter as someone dressed all in black. Can't give more detail because it was so dark."

Allison shuddered again, hating the weakness it revealed. *Her* weakness.

"Who do you think did it?" she asked.

"We don't know. The Major Case Squad will probably disband tomorrow because we're out of leads. Once the Squad disbands, the detectives at the Cape Girardeau Police Department will continue with the follow-up investigation since it happened in their jurisdiction. I imagine I'll still be involved since I'm the report writer for the Major Case Squad and since my boss likes me to keep tabs on all murder cases in our county."

Hearing his reference to his boss made her think of John Marshall Plimpton and the way he handled Gazing Woman as an exhibit at the preliminary hearing. "How's Plimpton's health these days?"

"Fine. Why do you ask?"

"No reason." She sighed. "What's going to happen to Gazing Woman now that Joey's stealing case is over?"

"She's already been returned to the museum. Clive Faulkner picked her up yesterday. Obviously, there's no longer any need to keep the statue for evidence since your client can't be extradited for criminal prosecution from wherever he is now."

Allison was surprised to feel a tear leaking from her right eye. She brushed it away, aggravated by the weakness she was showing.

"So, the bottom line is that the Major Case Squad doesn't know who killed Joey Red Horse?"

"Right."

"It's an unsolved murder?"

"That would be another way of putting it."

"Rex Tappinger paid me a visit today," she said.

"Did he? What did the old skirt-chaser want?"

"He wanted to hire me to do some legal work for him."

"He didn't ask you to represent him on a murder charge, did he? No confession to his attorney?"

"I couldn't tell you if a client confessed to me, you know that! No, just some landlord-tenant stuff. I turned him down."

"Sort of suspicious he would come to you now."

"That's what I thought." She glanced at Sullinger. "Did Rex Tappinger know about Marge's affair with Joey?"

236

"I shouldn't tell you details of the investigation. It's still active, and you're a key witness."

"You told me I'm no longer a suspect."

"You weaseled that fact out of me."

"Harry, I told you about Rex Tappinger coming to see me. Sharing can be a good thing, you know."

He smiled.

"Okay, just this one tidbit. Marge and Rex both say they had a big blowup when Marge got home. Rex was waiting up for her. She was still upset from her confrontation with Lolita. She ended up telling Rex all about the affair."

"I *knew* he knew," Allison said. "What else did they say?"

"Both claim that after the confrontation, Marge begged forgiveness and Rex magnanimously forgave her. They both claim that at the exact moment of the shooting they were vigorously engaged in a Viagra-aided alibi."

"I'm sorry I asked," Allison said. "Thanks for sharing, though."

Chapter 31

The girl working the front desk at the Heartland Mound Builder Museum waved Allison Culbertson through the turnstile without asking for the admission fee.

"Mr. Faulkner's expecting you," she said. "Do you know the way to his office?"

"Yes."

Allison Culbertson stared at the Bootheel Man exhibit as she walked past it. She wondered what Bootheel Man had been like. The real Bootheel Man. The *living* Bootheel Man. What were his hopes and dreams? How and when did his killer smash that axe into his brain? Where was his soul now? The passage of ten centuries had made these questions unanswerable.

Nearby, Gazing Woman had returned to her honored place in the museum, occupying her own glass case next to the tall skeleton with the stone axe embedded in his skull.

Oh, Joey. I feel your anger. I understand why you did what you did. It's not right that this man's skeleton is being displayed like this!

She listened to her high heels clicking on the bright, clean floor as she made her way down the wide hallway to the museum Director's office.

Clive Faulkner greeted her warmly when she arrived. "Miss Culbertson. I'm very glad to see you."

"I wasn't sure you would be. If I recall, the last time we spoke I was cross-examining you at Joey's preliminary hearing."

He winced. "Yes, that was a bit painful, and the headlines the next day were even worse, but cross-examination is supposed to be unpleasant, I imagine. You were just doing your job, seems to me."

"I'm glad you are so understanding about it."

"I've buried the hatchet," he grinned.

Allison found his word choice a bit too flip, all things considered, but decided not to get off on the wrong foot. He was trying to be nice.

"To what do I owe the pleasure?" he asked. "You were a bit vague when you called."

Allison had thought carefully about what she wanted to say to Clive Faulkner. She had even rehearsed her speech. She expected his reaction to be unfavorable, but she decided it was worth a try.

"Since Joey's death, I've been thinking a lot about what he was trying to accomplish," she began.

"Yes, it must have been awful," he interrupted. "I read about the shooting in the paper, and I spoke with the police when I got back to town. It must have been very hard for you, actually seeing it happen. I hope you're okay?"

"I'm fine, thank you."

She was pleasantly struck by his concern for her well-being. It seemed genuine. Empathy was written across his handsome face. She supposed he really had forgiven her for the rather nasty cross-examination.

"You've been out of town?" she asked, deciding her planned speech could wait.

"Yes. I gave a lecture about Bootheel Man at the University of Cundinamarca in Colombia. Surprisingly, most of the questions from the South American audience dealt with why he's called Bootheel Man. I spent most of the question-and-answer session explaining how the Missouri Bootheel got its name."

"I don't know that bit of history. Educate me."

"When Congress was setting up the boundary between the new State of Missouri and the Arkansas Territory, a wealthy Missourian named John Hardeman Walker wanted his land to be in Missouri, rather than Arkansas. He was a big landowner and cattle rancher who lived near Caruthersville. His nickname was the 'Czar of the Valley.' The Czar pulled some strings and the next thing you knew, the bottom corner of Missouri stuck into Arkansas like the heel of a boot. A patch of land that logically should have been part of Arkansas became part of Missouri. Money talks, you know."

"Always has," Allison agreed.

"As a matter of fact," Clive Faulkner said, "The university is sending me a videotape of my speech. Detective Sullinger wants it. All the speeches at the symposium were taped. Talk about an iron-clad alibi! I wasn't even in the same country when your client was killed, and I can prove where I was by an audience of two-hundred people and a videotape. So much for the theory that the sinister museum Director knocked off the young American Indian who stole an exhibit from his museum. I hope Sullinger speaks Spanish."

"Your speech was in Spanish?"

"Yes, Spanish was my minor in college, and I dated a girl from South America during my undergraduate years."

"I'm impressed," Allison said. "It's hard enough to give a speech in your own language, much less a second one. I can't imagine giving a closing argument in another language."

"I'm glad to have finally done something that impresses you," he smiled.

Allison decided it was time to fire her broadside shot. She hoped he would be receptive to the idea.

"Joey was very passionate about his belief that it's morally wrong for your museum to keep human remains on display as public exhibits. All he was trying to do, really, was convince you to voluntarily take steps to repatriate them."

Clive Faulkner nodded, but his happy expression hardened. "I suppose *repatriate* under your definition means to give away absolutely free, getting nothing in return?"

"Well, I don't think Joey was expecting the Osage Indians to pay ransom for the return of the remains of their *own* ancestors, especially since the bones were taken from graves without permission from the tribe."

Clive Faulkner rolled his eyes with exasperation. He looked at her, and his blue eyes drilled into hers. "May I call you Allison?"

"Okay."

"Well, Allison, I thought I explained to you before that Bootheel Man is the heart and soul of this museum. 'Mound Builders' is all we do. Without the Mound Builder bones and burial relics, we'd be Krispy Kreme without the doughnuts, McDonald's without the hamburgers, or Dairy Queen without the ice cream. If you've come here to ask me to give away our museum's invaluable collection of artifacts to the Osage Indians, you're wasting your time."

"At least think about it," Allison said. "The mission of your museum is to educate. You can still educate the public by displaying photographs and models of the items Alfred Dennison dug

240

up, by the wonderful picture boards and posters you already display throughout your museum and by videotapes and dioramas. You'd still have a first-rate museum, even without the real bones and burial items."

He shook his head. "If all my museum had was a photograph of Bootheel Man, the public might as well just watch a documentary on television or simply read my book. A museum is supposed to display real things from the past. That's what makes it a museum, as opposed to some sort of huge pop-up book. If you look up the definition of museum in a dictionary, you'll see it means an institution devoted to the procurement, care, and display of objects of lasting interest or value. Not just photographs of the objects or drawings of the objects. Not just educational videotapes. But the items themselves. Besides, the most zealous Indian activists protest even the display of photographs of the bones. They'd still be complaining, no matter what I did."

"It hurts many American Indians to see their ancestors made into museum exhibits," Allison said. "Doesn't it bother you to be causing pain to other people?"

"Of course it does. I don't like to hurt anyone's feelings. But what exactly are you asking me to do?"

"I want you to voluntarily return to the Osage tribe in Pawhuska, Oklahoma, all of the bones and burial relics currently housed in your museum. I'm not asking you to return anything that's not a funereal object."

"That would gut my museum," Faulkner said. "All I'd have left would be a bunch of pots and arrowheads found in prehistoric garbage pits and streams. Our best exhibits would be gone. They all came from burial mounds. You're asking for way too much, Allison."

"You'd be creating a tremendous amount of good will with American Indians," Allison said.

"I don't need their good will," Faulkner said. "Good will doesn't pay bills. I need tourist dollars. Our museum is the most popular tourist attraction in Cape Girardeau. We're one of the largest tourist attractions in the state. We're completely self-funded and self-sufficient. Most of our visitors aren't coming to see our nice paintings or our well-worded historical summaries. They aren't coming to buy a copy of my book. Quite simply, they want to see the guy with the axe in his skull. That's something you don't see every day. And while they might come to gawk, they leave a bit better educated. They leave with an appreciation for the Native American people who lived here thousands of years before the arrival of the Europeans. They leave with a better understanding of the shortness and sweetness of life on earth."

He threw up his hands. "Alfred Dennison spent his lifetime collecting these items. I'm not going to give them away. I'm not going to destroy everything he built."

"It wouldn't be destroying the museum," she insisted.

"Yes, it would! I've seen this coming ever since the Native American Graves Protection and Repatriation Act was passed in 1990. For now it just applies to museums receiving government money, but I know people like you and the American Indians are working to get NAGPRA extended so it covers private museums, too. That would be the end of everything we've built here. I know money talks. It's just a matter of time until someone influential convinces Congress to do it. That'll be the end of this museum."

He crossed his arms.

"You know, the ironic thing is that the archaeologists and museum directors are being made the bad guys here, and they're the ones who saved the Native American culture. By having people like Alice Fletcher and Francis La Flesche take a graphophone and record American Indians singing their old tribal songs, archaeologists preserved them for the present generations, including the Indians. By digging these excavations, archaeologists help all of us, Euro-Americans and Native Americans alike, to understand our past. Many American Indian tribes would have no inkling whatsoever about their history if it weren't for the work done by archaeologists. Men like Alfred Dennison were dedicated scientists who loved the Native American people. They worked hard to make a record of that vanishing culture before it passed into oblivion. People like me are preserving the artwork and culture of these Native Americans, not harming them."

Allison frowned. "I've got news for you, Faulkner. American Indians did not fade into oblivion. Open your eyes. They're still here. I'm not saying archaeologists are bad people or that archaeology as a science is not valuable. I'm saying that displaying human remains in your museum is every bit as offensive to American Indians as if we had a Holocaust museum in Cape Girardeau showing off the bones of Jewish people killed at Auschwitz. What if you were displaying one of those awful lampshades the Nazis made from Jewish skin? Can't you see why displaying these bones is hurtful? There are plenty of Holocaust museums, and they manage to get by just fine using photographs and other tasteful exhibits rather than the bones of human beings. There's a big difference between a human skull and a chunkey stone."

"I don't want to just *get by*," Faulkner said. "I want to have the *best* Mound Builder museum in the world, and I think we've accomplished it. I strive for excellence, Allison, in everything I do. Much like you, I imagine."

They stared at each other.

"Look," he said. "I wish you would read my book."

"I have."

"It didn't persuade you?"

"It convinced me that Alfred Dennison was a dedicated scientist, who nobly and generously donated his fortune to the creation of this museum and the collection of artifacts to be displayed in it. It didn't convince me that exhibiting human remains is not inherently wrong."

"Alfred Dennison was a great man," Faulkner said.

"I don't dispute it. But keep in mind that he lived in a different time. He found Bootheel Man less than thirty years after Custer was massacred at the Little Big Horn and only fifteen years after Chief Big Foot and his people were wiped out at Wounded Knee. He began displaying Bootheel Man at a time when lots of people thought American Indians and their cultures were going to become extinct. They wouldn't be around to complain. A lot has changed since then. For one thing, American Indians didn't disappear off the face of the earth. They are part of our American brotherhood. Many of them find displays like yours offensive. I'm not convinced that if Alfred Dennison was sitting right here today, I couldn't talk even him into admitting it is wrong to show off these human remains. If displaying bones is so great for a museum, let's drag Dennison out of his casket in Lorimier Cemetery and put his skeleton on display in your main foyer. His bones can be your second most popular exhibit. The founder himself!"

She nodded toward the oil painting of Dennison on the wall. "He doesn't look like an unreasonable guy. Neither do you. Won't you at least think about it?"

Faulkner removed his wire-rimmed glasses as he pondered his answer. "Don't hold your breath," he finally said. "I *will* promise to give the matter a great deal of thought. I'll discuss it at length with the Board of Directors. That's all I can do at this point."

"Thank you. It's better than nothing."

She glanced at his credenza and noticed that the framed photograph of Diedra Binzinger was gone. Perhaps Clive Faulkner was an eligible bachelor again.

Not that she was interested. Much.

Chapter 32

Joey Red Horse's funeral took place on a weekday morning at the Immaculate Conception Catholic Church in Pawhuska, Oklahoma. It was a red brick building standing tall and proud under the wide open sky. Large stained-glass windows adorned each side of the church. A cross topped its fortresslike cupola.

It surprised Allison that Joey had been Catholic. She had pictured him practicing some ancient American Indian religion. Instead, here she was, sitting in a Catholic church much like every other Catholic church in the world. Well, there were some differences. For instance, the stained glass in two tall windows near the front of the church depicted Osage Indians in Biblical scenes. She had never seen windows like that in any typical Catholic church.

As she sat in the wooden pew, she glanced around. Amid the towering white walls and tasteful red carpet, she recognized several faces scattered throughout the pews. Bear Smith and Lolita were in the row directly behind an elderly woman who had to be Joey's mother. Lolita wore a black dress. Its spaghetti straps were not exactly Emily Post attire for a funeral, but the dress may well have been her only black one. Allison willed herself not to be judgmental. She had expected to see Bear Smith and his daughter at the funeral. In fact, she had briefly considered calling them to see if they wanted to ride down from Cape Girardeau with her; but she finally decided to make the trip alone. Joe Black Dog sat with a group of middle-aged men and women in pews in the middle of the church. The men wore dark suits, with colorful blankets draped over their shoulders.

The surprises were Harry Sullinger, Cory Blaze, and Mark Windfoot, the head of the Angry Reformers Resisting Oppressive Whites organization from Washington DC. He was the ARROW spokesman interviewed on the *CBS Evening News* shortly after Joey's preliminary hearing. Allison was also surprised by the large number of people at the service. The church was packed with at least three-hundred mourners.

After the service, Allison stood in a long line, waiting to pay her respects to Louise Red Horse. When she finally got the chance to introduce herself, the woman's eyes brightened.

"I'm glad you came," she said. "Joey told me all about you. He greatly admired you. He was so glad you took his case."

"He was a good person," Allison said. She was aware that people around them were listening intently. Some probably knew she had been a witness to Joey's death. She had things she wanted to say to Louise Red Horse, but she did not want a bunch of eavesdroppers.

"I'm not planning to be in town long," Allison said, "but I'd like to talk with you some more about Joey, in a place where we'd have more privacy. Is there a time and place that would be convenient for you?"

"We'll be having a dinner at the Wikon Iron Community Center right after we take Joey to the cemetery. You're welcome to come. We'll have plenty of time to talk there."

Allison had been hoping for something even more private, but decided to take what she could get. "I'll be there," Allison said, squeezing her hand.

Outside, she spotted Harry Sullinger. He was standing next to a bald man. Each wore a sport coat and tie. They were videotaping people leaving the church. She walked over to them.

"You're a long way from your jurisdiction," she said.

"You can run but you can't hide, Culbertson," he grinned.

"Seriously, what are you doing here?"

"This is Detective Paul Burns," Sullinger said. "Cape Girardeau Police Department."

"Hi," said the bald man doing the videotaping, without taking his eye away from the viewfinder.

"We're making a record of everybody here today. You'd be surprised how often the killer shows up at the victim's funeral."

Allison put her hand over her mouth. "Is the sound on?" she mouthed.

"Why, are you about to confess?"

"I thought I wasn't a suspect."

"You weren't, until you showed up today. Now you're back on the list." He chuckled. "I'm kidding. Yeah, the sound's turned down."

He nodded toward the crowd. "You recognize any of the congregation?" he asked.

She pointed out Joe Black Dog and told about his aborted role as her expert witness. "I think you know anyone else I know," she added.

"Hey, look, Harry. We're not the only ones doing some videotaping," Burns said, eye still pressed to the camera.

Across the street, Cory Blaze and his KFVS-12 cameraman were setting up for an interview. The newsman was pinning a lapel microphone onto Mark Windfoot, the guy from ARROW. The television camera stood on a tripod, positioned so the church and the mourners would be in the background during the filming. A group of people were gathering behind Cory Blaze to watch the interview.

"Paul, keep shooting the church. I want to listen to this," Harry Sullinger said.

Allison tagged along with the big detective as they crossed the street and joined the small crowd behind Cory Blaze. Bear Smith and Lolita were among the spectators, but they didn't notice Allison.

Cory Blaze stood to the side of the cameraman, as the eye of the big, black camera focused on Windfoot.

"Tell us why you're here today, Mr. Windfoot."

"Joey Red Horse is an American hero," Windfoot said, "a true *Native* American hero. He saw the injustice of putting American Indian bones and burial objects on display in our country's museums, and he decided to do something about it. While the rest of us just complained, he took action. It cost him his freedom, and apparently his life!"

Mark Windfoot was wearing a dark suit, white shirt, and red tie. He looked like a man running for political office. "I didn't know Joey Red Horse personally, but I wish I had. I'm here on behalf of all American Indians of all tribes to show our respect for what this young man did."

Cory Blaze squinted in the unforgiving Oklahoma sunshine. "When you say Joey's actions cost him his life, do you mean he was murdered *because* he took Gazing Woman from the Heartland Mound Builder Museum?"

"Why else?" Windfoot said. "It's certainly a possibility. It wouldn't be the first time Euro-Americans killed an American Indian who posed a threat to their wallets."

"You don't have any proof *who* killed him, do you?"

"No, but many of us feel the police are dragging their feet in this investigation. Perhaps they'd be more concerned if the murder victim were white. Just like they'd be more concerned if the bones on display in the museum were those of pioneers or soldiers, instead of American Indians."

"Bull!" Sullinger said, under his breath.

"Tell me," Cory Blaze was asking, "is ARROW encouraging American Indians to do exactly what Joey did, to steal Native American remains and burial objects from private museums?"

Windfoot pointed toward the camera with a finger. "We would not encourage *any* American to break the law," he said. "But people can go to our website for a list of private museums that still display human remains and funerary objects. What each person does is up to him. Rosa Parks got African Americans *on* the bus! Joey Red Horse is getting Native American bones *out* of private museums!"

When the interview was over, Bear Smith was the first person to shake Windfoot's hand. Many others stood in line to congratulate him.

Cory Blaze spotted Allison Culbertson.

"Miss Culbertson! How about a few words?"

"No, thank you. I really have nothing to say."

Bear Smith turned and stared at her. He frowned. Over his shoulder, Lolita gave a brief wave.

"What about you, Detective Sullinger?" Cory Blaze called out. "May I ask you a few questions about the investigation? Are you dragging your feet?"

"Talk to my boss. He likes the bright lights. I never go on camera myself."

Allison noticed that the cameraman had removed his equipment from the tripod and was filming her as she and Harry Sullinger walked back to the church.

"I've got a meeting set up with a couple of Pawhuska County deputy sheriffs who're going to watch the videotape with me to try to identify everybody on it," Sullinger was saying. "That'll probably take a couple of hours. Do you have any lunch plans?"

"I'm going to visit Joey's mother. There's some kind of reception at the Osage community center."

"What a coincidence," he said. "I'm supposed to meet with her later today, too. Eventually, she's going to watch the videotape with me to see who she can identify. You're welcome to come to the Sheriff's Department with me. You can meet with her then."

"Thanks," Allison said, "but I think I'll catch up to her at the community center. I'll take a rain check on that lunch, though."

Sullinger looked disappointed as she walked away from him. She spotted Joe Black Dog standing near the front of the church, and she made her way over to him.

"Hi," she said.

"Miss Culbertson. I'm glad you came. I thought you'd decided not to."

"What made you think that?"

He looked a bit embarrassed. "Well, you weren't at the Indian Camp Family Ground earlier today. I thought that meant you weren't coming."

"I don't understand."

"I'm sorry. I should have told you. Under our traditions, the body of the deceased is laid out for four days, either at a relative's home or at the Indian Camp Family Ground. On the fourth day, a funeral service is conducted by an Osage Elder at the campground before the body and mourners move to the church for the Catholic service. Afterward, a burial is held at the cemetery, and then mourners gather at a private home or the community center to share a meal."

Allison winced. "So it was bad etiquette for me to miss the first service?"

"I'm sure Joey's mother is honored you made such a long trip at all. That's the important thing. Let me introduce you to my friends."

The people in the suits and blankets turned out to be the Chief, the Assistant Chief, and members of the Osage Congress. After polite conversation, they moved to cars waiting to drive in a procession to the cemetery. Before long, she and Joe Black Dog were out of earshot of anyone else.

"I'm surprised so many people attended Joey's funeral," Allison said. "The Osage Nation isn't big, and Joey hasn't lived here for a long time. I don't know what I was expecting, exactly, but it wasn't a packed church."

"Joey's mother grew up here before she married Joey's father and moved away," he said. "Most of the people at the funeral knew *her* rather than him, I guess. His father was part Osage, but never lived on the reservation. Joey grew up in Missouri, but his mother returned to Pawhuska after her husband died. As to the high attendance, you know human nature, Miss Culbertson. Many probably came because of the publicity about Joey's theft of Gazing Woman and his violent death. His name is suddenly rather well known. Notoriety will draw a crowd."

Joe Black Dog was staring at the cluster of people surrounding Mark Windfoot.

"What do you think about him?" Allison asked.

"Windfoot? He is an articulate and smart young man. He makes a good spokesperson for ARROW. They're a bit too radical for me, though. I'm a rancher and a historian. I just want to take care of my cattle, raise my family, read my books, and live a worthwhile life. ARROW goes around picking fights. That's not my style."

"I'm sure Joey would have loved the way today turned out," Allison said. "The minister did a wonderful job. Television cameras actually showed up for his funeral. And ARROW sent Mark Windfoot, who basically called Joey the Rosa Parks of the American Indian Movement."

"Seems like a bit of hyperbole," Joe Black Dog said, "but it's nice to be remembered after you're gone."

In the distance, Bear Smith was introducing Lolita to Mark Windfoot. The ARROW spokesman was shaking her hand enthusiastically.

"You told me once that you didn't know Joey, but you had heard of Bear Smith," Allison said. "Can you tell me more about Bear?"

250

"He was born and raised on the reservation. Got into all kinds of trouble as a kid. I remember he stole Roy Gray Wolf's truck when he was about fifteen. I think he may have even robbed a liquor store. He was sent off to some sort of reform school. He would come visit his mother every now and then over the years. He was always riding a big motorcycle. His parents are both dead now, though."

"Any idea where he would get fifty-thousand dollars cash?"

"Why do you ask?'

"That's what he posted for Joey's bail bond."

"Well, he's a full-blooded Osage. As a descendant of an original allottee he has a headshare of the mineral rights to the oil found on the reservation, so he'd get a check for several thousand dollars every year. Fifty thousand? His headshare wouldn't be that much, probably. What's his occupation?"

"He says he owns a junkyard. I haven't verified it."

"Well, I've told you all I know about him," Joe Black Dog said. "Would you care to ride with me to the cemetery?"

"I'd like that, thank you."

It was late in the day before Allison finally found a private moment with Louise Red Horse. It came after the dinner at the Wikon Iron Community Center. Most of the mourners had left. Allison was sitting next to Joey's mother at a table. Allison had told the elderly woman a little bit about Joey's case, about his zest for life, and about the contact she had with him while the case was pending. She had not provided a detailed description of Joey's death. She was hoping Joey's mother would not ask. She dreaded repeating the story of her cowardice. Yet, if she were Joey's mother, she would want to know how he died. The details. She suspected the woman was not asking because she wanted to spare Allison the pain of relating what she had seen. Louise Red Horse struck her as a woman who thought of others before herself.

"I'm sorry I missed the service at the Indian Camp Family Ground this morning," Allison said. "I didn't realize it was part of the funeral."

"Oh, sweetie, don't worry about it. I am truly grateful you came all the way to Pawhuska for Joey. It would have meant the world to him to know you took the trouble."

Allison sipped a Diet Coke and glanced around. The remaining mourners were temporarily out of earshot.

"I'm glad we have a moment alone," Allision said. "I thought you would want to hear directly from me how Joey died. I was there, you know."

Louise Red Horse nodded, tears escaping the corners of her eyes. She was a round woman, heavyset, with high cheekbones and a broad nose. She wore a simple, black dress.

Allison told her everything she knew about Joey's theft of Gazing Woman, and about his dramatic dive from the heights of the bridge. As discretely as possible, she described Joey's affair with Marge Tappinger, the blowup with Lolita, his request that Allison go with him to talk to Lolita, and the man in black gunning down Joey in the street. Allison left out the part about the man shooting at her and about her cowering helplessly in her Jeep. She was hoping that Joey's mother would not ask her how it was that the killer happened to leave her alive.

Louise Red Horse wept as Allison related the details.

"His last words to me were: 'They're grave robbers. Don't let them get away with it. Keep up my fight.'"

The woman's pillow-like shoulders shook. She looked at Allison. "You won't let them get away with killing Joey, will you?"

Allison once again felt helpless. "I'm doing everything I can to help the police solve his murder. I can tell you, they're working it hard."

"Good," she said. "But you help them, okay?"

"Okay," Allison promised.

Louise Red Horse buried her face in her handkerchief.

"Maybe I shouldn't have told you all the details," Allison said. "I'm sorry for upsetting you."

"No, I'm glad you told me. I'm trying so hard to understand why this happened to Joey. It makes no sense to me."

Louise Red Horse regained her composure, and patted Allison's hand. "I am better now," she said. "Thank you."

"I understand you're going to meet with the police this evening?" Allison said.

"Yes, but they don't know who did it. They want me to look at the tape of the people leaving the church, tell them who I recognize. So many people! Joey would have been pleased."

"What else do they want to ask you?"

"About Joey growing up. His father drove a cement truck. We lived in Crystal City up near St. Louis when Joey was young. Joey's father died when Joey was in eighth grade. I tried to keep him in school, but he ended up dropping out his sophomore year. He later got his GED. He was a very bright boy."

"I know," Allison said. "Joey *was* intelligent. What did he do after high school?"

"He worked several different jobs. He stayed in Missouri after I moved back to Oklahoma. He loved cars and motorcycles. He worked as a mechanic at a couple different places. He was a hard worker, never unemployed. His last job was working for a motorcycle dealership in Cape Girardeau."

"Do you know his friend, Bear Smith?"

"A bit. Bear is older than Joey. I think they met in Cape Girardeau. Bear rode down with him to visit me a few times. They'd come to motorcycle rallies down here, and Joey would drop by."

"Did you know Joey was romantically involved with Bear's daughter?"

"Heavens, no. I didn't even know Bear had a daughter. Joey never told me about his love life. But he sure told me about you. We talked a lot over the telephone. He was so excited about his big case."

"Yes, I've never known a criminal to be quite so happy about being caught and prosecuted," Allison said. "Most prefer to get away with their crimes, rather than calling the police to rat themselves out."

"Oh, Joey wasn't a criminal, not really," his mother said.

"I agree," Allison said. "He was the Rosa Parks of the American Indian Movement."

Louise Red Horse cocked her head. Allison could not believe she had just quoted Mark Windfoot. Had those words really come out of her mouth? Did she need to give him credit for the thought?

Did she need to attribute the source for Mrs. Red Horse? Was there such a thing as conversational plagiarism?

"What?"

Allison shrugged. If you're going to steal material, you might as well go whole hog. "Rosa Parks got African-Americans on the bus. Joey Red Horse got the bones of Native Americans out of private museums."

Joey's mother smiled. "What a beautiful thing to say. Joey told me you had a way with words."

Allison smiled humbly, a hopeful thought in mind: *Maybe when Louise Red Horse watches the news tonight she'll think Mark Windfoot stole the quote from me.*

Midway through Allison Culbertson's eight-hour drive home from Pawhuska to Cape Girardeau, her cell phone rang. She recognized the voice even before he identified himself.

"Allison? Glad to catch you. This is Clive Faulkner."

"What a surprise. Are you calling to say you give up? You're forking over the bones?"

"Not yet. But I *have* decided I want to make a trip to Cahokia to see what their museum's like nowadays. You know, they found lots of Native American skeletons in their mounds. They got some federal money, so NAGPRA applied to them. When I present the issue to my Board of Directors, I'd like to give a full report about what Cahokia has done since NAGPRA. I'm going to drive up tomorrow. Would you like to come, too? It isn't every day you get the chance to tag along while a museum director spies on another museum. I'll have you back by suppertime. I promise."

Allison Culbertson could think of many worse ways to spend a day than going to the most famous Mound Builder site in North America with a man who wrote a book about the topic. Especially one who looked like Clive Faulkner.

"I'd love to," she said. "Deal me in."

Chapter 33

Allison Culbertson never fully appreciated the immensity of the mounds at Cahokia until she stood at the top of Monk's Mound with Clive Faulkner, gazing off toward the gleaming St. Louis arch. The silver monument was a pinpoint glimmering in the distance, part of a blue haze in the skyline on the other side of the Mississippi River, eight miles away.

"I read that the biggest mound at Cahokia was one hundred feet tall," Allison said, "but it didn't sound like it would be this immense. I can't get over it. I'm afraid to get too close to the edges, the sides are so steep."

The mound was a gigantic quasi-pyramid, with its top shaved flat. Allison and Clive Faulkner had trudged up its various levels and terraces to reach its highest summit. Everything in the surrounding area was dwarfed.

Clive Faulkner smiled, obviously appreciating her awe. "Keep in mind the mound itself is as tall as a ten-story building. Experts believe the temple at its apex would have added another five stories in height to the overall structure. The temple was 104 feet long, 48 feet wide and probably 50 feet tall. Its main weight-bearing post was three feet thick, cut from a huge prehistoric tree. Three feet thick! Imagine that! But this mound was just the crown jewel in a carefully planned metropolis."

The hot summer sun shone on his white dress shirt. His sleeves were rolled up. His face was flushed. He looked as hot as Allison felt.

"How'd the biggest mound get the name 'Monk's Mound'?" Allison asked. "Did it have anything to do with the Mound Builders?"

"No," Faulker said. "It got its name from some Trappist monks who established a monastery on one of the mounds around 1811 and grew crops and vegetables on the terraces of Monk's Mound." He gestured toward the acres of hilly ground beneath them. "When you look at the aerial photos, you can see that Cahokia was a city covering six square miles. That's four-thousand acres. It was laid out in a diamond shape, with its tallest structure, Monk's Mound, at its center. This six-square-mile complex contained more than 120 carefully arranged mounds. It was a heavily populated city with urban neighborhoods consisting of thousands of homes. Blocks and blocks of them. The wealthier people probably lived in houses atop many of the mounds, but the biggest one was probably reserved for the rulers and the religious leaders. This city was carefully laid out, with a large, perfectly flat grand plaza in front of Monk's Mound. The plaza was undoubtedly used for big ceremonies and impressive events drawing thousands of people. It was the length of seven football fields. This metropolis on the Mississippi had a population of at least twenty thousand, maybe thirty thousand. But by the time the Europeans arrived, the city was completely gone. Everyone disappeared without a trace. Not a building left standing. The mounds marking the site struck early explorers as too immense to have been man-made. They mistook them for natural hills and mountains, never dreaming a civilization had flourished here centuries before. The question of what happened to the people of Cahokia is one of the great historical mysteries of all time."

Allison glanced in every direction, awed by the immensity of the mound.

"It's hard to imagine what it was like back then," Allison said. She gazed toward the horizon. The buildings of downtown St. Louis were purplish towers in the distant haze. "I know St. Louis used to be called Mound City because of the Indian mounds on its side of the river. Now all you see are skyscrapers and the arch."

"Oh, it was vastly different a thousand years ago," Faulkner said, "particularly the land itself. This part of the country, at the juncture of the Mississippi and Missouri Rivers, was known as the American Bottom. This lowland area was tremendously fertile, and its network of wetlands, swamps, and sloughs supported a tremendous supply of plant and animal resources for the Cahokia population. In addition to the corn crops, which were the main staple of their diet, the land provided sweet potatoes, pumpkins, persimmons, grapes, pecans, walnuts, mulberries, beans, squash, and lots of other herbs and plants. Their meat supply came from all sorts of animals, including white-tailed deer, squirrels, raccoons, bear, beaver, mink, muskrat, and wolves, as well as waterfowl like ducks, geese, and swans. The rivers and streams were filled with huge catfish, sunfish, sucker, gar, and bowfin. All of that is gone now, replaced by outlet malls, billboards, factories, asphalt parking lots, interstate highways, and oil-storage tanks. The wetlands are gone, and so is the wildlife. It's a different world now."

As they walked down the many steps of Monk's Mound, Clive Faulkner continued his one-man seminar. Allison was pleased to be his audience.

"The people who lived here were undoubtedly powerful," he said. "The inner two-hundred acres of the city, including Monk's Mound and seventeen other mounds, were surrounded by a huge palisade, built around 1150 A.D. This wall was made by standing thick logs upright side-by-side. They were sunk four feet deep into the ground, and probably rose twelve to fifteen feet in the air. No way anyone could climb over it. The wall was punctuated with 112 bastions at regular intervals, where rectangular portions of the wall projected away from it, allowing archers in the bastions to shoot arrows in three directions. The sides of the walls were plastered with a mixture of mud and straw to protect them from fire and weather. The man who inspired the building of Cahokia was a military and political leader whose charisma, leadership, and ruth-lessness would have matched or exceeded Alexander, Julius Caesar, Napoleon, or Hitler. The difference is that his subjects had not learned to write, so his achievements weren't recorded for posterity to study in history books."

"How could these people possibly build all of this with their bare hands?" Allison marveled.

"Well, they didn't have modern road graders and heavy equip-ment, but they were well organized and well led. Markings left in the soil show they carried the dirt in woven baskets, one basket at a time."

"That's astonishing," Allison said. "It's mind-boggling how much time and effort it must have taken."

"It wasn't just ignorant savages making a pile of dirt," Faulkner said. "It truly appears that one highly skillful architect designed Monk's Mound. Internally, its base is composed of a clay platform about twenty feet high. Deep inside this mound, the materials are carefully arranged, alternating weight-bearing hard rock or clay with massive softer fill units. An internal system designed to pull water into the mound by capillary action keeps the clay in the core in a perennially expanded condition and provides sufficient support for the tremendous weight above it. These ancient drains deep within the mound are still functioning, allowing water to drain off the mound without washing it away. The surfaces of the mounds were finished off with hard clay to prevent slumping and erosion. Whoever designed Cahokia had a genius-level understanding of geometry, units of measurement, and the building materials at his disposal, plus true architectural talent."

They were still going down the steps. Allison wished she had counted them.

"As to the manpower necessary to build Cahokia," Faulkner was saying, "you can get a glimpse of it just from studies done about the work necessary to build the wooden palisade surrounding Cahokia. It would have taken twenty-thousand logs to build each of the four walls. If one man using a stone axe can cut down two trees per hour, it would take ten-thousand man-hours to cut down the trees. It'd take another twenty- to forty-thousand hours to trim the trees, another twenty-thousand hours to dig the trenches, another forty- to eighty-thousand hours to move the logs, and at least another sixty-thousand hours to wedge them in the ground and plaster the whole construction. That's something like 190,000 man-hours or 23,750 eight-hour days. And that's just for the wall! You can see this was undoubtedly a highly-organized community with a population willing to follow the direction of its leaders."

"What makes you think Cahokia had a leader to rival Alexander and Napoleon?" Allison asked.

"Cahokia dwarfed all other Native American communities in size and organization, but it's clear these societies were connected. Shells from the Gulf were used as bead material at Cahokia, copper from the Great Lakes region was worked by Cahokia craftsmen. Pots and bowls and other artifacts manufactured at Cahokia were found throughout the smaller Mound Builder communities dotting the rivers of the midwestern and southeastern United States. But what really nails it down for me is the practice of human sacrifice. You don't convince people to perform human sacrifice on a grand scale unless you're tremendously powerful and persuasive."

"I've read a little bit about the signs of human sacrifice here at Cahokia," she said. "Tell me something I might not know."

He stroked his chin. "Something you might not know?"

He pointed to the south. "Mound 72 down there on the other side of the twin mounds sits on the north-south center line of the city, at the bottom corner of the diamond, on a straight line with Monk's Mound and the big post in the center of the plaza. It appears to be the tomb for more than one generation of the ruling family of Cahokia. You might call them the Cahokian Caesars. At one time, that particular mound was probably the showpiece of this dynasty's wealth and power. Most of the tomb was built during the first half of the eleventh century, but within two to four decades after the year 1000 A.D., its main building was emptied and the exterior of the mound was stripped clean. Sort of like the statue of Lenin being toppled in the Soviet Union when that government collapsed."

Allison followed his gaze toward Mound 72.

"The bones of nearly three hundred people were found buried in that mound. Sixty-two percent of them are believed to be human sacrifices. It seems likely that several generations of the same prominent family were buried there, in six separate burial episodes. But that era covered no more than a hundred years, probably less. Each time a ruler bit the dust, a bunch of sacrifices went with him."

"Was there one particular person you think might have been the Caesar, the Napoleon?"

"Yes. The man who must have been the elite ruler is nicknamed 'The Beaded Birdman' because his body was found lying face-up on a bed of twenty-thousand white beads made from sea shells. This platform of beads was laid out beneath him in the form of a bird, with a distinctive head, feathers, and wings. The beads were all drilled with holes and ready for stringing. Most had a diameter of about one inch. Maybe they once formed some type of huge cape, but the strings connecting them vanished with time. Under the bed of beads, another male body was found, lying facedown, perhaps guarding The Beaded Birdman's back. Not far from the body of this prominent man, archaeologists dug up the remains of three men and three women believed to have been his servants, sacrificed at the time of his burial to accompany him to the afterworld. Valuables accompanied them, including a three-foot-long sheet of rolled-up copper from the area around Lake Superior, several bushels of sheet mica from North Carolina, and several hundred exquisitely carved arrowheads, lying as if they had been mounted on wooden shafts and bundled in quivers. Near The Beaded Birdman, diggers also unearthed fifteen highly polished and carefully crafted chunkey stones. But the most disturbing things were discovered in the pits nearby."

"The women?" Allison asked.

"Right. At the same time The Beaded Birdman departed this world, he was accompanied by fifty-three young women, most between the ages of eighteen and twenty-three. They were all buried side-by-side in a nearby pit. Their bodies had been neatly arranged, originally separated by woven mats, but the mats had long since rotted away. These girls had not been mutilated, so precisely how they were killed is unclear. Examination of their teeth suggests they differed significantly from the other people buried in Mound 72 and may not have been from Cahokia at all, but rather from distant societies paying tribute to the central power at Cahokia. The lack of periostitis of the long bones of these girls indicates they probably had perfect complexions, since skin imperfections can leave distinctive indicators in those bones. The inescapable conclusion is that fifty-three beautiful young women from outlying areas under this ruler's control were selected to accompany him into the afterworld."

"Inescapable?" Allison asked.

"Well, inescapable for me. We'll never know for sure."

They reached the bottom of the steps and walked across the street toward the Interpretive Center.

"Also making the trip with The Beaded Birdman and his women," continued Faulkner, "were four men, buried nearby with interlocking arms. Their heads and hands were cut off and were not even buried with the bodies. Nicks on the upper spines showed that the heads had been hacked off, as you'd expect from a ritualistic but violent sacrifice."

Allison paused and glanced back at Monk's Mound. "It's amazing what science can tell us," she said. "This is fascinating. What a story must have taken place right on this spot one-thousand years ago! I wish we knew the details."

"That's what archaeology is all about," Faulkner said.

At that moment, his cell phone rang. He answered it. Allison could not help but overhear his side of the conversation.

"Hello. Hi, Diedra. Up in Cahokia, checking out the competition. No, I've got Allison Culbertson with me." He glanced at Allison and raised his eyebrows as he listened to whatever Diedra Binzinger was saying. "The topic hasn't come up." He nodded his head as she talked for another twenty seconds. "Okay. I'll call you when I get back to Cape. We can discuss it all you want. How's that? Fine. Bye."

He put his cell phone back into the clip on his belt.

"Sorry for the interruption," he told Allison, his eyes meeting hers.

"I didn't mean to eavesdrop," Allison said, "but I couldn't help it. What 'topic' hasn't come up? I suppose she meant some conversation between me and you."

Allison thought she saw Clive Faulkner blushing, but the redness in his face could have been from the exertion of walking up and down the hundreds of steps of Monk's Mound.

"She wanted to know if I'd talked with you about my relationship with her. Diedra and I were seeing each other, but we broke up a few days ago. It's completely over between us. We've still got some loose ends to wrap up, I guess. Now, where were we before my phone rang?"

Allison was surprised by the jolt of pleasure she felt at hearing that Clive Faulkner and his girlfriend had split up. Surely, the breakup was not due to any interest he might be harboring for a certain attorney who had made him look rather bad on the witness stand? She ignored her thoughts and went on with the conversation as if nothing had happened.

"I was saying," she said, "how impressed I am by what science can tell us about Cahokia, merely by studying artifacts the archaeologists have found."

"What excites me," Clive Faulker said, his eyes lighting up, "is that only a small fraction of one percent of the Cahokia site has been excavated. We will undoubtedly learn much more about this mysterious, prehistoric metropolis when future work is done. Right now the policy of the Illinois Historic Preservation Agency, however, is that no areas can be excavated where human burials are likely to be encountered. So it may be a while before we uncover any other startling revelations."

He touched her elbow with his hand as they entered the heavy bronze doors at the entrance to the Interpretive Center. *He touched me*, she thought. *Are we on some kind of date?* Until the phone call from Diedra Binzinger, Allison had supposed he had asked her on this trip merely as a combination propaganda exercise and peace-keeping mission.

Clive Faulkner was still talking.

"If activists like Joey Red Horse had their way, we'd know nothing about any of this ancient history. The Beaded Birdman would never have been discovered. Mound 72 would be just another peaceful, tree-covered hill. In fact, by now it would probably be under some highway or shopping center. Archaeologists haven't looted this site; they've saved it. It was once all privately owned. Archaeologists convinced the State of Illinois to buy the land to make it into a state park. Let me tell you, it wasn't easy to do. One legislator from Chicago named Bull Burke opposed spending taxpayer dollars to buy the land. In a famous speech, he even proclaimed: 'My district needs parks for live people, and the guys in that mound are all dead ones.'"

Allison gazed in wonder at the exhibits surrounding her. Clive Faulkner continued talking, keeping his voice low. "In 1982, the United Nations listed Cahokia as a World Heritage Site. None of it would have been possible if not for the archaeologists, men just like Alfred Dennison, who spent years trying to discover what the ancient community that lived here must have been like."

Allison stroked her chin. "Well, at least this place doesn't show off the real skeleton of The Beaded Birdman the way you exploit Bootheel Man."

She shot a glance at Clive Faulker. He wasn't smiling, but he didn't seem to be irritated, either.

They stopped in front of a beautiful mural depicting Cahokia as it would have looked in its heyday.

262

"Actually," Faulkner continued, "more bodies would have been recovered from Mound 72, but the archaeologists quit digging in that mound around 1972, when it was about two-thirds excavated. The northeast portion has remained largely untouched, and its secrets remain hidden to this day. The hope is that a time will come in the future when American Indians and archaeologists can come to an agreement about how science can acquire its information about the past without being disrespectful to the heritage and beliefs of the people whose ancestors are buried here. For now, the excavations of Mound 72 have been discontinued."

"What happened to the bones of the three-hundred individuals who were dug up from Mound 72 before the voluntary ceasefire?"

"Well, the dental anthropologist who was studying them carried them off to the University of Massachusetts, where he was completing his PhD. For years he studied them to determine sex and age. When he took a teaching position at the University of Alabama at Birmingham he carted the boxes of skeletons with him to continue his work on them. From there he moved to the University of Arkansas, and again the bones made the trip. Eventually, in 1986, he gave the Cahokia skeletons to the Illinois State Museum at Springfield."

"Where are they now?"

"Still at the museum in Springfield. Not on display, though."

Clive Faulkner lowered his voice. "They've done a nice job here, but imagine how dramatic this museum could be if they featured the real Beaded Birdman lying on his bed of shells for the public to see, instead of the obviously fake reproduction. It could all be in a glass case in the center of a room. Tourists could walk completely around it, viewing him from all sides. Now, that would be an exhibit! It could be tastefully done."

Allison winced. There was a Barnum & Bailey aspect to Clive Faulkner that just didn't get it, that just didn't understand the outrage he was causing American Indians by displaying Bootheel Man so shamelessly and callously.

"I hope you're joking," she said. "This is a wonderful museum, even without such a macabre spectacle. I love the murals. I really like the dioramas of the people working in their village. They've shown remarkably good taste in the way they're handling every-thing, Clive. Surely the Heartland Museum could follow suit."

Clive Faulkner shrugged. "Like I said, Allison, I'll talk to the Board of Directors about it. Perhaps we're behind the times. Maybe we need to be more politically correct. But I'm not making any promises. We won't do anything that will put us out of business."

Allison paused with Clive Faulkner in front of the life-size re-production of The Beaded Birdman. The leader was lying on a bed of white shells, his eyes closed. His face was serene and tattooed.

"Do you really think it would be better to have a real skeleton instead of this tasteful reproduction?" Allison asked.

"Yes. Museums should show authentic objects, when possible. That's what museums do."

"You'll never convince me," Allison said. She changed the sub-ject. "So, you think this ancient chief at Cahokia was comparable to Napoleon?"

"Had to be," Faulkner said. "He ruled the entire heartland of this continent, a huge area. He was the dynamic force who joined together these separate tribes of Indians into a cohesive and con-nected society. He must have been an extraordinary man."

Allison touched Clive Faulkner's arm. "Have you ever been to Napoleon's tomb in France?" she asked.

"No."

"Well, I have. For your information, all you see is the tomb. His body isn't wheeled out for public display."

"Score one for your side."

"And Abraham Lincoln?" Allison said. "You haven't gawked at his skeleton lately, have you?"

"Okay, okay. You've made your point. Don't push it or you'll find yourself walking home." The words were said with a smile, though.

I just might be able to convince him to do this, she thought. *I just might be able to win Joey's fight. All without firing a single shot!*

Chapter 34

Allison Culbertson closed the driver's door of her newly repaired Jeep Cherokee and checked the lot number on the front of the brown-and-beige mobile home. Yes, this was where Bear and Lolita Smith lived. It was on the last row of the Star-Vue Mobile Home Park on Kingshighway. The neighborhood got its name from the drive-in movie theater formerly occupying the tract of land.

Drive-in theaters are as extinct around here as Mound Builders, Allison thought as she walked toward the double-wide. *Another victim of the everchanging world.*

She had called Lolita earlier that morning and asked to speak with her. Lolita invited her to come by for lunch. Allison bought two white-chocolate cappuccinos on the way over. She carried them in her hands, as she climbed the steps of the small wooden porch and knocked on the door.

"Lolita?"

When the girl opened the door, she was wearing her CUSTER DIED FOR YOUR SINS t-shirt. Allison suspected she was wearing it for her benefit. Lolita also wore gym shorts. Her legs were tan and muscular. Her feet were bare. The girl gave Allison a big hug, nearly spilling the cappuccinos.

"I'm glad you called," Lolita said. "I need somebody to talk to. All I've felt like doing since Joey died is lie around, crying."

"I want to talk some more about Joey," Allison said. "Thanks for letting me come over. What smells so good?"

Lolita brightened a bit. "Banana bread. It's one of my specialties. Comfort food. I thought it would go well with a Caesar salad."

"Sounds great," Allison said, holding up the cappuccinos. "I brought something, too."

Allison glanced around as she followed Lolita to the dining table. The living room was clean and surprisingly spacious. Nothing seemed out of place. It looked more like the living quarters of a certified public accountant than a biker who owned a junkyard.

Allison spotted a framed color print of an Indian chief on the wall near the entertainment center.

"Is that a relative?" she asked, pointing to the picture.

"No," Lolita said. She pointed to the lettering on her t-shirt. "That's Sitting Bull. He's the one who rubbed out Custer."

"Right," Allison said. *Well, so much for the CPA living room*, she thought.

Allison sat at the table while Lolita worked in the open kitchen area, putting the salad in bowls and taking the banana bread off its cooling rack.

"Have the police figured out who killed Joey?" Lolita asked, her back to Allison.

"No, that's why I'm here. The last I heard, the Major Case Squad had disbanded. The case is still unsolved."

"Are you trying to solve his murder yourself?" Lolita asked.

"Sort of. The last thing Joey said to me was, 'Don't let them get away with it.' If I can help the police figure out who killed him, I'll feel better about myself. It makes you feel pretty helpless, seeing someone killed right in front of your eyes. In hindsight, I wish I'd done a lot of things differently, like getting a good look at whoever did it."

Lolita's shoulders began to shake. She was crying.

"I'm sorry," Allison said. "I didn't mean to upset you."

Lolita tore a paper towel from a spool and dabbed her eyes. "That's okay. Like I said, all I do these days is cry. I loved Joey so much."

Lolita tossed the paper towel into a trash can under the kitchen sink and carried the salads to the table.

"I don't know what I can do to help out," Lolita said, "but I want his killer caught. I'll tell you anything. Ask away."

She returned to the kitchen counter to get the banana bread.

"First of all," Allison said, "the police questioned me about Joey's drug use. Evidently they found some illegal drugs in his apartment. What can you tell me about Joey and drugs?"

Lolita put the fragrant banana bread on the table and sat down.

"Joey wasn't into hard drugs at all," she said. "He was experimenting a little bit with peyote. He got involved with it because of his interest in Osage history."

266

Lolita paused as she rose to get butter from the refrigerator. "Peyote is a cactus that grows out West. Around 1891, a man named John Wilson, a Caddo-Delaware, converted many Osages to the Big Moon Peyotism religion. The peyote religion talks about Christ and how he rose from the grave and went back to his father in heaven. Joey read how the peyote religion played a part in cutting down alcoholism among the Osages. The use of peyote induces a beautiful state, much more mellow than intoxication from alcohol. It lets you focus inwardly. For some, it stimulates awareness and heightens mental capacity. For others, it has the opposite effect. The Native American Church uses it as part of their religious ceremonies. Joey got involved with it when he visited their church. He used it, sure. But it's not like he was a drug addict or anything. It's no more addictive than marijuana. In fact, it's legal for people in the Native American Church to use."

"Have you tried it?" Allison asked.

She nodded. "Joey and I did it together several times."

"How do you use it, exactly?"

"Parts of the cactus are dried into little pieces, called mescal buttons or peyote buttons. You eat them. Want to try it?"

"No, thank you," Allison said. "Did Joey sell or distribute peyote? Was he a dealer?"

"Dealer sounds harsh," Lolita said. "Joey would bring peyote back with him when he made trips out West. He was even starting to grow some in his apartment. He shared it with other people. But a mescal button only sells for ten dollars, a whole bag for a hundred. So Joey wasn't making big money on it. He was basically just sharing the glow with friends."

"Was your father involved in this enterprise with him?"

"What, selling a bag or two of mescal buttons here or there? I guess so. They'd take it with them when they went to their biker rallies. But don't get the wrong idea. We're not talking big money here."

"Can you think of any way his involvement with peyote could have caused someone to want to kill him?"

"No. There wasn't any big-time peyote drug ring whose turf they were invading. It's not like cocaine and Colombian drug lords and all that."

"Was Joey involved with any other illegal drugs, either as a user or a dealer?"

"No, and I would have known if he were. After all, we used the peyote together. We hung out a lot."

"Did your father know Joey introduced you to peyote?"

She looked down. "I don't think so. But he didn't know we were sexually involved, either. At least not until that last night."

"What happened that night?"

"After you dropped me off?"

"Right."

"Well, I went into Joey's apartment. I let myself in with a key he gave me. I caught him in bed with Mrs. Tappinger."

"What happened next?"

"Well, I kind of lost it. I started screaming and throwing things. I hit Joey. I called Mrs. Tappinger a bunch of names. She got dressed and ran out. I saw a framed picture of me on Joey's dresser, one I gave him for his birthday. I smashed it. Then I started smashing anything that would break. He finally begged me not to leave until you could talk to me, and he ran off to get you."

Lolita's lower lip quivered. "That was the last time I ever saw him alive. I never even got to say goodbye." She buried her face in her hands.

Allison waited for her to compose herself.

"How long did you stay at his apartment?"

"Maybe thirty minutes. I was hoping he'd come back with you. I was hoping something you'd do or say would make everything better, but I didn't see how it could, not really. When he didn't come back, I finally just went home."

"How'd you get home?'

"On my motorcycle. I parked it at Joey's before you and I left for Oklahoma."

"What happened when you got home?"

"Well, I turned off the cycle when I got to the Star-Vue entrance, and pushed it to our driveway. I didn't want my dad to hear me coming home." She sniffed. "He heard me, anyway. You can't sneak up on anybody with a motorcycle. He came out of his bedroom the minute I came through the door. He started grilling me about where I'd been. Like a fool, I told him."

268

"Then what?"

"He slapped me. Said I was stupid for getting involved with Joey. He ranted and raved for a while, but finally calmed down. He felt bad about hitting me and apologized. We ended up hugging and crying."

"Did he leave your home that night?"

"I can't say for sure. I went to bed right after our fight."

"I thought you and he told the police you were together all night."

"Well, we talked it over before we spoke to the cops. We thought it would be better if we each claimed we had talked throughout the entire night."

"Was that your idea or his?"

"His," she said. "He said we were obvious suspects, both of us."

"Where's your father right now?"

"At the junkyard. He's almost always there until at least five." Lolita dabbed her eyes. "Miss Culbertson, I know what you're thinking, but my dad would never hurt Joey. He liked him. He liked him a lot. Besides, I don't know exactly when Joey got shot, but my dad and I really did talk for a long time before I went to bed."

"Does your father have a gun?"

"No. He's a convicted felon, remember?"

"What about Mark Windfoot," Allison asked. "I saw you talking with him at the funeral the other day. How long have you known him?"

"I just met him that day."

"What about Joey and your father? Did either of them know Windfoot?"

"I don't think so. If they did, they never told me. You know Joey. He'd have been bragging his head off if Mark Windfoot, the President of ARROW, was a buddy of his. He would've told me."

"Did you know beforehand that Joey was going to break into the Heartland Mound Builder Museum and steal Gazing Woman?"

"No," Lolita said. "I sure didn't."

"So, Joey *didn't* tell you everything?"

"I guess not."

"Was your father surprised when Joey stole Gazing Woman? Did your father know in advance it would happen?"

Lolita paused several seconds before giving her answer.

"Neither of them ever *told* me that my father knew what Joey was going to do. I sort of think he did, though. He was very proud of Joey. He called it the 'righteous heist.' He said it was the sort of thing he would have done himself if he didn't have a kid to put through college."

"Where did your father come up with the bond money to get Joey out of jail?"

Lolita shook her head. "I really don't know. My dad and I never talk about money. We're not rich, but we're not poor, either. I've never been interested in his junkyard business, so we've never really talked about how much money he makes or what he does with it. He's always been able to get me what I wanted or needed. He's made it clear to me that I'm going to college. He said he'd pay for wherever I wanted to go, as long as I could get in. I've been sending out applications, checking the box that I'm an Indian. For once in my life, it might be an advantage."

Back at her office, Allison tracked down the phone number of the headquarters for Angry Reformers Resisting Oppressive Whites in Washington DC. She dialed the number. After fencing politely with a secretary obviously well trained and vastly experienced in screening calls, she eventually reached Mark Windfoot.

"This is Allison Culbertson. I was Joey Red Horse's lawyer."

"Miss Culbertson, good to hear from you! I saw you at Joey's funeral, but we never got the chance to hook up."

Right, Allison thought. *You were too busy preening for the TV cameras.*

"I want you to know," he was saying, "that we here at ARROW appreciate all you did for Joey and all you did for our cause. In fact, we've added you to our list of approved lawyers. If someone we know ever needs a lawyer in Missouri, you'll be the first one we recommend."

"I appreciate that," Allison said. "In a way it relates to why I'm calling."

"Oh?"

"I saw your television interview."

270

"Which one?"

"The one from Joey's funeral, the one where you speculated that Joey might have been killed because he stole Gazing Woman. For the past week, I've been trying to figure out why someone was shooting at me and Joey that night. So far I haven't been able to piece it together. Do you have any specific proof as to who killed Joey or why? You were pretty vague with the media, but maybe there's more you could tell me."

"I gave a full statement to the police," Windfoot said. "Haven't they solved it yet?"

"Not that I can tell. Nobody's been arrested or charged, anyway."

"To be perfectly honest," he said, "I don't have any proof of anything. I was shooting from the hip, taking advantage of the chance to promote our side of the fight. You know, I've been butting heads with private museums for the entire time I've been the President of ARROW. Some are cooperative and understand our viewpoint. Others, like Clive Faulkner, make it clear they don't give a rat's ass how American Indians feel about their exhibits."

"I'm working on him," Allison said.

"Who?"

"Clive Faulkner. I'm trying to convince him to repatriate Bootheel Man and the other human skeletons. I sort of feel it's something I can do for Joey."

"More power to you, Miss Culbertson. I hope you have better luck than I did talking with Faulkner. He's stubborn as a mule, but smart, too. You won't get him to budge if he doesn't want to do."

"Do you think he or some other museum-type with a beef against American Indian activists might have come after Joey?"

"Who knows? There are museum people whose jobs might be on the line. There are archaeologists who are mad because they can no longer dig everywhere they want to dig. There are collectors who pay top dollar for stolen American Indian art. Lots of people might have been mad at Joey for what he did. What I say to the media, though, is often geared toward drawing attention to injustice. I've got to keep my sound bites under thirty seconds, too, if I want them to air. In the big picture, yeah, I think somebody killed Joey because he broke into the museum. Specifically who or why? I don't know. Do I think Clive Faulkner shot him? From my contact with Mr. Bow Tie, he strikes me as a talker, not a fighter. In spite of what I said to the media, I doubt he's the killer. But he and people like him have been butting heads with ARROW for years. Who's to say whether he or one of his colleagues finally blew a fuse?"

Mark Windfoot's radio-caliber voice went silent. After a pause, Allison changed the subject.

"How many times would you estimate you personally talked with Clive Faulkner?"

"Ever?"

"Right."

"I met him in person once, at a convention for museum professionals in Tucson, Arizona. This was a couple of years ago. To their credit, the museum people put me on their program and let me speak about the emotional hurt many Americans Indians feel when the bones of their ancestors are displayed. I also warned them about their own physical danger."

"You threatened the museum directors?"

"No, no. I told them about the American Indian belief that those who tamper with graves and handle the bones and burial relics of the dead put themselves at risk. I wasn't making threats. No one took it that way."

"What other contact have you had with him?"

"Maybe a dozen phone conversations. Every time an American Indian would complain to me about Bootheel Man, I'd call Clive Faulkner personally, just to remind him about the pain he's causing other people and the fact that I'm over here in Washington DC, keeping my eye on him, lobbying to get laws passed that would eventually force even private museums like his to get rid of their human remains. To his credit, he took my calls. They couldn't have been pleasant for him. I can be rather abusive."

"Did he ever say he'd think about repatriating the remains, or at least put the question to his Board of Directors?"

"No. I never made any progress whatsoever. We pretty much agreed to disagree."

"What about Joey Red Horse?" she asked. "Did you know him before the theft?"

272

"Never met him. That's the same thing the police asked, by the way."

"What about Bear Smith? Did you know him?"

"First time I met him was Joey's funeral."

"Did any of the money for Joey's attorney fee come from ARROW?"

"You're the attorney. You tell me? Where did your fee come from?"

"Bear Smith put up Joey's bond. My fee came out of that money."

"There you go."

"You still haven't answered my question," Allison pressed. "Did any of that fifty-thousand dollars come from ARROW?"

"No. We don't have a line item in our budget for breaking and entering."

In the ensuing silence, Allison knew it was time for her last question, one that could end the friendliness of their conversation. "Where were you on the night Joey was killed?" she asked.

He chuckled. "The police covered that ground, too. I was being interviewed live on *Nightline* about a squabble between a private museum and our movement out in New Mexico. It was a satellite feed. I was sitting in a newsroom in Washington DC. I believe my alibi is what your profession calls 'iron-clad.'"

Allison was glad he didn't sound offended by the question. "Well, I'm not a detective, but it sounds pretty good to me. Can you think of anything else that might help me track down Joey's killer? Is there some bit of relevant information you didn't tell the police?"

"No."

"Thanks for taking my call," Allison said.

"Any time. By the way, you might want to watch the *Ted Stryker Show* on cable tomorrow night. An archaeologist and the very opinionated host are going to spar with me about Injuns versus private museums. I'll be outnumbered, but justice is on my side. I'm sure Joey's name will come up. If the opportunity presents itself, I'll mention yours, too."

The moment Allison hung up from talking to Mark Windfoot, Rita buzzed her that she had a call from Bear Smith.

"Hello?"

"I heard you came to my house today and talked to Lolita when I wasn't home."

"We had lunch together."

"Listen to me, and listen good because I'm only going to say it once. Stay out of my home and stay away from my daughter. Leave us alone. Your fee is paid and your job is done. Don't come out here again. I mean it."

The line went dead.

Allison shuddered involuntarily. The malevolence in his voice warned her that the big man was fully capable of making good on any threats of violence. Was she getting in over her head?

Chapter 35

Allison Culbertson's eyes popped open. She glanced at the glowing red numerals of the clock on her bedside table. It was three o'clock in the morning.

What had awakened her? She could have sworn she heard breaking glass.

She lay in bed listening. Was somebody breaking into her home?

I should have called Harry Sullinger about getting that gun, she thought. *I need to move firearm acquisition higher on my list of things to do.*

Allison slipped from her bed and reached underneath it. Her fingers gripped the Silver Slugger aluminum bat she had used throughout her softball years. *Thank goodness I put it under the bed.*

Allison raised the bat and stood absolutely still in her bedroom, poised like the statute of Stan Musial outside Busch Stadium in St. Louis. She faced her bedroom door as if it were the pitcher's mound. She listened with every fiber of her body, searching for any noise that was not part of the normal chorus of night sounds of her two-story frame house.

What was that! she asked herself. *That would be the ice-maker in the refrigerator,* she answered. More time passed. *What about that!* She listened intently. *Don't get your panties in a wad. That's just the clock over the fireplace mantel.*

After what seemed like forever, Allison glanced again at the alarm clock by the bed. A mere four minutes had passed.

This is ridiculous, she thought. *I can't stand here all night. I should call 911. But what if it's nothing? How stupid would I look?* A horrible thought occurred to her. *Maybe they've cut the phone line!* She inched her way quietly toward the telephone on her bedside table. She would pick up the phone. If the line was dead she could still call the police with the cell phone recharging on her dresser. She put the regular phone to her ear and heard the reassuring dial tone. *Okay, maybe I'm imagining things.* Nevertheless, she crept to her cell phone, unplugged it, and clipped it to the waistband of her shorts.

After five more minutes of Stan the Man impersonation, she decided to check out the house. Other questions presented themselves. Did she want to walk through the house with the lights out, so an intruder wouldn't see her coming? Or did she want to go through the house flipping light switches like crazy? Did she want to sneak though the house stealthily? Or did she want to charge through it like a whirling dervish? To whirl or not to whirl, that was the question.

After much consideration, she chose the light-flipping whirling-dervish option. The worst part was opening the door to her bedroom, not knowing what might be on the other side. Once that heart-stopping moment was accomplished, she sped through the rooms on the second floor, snapping on lights and checking windows and closets. Within minutes, she knew she was alone on the second floor, standing at the head of the staircase leading to the first floor.

Now came another hard part.

She inched down the stairs, keenly aware that the walls on each side of the staircase blocked the view at the bottom of the steps. Someone could be lurking on either side.

When she neared the bottom, she leaped down the last steps and darted to the middle of the foyer between the staircase and her front door. She spun a quick circle, fully prepared to bat-bash anyone who might lunge at her.

Thankfully, the room appeared to be empty. She checked the front door and the narrow windows next to it. Everything was fine.

She moved to the wall near the living room and flipped on the foyer and living-room lights. Once more, she stood poised with her bat. Again, everything was normal.

Yet, as she stood in the living room, something didn't feel right. It took a moment for it to register. A breeze was tickling her bare legs.

Allison felt a shot of adrenaline charge up her back.

She gripped the bat with both hands and inched quietly toward the source of the breeze—the dining room.

At the dining-room door, she flipped on the overhead chandelier. Its flame-shaped lightbulbs lit the room. At first, nothing seemed wrong. Certainly, no one was hiding under the table or in any of the corners. No one would fit inside the buffet or china cabinet she'd inherited from her parents. But then she saw it. The curtain was rustling gently with the breeze.

But her window had been closed when she went to bed. She knew it. She had checked the doors and windows three times the other night and had not opened any of the windows since.

Allison pulled her cell phone and dialed 911.

"What's your emergency?"

"This is Allison Culbertson. I think my home is being burglarized. A window has been opened."

"What's your address?"

Allison told her.

"I'm sending a patrol car right now. Please stay on the line."

Allison felt panic rising from her gut. She fought the image of herself lying helpless on her car seat as the shooter calmly considered whether or not to take her life. *I am going to handle it better this time!*

"The window in my dining room appears to be open," she told the 911 operator, moving carefully toward the undulating curtain. The curtain didn't reach the floor. Allison confirmed that nobody's feet were at its bottom. No killer lay in wait behind it.

When she got to the window she pulled the cord, opening the curtain. She stared at what she saw. A pane of glass at the bottom of the window had been broken out. Pieces of glass lay on the windowsill. Sitting amid the glass was a six-inch-tall figurine of a bare-chested Native American man rolling a chunkey stone. Lying next to him was a piece of white typewriter paper, folded in half.

"My dining room window has been broken," Allison told the 911 operator. "Someone has left me some kind of little statue, and maybe a note." She glanced at the latch on her window. "My window is still locked. It doesn't look like anybody got in. The hole is too small."

"Don't touch anything," the 911 operator said. "The officers will want to fingerprint everything. Why don't you go to your front door? An officer is pulling up to your house right now."

Allison spent the next few hours with the dark-uniformed officers of the midnight shift. The first patrolman was quickly followed by two other street officers. The three police officers, two men and one woman, walked through her house, checking for any unwanted guests. It didn't take long to determine that the broken window was the only point of entry, and that the only intruder was the ceramic chunkey player.

One of the officers was an evidence technician. He spent a great deal of time photographing and fingerprinting everything in and around her window. He used three cameras: a Polaroid, a 35-millimeter, and a digital. He also examined and photographed the ground outside the window, searching closely for footprints.

The female officer sat with her at the kitchen counter as Allison laboriously wrote out her statement. As she was writing a detailed account by hand, it occurred to her that it would have been far easier to type her statement on her computer, but since she had already started filling out the form and didn't really have much to say, she kept going, writing slowly and carefully to make her handwriting legible.

She was pleasantly surprised when, shortly after 7:00 A.M., Harry Sullinger joined the uniformed officers in the informal get-together at her house. He brought doughnuts. The young street officers, their work mostly done and their shift about to end, deferred to him when he arrived, letting him take charge of the interview with Allison.

Sullinger spread out the Polariod photographs on the tabletop. The chunkey-player statue and the note had already been bagged as evidence. They also lay on the table.

"So, the up-and-coming lawyer adds burglary victim to her resume," Sullinger said, smiling. "What happened? I heard a little bit about it at the station, but nobody knew all the juicy stuff."

Allison was suddenly aware that she was wearing only a pair of gym shorts and a t-shirt. He, on the other hand, was looking quite presentable in his khaki slacks, navy sport coat, and tie. She crossed her arms over her chest, wishing the cloth of her t-shirt were a bit thicker. Why did this man have such a powerful effect on her?

He offered her a doughnut, and she reached into the box and took a carmel-covered cinnamon roll. As she leaned toward him, she peered at the design on his tie. What was the pattern? Small cartoons of guys in striped jail uniforms, peering out from behind barred jailhouse windows. *Clever.*

"How you holding up, Allison?" he asked as he handed the balance of the doughnuts to the other officers.

"Surprisingly well." She nodded to the horizontal rows of convicts. "Nice tie."

"Thanks. It was a gift."

"Let me guess. It came from one of your ex-wives?"

"Number five. Ties were her thing. But I'd rather not talk about her. Let's have a look at your trespasser, there."

The chunkey player now inhabited a clear plastic police-evidence bag on the dining table near Allison's elbow.

"Why would somebody leave this guy with you?" Sullinger said.

"I don't know. That's why I called 911. You professionals are supposed to have all the answers."

"No, we just serve and protect," Sullinger said. "Sometimes we figure things out; sometimes we don't." He leaned his head so far to one side his ear practically rested on the table. "Man, this is another fine piece of pottery. Reminds me a lot of Gazing Woman. Same reddish color. Same attention to detail."

"If I'm right," Allison said, "my chunkey player visitor is made of flint clay, just like Gazing Woman."

Harry Sullinger grunted. He studied the Polaroid photographs taken of the windowsill before anything had been moved.

"He wasn't *thrown* through the window," Sullinger said. "Looks like somebody broke out the glass, then reached through and placed him carefully on the windowsill. Too bad your vandal didn't cut himself. We could have gotten a DNA sample. Let's have a look at that note."

The white piece of paper had been opened and placed inside a flat plastic evidence bag. Allison's unknown visitor had left a message by cutting out letters from magazines and gluing them to a blank sheet of white paper.

"We don't get handwriting samples when they do it this way," Sullinger said. "Nor can we match it to a typewriter ribbon or computer memory. Somebody's wanting to stay anonymous."

Allison read the note again as Sullinger peered at it.

MISS CULbErtSoN
QUIt aSKiNG QuEStiOnS
YoU Are NOT iN DaNGeR NOw
BUt WiLL bE If YoU Don'T
LeT it go

"Like the bald guy in *The King and I* kept saying, this is a puzzlement," Sullinger said.

"That was Yul Brenner." She smiled. "I wouldn't have pegged you for the type of guy who likes musicals."

"Oh, I'm a regular musical aficionado," he said. "I've seen *The Phantom of the Opera* six times. I just love it when you figure out why the old guy's bidding so high for the mechanical monkey."

Sullinger carefully held up the evidence bag containing the note, gripping it by a corner. "So, you've been asking questions. What questions have you been asking, my dear, and of whom?"

Allison told him about her amateurish quest to discover the identity of Joey's killer, detailing who she had spoken to and when, all the while humbly emphasizing that she didn't really have a clue what she was doing.

"Well, you must have made somebody nervous. The crime lab will test the paper. Every now and then they succeed in lifting a fingerprint or DNA off a document. It's a long shot, but maybe your pen pal got careless and left an inadvertent calling card. Wish he'd used tape. You can get a good print off the sticky side."

Sullinger frowned as he studied the note again. "I don't like this reference to danger," he said. "Maybe you'd better cool it with your snooping."

"I'm not particularly thrilled about that part of the note, either," she said. "I've got a better idea, though. How about I keep snooping around, but I take you up on your offer of helping me pick out a gun. If I recall correctly, you volunteered to teach me how to use one."

He grinned. "I wouldn't have pegged you for the gunslinger type."

"I became a lethal weapons buff somewhere around three o'clock this morning," she said, "when I thought someone who wanted to kill me was in my house and all I had for self-defense was a softball bat."

He reached over and felt her bicep.

"I'll bet you pack a wallop, Counselor. I wouldn't want to be on the receiving end of one of your bat swings."

His hand lingered a moment longer than necessary before leaving her arm. They both stood and watched as the evidence technician gathered the photographs and bags of physical evidence and left for the police station.

"So," he said, when they were alone, "I get off at four-thirty this evening. If you're serious, I'll pick you up at your office, take you to the firing range, and teach you Firearms 101."

"It's a date," she said, liking the sparkle of happiness she detected in his eyes.

"I suppose as a fan of musicals you've seen *Chicago*?" she asked him.

"Only about four times."

"There's a few ladies in that particular show who knew how to use guns," Allison said. "I want you to make me dangerous, like them."

"I don't know," he said. "Some of those beautiful dames were public enemies. You'll have to promise to follow their same rigid guidelines about determining when and whom to shoot."

"What guidelines?"

"Don't you remember the song? They only killed guys *who had it comin'*."

"I'll try to remember that," she said.

Chapter 36

Allison Culbertson aimed Harry Sullinger's 9-millimeter Beretta handgun at the target, a rectangular piece of paper about a yard wide featuring a black and white photograph of Osama bin Laden. She pulled the trigger. Simultaneously with the blast from the gun, a hole appeared in bin Laden's forehead.

"Nice!" Sullinger said. "You're a natural."

"I was aiming at his chest."

"Oh," Sullinger said. "Well, don't forget to position the gun so the white dot on the nub at the far end of the barrel is right smack in the middle of the groove in the sight at your end of the barrel. It should make a horizontal line. Put what you're shooting at right on top of the white dot."

She aimed again and pulled the trigger.

A hole appeared in bin Laden's upper chest. She pulled the trigger three more times, placing additional holes near her first one.

"Are you sure you haven't done this before?" Sullinger's voice was slightly muffled by the earplugs she was wearing.

"Never. I'm afraid of guns. They kill people."

"Guns don't kill people, people ..."

"Don't say it!" Alison waved him quiet. "I've heard the NRA propaganda before."

They were at Harry Sullinger's private firing range. He lived in rural Cape Girardeau County, on a ten-acre, forested hill near Whitewater, Missouri. His firing range consisted of two posts driven into the ground in front of a steep hillside at the bottom of a ravine. Bullets fired at his targets would disappear harmlessly into the earthen wall of the ravine.

"Don't the neighbors mind the noise?" Allison asked.

"What neighbors? It's mostly farms out here."

He adjusted the position of her hands. Her right hand gripped the gun and her left hand steadied it.

"Your stance is perfect," he said. "Go ahead and fire the rest of the clip."

She glanced at him. Thanks to the protective goggles, he looked like either a chemistry professor or a muscle-bound frog. She decided not to be too critical. She was wearing a set herself.

She fired ten more shots. Most grouped in a cluster the size of a basketball.

"I'm impressed," Sullinger said.

"Well, you said it was like pointing your index finger at someone. I've been rudely pointing at people my whole life."

"Okay, let's reload."

He showed her how to push the button on the side of the gun to drop the cartridge clip out of the gun's handle.

He took another clip from a leather pouch on his belt. "I always carry this pouch with two extra clips. With fifteen shots per clip and a full one in the gun, I know I've got forty-five shots."

"Sounds like police brutality waiting to happen," Allison murmured.

"I heard that! Truth is, you never know how many guys are going to be on the other side of a fight or how many times you're going to miss." He snapped a fresh clip into the Beretta. "I always wear my extra ammunition in exactly the same place on my belt. Whenever I go to the range, I always reload by reaching to exactly the same spot for my new clip. You train so everything comes automatically, without even thinking about it. In the stress of a gunfight, you need to be reacting instinctively."

He pointed to the expended shellcasings strewn all over the ground. "And never pick up your spent shellcasings as you go. A police officer once got killed because he kept stopping to pick up his expended shellcasings during a gunfight. His firearms instructor at the firing range always made his students pick up after themselves as they went. When the cop found himself in a real gunfight, he couldn't shake that instinctive training of picking up his shellcasings. They found him dead, his empty gun in one hand and a bunch of spent shellcasings in the other, with lots of unused ammo still on his belt."

Allison remembered seeing the man in black shooting Joey Red Horse. Could she have shot that man? Could she have made herself pull the trigger? Would she have been able to hit him from clear across the street? She closed her eyes.

"You've had a taste of what it's like," Sullinger said, almost as if he were reading her mind. "In the intense fear and excitement caused by being in a gunfight, your body is going to be releasing chemicals that take your brain to another level. You're focusing so much on your target, on the man who is out to kill you, that you lose track of everything else. I can't tell you how many times an officer at the end of a gunfight is flabbergasted to discover he emptied his gun. He thinks he fired only two or three times. Turns out he shot the entire magazine."

"If it ever happens to me," Allison said, "I hope I don't freeze up."

"You won't. We're going to come out here twice a week until using this gun feels as comfortable for you as brushing your teeth. Which hand did you use to brush your teeth this morning?"

"My right, why?"

"I guess you squeezed the toothpaste onto the brush with your left hand?"

"Yes."

"And you probably started brushing the teeth on the left side of your mouth first?"

Allison thought about it a moment.

"That's right."

"And you did it without even thinking about it, like you were on autopilot?"

"I guess so."

He handed her the Beretta.

"Here's your new toothbrush. Now, remember what I told you about the safety?"

"It's that switch near the sight. If the safety's on, the gun won't shoot. If the red dot's showing, the safety's off."

"Right. Okay, this time aim at Osama's nose. Pause about five seconds between each shot, adjusting your aim each time. I want you to get a feel for what you're doing."

Her first three shots all went high, perforating the paper right above bin Laden's turbin.

"You're jerking the gun up just a fraction," Sullinger said. "Pull the trigger smoothly. Don't jerk it."

Her next shot hit the turban.

"That's better," he said.

As she fired the rest of the clip, her protective goggles slid down her nose. She realized she was sweating.

"Reload," he said, handing her the third clip.

She hit the button, dropped the empty clip from the gun, and shoved the new one into its handle.

"There you go," he said. "This time, fire two shots at a time, first at his chest, then the head."

Most of Allison's shots hit pretty close to where she'd been aiming. When she finished, she handed the empty gun to Sullinger.

"Allison, I'm not just saying this. I've taught lots of people to shoot, but no one has ever been as accurate as you the first time out."

"Must be something to do with my high LSAT score."

"Okay, genius, pop-quiz time. What's your primary responsibility to the public once you start carrying a gun? It's the first thing I told you today."

"Don't let somebody take the gun away from you."

"Right. If you're going to carry a gun, you have to be aware of where it is at all times. You have to protect it. You can't let somebody take it away from you. They could use it on you, but worse yet, they could use it on innocent bystanders. Then you've done more harm than good by carrying a weapon. You absolutely can't let it get taken away."

He held up two fingers. "What's the second rule?"

"Never point it at someone unless you're prepared to shoot him."

"Right. Not even playing around. Most gun accidents happen when someone thinks a gun is empty and horses around with it. Always assume it's loaded. Never point it at another person unless you mean business."

He held up three fingers. "And what's Sullinger's Rule Number Three of Firearms 101?"

"If you've made the decision to shoot, always shoot to kill."

"Right. The movie stuff about shooting the gun out of someone's hand or just wounding the bad guy in the arm is pure fiction. If the bad guy is shooting at you and you're shooting at him, you're both very likely to get shot. Just because you hit him first doesn't mean he's going down. Even when the heart stops, a person still has enough oxygen in his brain to function for another five to seven seconds. A documented case exists where a man shot in the heart still managed to run fifty yards before he fell. Think how many shots he could have fired! Your assailant will keep shooting at you until you disable him. You disable him by hitting him on the perpendicular line from his head to his navel. In other words, you need to hit his brain or his spine. Otherwise, he'll still be a threat and can put a bullet in you while you're celebrating your accurate shooting."

Harry Sullinger reloaded all three clips for Allison and replaced the shot-up target with a fresh one. This one featured a photograph of Adolph Hitler.

As he was walking back to her, Allison studied their surroundings. His house was off in the distance at the top of the steep slope. A brook ran through the woods at the bottom of one side of the hill. Except for the gravel driveway leading to his rather dumpy house, the entire hill was covered with woods. Birds had filled the trees until the target-practice session began, but they quickly took flight when the shooting started.

"How did you happen to find this place, anyway?" she asked.

"I call my humble abode 'Fort Sullinger.' It's not much on the outside, but it's got a great burglar alarm system and thick walls. It was a drug-dealer's house. It was forfeited by the government and sold at a public auction on the courthouse steps. I got a good deal on it. The landscaping is one hundred percent natural, all trees and rocks, not to mention the stream. It was too hilly for farming, so this piece of property still has its trees. My bank pretty much owns the place now, but once the mortgage is paid off, Fort Sullinger will be all mine."

Allison Culbertson frowned. "Have you ever thought that maybe too much of your life is centered around violence, Harry? You carry a gun all the time, you've got your own firing range and your house is a fortress. Do you ever think that maybe you overdo it a bit?"

Sullinger regarded her thoughtfully. "I'll tell you something a veteran cop once told me. The world consists of three kinds of people: sheep, wolves, and sheepdogs." He handed her the reloaded

286

clips. "Most people in our society are sheep. I don't mean it in a derogatory way. They're gentle people, good citizens who go about living their lives, oblivious to the wolves in the world. In fact, they often coast along in outright denial, refusing to believe the wolves even exist, in spite of nightly newscasts full of their predatory exploits."

He raised an eyebrow. "I don't mean this as an insult, but *you* were a sheep on the night Joey Red Horse died."

She felt herself blushing.

"On the other hand," he continued, "the world has its share of wolves, people who are just plain mean and evil. They prey on the sheep. When they attack a sheep, it's easy pickings, because the sheep just runs for its life until it is caught and killed. The wolves have nothing to fear from the sheep." He held up his gun. "Then you've got your sheepdogs. They live to protect the sheep. They are warriors. They confront the wolves. Like the wolves, they have sharp teeth and a capacity for violence. The sheepdogs don't back down from the wolves. In fact, they run toward them when they hear them attacking the sheep. Cops are the only people in society who run toward the sound of gunfire, Allison. Every other sane person runs the other way."

He gestured at his firing range, at his house equipped with its burglar alarm system.

"Most of my life is spent preparing to face the wolves. If somebody wants to be a sheep, that's okay by me. We need sheep. They're productive members of society. But that person needs to understand the price he's paying. When the wolf comes to his door, he and his loved ones are going to die if no sheepdog is around to save them. On the other hand, if you want to be a sheepdog, you must make a conscious decision every single day to prepare yourself physically and mentally. You need to be ready for that eventual fight with the wolves, because they won't tell you in advance when they're coming."

They stood in silence for several seconds. It was the longest speech she had ever heard Harry Sullinger make.

"I guess I never thought of it that way," she said.

He grinned at her self-consciously. "I'm teaching you how to be a sheepdog. When the wolf bites the sheepdog, the sheepdog bites right back. You've got to decide for yourself whether you want the burden of being a sheepdog. It is a big responsibility. It's a lot easier to run away from the sound of gunfire." He smiled. "Once you're carrying a gun, you can't just bebop along, oblivious to what's going on around you. You've got to stay alert, always ready to confront the wolves."

He motioned for her to follow him. "Let's move farther back," he said. "We've been shooting from twenty feet, but not all bad guys will considerately position themselves exactly twenty feet from you. Let's try thirty for a while."

Over the next hour, Sullinger introduced her to several different weapons, both revolvers and semiautomatics and even a shotgun. After one shoulder-numbing experience firing a twelve-gauge shotgun, she abandoned the idea of having one in her home. Of all the guns she tried, she kept coming back to the Beretta. Its weight and size felt right for her hand. She was more accurate with it than with the other guns.

"It's what I carry, a Beretta Model 92F Parabellum," Sullinger said. "Many local police departments have gone to Glocks, but I've carried this one for years. I've gotten used to it. Like I said, in a gunfight you want to use a gun you're comfortable with."

"I like it," Allison said, taking out her earplugs. "Will you sell it to me?"

"No. This one is mine. We can order you one exactly like it, though."

"The sooner the better," she said.

Allison examined the handle of the Beretta. "I don't see any notches. I thought you cowboys always put notches on the handle for each villain you killed. I guess you've never killed anybody?"

She was surprised by his silence.

He took off his goggles and wiped his face with a shirtsleeved forearm.

"Yeah, I killed somebody. Two somebodies, to be exact. One of them shot me."

He was quiet for a long time. Allison thought he was getting ready to tell her about it. She was surprised by how much she wanted to know the details. Instead, he ended up shrugging. "I've got a nice scar five inches to the left of my navel. I can show it to you sometime. It's shaped like the country of Panama. But I'm not sure I know you well enough yet to show it to you. Maybe we'll save it for another day?"

Allison nodded. "I'm a long way from being ready to visit Panama, Harry."

She removed her own goggles.

"Actually, at this point I'm just using you for firearms training and to pump you for information about Joey's case."

He smiled. "I'm here to serve and protect."

"So," she said, "tell me about the people you killed? Arch-fiends, I suppose?"

He shook his head.

"Let's talk about them some other time. Right now, wouldn't you rather hear a couple of top-secret tidbits about Joey Red Horse's murder?"

Sullinger opened a small Igloo cooler and handed her a cold Diet Coke. "Can you keep a secret?" he asked.

"Of course I can. Next to billing for time, that's what lawyers do best."

"Well, three things of interest occurred this afternoon. Do you want to hear about firearms testing or telephone records or pottery?"

"Aren't you going to tell me about all three? Do I have to choose?"

"I'll tell you about each of them, but one at a time. Which do you want to hear first?"

"I'll take firearms testing for five hundred, Alex," she said.

Sullinger held up a bullet. "This is a typical nine-millimeter bullet," he said. "Let's call it Exhibit One."

"Okay."

"Note how the bullet consists of separate parts. You have the pointed slug at one end. It speeds through the air and hits the target?"

"Yes, I see the slug."

"And you have the brass shellcasing. It holds the gunpowder and provides the chamber for the explosion that propels the slug forward at a high rate of speed?"

"Yes, I see the brass shellcasing."

"Now, look at the back of the bullet, the flat bottom of the shellcasing. You see the small circle in the middle?"

"Yes."

"That's the primer. The metal end of the firing pin of the gun hits the primer, causes a tiny spark inside the bullet, the gunpowder explodes, and off goes the slug."

He reached down to the ground and picked up an expended shellcasing.

"Remember how the Beretta was ejecting these spent shellcasings as you were firing shot after shot?"

"Yes. They came out of the side of the gun."

"Well, look at the back of the shellcasing."

Allison saw a tiny dent on the primer.

"Look, too, at the little scratches on the sides of the brass shellcasing."

Allison rolled the spent bullet over and over in her hands, examining the tiny marks.

"Every gun is a bit different," Sullinger said. "Each one will leave slightly different tool markings on the shellcasings it ejects. An expert can compare ejected shellcasings to a known gun and can tell whether or not that gun fired that shellcasing."

"Wow, I knew you could do ballistics and compare a slug to see if it had been fired from a particular gun by the markings the barrel would leave on the slug, but I never heard about comparing shellcasings."

"It's done all the time. In fact, our local crime lab is now part of a network called Drug-Fire, where the information from expended shellcasings is entered into a permanent database in a nationwide computer system and compared to shootings from all over the country. You can find out if the shellcasings from your crime scene match ejected shellcasings from shootings elsewhere in the country, or from older shootings in your own jurisdiction."

"Was that done here?"

"Yes."

"Well, don't keep me in suspense. What did you find?"

"The gun that killed Joey Red Horse, a semiautomatic much like this Beretta, was involved in two other shootings during the past three years, one in Los Angeles and one in Miami."

290

"What?"

"Whoever shot Joey Red Horse is probably the same person who shot two drug dealers, one in Los Angeles and one in Miami. At least, the same gun was used. The shooters might have been different people. As I told you before, guns don't kill people, people . . ."

"All right, all right. Same gun. I get the point. But you say these two dead guys were drug dealers? Not peyote, I hope?"

"No, cocaine. Both were known cocaine dealers. The DEA says the cocaine they dealt was especially pure stuff, very high-quality, very high-dollar. They were big-level dealers."

"What do big-time drug dealers from Los Angeles and Miami have in common with little old Joey Red Horse in Cape Girardeau, Missouri?"

"That's what we're trying to find out. We didn't think he swam with such big fish. But there may have been a lot about Joey Red Horse we don't know. What about it? Do you have any ideas?"

"I know Joey used and sold peyote. Since you first asked me about his drug use, I've looked into it some more. I found out Joey would bring peyote back from trips out West and was trying to grow some in his apartment. He'd sell it for ten dollars a pop or a hundred dollars a bag, but apparently this was a small-level operation. You guys didn't find any cocaine in his apartment, did you?"

"No. Just those nasty-looking cactus plants in various stages of development, plus scads of mescal buttons."

"Are major drug dealers like those corpses in Los Angeles and Miami involved in peyote distribution?" Allison asked. "Could the market for peyote be evolving into a big-time thing?"

"The DEA doesn't think so," Sullinger said, "but there's a first time for everything. Maybe Joey was on the cutting edge of some developing trend."

"Wow, this is a shock," Allison said. "Does Bear Smith have any connections to Los Angeles or Miami?"

"Not that we can find."

"What about Clive Faulkner or Rex Tappinger?"

"Nothing."

Allison decided it was time to hear the second bit of big news. "Harry, this time I'll take pottery for two hundred."

"Well, we've got some preliminary news back about that piece of pottery your unknown visitor stuck inside your window last night."

"Oh?"

"It's a fake. I mean, it's real pottery, but it's not really a relic from the Mound Builders. I showed it to Clive Faulkner. He said it didn't come from his museum. He could tell it wasn't ancient, either. He suggested I show it to Diedra Binzinger. I took it to her and she identified it as something she made years ago. She sold it through her store. She's made several just like it. Unfortunately, she didn't have records of any names of people who bought them. Lots go to tourists visiting Cape from one of the vacation boats on the Mississippi."

"So, it's not a priceless relic?"

"No."

"Well, there goes my early retirement. I was hoping it was worth millions and somebody left it for me under my Christmas tree."

"Looks like you'll have to keep your day job."

Allison switched to the last bit of news. "Okay, Harry, I think I'll take phone records for four hundred."

"Well, to phrase it in your *Jeopardy* format, this prominent Native American activist organization in Washington DC received three phone calls from Joey Red Horse's telephone during the month prior to Joey's death."

"Mark Windfoot?" Allison asked.

"Sorry, but you don't get credit for that answer. You didn't phrase it in the form of a question. The correct answer should have been, 'What is ARROW?'"

"You lost me there," Allison said.

"In plain English, we subpoenaed Joey's phone records. They show that he made three calls to ARROW headquarters in Washington DC in the month prior to his death. Now, this only shows that *his* telephone called *their* telephone. It doesn't tell us which human talked with which human. Mark Windfoot denies getting any calls from Joey Red Horse or even knowing him. Windfoot's secretary says they get calls from people all the time, wanting to make donations or ask questions. She often refers callers to

ARROW's webpage. She gets several calls a year from American Indians complaining about Bootheel Man and wanting to make sure ARROW knows about it. She can't recall any of those calls in particular. Who knows? Maybe Joey was just calling as part of the research he was doing."

"That's very possible," Allison said. "He sure knew a lot about the Native American Graves and Repatriation Act. He and Lolita are the ones who educated me."

"So, what do you think?" Sullinger asked. "Is Mark Windfoot lying when he says he didn't know Joey?"

Allison shrugged. "That reminds me," she said. "Windfoot is going to be on the *Ted Stryker Show* tonight. He said to be sure to watch."

Sullinger held up the Beretta. "We have just enough time to shoot another hundred rounds or so, grill some hamburgers, and watch the show with my satellite dish. How does that sound?"

Allison wasn't sure. This came awfully close to being a real date, and this man had been married and divorced five times. That was a lot of emotional baggage.

"I won't show you my scar." Sullinger grinned. "I promise."

"Okay. But only if you can teach me to nail Adolph Hitler with at least ninety-five percent accuracy from thirty yards."

"You've got a date."

That's what she was afraid of.

Chapter 37

The odor of burnt gunpowder still clung to Allison's clothing as she sat in Harry Sullinger's living room, watching the beginning of the *Ted Stryker Show*. Stryker, who prided himself on staking out the most controversial position on any current event, always produced a lively broadcast by bringing on guests with widely divergent viewpoints. Sometimes they physically sat in his studio arguing across a table. Other times they duked it out by satellite hookup. He took obvious pride in the shouting matches he provoked. His formula worked. His show was the highest-rated talk show in America.

As his theme song wound down, Stryker's face filled the television screen. His square face was handsome, but his blow-dried hair was thinning on top.

"I'm Ted Stryker, live from Washington DC. Tonight's 'Strike Out' segment focuses on the ongoing conflict between American Indians and American museums. The issue drew national attention this month because of a Missouri criminal case where a twenty-four-year-old Osage Indian stole a burial relic from a local museum."

Stryker played the KFVS-12 clip of Joey Red Horse standing at the edge of the Bill Emerson Memorial Bridge. As the tape showed Joey gesticulating with the artifact and finally throwing it into the river, Stryker told the story of Joey's theft of Gazing Woman, culminating with the KFVS-12 footage of Joey's breathtaking dive from the bridge. The pictures on screen switched to courtroom shots from the preliminary hearing, with Stryker describing Joey's claim-of-right defense. A close-up shot of Bootheel Man standing in the Heartland Mound Builder Museum took center stage as Stryker explained that the museum's use of the bones and burial relics offended many American Indians. Stryker lamented that Joey's case would never make it to court because the young man had been tragically murdered shortly after his preliminary hearing.

Stryker's face filled the screen again. "Tonight I say to American Indians across the country, just calm down! Get a grip! The battle between the cowboys and Indians has been over for a century! Quit trying to pick a fight! Especially one you can't win!"

The television screen went to a split-screen format. Mark Windfoot was on one side of the screen. Allison's eyes widened with astonishment. Clive Faulkner was on the other side.

"This evening," Ted Stryker was saying, "I'm joined by two experts on this explosive issue, men who have staked out opposite positions on the front lines of this battlefield. Mark Windfoot, President of Angry Reformers Resisting Oppressive Whites, known as ARROW, joins us from the studio here in Washington DC. Clive Faulkner, the Director of the Heartland Mound Builder Museum in Cape Girardeau, Missouri, and author of the book *Alfred Dennison and the Bootheel Man*, joins us by satellite hookup from his museum in Missouri's bootheel."

Stryker's face again filled the screen. "The way I see it, gentlemen, history is important. As a people, we want to know who came before us and what happened in the past. The bones in these mounds are one-thousand years old. No written history tells us who they were or how they lived and died. Particularly in a place like Cahokia, where human sacrifice was practiced and a highly populated city vanished off the face of the earth, things went on in those days that people want to know more about. The only way to find out is archaeology. What's your beef, Mark Windfoot?"

Windfoot's carefully coiffed head and blue-suited torso appeared on one side of the television screen. Stryker was on the other side, thoughtfully stroking his chin.

"My beef? We American Indians find it offensive for our dead to be put on public display. Is that so hard to understand? The Heartland Mound Builder Museum, for instance, features as its main exhibit the skeleton of a dead man, wired together and standing upright in a big glass case, with a stone axe embedded in his skull. This man's bones were resting peacefully in his grave until archaeologists dug him up and put him on public display like a stuffed buffalo. That bothers me."

"Well, I don't know how *peacefully* this guy was resting," Stryker said. "He did have that axe in his head, after all." Windfoot was replaced by Clive Faulkner on the television screen. Faulkner was wearing his tweed sport coat and his bow tie. He had not had time to rearrange the clutter on his desk.

"What a mess," Sullinger said. "You'd think a guy who knew he was going to be on national television would at least clean off his desk a bit, put the junk on the floor, anyway."

Allison felt oddly defensive. "He's really busy."

"Thinking great thoughts, no doubt." Sullinger rolled his eyes.

"Tell me, Clive Faulkner," Stryker was saying, "what kind of huckster digs up the bones of a dead man and puts them on display? Why aren't you just as much a grave robber as someone who might sneak into Arlington National Cemetery tonight and dig up a president or a general?"

"You hit it on the head earlier, Ted," Faulkner said. "Whoever Bootheel Man was, he died ten centuries ago. From his mound and from other archaeological digs throughout the Midwest over the past ten decades, we've learned for a fact that America was populated with a huge number of people long before Columbus got here. We've learned these people were American Indians, not some tribe of Europeans who happened to wander over here. We've learned they built great cities and accumulated detailed knowledge of astronomy and agriculture, that their corn-growing farming operations fed thousands of people, and that they built temples that rivaled the pyramids of Egypt. We wouldn't know any of this if we just said, 'Oops, this is a grave. Let's go dig someplace else.'"

"Oh, he's thrown a strike, Mark Windfoot," Stryker said. "A high, hard one! How do you respond to that?"

Now both Clive Faulkner and Mark Windfoot appeared onscreen, side by side, each facing the camera. Both were calm and collected. Allison wasn't sure she would have been able to stay so cool.

Windfoot was patiently speaking directly into the camera: "Many Native American religions believe that when a person's bones have been tampered with, his spirit's journey through the afterworld is interrupted, and he's thereby spiritually harmed. So we're not just talking about hurt feelings. We believe significant injury is occurring here, and we don't believe curiosity justifies grave robbery."

296

"There's a strike," Stryker crowed.

"Archaeology is not just idle curiosity," Faulkner interrupted. "It's trying to understand the world and its past. Newton may have been curious why the apple fell from the tree, but his research into gravity went far beyond mere curiosity. All branches of science are essentially a search for truth."

Windfoot snorted. "It's all physics envy. The greatest archaeologist in the world can't hold a candle to Isaac Newton. You archaeologists aren't espousing a real science like physics or chemistry, dealing with equations that can be proven over and over again. Your field is mere speculation and guesswork. Your research methodology consists of poking through the remains of dead human beings, as if you were worms. But you, Faulkner, you're the worst of the lot, because the Heartland Mound Builder Museum is the most egregious example. You aren't just studying Bootheel Man, you're putting him on public display like a freak at a carnival and charging money to see him. I'll bet you've made a fortune off his bones."

Ted Stryker's voice cut in. "Physics envy, that's good! We'll call that a strike! Tell me, Clive Faulkner. What would you do if someone conclusively proved through DNA or some other reliable method of scientific evidence that he was a direct descendant of Bootheel Man and that the exhibit offended him, and he wanted to take his ancestor out of the museum and rebury him? Would you do it? Would you take it down?"

"Absolutely. But that's the whole point. *Nobody* can say Bootheel Man is his direct ancestor. All this garbage about how would you feel if your grandmother or a Holocaust victim were put on display is just hyperbole. This is *ancient* history we're talking about, not somebody's grandma. All archaeologists agree that any bones of known relatives should be returned to provable descendants. The disagreement is over what to do with remains when no living person can demonstrate any direct kinship. The goal of organizations like ARROW is to strip museums of all their American Indian artifacts."

Ted Stryker threw another question to Windfoot.

"What about it, Mark Windfoot, don't American Indians want to know who these Mound Builders were?"

"We already know who they were. Our oral traditions tell us. True Native Americans know we inhabited this land from the beginning of time. We don't need some two-bit archaeologist to tell us the same thing."

"Clive Faulkner? One last comment from you?" Stryker said.

"If the question is whether to seek knowledge or to make a deliberate choice to remain ignorant of the ancient past, then I choose knowledge," Faulkner said.

"Strike two! Mark Windfoot? Your last word?"

"ARROW is committed to closing every single private museum that still displays human bones of American Indians. We may do it by legislation or by public pressure or by boycotts or sit-ins or lawsuits. I applaud what the late Joey Red Horse did, even though his actions may technically have constituted a crime. I'm glad to say that in every state of the Union, our organization has developed strong ties to dedicated lawyers like Allison Culbertson, Joey's lawyer. These bright, young attorneys are willing to fight against the injustice of desecrating human burials, in the same way Thurgood Marshall and his dedicated young lawyers fought the good fight nationwide against racial discrimination."

Allison's mouth dropped open.

"Strong ties?" Sullinger said.

"One phone conversation," Allison muttered, wondering if any of her old law-school professors were watching. That was pretty heady stuff, being compared to Thurgood Marshall on national television. She wished she had recorded the show.

Ted Stryker was summing up. "Ladies and gentlemen, you've heard both sides, and I'm ready to make my call. Mark Windfoot, strike three for you! I side with the quest for knowledge. The best point of the night went to Clive Faulkner, when he said that as a society, we are not ready to say, 'Oops, this is a grave, let's go dig someplace else.' No, sir, it is a choice between knowledge and ignorance, and I side with knowledge. Sorry, Mark Windfoot, but you have struck out!"

As the *Ted Stryker Show* moved into its national news bloopers segment, Sullinger flicked off the television.

"Man, you couldn't pay me to go on that show," he said. "Imagine listening to that arrogant blowhard telling you you'd just struck out."

"I'm sort of surprised Clive Faulker agreed to it," Allison said. "I thought he was seriously considering turning over the bones in his museum to American Indians."

Sullinger snorted.

"Well, if he is, he did a good job of hiding his intentions. Maybe they're buried somewhere in that mess on his desk."

Chapter 38

Allison Culbertson was reading the police reports in a new client's shoplifting case when Rita buzzed her that Clive Faulkner was calling.

She felt a surprising jolt of adrenaline as she answered the phone. "I saw you on the *Ted Stryker Show* last night," she said. "You came across as quite the impassioned zealot. What happened to your big talk about giving serious thought to taking the bones out of your museum?"

He chuckled. "Nice to talk to you, too, Allison. Going on that show was a last-minute thing. Somebody else canceled on them. They called and I said I'd do it. They wanted me to give the museum's side of the issue. That's what I did. Doesn't mean I'm still not considering everything we discussed. I still promise I'm going to take the matter up with the Board of Directors. Obviously, I couldn't talk about it on national TV before I find out what the Board wants to do."

Allison felt her irritation melt. "I don't know why you even went on a show like that. His whole 'Strike Out' segment is pure sensationalism. He goads people into arguing and then insults them by telling them they've struck out. I can't believe you did it."

"Well, I suppose you notice how I managed to get my book mentioned on national television. Hopefully, I'll see a spike in sales. Plus, Windfoot was the one who struck out, not me. I could tell the moment the producer called that Stryker agreed with my viewpoint, so the risk that I would be ridiculed coast-to-coast seemed pretty small. I did take a couple of nasty shots from Windfoot, though. The guy's a real jerk."

"I can't say I agreed with the content of what you said, but you looked good," Allison said.

"Thanks."

"Except for your desk."

He chuckled again. "It would have been intellectually dishonest for me to clean it off. As you know, my desk can't be called uncluttered."

"So, why are you calling? Did you just want to make sure I saw you on the Stryker show? Are you fishing for compliments?"

"No. I'm extending another invitation."

"Oh?"

"This Friday is the annual 'Mound Builder Days' festival at the museum. Each year we invite sixth-graders from area schools to spend half a day at the museum. We bring in volunteers and extra staff to run the program. The kids tour the museum in small groups with specially trained tour guides. They watch a documentary about the Mound Builders. They watch an artist making pottery the same way the Mound Builders made it. They study our authentic woodhenge while an astrologer explains to them how it works. They eat beef jerky, popcorn, and corn soup. They compete in a Mound Builder Trivia Bowl. The day ends with athletes from each school participating in a chunkey tournament on our replica chunkey field."

"All that in half a day?"

"We operate with an efficiency Disney would envy. We've been doing this since Alfred Dennison thought it up before Disney World even existed. So, will you come? I still need an emcee for the trivia bowl and another referee for the chunkey game."

"You're putting me to work?"

"If you'll do it."

"Why not? I don't have court on Friday. Put me down as one of the chunkey-game refs. Of course, somebody will need to explain the rules to me first."

"Don't worry. I'll get you a copy of the rules manual, the referee training video, and your uniform."

"Uniform?"

"Yeah. We have our refs wear white- and black-striped outfits like football referees. It gives the feel of a real sporting event. The kids really get into it. The chunkey game is explained to them in the documentary earlier in the day, and each school chooses its own team. It can get pretty competitive. It's probably the most fun the kids have all day, next to gawking at Bootheel Man, of course."

Allison did not particularly like the thought of wearing a referee's uniform.

"Maybe I'll be the emcee of the trivia-bowl thing instead. You don't put the emcee in a uniform, do you?"

"Matter of fact, we do. The emcee wears traditional Mound Builder attire. If it's a man, he wears a breechcloth and leggings. If it's chilly, he gets a fur robe, too. A woman wears a traditional Native American dress. In real life, the native women went topless in warm weather, but we provide a blouse for our costume. These are sixth-graders, after all."

"I'll stick with the ref's outfit."

The weather was perfect for Mound Builder Days. It was a warm, sunny September day. Allison arrived at the museum parking lot fully prepared. She had studied the referee training video, memorized the rule book, and, in general, felt ready to referee a sporting event she had never played. Her only consolation was that none of the contestants would have ever played the sport, either, so bad calls might not be recognized.

Allison felt a bit self-conscious as she parked her Jeep Cherokee and walked toward the museum in her referee outfit. She saw kids staring at her from buses pulling onto the lot. Jackson, Sikeston, Carbondale, Poplar Bluff, Paducah, New Madrid, Ste. Genevieve; these kids were coming from all over.

The first person Allison met upon entering the museum was Marge Tappinger, dressed in American Indian attire, greeting people at the front door. She wore a nametag identifying herself as the President of the museum's Board of Directors.

"Why, Miss Culbertson, it's so nice to see you," she gushed. "Thank you for helping us out."

As they shook hands, Joey Red Horse's former lover leaned forward and whispered to Allison, "I need to talk to you. Maybe I can catch you for a private moment later in the day?"

"Sure," Allison said, disengaging her hand and pulling away as Marge Tappinger launched into an effusive greeting to a class of kids from Sparta, Illinois. The children were giddy with excitement. Allison could barely remember what it was like to be that age on a field trip. It had been a long time since she had giggled, she reflected.

302

Marge Tappinger was consulting a clipboard. She checked a form and directed the noisy kids toward the auditorium.

Clive Faulkner appeared at Allison's side and shook her hand warmly. "Allison, thanks again for doing this. You look . . ." he shook his head and shrugged, "like a zebra, actually, but a really good-looking zebra."

"Yeah, well, the outfit's your fault. I hold you personally responsible for any negative feedback I receive."

He took her by the elbow. "The kids all start out in the auditorium for an orientation session and documentary video. From there they'll break into groups for smaller sessions at different stations. Let me escort you to your domain—the chunkey field."

As more sixth-graders entered the museum from various schools, the noise level continued to grow.

"This is a big deal, isn't it?" Allison marveled.

"Always has been. Two schools cancelled out this year, though: St. Mary's and Perryville. They got scared off by all the bad publicity about Joey Red Horse. They begged off to show their sensitivity toward American Indians."

"Maybe they'll come back next year if you repatriate the skeletons."

"That's exactly what the principals said."

When they went outside and passed the pottery station, Allison noticed Diedra Binzinger manning that particular exhibit. Her reproduction of an ancient covered fire was already baking one work-in-progress while she was busily making another from her reddish clay. When the artist glanced up, she glared at Allison. Or maybe she was glaring at Clive Faulkner, and Allison was an innocent bystander struck by a stray hate vibe.

"Looks like somebody has some hard feelings," Allison said softly when they were out of earshot.

"She didn't take our breakup well," Faulkner said. "To her credit, though, she was still willing to help out the museum today. She's done this many times. Her session is always one of the most popular. Kids love pottery. She even carved the chunkey stones you'll be using today. Exact replicas."

"You know, Clive, speaking of replicas, somebody threw one of her pieces of pottery through my window the other night."

"I know. Harry Sullinger told me. He showed it to me. It looked like one of hers, but I wasn't sure. I suggested he talk to her."

"He did. She identified it as one she made, but said she's done a bunch just like it and sold them through her gallery. She apparently doesn't keep specific records of the names of people who buy her work."

"Well, she's painted hundreds of pictures and made thousands of pieces of pottery, lots with Native American themes. I wouldn't expect her to remember who bought each one."

"Can you think of any reason why *she* would leave it at my house?" Allison asked.

"Diedra? No. She's not the confrontational type. Even if she were jealous of you, she'd avoid you rather than harass you."

"Jealous? Why would she be jealous of me?"

"Well, you're beautiful, you're smart, you're successful, and maybe I've let it slip a time or two how much I admire you. Who knows? Maybe she thinks I have a thing for you."

He was studying her face, obviously hoping for a response. She didn't give him one.

The chunkey field was located in the middle of a flat grassy plaza at the back of the museum. The plaza was a square, fifty yards in diameter. The chunkey field itself was made of hard, packed clay, much like the dirt of a baseball infield, but firmer. It was one hundred feet long and fifteen feet wide. It reminded Allison of a triple-wide bowling alley with no gutters.

Allison knew the chunkey rules from watching the training video and from studying the rule book. She'd also watched the documentary the children would be shown, so she knew beforehand exactly what they had been taught about the game. Each team would consist of five players. One from each team would take positions next to each other at the starting line at one end of the chunkey alley. Each held a six-foot-long pole, made from a broom handle with a weight at one end. The weight was a hollow cylinder of rock slipped over the pole and fastened to it about six inches from one end. A server from one of the teams would roll the chunkey stone down the middle of the hard-packed field. Both contestants would throw their poles at the rolling chunkey stone. A direct hit was worth two points. If neither hit it, the pole ending up closest to the place where the stone came to rest was worth one point. If the server rolled the chunkey stone out of bounds, the other team got two points. The game would go through five rounds, until each teammate had faced off against an opponent from the other team. Each player had to take at least one turn serving. At the end, the team with the most points won. It sounded pretty uncomplicated to Allison.

She was surprised and pleased when she recognized the other referee. He also appeared a bit self-conscious in his referee getup.

"He got you, too, huh?" Harry Sullinger said.

"I believe you two know each other," Faulkner smiled. "Back at that preliminary hearing, I seem to recall that she went a bit easier on you than she did on me."

"Yeah, her bark's worse than her bite," Sullinger said.

"You just better watch out, buddy," Allison said. "You might get a chunkey stone in your ear."

Sullinger's bodybuilder physique was popping out of the black-and white-striped shirt.

"Good thing the museum didn't try to give us one-size-fits-all uniforms," she said. His shirt had to be four times the size of hers.

"I'm not sure they didn't," Sullinger said, pulling at the neck of his jersey to make it less tight.

"You guys need any last-minute pointers?" Faulkner asked. "As you know, the kids will come to you throughout the morning in groups from each school. Line them up and get them playing. You'll have just twenty minutes per school. At the end, the teacher will choose the five athletes who'll represent that school in the tournament. In the duffel bag over there we have five jerseys for you to hand out to each team. The jerseys are in their school colors and have the school names on the back."

"How'd you come up with the rules, anyway?" Sullinger asked. "After all, no Mound Builders were left to write your manual."

"You didn't watch the documentary, did you?" Faulkner said.

Sullinger winced.

"Caught me. I read the manual and watched the referee train-ing video. I thought the documentary was maybe an optional thing."

"It was, but on it I explained how we came up with our rules. Many American Indian tribes were still playing a variant of chunkey when the Europeans arrived on the continent, so written accounts really exist about the game. The rules varied from place to place, though. In some tribes, one of the throwers rolled the chunkey stone before throwing at it himself. In other places, the contestants didn't actually try to hit the chunkey stone but rather threw their poles to the place where they thought it would land. We experimented with different versions of the rules. Quite frankly, we came up with a version that is the most fun to play."

"I'm ready to rumble," Sullinger said, flexing his muscles. "Bring on the kids."

"You're a ref, not a contestant," Allison said.

"Right."

Faulkner was smiling as he headed back inside to give his opening remarks to the students.

"Was he grinning because he's having so much fun or because he's so pleased to put us in these zebra suits?" Sullinger asked.

"I was wondering the same thing myself," Allison said.

To her horror, she saw a photographer from the *Southeast Missourian* approaching.

The morning passed quickly. The children grasped the game instantly, and even developed individualized strategy. Under the rules, the two contestants could chase the chunkey stone for the first twenty feet, but had to stop at the twenty-foot line. They couldn't throw at the chunkey stone until it had crossed that line. Some chose to go for the all-or-nothing strategy of running as fast as they could to stay close to the rolling stone and throwing at it immediately after it crossed the twenty-foot line, going for a direct hit. There was an advantage to this approach, because if two players actually hit the stone, only the first one to hit it would get the points. Others held back, though, waiting to see if the opponent scored a direct hit. If the opponent missed, it was often easy for the more patient player to pick up an easy point by throwing the pole nearest the place where the stone came to rest. Sullinger began calling this strategy the "girlie" plan.

Allison was glad she brought her tube of sunblock, because as the morning wore on, the September sunshine grew brighter and brighter and hotter and hotter. She and the big detective both worked up sweats. It was hard work teaching the kids the fundamental skills. It was logistically difficult to make sure nobody stepped over the starting line too soon or crossed the twenty-foot line before throwing, while keeping a close eye on the rolling stone to tell whether a pole actually touched it. Normally, the stone would go down when hit, but a nick didn't always knock it over.

The photographer from the newspaper seemed to particularly like the chunkey game. He must have taken fifty pictures. With strands of sweaty hair hanging down the sides of her face, Allison dreaded tomorrow's edition.

At one point during the morning, Marge Tappinger approached Allison, obviously itching to talk. When she noticed Harry Sullinger, she turned and retreated back inside the museum. Whatever she had to say could apparently wait for a more private moment.

At midmorning, a museum volunteer in a blue jersey brought Allison a pan of popcorn. It was called "Mound-O-Corn" and was sold in the gift shop. It reminded her of the Jiffy-Pop she'd made as a kid. For both products, you started out with a covered aluminum pan with a handle and jiggled it over a heat source. Within minutes, the popcorn inside popped and forced the thin aluminum cover into a big, popcorn-filled sphere the size of a soccer ball.

The kids were getting all the free popcorn, beef jerky, corn soup, and soda they could hold. Allison had to admit it would be a fun day for a twelve-year-old.

Many of the sixth-graders were carrying around little plastic skulls with axes embedded in them. When she got a chance, she borrowed one from a Kennett student.

"Where'd you get this?" she asked.

"We all got them. Free."

Allison examined it closely. About the size of a Barbie-doll head, it was made of cheap plastic. It was actually a good replica of Bootheel Man's head, even down to the crack in the skull around the axe. Allison was not surprised to find an advertisement for the museum in tiny writing, molded on the inside of the skull.

The climax of the day proved to be the chunkey tournament. The sixteen schools were set up in a single-elimination bracket, the losers of each round being knocked out of the tournament. The last team standing would win a trophy and have its picture taken.

The photo of the winners would be framed and added to those already on a wall in the museum. The kids knew they had the chance to have their picture added to the museum wall. The photos went back more than seventy-five years. Allison spotted the current mayor of Cape Girardeau grinning as a victorious sixth-grader in one of the black and white photos from a long-ago September afternoon. Rush Limbaugh, the radio talk-show host, was in another. He had been talking when the photo was taken.

It was interesting to watch the different methods used by teachers to select the teams. After scouting the talent, some would simply name the five members of the team. Others would select a captain and delegate the team selection to that student. Others would let the class do a quick vote to choose their representatives.

The chunkey field was roped off on all sides to prevent spectators from crowding so close to the chunkey alley that they might be struck by a thrown pole. Four-hundred students and teachers vied for positions behind the ropes, positioning themselves for a good view of the action.

At first, Allison was nervous, afraid she would blow a call. Harry Sullinger took the position near the starting line. His responsibility included making sure nobody stepped over one of the lines, as well as watching for a direct hit on the chunkey stone. Allison was more of an outfield judge, looking for direct hits on the chunkey stone and using a tape measure to make the call as to which pole was closer to the stone, if she couldn't tell by her naked eye.

Another volunteer manned the scoreboard, using the same white-on-black rectangular numbers manufactured for little league scoreboards.

As the bracket narrowed, the intensity level of the crowd grew. Children from different schools quickly picked favorite players on the remaining teams and rooted loudly for them. At the end, the championship game came down to Cape Girardeau versus Jackson.

"This is perfect!" Allison heard the newspaper photographer tell someone. "Their football teams are playing each other this weekend. It's the biggest rivalry of the year. Now the sixth-graders can give us a preview of the big game. My editor's going to love this."

Both the Cape Girardeau and Jackson teams reached the finals because of one particularly outstanding player on each team. The Cape Girardeau star was a slender blonde girl who wore her hair in a ponytail. She took the strategy of tearing pell-mell after the chunkey stone and launching a vicious strike at it as soon as possible. So far, she had hit it every time. Her counterpart on the Jackson team was a cherubic-faced black boy, who employed the same strategy and was every bit as accurate. In the championship match, each team saved its best player for last.

When it came down to the final match-up, the score was tied 3 to 3. Cape had scored its points by one direct hit and one closest-to-the-stone. Jackson had scored its points by one closest-to-the-stone and one out-of-bounds throw by Cape.

With the score tied, the Jackson server took the stone and rubbed it with her jersey. Both the girl from Cape and the boy from Jackson waited expectantly, their backs to the server, their poles clutched in their hands.

The server raced forward and propelled the chunkey stone into a perfectly straight and incredibly fast roll down the middle of the chunkey alley. The throwers raced wildly behind it.

They threw their poles at exactly the same moment. Allison watched closely as the two poles sped toward the rolling stone. The Cape player's pole was orange. The Jackson player's pole was red. They descended on the stone like guided missiles. One struck the top of the stone and sent it flying. The other skimmed over the top of the pole that struck the stone, but didn't seem to touch the stone.

Allison stood frozen in place as she watched the poles skitter to their stops while the chunkey stone spun a dying circle.

Which pole hit it?

The poles were close in color. The orange was a dark shade, almost red. They looked a lot alike.

Allison glanced at Harry Sullinger for help.

He shook his head, almost imperceptibly, but clearly indicating to her that he had no idea which pole hit the chunkey stone and didn't want to be involved in making the call.

The wild cheering of the large crowd died to a murmur as all eyes turned to Allison.

She walked to the chunkey stone and picked it up. Maybe a paint transfer would give a clue. No such luck.

Oh, well, it's just a game, she thought. She picked up the red Jackson pole.

"Two points for Jackson," she announced. "Direct hit."

The blonde-haired girl from Cape Girardeau burst into tears. "It's not fair!" she cried. "I hit it!"

Her four orange-jerseyed teammates clustered around her, consoling their distraught star, and giving Allison malevolent looks.

The rest of the Cape Girardeau students, in a remarkable display of bad sportsmanship, began booing Allison vigorously. They were soon joined by students from other schools.

Teachers were scolding students, trying to stop the booing, but the noise level grew in intensity as sympathetic children watched the girl from Cape Girardeau crying her eyes out. The booing intensified even more when the scorekeeper put up the final score, Jackson 5, Cape 3.

Students cupped their hands to their mouths, lustily booing, really putting effort into achieving maximum boo-volume. Their eyes were flashing disgust and malice at her. It was a new sensation for Allison. She couldn't recall ever being quite so unpopular.

The *Southeast Missourian* photographer was shooting pictures of Allison and the irate crowd. Allison tried her best not to look sweaty, hot, tired, befuddled, and irritated. Her efforts were unsuccessful.

"I made my call," Allison said, in a voice barely audible above the chorus of soprano boos. "The game is over."

At least they're not throwing things. As soon as the thought occurred to her, she checked to make sure it was still true. Those plastic skulls could hurt if thrown hard enough, and every kid had one. She hoped they didn't think of it.

A Jackson teacher was approaching her. The black boy in his red jersey was at her side. He was looking at Allison, shyly.

310

The crowd quieted as the pair reached her.

"Timmy has something he'd like to tell you," the teacher said.

The boy squared his small shoulders and looked up at her.

"Ma'am, I missed the chunkey stone. The Cape girl's the one hit it."

Allison shook his hand.

"Thank you, young man, for being so honest," she said. She put up her arms in the parallel signal used to show a touchdown in football.

"Correction!" she yelled. "Direct hit by Cape Girardeau. Cape wins 5 to 3."

As the sixth-graders yelled their approval, the score on the scoreboard was changed.

Harry Sullinger sauntered close to her and said, "What's with the touchdown signal? I didn't see that in the rule book."

"I made it up. It seemed appropriate."

"By the way," he said. "The gun shop called. Your Beretta's in. For a minute I was thinking you'd be needing it today. I didn't know sixth-graders could be so fierce. I gotta tell you, you were gonna be on your own. I wasn't sticking around to get my butt kicked by a bunch of irate twelve-year-olds."

"My hero," she said.

Chapter 39

Allison Culbertson let her hand dangle from the passenger side of Clive Faulkner's metallic red Mercedes-Benz convertible as they sped along Highway 3 in Illinois, zipping over a scenic stretch of blacktop road running along a ridge crest parallel to and overlooking the Mississippi River. They were heading for the Wickliffe Mounds State Historical Site, located in the hilly lowlands where the sharp point of Kentucky tickled Missouri's Bootheel. The site was forty-one miles from Cape Girardeau, a one-hour drive.

Allison opened her palm and felt the breeze beating against her hand. It felt good. Refreshing. Then she remembered the newspaper article.

She had resisted the temptation for several miles, but for the third time, Allison succumbed to an overwhelming urge. She brought her hand back into the car and opened the glove compartment. She pulled out the morning's *Southeast Missourian* newspaper and studied her photograph. It was, indeed, every bit as awful as she had feared.

The picture must have been snapped at the very moment Allison was telling the irate crowd that she was not going to change her call, right before the Jackson teacher and the honest student had convinced her to do so. Allison's sweaty face and torso took up the entire left side of the photo. She was brandishing the chunkey stone and speaking over her shoulder to the irate crowd of kids. Booing children filled the right side of the picture, many with hands cupped to their mouths, savaging her with gusto. All bore cross and irate expressions on otherwise cherubic faces.

"No one looks good when a picture is taken while they're talking," Clive Faulkner said consolingly, without looking away from the road. "People understand that."

In the photograph, Allison's mouth looked like Mick Jagger's distorted lips caught in full screeching howl during a Rolling Stones concert. It was unbelievably large and grotesquely twisted. Sweaty strands of hair hung down over her forehead, unruly renegades escaping from her worthless twisty, adding to an image of

312

general dishevelment. It was not a good look. And her eyes! You just don't have an attractive expression on your face when you're being booed by belligerent preteens. She hoped she hadn't really looked so angry in person. To top things off, holding up the chunkey stone had caused the oversized referee's jersey to gape open at the neck. Her bra strap and an alarming amount of bare skin showed.

"Besides," Faulkner added, "the black bra goes really well with the ref outfit. I'm sure that's why the editors chose that picture. You're just lucky the headline writers didn't think of a pun having to do with mounds."

She shot him a glare. "You really *don't* want me to ref one of your chunkey games again, do you?"

"Of course I do," he chuckled. "It's the first time Mound Builder Days ever made the top half of the front page."

"Well, then, stifle yourself. You're not helping my disposition."

She stared again at the newspaper. "I can't believe they put it on the front page," she said. "Wasn't there bigger news going on somewhere in the world yesterday?"

"Bra straps and cleavage sell newspapers," Faulkner said.

"I'm warning you. Don't say another word."

The color photograph was prominently featured on the left side of the page. The large headline on the right read: FUNKY CHUNKEY CALL!

"Listen to this first paragraph," Allison said with indignation. She read aloud: "Allison Culbertson, well-known local attorney, may choose to stay in the comparative safety of the courtroom from now on. In a volunteer stint as a referee for the chunkey tournament at Mound Builder Days at the Heartland Mound Builder Museum's annual field trip for area sixth-graders, she was vociferously booed after making a bad call. 'I knew she blew the call,' Harry Sullinger, the other referee, said afterward, 'but it isn't every day you get to see a lawyer undergo such thorough public castigation. I was enjoying the moment so much I kept my mouth shut.'"

Faulkner grinned. "You know, if they hadn't got that quote from Sullinger, they wouldn't have had much of a story."

"Yeah, he really did me a favor there," Allison said. "I guarantee you he had no clue which pole hit the chunkey stone."

"Those who talk to the press write the first draft of history," Faulkner said.

Allison silently reread the entire article. Most of it simply talked about Mound Builder Days and the Heartland Mound Builder Museum, but the reporter and editors used Allison's bad call to begin and end the story. Nothing like a little humor to liven up a human-interest bit, particularly at the expense of a lawyer.

"They end it with that other clever Sullinger witticism," she said. "'They obviously hired her for her looks, not her eyesight.'"

"Well, he got that right," Faulkner said. "I don't care a whit about your eyesight. Mine's not perfect, either."

Allison folded up the newspaper and shoved it back into the glove compartment.

"So," she said, settling into the bucket seat, "are you still giving serious thought to voluntarily repatriating the bones and burial relics from the Heartland Museum?"

She glanced at Clive Faulkner. His chiseled profile stared straight ahead.

"I promise you, it's a real possibility. My meeting with the Board of Directors is next week. Like I told you when I invited you on today's trip, I want to see firsthand how the Wickliffe Mounds site is handling these things. They removed the real bones from their museum several years ago."

"They must have a very progressive museum director," Allison said. "I can hardly wait to meet him."

"She's off today," Faulkner said. "You'll have to make do with me."

The Wickliffe Mounds State Historical Site was smaller than Allison had expected. Its well-manicured cluster of green, grassy hills and small buildings nestled upon a sloping hillside, surrounded by a thick and shady expanse of densely wooded forest. It reminded her of a tree-lined fairway at a secluded golf course. The entire Wickliffe site could have fit underneath Cahokia's Monk's Mound, like gum on the bottom of a shoe. The park was tiny by comparison, but welcoming and accessible. Peaceful and pretty, its mounds were a gentle and attractive part of the hilly landscape, rather than awe-inspiring earthworks. The overall feeling was a sense of nature's beauty, of a trip into unspoiled Midwestern wilderness.

Three of the mounds featured small buildings cutting into them, allowing visitors to walk inside and study the excavations at the heart of each mound. Inside the mounds, the air was cool and smelled earthy.

Clive Faulkner proved to be an exceptional tour guide as he led Allison through the Wickliffe Mounds site. They first took a neatly tended asphalt path to the top of the largest mound and enjoyed a panoramic view of the two platform mounds, the eight smaller mounds, and the central plaza area, now the site of the Visitor Center and parking lot. Faulkner pointed west, toward the Mississippi River. Allison could barely glimpse snippets of its distant blue surface between the branches of thickly foliaged trees.

"Like Cahokia and Cape Girardeau, the mounds here were built near the river. This site is three miles downstream from the confluence of the Mississippi and Ohio Rivers. The village at this spot was occupied from 1100 to 1350 A.D. It was nowhere near the size of Cahokia. It probably had a population of three hundred people. This whole area around the mound would have been packed with homes. But like the sites at Cape Girardeau and Cahokia, all traces of this village were completely gone by the time Europeans came through."

"Who discovered this place?" Allison asked, still surprised by the thick, vine-filled woods surrounding the small site of the former ancient village. The whole place had an uncivilized feel to it, as if the forest was reclaiming the site.

"Much like the Heartland Mound Builder Museum, this one started out as a completely private operation," Faulkner said. "In 1932, a man named Fain King, from Paducah, bought the property. He used his own money to finance the archaeological work. Over the next decade, he and his wife, Blanche, carefully dug up parts of the mounds and found hundreds of artifacts and human skeletons. They continued their excavations for years and turned it into a tourist attraction called the Ancient Buried City."

"Did Fain King and Alfred Dennison know each other?" Allison asked.

"King came to see him shortly before Dennison died. Even though there was a big age difference, and, in a way, they were competitors as well as colleagues, they had a high degree of mutual respect."

"How long did Fain King work the site?"

"Until 1946, when he donated the 'Ancient Buried City' to a Paducah hospital. Later, in 1983, the hospital gave it to Murray State University. Finally, in 2004, the University turned it over to the State of Kentucky. It's now part of the Kentucky State Department of Parks. It's listed on the National Register of Historic Places and is considered Kentucky's first archaeological landmark."

They made their way down the grassy slope of the mound and Faulkner led her to a tan building with a green roof. Its sign read: "Lifeways."

Inside, he guided her past a large mural to an exhibit featuring a pottery bowl. "See the design on the side of that bowl?" he said.

"Yes."

"Its design is a perfect match to several made at Cahokia. The shards and tools at the Cahokia site lead us to believe these bowls were actually made at Cahokia. One just like it was found with Bootheel Man in Cape Girardeau, and this one was found down here at Wickliffe. There's really no doubt that the villages here and at Cape were in direct contact with Cahokia. In my opinion, the ruler at Cahokia was the ruler over all of the villages along the Mississippi."

"I know. Like Napoleon or Caesar. I've heard this speech before."

They walked a few feet forward on the wooden-plank floor and paused in front of a glass case containing several pieces of pottery.

"Look at that one," Faulkner said. "It's probably the most famous artifact from this site, the owl effigy."

Allison leaned closer, studying the piece. It was a circular pot the size of a bowling ball, but its head and legs and tail made it an owl. The tennis-ball-sized head featured large eyes, a pointed beak, and stubby ears.

"I wonder how old it is," Allison said. "What would you guess? One-thousand years?"

"Closer to twenty."

"Twenty thousand!"

"No, twenty. It's just a replica. The original was stolen by burglars in 1988. Never been recovered. No doubt, the owl pot is now part of the private collection of some wealthy and unscrupulous collector."

"Well, you can't pin *that* one on Joey," Allison said. "That was before his time."

When they finished studying the arrowheads, drill points, grinding tools, and other items in the Lifeways exhibit, Faulkner touched her arm. "Now, let's go to the part we really came for," Faulker said, "the Cemetery Building. Let's see the Wickliffe equivalent of Bootheel Man."

They went outside and made their way to another small, tan building. Like the rest, it cut into the side of a mound, letting the visitors enter into its ancient depths.

Inside the Cemetery Building, they stood on a wooden walkway, hands on a wooden rail, looking down at an excavated area where numerous skeletons lay at various angles, each on its back in an unearthed grave, each buried amid various pieces of pottery and mussel shells. They looked like they were laid out on butcher blocks, since the diggers had dug deeper on all sides of each grave, leaving the skeletons lying on rectangular slabs of earth.

"This is every bit as creepy as Bootheel Man," Allison said, looking away from the graves and studying Faulkner's handsome face. Surely this was not the reaction he had been seeking.

"Good! That's wonderful."

"You are warped," she said.

He laughed. "No, I mean it's good news you found these skeletons appalling because they aren't real skeletons. Since this isn't a private site, anymore, Wickliffe had to comply with NAGPRA. They removed all the real skeletons and replaced them with plastic ones. They arranged them in exactly the same positions the real ones formerly occupied. They're obvious fakes to me, but I'm glad a lay person like you didn't immediately notice a difference."

Allison let her gaze wander over the plastic skeletons.

"What did they do with the real ones?"

"They're working with American Indian tribes to repatriate them."

Allison moved to a display on a wall of the building and read about the efforts of the Wickliffe site to repatriate its human remains. Apparently, it was still a work in progress. Clearly, though, the eventual goal was to return the human skeletons to final resting places. If only Bootheel Man had the same thing in store for him.

Outside, in the bright sunshine, they walked back to the top of the highest mound, the "Ceremonial Mound."

Clive Faulker took off his glasses and rubbed his eyes. "So, Allison, what do you think?"

"Of the park? Well, I have to admit, it doesn't have the Disney World feel of the Heartland Mound Builder Museum. But maybe crass commercialism isn't always a good thing."

Faulkner slipped his glasses into his pocket. "They've operated on a shoestring budget compared to us," he said. "They've done a professional job, though. Fain King was a talented amateur archaeologist, but he didn't have the marketing genius of Alfred Dennison, so this place never developed into nearly the tourist attraction of my museum. But you can learn a lot of history by visiting here. There's something to be said for its comfortable feel."

Allison studied his face. Without his glasses, he was quite possibly the most handsome man she had ever seen. "You could replace Bootheel Man with a replica and still keep the Heartland Mound Builder Museum a world-class attraction, Clive. Those plastic skeletons in the Cemetery Mound look plenty real. People would still flock to your museum even if your Bootheel Man was just a replica."

He shook his head, sadly. "I don't think they would, Allison. I'm convinced a large percentage of our visitors are coming specifically to see Bootheel Man. They want to see that stone axe embedded in his skull. They've heard about it. They've read about it. Now they want to see it for themselves. You've been in my museum. You've seen how people always cluster around Bootheel Man. He's my Elvis. Everything else in the museum is just the backup band."

Allison folded her arms across her chest and turned away from him. Her gaze landed on a tacky "Indian" trading post across the highway from the ancient mounds. It was a standard convenience store, transformed into an Indian trading post by the addition of large red and white signs hawking cigarettes, lottery tickets, souvenirs, liquor, food, and gifts. She doubted that a real American Indian had ever set foot in the place.

But the tawdry store reminded Allison of the passion of Joey Red Horse and the eloquence of Joe Black Dog. She pressed her case.

"Bootheel Man was a living, breathing human being. Some people believe his soul is in torment from being publicly displayed. Maybe it's true. Maybe he is suffering. Please, Clive, take him down. Give him back to the Osages."

Clive Faulkner rolled his eyes.

"Don't roll your eyes at me," she said, "I've been watching you closely for a month. It's clear to me you're every bit the marketing genius Alfred Dennison was. You could keep the museum thriving. Disney World survived the death of Walt Disney."

Faulkner shook his head. "Walt Disney was the *founder* of Disney World, not its main attraction. We survived the death of Alfred Dennison, too. But could Disney World survive the loss of Mickey Mouse? That's a more relevant question."

Allison pressed on, sensing a crack in his resolve. "You've made the Heartland Mound Builder Museum a beautiful place, Clive. You've made it a fun place. You've built a museum where a person can learn history while having a really good time. You'll keep coming up with ways to draw people to the museum. I know you will. Like I said, you're a marketing genius."

He took one of her hands in his. "Now you call me a marketing genius? At Joey Red Horse's preliminary hearing you were calling me a grave robber. Has my stock gone up?"

"Your stock will soar if you take those bones out of your museum."

"I suppose you'd want the burial artifacts to go, too?"

"Of course. Couldn't you get reproductions made?"

"I suppose so, but, like I told you, the whole point of a museum is to house original items of historical importance, not facsimiles."

She squeezed his hand.

"You'll still have lots of original artifacts. You just won't be hawking human burial remains."

Clive Faulkner let go of her hand. "Allison, you're a beautiful woman, especially when you're worked up about something."

"Thank you, but I want you to take the bones out of the museum because it's the right thing to do, not because you think I'm pretty."

He stepped forward, his eyes gazing into hers. "All right, Allison, you've finally won your case. I'm going to recommend to the Board of Directors that we make a replica of Bootheel Man and replace his real skeleton with a reproduction." He shook his head, almost in disbelief. "This may be the worst decision made by a white man involving Indians since Custer decided to chase that band of defenseless-looking Indians toward the Little Big Horn, but I'm going to take the risk."

"Thank you, Clive!"

Allison seized both of his hands in hers and squeezed them. He reached up and touched her chin with a curled forefinger, tilting her face upward.

Before she had time to react, he was kissing her.

Her first inclination was to pull away, but within moments the urge passed and she thrilled to the sensation of his lips upon hers.

When they pulled apart, she took a breath and smiled at him. "You know," she said, "this archaeology stuff gets more interesting every day."

Chapter 40

A bell on the door jingled brightly as Allison Culbertson entered Diedra Binzinger's art gallery and studio. It was just a block from Allison's law office, but she'd never set foot in it. *Another price paid for always being immersed in work.* How many other Cape Girardeau cultural activities had she passed up due to her self-imposed exile at the grindstone?

"I'll be down in a minute!" a voice called from above.

Allison looked up. She was stuck by the beauty of the room.

Binzinger's business was a long, narrow, two-story room, completely open. The back third of the room featured an upstairs loft, much like a huge church balcony. Binzinger's art gallery filled the lower level of the big room; her art studio took up the upper level. The tall, long, red-brick side walls of the room bore no windows since they shared common walls with neighboring Main Street businesses, but the back wall of the upper level consisted almost completely of a huge picture window overlooking the Mississippi River. Its light bathed and brightened the entire studio. In the natural light from the window, Diedra Binzinger stood at an easel, painting. A recording of Debussy's piano solo *Clair de Lune* played softly in the background.

The walls of the gallery were covered with paintings, both oils and watercolors. Tables and multileveled shelves filled the open space of the lower level, displaying all sorts of pottery and stone carvings. An old-fashioned cash register stood on a counter at the back of the gallery, the only piece of non-artwork visible in the room.

Allison moved to a shelf containing Mound Builder-type pottery and saw a chunkey player just like the one left on her windowsill. She picked it up. She had to admit it was a beautiful piece of work. She checked its price tag: $550.00.

"Oh, it's you," said a voice from above.

Allison looked up, the chunkey player still in her hands.

Diedra Binzinger stood in the middle of the loft, looking down at her, wiping her hands with a cloth. She wore a pastel-purple smock. A ribbon in her hair gathered her blonde curls into an impossible pile on top of her head. "What are *you* doing here?"

"Someone left a piece of your artwork at my house," Allison said. "I'd like to ask you a few questions."

"I'm sort of busy."

"I can ask questions while you paint."

"That's nice, but I'm not sure I can paint while you ask questions." Diedra Binzinger folded her arms across her chest and stared at Allison. "What makes you think I'm interested in talking to you?"

"I can't pretend to be worthy of your interest," Allison said, "but I was hoping you'd talk to me, anyway."

Diedra Binzinger studied Allison for several heartbeats. "Oh, you're interesting all right, like a shark."

"Is that a lawyer joke?" Allison asked.

"You catch on quick."

Diedra Binzinger's arms were still crossed in front of her. "What the hell, come on up," she said. "There's two ways to get up here, either the steps or the pole. Pick your poison."

On the left side of the room, an open black metal spiral staircase wound its way to the second level. On the opposite side of the room, a shiny brass fireman's pole reached from floor to ceiling.

"I'll take the steps," Allison said.

She carefully made her way up the spiral staircase. Diedra Binzinger had returned to her easel by the time Allison reached the top.

The smell of oils and paint-thinner was stronger on this level. Allison stood still for a moment, taking it all in.

The second-story loft was crammed with artwork in various stages of completion. A dozen wooden easels held works-in-progress, from bare pencil sketches to oil paintings nearly completed. A kiln rested in one corner, bordered by tables bearing dozens of pottery projects. A white-pine desk was affixed to the wall on the left side of the room, running its length. A computer sat at one end. A sloping draftsman's table was mounted in its center. A counter ran the entire length of opposite wall, completely covered by drop cloths spread out like blankets on a bed. Above the drop cloths ran a mural of the Cape Girardeau riverfront, as seen from the water.

The center of the mural was finished. It depicted the *Delta Queen* riverboat docked near one of the floodwall gates. The finished painting in the middle tapered into incomplete pencil work at each end. She obviously had much yet to add to the extremely long piece of artwork.

"Everything is beautiful," Allison said. "You're a wonderful artist."

"Come here," Diedra Binzinger said. "I think you'll particularly like the project I'm working on today."

Allison made her way between tables and easels until she stood next to Diedra Binzinger.

"What do you think?" the artist asked.

Allison almost gasped.

The painting was of Joey Red Horse.

He was standing on the ledge of the Bill Emerson Memorial Bridge, extending the statue of Gazing Woman toward the sky. The viewpoint was from an impossible angle. You were facing him, looking down at him from above. His face filled the middle of the picture, looking up. Gazing Woman was in close-up perspective in the upper left-hand corner of the picture. Her clay face also looked up.

"I call it 'God's View.'"

Joey's face, a perfect likeness, was positioned at an angle much the same as the head of Bootheel Man, his mouth stretched wide in an anguished scream. His eyes bulged open, staring upward, right at you. His chest was naked. She had captured the exact color of his skin tone. But somehow, throughout his entire body, even beneath his face when you studied it closely, you could faintly see the glow of Joey's skeleton, ghostlike through his flesh and features. Skull's eye sockets lurked beneath Joey's eyes.

Allison felt tears on her cheeks.

"What do you think?" Binzinger asked.

"It's disturbing," Allison said.

"Thank you. It was meant to be."

"Did you know him?" Allison asked. "Did you know Joey?"

"No, but I feel like I did."

Allison tore her eyes away from the painting and studied the photographs on the tabletop to the immediate right of the easel.

Many were stills made from the KFVS-12 broadcast of Joey's big moment on the bridge. Several close-ups of his face were scattered among the bridge photographs.

Allison turned again to the painting. Even Gazing Woman looked real. The detail and lighting were perfect. Allison remembered reading somewhere that the use of light was what separated a great artist from a mediocre one. Diedra Binzinger clearly knew what she was doing with light. Allison imagined she would be able to feel the cool surface of the flint clay if she reached up and touched the Gazing Woman on the canvas.

"Why?" Allison asked. "Why are you doing it? Why are you painting Joey?"

"Why does any artist paint any picture?" Diedra Binzinger said. "The muse grabbed me by the throat and made me paint. This young man dreamed of returning the bones of his ancestors to a peaceful resting place. Yet he failed tragically. In the blink of an eye, he left nothing in this world but his own bones. We human beings burn with passion and desire, brightly and briefly, for one fleeting moment. But not one of us succeeds in leaving more than a mere smudge on the stained-glass window of time."

Allison was silent for several seconds, replaying in her mind the words she'd just heard.

"I see your point," she said, finally, "but I have a few other questions."

Diedra Binzinger picked up a brush and started adding shadings of color to the small part that could be seen of Joey's breechcloth.

"He's not the right man for you," Diedra Binzinger said.

"I beg your pardon?"

"He's not the right man for you."

"Who? What man?"

"Clive Faulkner."

Allison remembered the kiss and the confusion she felt afterward during the drive back from Wickliffe, Kentucky. After years with no love life whatsoever, she suddenly found herself with conflicting feelings for two men: Clive Faulkner and Harry Sullinger. But she certainly wasn't going to share her budding soap-opera predicament with Diedra Binzinger. She was here to *get* information from her, not give it.

"I'm not sure I ever thought he *was* the right man for me," Allison said. "I don't know how I feel about him, really. I know the two of you recently broke up. Please understand I didn't do anything to try to steal him from you."

"I know you didn't. It's him. He can't commit. Not to any relationship. Not to any person. Nothing matters to him but his precious museum and his research and the memory of Alfred Dennison. Well, money and the fine things it buys, he likes that stuff. But you don't want to start a relationship with Clive Faulkner. Believe me. I did, and I wish I hadn't."

Allison wondered exactly how close this woman and Clive Faulkner had been. When had they first kissed? More importantly, when had they last kissed? Allison tried to separate her own feelings for Clive Faulkner from the conversation.

"It must have hurt when he broke up with you," Allison said.

Diedra Binzinger gave a sharp laugh. "*He* broke up with me? Is that what he told you? No, it was the other way around. I told *him* it was over."

"Well, maybe he never specifically said which of you initiated the breakup," Allison said. "I may have jumped to conclusions."

"Of course. What woman in her right mind could possibly resist the charms of suave and handsome Clive Faulkner? He's a regular Indiana Jones, a combination of erudite professor and sexy glamour boy. What woman would ever break off a relationship with *him?*" Binzinger's voice was filled with sarcasm. She put her hands on her hips. "I'm telling you," she said. "You'll be making a big mistake if you think he's the right man for you. He'll bring you nothing but disappointment and heartache."

"So, it is over between the two of you?"

"Most definitely."

Allison glanced again at the painting of Joey on the bridge. Now that the initial shock was over, she could look at it as a piece of art. Almost.

"What are you going to do with this picture when it's done?"

"Same thing I do with everything I make. That's what an artist does, you know. You create art, you put your soul into it, and then you peddle it to others. If you do it right, you have nothing left for yourself but a stack of empty canvases awaiting your paint, plus a bank account full of money."

"You must be pretty successful," Allison said. "You've done wonders with this old building. Didn't it used to be a jewelry store?"

Diedra Binzinger leaned forward as she touched up a spot of fringe on the buckskins.

"This old storefront has evolved through several reincarnations, but it's better than ever now. The window alone cost me a fortune."

"Tell me about it," Allison said. "I remodeled my office, too. I also have a window with a great view of the Mississippi. You should come see it sometime."

"Maybe I will. For now, let's go downstairs for a drink. I'm ready for a break."

Diedra Binzinger put down her brush and wiped her hands on a cloth.

"Stairs or pole?" she asked.

"Stairs," Allison answered immediately.

"Meet you at the bottom," Diedra Binzinger said. She walked to the fireman's pole. Like Batman's cape, her smock billowed on each side as she grasped the pole and whooshed to the first floor.

Allison was impressed by the artist's flair. Meanwhile, she tentatively descended the spiral staircase, thanking her lucky stars she wasn't wearing high heels as she placed each foot on the narrow fretwork steps.

By the time Allison reached the first floor, Diedra Binzinger was already kneeling in front of a small refrigerator hidden in a nook behind the cash register.

"Green tea or Heineken? I can't offer much of a choice."

"Tea, thank you."

Binzinger handed her a cold bottle of green tea, and Allison unscrewed its top. Binzinger was opening a Heineken beer for herself. She fixed her bright eyes on Allison.

"So, what other questions do you have for me?"

"Well, for one thing, somebody left a piece of your artwork at my home recently. I wondered what you know about it."

The artist took a swig of the beer. "All I know is what the cops told me. It was one of my chunkey player effigies. I've probably made fifty over the years. That piece is one of my bestsellers. They're all pretty much alike, though. Once I design a figurine that proves to be popular, I tend to do it over and over. Pays the bills, you know. I couldn't tell from the one the police showed me who bought it. The date and my initials show I made it three years ago. That's all I can tell you. Sorry I can't be more help."

Allison studied Diedra Binzinger's face, but detected nothing to indicate deception. The woman was looking at her expectantly, waiting for the next question. She did not appear to be nervous, at least not that Allison could tell.

"Whoever left the chunkey player also left a note," Allison said.

"The police told me that, too, but didn't say what it said. Tell me."

"It said I wasn't in danger right now, but I would be if I kept asking questions."

Diedra Binzinger smiled coolly. "Yet here you are today, still asking questions. Guess you didn't take the note seriously. Did you think it was a joke?"

"It was no joke," Allison said. "It was a threat."

Binzinger raised her eyebrows. "A threat? Maybe it was meant more as a friendly warning."

"How so?"

"I don't know. What sort of questions have you been asking?"

"I've been trying to find out who killed Joey."

"There you go. Someone's telling you to quit searching for the answer to that question."

"Are you that someone?" Allison asked.

Diedra Binzinger stared at her silently, taking another long pull from the green Heineken bottle.

"My only warning to you, Allison Culbertson, was the very first thing I said to you when you came through that door today. Don't fall in love with Clive Faulkner. He'll break your heart."

"Did he break yours?"

"Do I look like a woman with a broken heart?"

Allison took a moment to study her. Diedra Binzinger's face was pretty, but wrinkles were already forming at the corners of her eyes. Her face bore no makeup, revealing washed-out skin that could have used some. Her blonde hair was obviously dyed, a secret not-so-subtly betrayed by untended dark roots near her scalp. Her sharp eyes did not hold much happiness.

And that half-empty beer bottle appeared very much at home in her hand during midmorning of a day smack in the middle of a workweek.

"Yes," Allison answered. "I'd say you do."

Diedra Binzinger drained the remainder of the beer and stood up. "Got to get back to work. Don't let the door hit your ass on the way out. Come back and see me again, though, if you want."

With those mixed messages ringing in her ears, Allison left the gallery. As she walked up the sidewalk toward her office, she passed the spot where she had cradled Joey Red Horse's head in her lap. She kept her eyes fixed straight ahead, hoping the city's maintenance crew had finally scrubbed out the last of the bloodstain.

Chapter 41

"Tell me how you got shot."

Allison Culbertson was trying out her brand-spanking-new Beretta handgun at Harry Sullinger's firing range. She hadn't talked with him for several days because his work had taken him to Los Angeles and Miami. He and Paul Burns, the detective from the Cape Girardeau Police Department, had traveled coast-to-coast to peruse police-department files pertaining to the unsolved shootings involving the gun that killed Joey Red Horse. So far, she had not pried any new information out of her favorite detective, but the afternoon was still young and he usually proved vulnerable to her interrogational charms.

Both had taken off from work early. He had chauffeured her through the process of obtaining from the Sheriff's Department a permit to carry a concealed weapon.

"You're dangerous now," he had said as they drove out to his place.

She believed it, but hoped she might prove dangerous to someone other than herself.

She had just fired 150 rounds into an Osama bin Laden target when she threw the question at him.

"What?" he said, taking out his earplugs.

"Tell me how you got shot. You've kept me in suspense long enough."

She took off her goggles and earplugs and ran a hand through her hair.

He winced. "Wouldn't you rather hear some news about my trips to Miami and Los Angeles?"

"I figured you wouldn't tell me," she said. "Top-secret police business and all that."

"Well, the way I see it, you were a victim, too, since the killer shot at you. I don't see any harm in keeping you informed, as long as you don't go around telling people."

"My lips are sealed."

He glanced at her lips. His intense interest in them was written across his face. She looked down, most likely blushing.

He began gathering the empty magazines she'd dropped each time she'd fired a full clip.

"I guess the most intriguing part of the trip was that both the shooting in Miami and the shooting in Los Angeles have ties to a Colombian drug lord named Pablo Ramirez. He's one of the major drug dealers in the world. We're talking about the kind of guy who smuggles boatloads of cocaine into Florida, who airdrops bails of it into the ocean to be picked up by other smugglers, and whose hit men have been assassinating Colombian political leaders, police officers, and rival gangsters for years. He's near the top of the drug-dealer food chain. The DEA, through informants, is positive that both the guy in Miami and the guy in Los Angeles were buying their cocaine from Ramirez. According to the informants, Ramirez thought they had ratted him out to the feds."

"Do they think Ramirez killed these guys?"

"Not personally. He's never even been in the United States, so far as we know. But he's got lots of people who work for him, the kind who kill for a living. He's certainly a suspect in each death."

Allison remembered watching the man in black shooting Joey Red Horse. Could the killer have been a hired assassin? A hit man for a Colombian drug lord, carrying out an assassination in Cape Girardeau, Missouri?

"Surely Joey wasn't of interest to Pablo Ramirez?" Allison said. "I mean, even if Joey were a drug dealer, he's not likely to have angered one of the biggest drug lords in the world, is he?"

"Well, so far, the only tie we've come up with is that he was killed by the same gun that killed two of Pablo Ramirez's enemies. Coincidence? In my job we are suspicious of coincidences."

"Were there any other similarities to those killings and Joey's?"

"No. Neither of the others had any living eyewitnesses, unless you count the traumatized dog of the Miami victim. The cops in Los Angeles and Miami were ecstatic to hear we had two live witnesses in Cape, you and the designated driver, until I let them know that neither of you can say, really, whether the shooter was big or small, white or black, or even male or female. I have to tell you, they were unimpressed with your powers of observation."

"So am I," Allison said. "That's one reason we're here on this firing range. I'm through being one of the sheep. There's going to be a new me. Beware of the sheepdog!"

She ejected the empty clip from her new Beretta. "Tell me about the two notches you *could* have put on your gun, if you were the notch-carving type."

He was kneeling, taking new bullets from a box and refilling empty clips.

"It's a sad story," he said.

"I revel in sad stories," Allison said. "I've handled divorce cases, remember? Maybe it will earn you some sympathy points. You could use them. So far, you come across as a bit too cocky, a bit too self-assured. I wasn't entirely pleased, you know, about your quotes in the newspaper after the chunkey game."

"Oh, you saw those?"

"Playing dumb now, huh? Telling the newspaper you could have made the correct call! I saw your face. You didn't have a clue."

"Well, you had the better angle," he said.

"And your quip that I wasn't hired for my eyesight! Very funny."

"Hey, that was a compliment. I thought you'd like it. Remember what P. T. Barnum said about publicity for lawyers?"

"No, what *did* P.T. Barnum say about publicity for lawyers?"

"He said any publicity is good publicity."

"I think you've got your quotes mixed up, Harry. P.T. Barnum is the one who said, 'There's a sucker born every minute.'"

"And he was right," he said. He stroked his strong chin and nodded thoughtfully. "I guess telling you about the people I killed relates to your firearms training."

"I don't care how bad it was," Allison said, "Whatever you went through has got to be better than pressing your face to a car seat, peeing your own pants, waiting to be capped in the back of the head."

"Capped?" Sullinger said. "Where'd you hear that term?"

"From my buddy, Bear Smith."

"I'll have to ask you more about that later." He pursed his lips and glanced into the distance. A full minute passed before he began talking.

"It was my second year on the police force," he said. "I was working nights. Shortly before dawn one summer night, I was dispatched to a domestic disturbance."

He kept his eyes focused on something far away as his fingers pressed bullet after bullet into an empty clip.

"I was alone in my patrol car, the first officer at the scene. I'd just arrived when the dispatcher broadcast an update telling us that the woman in the house was frantic. She was saying her husband was waving a gun around, threatening to shoot her." Sullinger put down the full clip and started filling another. "I got out of my car, drew my gun, and hurried to the front door. It was a dinky little house with a concrete front porch. I stood by the front door, listening, trying to decide whether to try the knob, ring the doorbell, kick in the door, or wait for backup. I was careful to stand where I couldn't be shot from one of the windows. I could hear the yelling and screaming going on inside the house, angry shouts by both a man and a woman. I was glad to hear both voices. I thought to myself, 'Well, nobody's shot anybody, yet. If I go in, it might make things worse.' So, I stayed there by the door, listening."

His hands stopped moving, even though the clip was not yet full.

"Then I heard it, a gunshot. To this day I remember exactly what went through my mind: 'Oh, hell, he killed her while I was standing out here with my thumb up my ass!' I turned the door-knob. It was unlocked. I flung it open and barged in, gun drawn, ready to fire. They were both right there in the living room, the wife and her husband. The gun was in his right hand, pointing toward the ceiling. I spotted a hole in the plaster. He had fired in the air. The wife was on her knees by the couch, sobbing. If his goal was to scare her, he succeeded. She was hysterical, begging him not to shoot. He looked over at me and our eyes met. We stared at each other across that small living room, seemed like forever. My gun was aimed right at him. I had him in my sights. His gun was still pointing straight up."

Sullinger noticed the clip and once again started refilling it with bullets. "'Drop it,' I yelled, but he just kept looking at me. 'Please don't shoot me, Jesse,' the lady was saying, over and over. His gun was still pointed upward. They were both in their twenties, about my age at the time. Jesse was bare-chested, with lots of thick, black hair on his chest, and a tattoo of a joker on his arm. The joker's face was red. I'll never forget it. Weird tattoo. The wife, her name was Carrie, she was sobbing this whole time.

"'Drop the gun,' I told him. 'I'll shoot you if you don't drop the gun. I mean it. I'll shoot.' Jesse glanced down at his wife and said, 'This is your fault, all your fault.' He called her a filthy name and whipped his gun down toward me. I fired twice as he was bringing it down. The first shot hit him in the chest and the second hit him in the head as he was falling. His shot went wild and hit the ceiling behind me, above the door."

He paused, remembering. He was quiet for a long time.

"Well, you were clearly justified in shooting him," Allison said. "It was self-defense, no doubt. Now, tell me about your other gunfight, the one where you got shot."

"I haven't finished," Sullinger said. "There's more." He frowned.

"After I shot Jesse, I wasn't sure I had disabled him. I wasn't positive he wouldn't pop up any minute and start shooting. So I kept my gun pointed at him. Carrie, the wife, started screaming and caterwauling. She threw herself on top of him, calling out his name, telling him she loved him. She was getting all covered with his blood. I'll never forget how I felt standing there, watching her grief and knowing I caused it. I stood there like a bump on a log, pointing my gun at both of them, not knowing what to do. Like I said, I'd only been a police officer for two years. Then a child upstairs called out, 'Daddy?' It was a young voice, a girl maybe five or six years old. At the sound of the voice, Carrie's face changed. She got this look of pure hatred in her eyes. Next thing I knew she had Jesse's gun in her hand and was raising it. I could have shot her right then, before she even got it up, but I was processing it through my mind, as if it were happening in slow motion. I was thinking how I'd just killed that little girl's father, and if I shot her mother, too, I'd make her an orphan. I yelled out, 'Drop the gun! Drop it! Don't shoot!'"

Harry Sullinger paused and took a deep breath.

"I don't like to tell this story," he said.

"I'm sorry," Allison said. "I made you do it. You don't have to finish."

"Don't you want to know what happened?"

"Of course I do, but not if you don't want to tell me."

His eyes welled with tears. "I could've shot her as the gun was coming up. It would've been an easy shot. I could have drilled her right between the eyes, but I just couldn't pull the trigger. I kept thinking that maybe she wouldn't do it. Maybe she'd realize the enormity of what she was doing. After all, I was there to protect her. I had shot her man to protect her. Saved her life, maybe. All of this was going through my mind when, before I knew it, she fired. I felt a bullet punch me in the gut, below my bulletproof vest. I knew I was hit, and I knew she wasn't through shooting. I never saw such hate in a person's eyes. I fired and she fired again. We fired at the same time. Her second shot slammed into my bulletproof vest. It felt like someone hit me with a hammer. My shot hit her smack in the middle of her forehead. She dropped like a sack of potatoes. Right there in her own living room. Across her dead husband."

"It must have been terrible," Allison said.

"I haven't told you the worst part.'"

"The child?"

"Right. The little girl, her name's Susan, had seen the whole thing. She came down the stairs and walked into the room and stood looking up at me. I was still holding my gun, and her parents were lying lifeless on the living room carpet. Turned out I was right about her age; she was five years old. She looked at them, looked at me, looked back at them, looked up at me, and finally said, 'Why did you hurt my mommy and daddy?' I couldn't answer. She went and sat down next to them, and held her mother's hand."

"I'm sorry, Harry."

"Sorry for me? I was twenty-four years old at the time. I'm thirty-four now. Susan Torrence just turned fifteen last month. She's a sophomore in high school. She's been raised by her maternal grandmother. She's had to grow up without parents. She's the one to feel sorry for. I've told myself over and over that if I'd let Carrie Torrence kill me, she would've either gotten the death penalty or would've spent the rest of her life in prison, so Susan would've been raised by her grandmother, anyway. But it doesn't make it any better. If I'd died instead of her mother, at least she would still have a mother."

He hung his head.

"Both shootings were clearly self-defense," Allison said. "They were completely lawful."

"Oh, yeah, they were righteous shootings, completely justified under the law," Harry said. "Still, I got investigated, suspended, and sued."

"You did?"

"Yeah, the Missouri Highway Patrol conducted a criminal investigation of the shooting. Recall that there were no living witnesses except me and a five-year-old. Here's two people shot dead in their home by a cop, who, by the way, went into their house without a warrant. Fortunately for me, that sweet, innocent kid gave a video-taped interview to an investigator from the Highway Patrol, telling how Daddy had been hitting Mommy and pointing a gun at Mommy so Mommy called the police. The ballistics, of course, fully supported my account, too. Also, the phone was off the hook, so the whole thing was recorded by the 911 call. Still, the coroner called a coroner's inquest, mostly so the public could hear the facts and see that the shootings were justified. I had to testify in front of a coroner's jury about the whole thing. A ballistics expert and the medical examiner also testified. The little girl's videotaped statement was played. I was fully exonerated as far as any criminal charges went. Nevertheless, I was suspended while the investigation went on and was forced to go through some mandatory psychological counseling. But the suspension was with pay and didn't last too long, so it wasn't too bad. Of course, the lawyer for the little girl sued me for the 'wrongful death' of her parents. The city's insurance company settled it out of court. Frankly, I was glad Susan Torrence got a little something, even though I wasn't at fault, legally. I did kill her parents, after all. I made a conscious choice that it would be her mother who died that night, not me."

A tear worked its way down his cheek. "So, Allison, this concludes the lecture part of your Firearms 101 class. Keep in mind that by carrying a gun, you assume the risk of being investigated, prosecuted, fired, and sued for a choice you make in a split second, even if the choice you make proves to be completely legal."

"Well, nobody can fire me, anyway," Allison said, trying to lighten the mood. "I'm self-employed."

Harry Sullinger ignored the tear as it meandered toward his strong jaw. If he knew it was there, he was pretending he didn't.

"One last bit of advice?" he said.

"What?"

"Always carry an extra clip. Practice ejecting your empty magazine and replacing it with the extra one."

Allison pictured herself firing 30 shots on purpose at anybody or anything and practically laughed at the absurdity of it. "I think it will be hard enough for me to carry the gun itself, much less extra ammo. Let's face it, Harry. If I can't hit what I'm shooting at with 15 shots, I'm in real trouble."

Sullinger nodded. "Exactly. That's why you should carry the extra magazine."

Allison got into her purse and pulled out one of her business cards and a pen.

"Say, Harry, I've got something I want to give you. I ran across it in a book one time. It's a prayer Jews say on Yom Kippur. Here, I want you to carry it with you. Pull it out and read it when you're feeling the way you feel right now."

"How do you think I'm feeling right now?"

"Guilty. As if you did something wrong."

She wrote the words on the back of her business card, printing slowly. She handed it to him. "Read it," she ordered.

He studied it. "You print like a little kid."

"I wanted it to be legible. My handwriting's awful. Now, read it."

He read aloud, slowly: "Purify me, revive me, uplift me. Forgive my past and lead me into the future."

Allison touched his hand. "Whenever you start thinking about Susan Torrence, Harry, and what happened to her parents ten years ago, pull that card and say those words."

"Thanks, Allison," he said. He took a deep breath and let it out slowly. He glanced at her and shook his head. "Now I almost feel bad about the things I said about you in the newspaper. Truth is, I didn't know which pole hit the chunkey stone, either."

Chapter 42

"Hurry, get in the car!"

Allison Culbertson was standing at the bottom of the sixty-one concrete steps leading from the Common Pleas Courthouse to the sidewalk on Spanish Street. She had been walking back to her office from a trip to the courthouse to handle a probate matter when a car screeched to a stop next to her.

"Get in!"

Marge Tappinger pulled her silver Lincoln sedan to a stop. She was talking to Allison through the open window on the driver's side of the luxury car.

"Quick, get in! I don't want people to see us together!"

Allison was not keen on the idea of getting inside Marge Tappinger's Lincoln. She had an appointment with a client in thirty minutes, she hadn't eaten lunch yet, and she didn't like the frantic look on Marge Tappinger's face. Still, curiosity and a desire not to appear frightened overrode her caution. After all, she was the new Allison Culbertson: fearless and dangerous. Her gun, however, was back at the office. Weapons were not allowed in the courthouse, so she'd left it in her desk drawer.

She circled around the Lincoln and opened the passenger door.

"I have to be back in thirty minutes," she said. "If this is going to take longer than that, it will have to wait."

"It won't take long," Marge Tappinger said. "Get in!"

Allison slid onto the expensive leather seat. Marge pulled away from the curb while Allison was still closing the door.

"What's the rush?" Allison said.

"I don't want anybody to see us. I think Rex might be having me followed."

The Lincoln shot down Spanish Street. At the intersection with Broadway, Marge Tappinger made a hard right, barely slowing for the stop sign. Allison swayed to her left, struggling to buckle her seat belt.

She had just managed to fasten it, when Marge came to the intersection with Main Street. She made a rolling stop and turned left.

"Where are we going?" Allison asked.

"Cape Rock Park. It's nice and private. We can talk. We can make sure we're alone."

Within minutes, the silver Lincoln rolled to a stop in the circular drive of Cape Rock Park. The high spot over the Mississippi provided the town's best view of the river. The high park featuring its chunk of rock and a plaque was all that remained of a huge rock promontory that once shot out into the water, forming the cape that had given the town its name. Engineers had dynamited the landmark around 1900, when railroads called the shots for local communities, in order to make a flat path next to the river for the railroad tracks.

Marge Tappinger looked around, nervously.

"Nobody followed us," she said.

"You're lucky you didn't get a ticket," Allison said. "I counted two dozen traffic violations. Reckless driving doesn't strike me as a good way to stay incognito."

"Well, it worked." Marge Tappinger put the car in park. "Look, I've got something really important to tell you, but it's got to remain a secret."

Allison frowned. "I can't absolutely guarantee secrecy, Marge. You're not my client, so the attorney-client privilege doesn't apply. I don't want to be your lawyer, so don't even ask. Does this involve Joey?"

"Yes. Very much so."

"Well, even though I can't promise absolute secrecy, I *can* tell you that I'm pretty good at keeping secrets and I'm no gossip. So, unless I have a darn good reason for telling somebody, whatever you tell me will remain between us. If that's good enough for you, tell me your big secret."

Marge Tappinger clasped her hands together. "I'm pregnant. With Joey's child."

Allison kept her face expressionless. It was a difficult task. "Pregnant? Are you sure?"

"Oh, yes. Home pregnancy tests are very reliable these days."

338

"How do you know it's Joey's?"

"He's the only man I had sex with in the past month."

Allison recalled a previous conversation with Harry Sullinger.

"I thought you and Rex did some hanky-panky when you got home on the night Joey died. I thought that was your alibi? Somebody called it a Viagra alibi."

"That was Rex's idea."

"The sex?"

"No, the story we told the police. To tell the truth, we fought like cats and dogs the minute I got home, and he slept in the guest room."

"So, you can't say for sure that Rex was home when Joey was shot?"

"No, and frankly, I'm developing some suspicions about Rex, myself."

"What do you mean?"

"Well, making me lie to the police? That got me thinking. Did Rex leave the house after he stormed off for the guest room? I can't say he didn't."

"Did Rex know you were pregnant with Joey's child?"

"He does. I told him. He wants me to get an abortion."

"I mean, did he know that night?"

"Yes. I had just found out myself. That's why I went to Joey's apartment that night. I wanted him to be the first to know. Before I could tell him, though, he started talking about how it was time for us to stop seeing each other. I started crying and told him the news. When he found out I was pregnant, everything seemed to change. He took me in his arms. He said he'd always wanted children. He made it seem like everything would be okay. In fact, things were going wonderfully until that little slut showed up."

"Were you and Joey in bed when Lolita let herself in?"

"Yes. Like I said, my big news really seemed to affect Joey. He went from talking about breaking up to gushing about being a father."

"What happened next?"

"That psycho twit attacked Joey and started smashing things. I tried to calm her down, but she started screaming and yelling at me. Joey suggested I should leave, and I got out of there. I drove straight home. Unfortunately for me, Rex was waiting up. He could tell I was upset. Before I knew it, I had told him everything. He started yelling about how I had to get an abortion, how he wasn't going to have some half-breed kid in his house. I explained to him that Joey wasn't a full-blooded Indian, so my child would not be a half-breed, but the math didn't matter to him."

Marge Tappinger let her hand rest on her stomach. She didn't look pregnant. She looked like a society matron in an expensive suit, perhaps suffering from a slight case of indigestion.

"I want Joey's baby," she said. "I'm glad I'm pregnant."

Allison didn't know if congratulations were in order. She was sure Marge Tappinger might be the only person in the world who would consider this a good bit of news. She couldn't think of a single other person who would be pleased by this development.

"So, Rex finds out Joey has impregnated his wife. Less than an hour later, Joey is shot dead. And you can't swear Rex didn't dash out of the house in a fit of anger?"

"Right. Now you see why I'm so afraid."

"Afraid?"

"Yes. Since I told Rex I wouldn't get the abortion, he's been having me followed. There's a private security company he used for his first divorce. I think he hired them again. Those guys are pretty good. But I've spotted them following me a couple of times. I lost them this morning, though, when I waved over a police car, pointed out the van, and told the cop I was being followed by a stalker."

Marge Tappinger took a handkerchief from her purse and blew her nose. "Rex told me I'd better not tell anyone I was pregnant, that I'd better think again about getting the abortion."

"He didn't know you were planning to meet with me today, did he?"

"No. He thinks I went to the beauty parlor. In fact, I need to get there really soon. I didn't want to come to the front door of your office, though, in case he's having it watched. He's smart. He'd figure out you're the first person I'd want to tell about this."

"Why? Why am I the first person?"

"Because you were Joey's lawyer. You knew him. You know how much I loved him. You're the one person who knows how much this means to me. A part of Joey is still going to be alive!"

340

Marge Tappinger dabbed at her eyes with the handkerchief.

"I didn't go to Joey's funeral because of Rex. He wouldn't let me. He said the police go to murder victim's funerals, looking for suspects. He didn't want us sitting there. But I read in the obituary that Joey was survived by his mother. Did you meet her?"

"Yes."

"Tell me," Marge Tappinger said. "From what you know about her, will it be good news or bad news for her that she's going to be a grandmother?"

Allison recalled Louise Red Horse sitting at the Wikon Iron Community Center, talking wistfully about her son. It dawned on her that Louise Red Horse might actually consider the pregnancy good news.

"You know, I think she'll find your news very welcome."

"Oh, you don't know how happy that makes me!" Marge Tappinger started fumbling with her purse. "I need your advice, though."

"I'm not going to handle your divorce."

"I'm not talking about that. In fact, if Rex isn't a murderer, I'm not sure I'll be getting a divorce. Here's what I want from you."

Marge Tappinger pulled a semiautomatic handgun from her purse.

Allison's eyes widened as her mind raced. *I should have brought my gun. I'm going to get shot to death in Marge Tappinger's Lincoln while my brand-new Beretta is back in a drawer at my desk. What a waste of money! Some sheepdog!*

Marge handed the gun to Allison. "I want you to get this gun checked out. See if it might be the one that killed Joey. It's Rex's. I got it out of his desk at home."

Allison held the gun as if it were a scorpion. "Let me get this straight. You stole it from your husband's desk, and you're giving it to me. That puts me in possession of stolen property."

Allison handed it back.

Marge shoved it toward Allison. When Allison wouldn't take it, she dropped it in Allison's lap.

"No, it was in my own house, so I didn't steal it. I'm loaning it to you to get it checked out."

Allison picked it up again. "Did Rex buy this gun after you were married, or did he own it before you got married?"

"Oh, he had it years before we got married."

Allison thrust it back to Marge.

"Then it's not marital property. It's not yours to give away."

Marge placed it firmly back in Allison's lap.

"I'm not giving it to you permanently. I'm providing it to a lawyer for testing. Have somebody do whatever magic they do to see whether it fired the bullets that killed Joey."

Allison picked it up again. How stupid would she look if she gave the gun back to Marge and it later turned out that it was, in fact, the murder weapon? Or if she gave it back and the murder never got solved and this one ballistics test could have solved it? Or if she gave the gun back to Marge and Marge killed Rex with it or Rex killed Marge with it? On the other hand, how bad would it look if Rex Tappinger reported the gun stolen (maybe he already had!) and she got caught with it in her possession before she managed to turn it over to the police?

She eyed Marge Tappinger closely. Was it possible both Tappingers were in cahoots to set her up? Provide her with the murder weapon, tip off the police, and then lie and say they had no idea what she was talking about?

No, Marge Tappinger was distraught. Surely she wasn't a good enough actress to pull off such a stunt. *At least I hope she's not*, Allison thought.

Harry Sullinger! His rugged face popped into her mind. That was it. She'd get the gun to Sullinger. He could take it to the crime lab for analysis.

"I'll take it on one condition," Allison said.

"What's that?"

"Let me turn it over to Harry Sullinger, the investigator for the prosecutor's office. He can have the tests run on it. I won't take possession of it unless you'll authorize me to turn it over to him."

"Okay, give it to him."

"Here, write that down," Allison said.

"Why?"

"Because I'm a lawyer and I like things in writing."

She handed one of her business cards to Marge Tappinger and dictated what she wanted her to write: "I, Marge Tappinger, voluntarily turn over my husband's 9-millimeter pistol to Allison Culbertson and consent that she may give it to Harry Sullinger for testing."

Marge Tappinger began writing the words.

"It's hard to fit all that on this little card."

"Write small."

When she finished, Marge Tappinger handed the business card to Allison. Her handwriting was much nicer than Allison's. Although tiny, her words were clearly legible.

"Okay," Allison said. "I'll do it."

"Great."

Allison's head rocked back as Marge Tappinger accelerated and the Lincoln's tires squealed.

"Slow down, for God's sake!" Allison said. "If we get pulled over and the police find this gun sitting on the front seat, we'll both have a lot of explaining to do."

Chapter 43

The chance to win an award from ARROW was an offer Allison Culbertson couldn't refuse. Mark Windfoot reached her on her cell phone while she was reading microfilm at the Cape Girardeau Public Library. She moved outside to take the call. She stood near the rear entrance of the library, facing its back parking lot, as she listened to Mark Windfoot's voice.

"We want to give Joey Red Horse this year's Crazy Horse Award and we want to present you the Legal Eagle Award," he explained.

"What's the Crazy Horse Award?"

"It goes to the American Indian who did the most that year to stand up for the rights of American Indians."

"What about the Legal Eagle Award?"

"It goes to the lawyer whose legal work made a significant difference in fighting for the rights of American Indians."

"Well, you know, I didn't exactly win Joey's case. In fact, we didn't even get to trial."

"I know, but your championing of Joey's cause, and your use of the claim-of-right defense, brought nationwide attention to the problem. You were outstanding at the preliminary hearing. We've had more success negotiating with private museums nationwide ever since. Your legal work really did make a difference."

"Well," said Allison, "I'm honored. Thank you."

Allison's eyes scanned the library's parking lot as she spoke on her cell phone. She noticed a white van parked by itself on the back row of the parking lot. It faced her Jeep Cherokee. Someone sat in the driver's seat, but because of the tinted glass she couldn't make him out.

"What we'd like to do," Windfoot was saying, "is come to Cape Girardeau to present both awards. We'll make a big deal of it. We're finalizing details, but we're hoping Joey's mother can travel to Missouri for the presentation, and, of course, we'll do it at a time you're free. I'm looking at a couple of significant historical dates, both of which might be hooks to garner a bit more national public-

344

ity. We already missed the date Crazy Horse was bayoneted while a prisoner of the U.S. Army. That was September 5. We might do it on October 4, the anniversary of the death of John Chivington. He was the minister from Missouri who massacred the Cheyenne women and children at Sand Creek. That might be good because of the Missouri ties. Or we might do it on the exact anniversary of the Sand Creek Massacre, which was November 29. Then again, we might do it on the anniversary of the Wounded Knee Massacre, which is December 29. How do those dates look for you?"

Allison checked her pocket calendar.

"They're all free right now. Let me know which one you pick and I'll keep it open."

As Allison slipped her cell phone back into her purse, she looked again at the white van. Why would someone be sitting on the empty back row of the library parking lot? If the van was still there when she left the library, she'd check into it. She walked back into the library and returned to her seat in front of the microfilm reader.

She was reading old *Southeast Missourian* stories about Harry Sullinger's shooting of Jesse and Carrie Torrence, and the ensuing coroner's inquest. She also read the obituary for each Torrence. She took notes as she did so.

When she finished, she went outside. The white van still sat by itself on the back row of the parking lot. Now, a black Chevy Tahoe was parked next to it. Its windows were also tinted.

She had left her gun in the console of the Jeep because the library doors were posted with large signs proclaiming that firearms were prohibited in the building. Trying not to glance at the van, Allison walked to her car and got into the driver's seat. She started her engine, opened the console, took out the Beretta, flipped off its safety, and backed the Jeep out of her parking space. She hit the speed-dial button on her telephone. In a moment she heard Sullinger's voice.

"Hello?"

"Harry, this is Allison Culbertson. Do you have a minute?"

"Sure. What's up?"

"I'm on the parking lot of the public library. Some guy has been sitting in a van for the past hour. I've got the feeling he's following me. I'm going over to talk to him. Would it be okay if I keep this line open so you can listen in?"

"Better yet," Sullinger said, "why don't you wait for me? I'm at the station. I can be there in five minutes."

"I'd rather do it alone, Harry. It's a sheepdog thing."

"Well, be careful."

As she drove slowly toward the white van and the black Tahoe, she recited their license-plate numbers for Harry Sullinger. She pulled directly in front of the van, blocking it in. She lowered her window and motioned for the driver to come to her window. She kept her gun out of sight under her right thigh, where she could grab it if necessary.

After a long pause, the man in the van climbed out and walked toward Allison's open window. He was a fat, middle-aged, big-bellied white man, wearing a too-small shirt and a too-short tie.

"That's close enough," she said, when he was about six feet away. "Who are you?"

"Who are you?" he countered.

"I'm Allison Culbertson, a lawyer. Now it's your turn. Who are you?"

"I don't see how that's any of your business," he said. "Why do you want to know?"

"Have you been following me?" she asked.

"No. I've just been sitting here."

"Why have you been parked on this parking lot for the past hour, facing my car?"

Before the man could answer, the door of the black Tahoe opened. Rex Tappinger got out.

His eyes were angry under his mane of white hair.

"I'll take it from here, Pete."

Rex Tappinger walked to Allison's window.

"He works for me. He's a private investigator. I had him follow you because I believe you've been meeting with my wife. My gun has turned up missing. Pete here saw you get into my wife's car the other day. I think you have my gun and I want it back."

"I don't have your gun."

"Don't lie to me, Miss Culbertson. I guess I neglected to tell you that Marge has already admitted she gave it to you. You know, you are possessing stolen property. I just might file a police report. I want the gun back now. If you don't have it with you, I'll be glad to accompany you wherever you need to go to get it."

"You would report me to the police?" Allison said.

"I will if you don't return my gun immediately."

"Well, I happen to have the police on the line right now. Here, make your report."

She held out the cell phone.

Rex Tappinger showed no interest in taking it.

"You're bluffing," he said.

Allison Culbertson spoke into the phone.

"Harry, he doesn't believe you're really on the line. What should I tell him?"

She listened and nodded.

"He says he ran the plates on both the van and the Tahoe. He says Pete's last name is Gerringer and he lives in Scott City. Harry would be glad to talk to you if you want. In fact, he has a few questions for you."

She held out the phone again.

"I don't want to talk to him. I just want my gun back," Tappinger said.

"It's at the police station. Take it up with them. One other thing: If either of you bozos ever follows me again, I'll file a complaint against you for stalking."

Allison put the Jeep Cherokee in gear and roared off.

"My, you're a forceful woman," Harry Sullinger said into her ear.

"Yeah, that felt pretty good."

"Bozos," Sullinger said. "I liked that part. Is that a legal term?"

"Right. It's legalese for incompetent buffoon."

"It's a shame he didn't want to talk to me," Sullinger said. "I could have given him the good news that the ballistics tests show his gun was *not* the gun that killed Joey Red Horse."

"In that case I'm glad I didn't shoot him."

"Yeah, probably a good thing you didn't. As far as the police and prosecutor are concerned, he can have his gun back. All he has to do is ask."

"That's between him and you. I don't intend to talk to him again. I just hope Marge is okay."

"Say," Sullinger said, "I have another bit of interesting news for you. Once again, it goes into the category of things you need to keep under your hat."

"I haven't blabbed one of your secrets yet, Harry."

"We checked Bear Smith's Visa bill. It shows he rented a motel room in Los Angeles around the same time the drug dealer out there was killed."

"Maybe it's just a coincidence," Allison said.

"In my job, we are deeply suspicious of coincidences."

"Yeah, so you told me."

"So far, though," Sullinger said, "we don't find any connections between Bear Smith and Miami. We're still working it hard, though."

"Please let me know what you find out. I really appreciate the way you're keeping me in the loop."

"Think nothing of it, Allison. To tell the truth, I enjoy having an excuse to talk to you."

"Knock it off, Harry. Our relationship is strictly professional."

When she hung up, she wondered about the truth of those words.

Back at her office, Allison examined the notes she'd taken at the library and leafed through the phone book. Finding the name she was seeking, she dialed the number.

"Hello?"

"This is Allison Culbertson. May I speak to Betty Clinkscale."

"This is she."

"Mrs. Clinkscale, I'm a lawyer in Cape Girardeau. I was wondering if I might be able to talk with you for a few minutes?"

"Oh, I saw your picture in the paper recently! You're the one all the kids were booing! The one with the black bra strap."

"Yes, I'm that Allison Culbertson."

"Well, honey, I read those awful things that policeman, Harry Sullinger, said about you in the newspaper. It wasn't very nice of him to make fun of you like that. But what would you expect from the likes of him!"

Allison grimaced into the phone. "That's sort of what I wanted to talk to you about," Allison said. "You're Susan Torrence's grandmother, aren't you?"

"Yes. Is she in some sort of trouble?"

"No, no. Actually, I was hoping to talk with you a bit about Harry Sullinger and what happened ten years ago."

"You mean his killing my son and daughter-in-law?"

"Yes."

"Honey, we settled our lawsuit over that shooting a long time ago. We don't need a lawyer for that, now."

"I know, Mrs. Clinkscale. I was hoping you might give me a few minutes of your time, anyway."

"Well, sure. Anytime. You've got me curious now."

Chapter 44

Allison Culbertson sat with Clive Faulkner in a Cajun restaurant a few storefronts down the street from her office.

They were in a window booth, sitting right behind the alligator painted on the window. Clive Faulkner wore his usual bow tie. He was as handsome as ever.

"So, what's your big news?" she asked.

He leaned toward her, looking directly into her eyes. "It's official. The Board of Directors voted last night. We're going to replace the real skeletons and burial artifacts with reproductions. We're going to return the funereal objects to Native Americans."

She gasped. "Oh, Clive, that's wonderful. Thank you!"

He leaned back, a slight smile playing with the corner of his mouth. "It probably won't happen until next year. We won't do it until the replacement objects are made. We want to make sure they're perfect, so people can't tell the difference. Also, we want to make sure we return each item to the correct Indian tribe. It looks like most will probably go to the Osages, but the Mound Builders likely split into several tribes when they broke up. More than one modern tribe can make a good argument that Bootheel Man and his roommates are its ancestors. We want to make sure all American Indians are happy with the outcome, and no one feels left out."

Clive Faulkner reached across the table and took her hand. She didn't pull away. She was enjoying the moment. She wished Joey were around to share it. Joey had won. Even after his death, he had accomplished his dream.

"I may need your help," Faulkner said.

"In what way?"

"Well, the Board says if we're giving the skeletons back, we want guarantees they're getting reburied. I mean, that's the whole point, isn't it? We don't want Bootheel Man being put on display in some Native American museum or, worse yet, in some reservation casino. We don't want to give away the main attraction of our museum, only to find ourselves competing with it down the road."

"You don't need to worry about that," Allison said. "There's no chance in hell true American Indians would display the bones of their ancestors. Frankly, your casino comment would get you punched in the nose if you said it in front of the wrong people. They don't even want to touch them, much less display them. It's bad karma, you know?"

Faulkner nodded. "Also, we also want the American Indians to agree that we can continue to display photographs of Bootheel Man, as well as our reproduction of him and the other artifacts. We want this agreement in writing. If they're going to keep badmouthing us for displaying photographs and facsimiles, we might as well keep the original items."

"I see your point," Allison said. "I'm not sure they'll agree to keep their thoughts to themselves, but you can try to make that part of the agreement."

"Finally, we want to make absolutely certain adequate steps are taken to protect the grave of Bootheel Man. We don't want some collector or real grave robber digging him up in the middle of the night. We'd be willing to pay for a concrete tomb or whatever else might be necessary to ensure he stays buried this time."

"Clive, this is wonderful news. I'll tell Joe Black Dog and Mark Windfoot as soon as possible."

"The Board would rather not go public with this for a couple of weeks. We want to make sure we can find the right company to make the reproductions."

"What about Diedra Binzinger? She could probably do it."

He winced. "She's one possibility, but this is too big a job for one person. I mean, we're talking about lots of items. Plus, she and I aren't on the best of terms right now. The museum is going to contact several artists and companies, maybe get some bids."

The waitress, a busty girl with a tight t-shirt and numerous ear-piercings, delivered their salads to the table, forcing Faulkner to release Allison's hand.

As the waitress left, Allison picked up the red plastic drinking cup. "To Clive Faulkner," she toasted, "for doing the right thing."

He touched his cup to hers. "To Allison Culbertson, who made me do it."

Their eyes held for a moment. She remembered the kiss they'd shared at the Wickliffe Mounds site and felt a glow deep inside her body.

He put down the cup. "The Board needs your help, Allison. You're on pretty good terms with some of the key players in the Osage Nation, aren't you?"

Allison thought of Joe Black Dog. "I know one of them pretty well."

"And you're friendly with Mark Windfoot and ARROW?"

"He's a fan. He's giving me an award, as a matter of fact."

"What award?"

"The Legal Eagle. It looks like they're going to present it to me on October 4."

"Congratulations."

He raised his plastic cup again. "To Allison Culbertson, the most breathtaking lawyer I've ever met, whose legal skills have proved to be far above mere adequacy."

"I'll drink to that," Allison said, clinking cups with him.

His eyes were twinkling, but after a few moments he grew more serious. "The Board would like you to serve as a middleman for us. We want to make sure everything goes smoothly in this transfer. We're hoping the Osages would allow a public funeral ceremony or memorial service for Bootheel Man, something that could be filmed and might be suitable for the *Discovery Channel* or *National Geographic*. We're also hoping they'll work with us in the future by arranging guest speakers from their tribe to periodically appear at our museum. Quite frankly, losing Bootheel Man is going to be a tremendous blow. We're not sure we'll recover from it. We're hoping to offset the damage by creating new exhibits and by involving authentic American Indians in our educational programs. We want to get the maximum possible favorable publicity about our change of heart. We want to avoid anything negative whatsoever."

"Clive, if the museum is offering to hire me, I'll have to turn you down. My loyalties in this fight will always be with Joey and the Osages. But I'm willing to unofficially do my best to help things go smoothly."

352

"Anything you can do will be greatly appreciated." He leaned forward. "You know, none of this would have happened if it hadn't been for you."

Allison felt good. Perhaps she truly *was* a big part of the reason the museum had decided to return the human remains to their final resting places. She tried to make light of the pride she was feeling.

"I know. I was a real courtroom whiz at the preliminary hearing. That's why I'm getting the prestigious Legal Eagle Award. It ranks right up there with the Nobel Peace Prize, you know."

He chuckled. "Well, that wasn't exactly what I meant. What I mean to say is, I think I'm falling in love with you, Allison. For the first time in my life, something is more important to me than my work at the museum. I want to be a man you'd consider spending your happily-ever-afters with."

"Oh," Allison said. The inarticulate grunt came out like she'd been kicked. She was not sure what to say. She found Clive Faulkner extraordinarily attractive and enticingly brilliant, but she was a long way from seriously considering lifetimes and forevers. Plus, even though Harry Sullinger came packaged with his assortment of failed marriages, dragging ex-wives behind him like tin cans tied to a cat's tail, she had to admit she felt a spark every time she was around the big guy. Still, she probably had more in common with Clive Faulkner. Books. Education. Ambition. It was all very confusing.

"Clive, I don't know how I feel about you just yet. Let's not jump into things too quickly, okay?"

His blue eyes met hers. "You can't rule out the possibility of falling in love with me, can you?"

"No, I can't."

"Well, that's good enough for now. I'll be patient."

Chapter 45

Allison Culbertson had to hand it to Mark Windfoot. He knew how to stage a "media friendly" event. It was a bright October morning. The ARROW award ceremony was taking place in Indian Park in Cape Girardeau at the intersection of Lorimier and William Streets, three blocks from the Mississippi River. The small park was the perfect choice, since it had been given to the town by the city's founder, Louis Lorimier, and was dedicated to the American Indians who had used the site for a campground during their numerous visits to Lorimier and his Shawnee wife prior to her death in 1808. Windfoot scheduled the big event for 10 A.M., the most convenient time for network television, since it allowed plenty of time to prepare stories for the evening news. He provided slick information packets for each media person, complete with a brief history of ARROW, a list of previous ARROW award-winners, a synopsis of the legal battles waged by American Indians to force museums into repatriating human remains and funereal objects, a description of why Joey Red Horse and Allison Culbertson were winning this year's awards, and his own detailed biography. He had prevailed upon Allison to let him use her office to send sound bites from his speech to radio stations across the country immediately afterward. He had rented a flatbed trailer. His volunteers added crepe paper, a podium, and a microphone to the trailer, and unfurled a huge red ARROW banner behind the podium, transforming the ugly trailer into an aesthetically pleasing outdoor stage. He jump-started the size of his crowd by encouraging local grade schools, high schools, and sympathetic college professors at Southeast Missouri State University to award extra credit for attending his talk and writing reports about the issues involved. Finally, he convinced American Indians from all over the Midwest to attend the event. Many members of the Osage Nation made the trip to Cape Girardeau from Pawhuska, including Louise Red Horse and Joe Black Dog.

Allison watched the CNN news team interview Windfoot thirty minutes before the event was scheduled to begin. She marveled at his ease in turning the presentation of two plaques into a big event. Somehow he had even brokered perfect October weather from *Wah'Kon-Tah* or whoever controlled such things.

When the bus arrived, bringing the Osage contingent from their motel, Allison made her way to it.

Joe Black Dog was helping Louise Red Horse down the steps of the bus.

"Welcome to Cape Girardeau," Allison said.

"Hello, Miss Culbertson!" Louise Red Horse gave her a hug. "Isn't it nice what ARROW is doing for Joey?"

"Yes, he'd definitely like it."

Joe Black Dog's face was less enthusiastic. "I am reserving judgment," he said. "I want to believe this is about Joey and not about Mark Windfoot. We'll find out soon enough, I imagine."

Louise Red Horse touched Allison's arm. "Have you figured out who killed my Joey?"

"Well, the police are the ones actually doing the investigation, but, no, I don't think his murder is solved yet."

Her bright, wet eyes gazed at Allison. "Can you prosecute the killer? Can you do it for Joey? For me?"

"The elected public prosecutor would be responsible for handling any criminal prosecution. We don't have private prosecutors in America. It's possible, though, that Joey's family might want to file a wrongful death civil suit against the killer. Remember how O.J. Simpson was prosecuted criminally and sued civilly for the deaths of Nicole Brown Simpson and Ronald Goldman?"

"O. J. Simpson," she sniffed. "Who can forget him?" She patted Allison's arm. "You keep that civil suit in the back of your mind, honey. If I live long enough, we'll file one when they catch Joey's killer."

"I won't forget what you said, Mrs. Red Horse," Allison promised.

She and Joe Black Dog helped Joey's mother to a seat on the stage.

When Allison had a moment to speak with Joe Black Dog, she told him about her recent conversation with Clive Faulkner.

"The Heartland Mound Builder Museum is seriously considering voluntarily returning the bones and funerary objects in its possession to the Osage Nation," she said. "He's hoping the details can be worked out."

"What sort of details? Transportation arrangements? Several of us have pickup trucks, if that's what he's worried about." Joe Black Dog's habit of speaking without varying his intonation made it difficult to tell when he was joking.

"No," Allison said, "Clive Faulkner wants assurances that the Osages will rebury the items and not put them on display."

Joe Black Dog grunted. "He actually worries that we would tamper with the human remains of our ancestors ourselves, after working so hard to bring peace to the souls of these dead people? I will speak with our elders and our tribal government, but I am sure we can agree to those terms. Anything else?"

"He's also hoping the Osage Nation will hold some type of public funeral or memorial service for Bootheel Man, something suitable for primetime news."

"Primetime news?" Joe Black Dog frowned.

"Well, he wants publicity for his good deed."

Joe Black Dog nodded. "I doubt we would let the media attend our private ceremonies, but perhaps something superficial enough for the media could be done outside the museum before the bones are returned to us. Anything else?"

"He is going to insist that part of the deal be that he can display photographs of Bootheel Man, as well as a replica."

"Tell him we will get back to him, but it looks promising." Joe Black Dog took her hand. "Thank you for everything you have done, Miss Culbertson. Let's hope it works out."

"May I ask you something else?" she said.

"Certainly."

"Can you think of any connection between Joey and a Colombian drug lord named Pablo Ramirez?"

"No. Why?"

Allison recalled that Harry Sullinger did not want her to share the details he had told her, so she carefully worded her answer.

"This drug lord's name has come up in the investigation. I'm not sure I can explain precisely how. But is there any way Joey's involvement with peyote could have trickled over into cocaine? Has it ever happened before?"

Joe Black Dog thoughtfully considered his answer before speaking.

"Ever? How can I answer that? Peyote is nothing like cocaine, though, Miss Culbertson. It produces a calming experience. In fact, at the height of its use in the Church, it actually cut down on alcoholism. It is cheap, too. There would not be enough money in peyote to interest a big-time drug dealer. I don't see how Joey's involvement with peyote could bring him into contact with a Colombian drug lord, unless the drug lord was converting to Peyotism as a religion."

Mark Windfoot and the mayor of Cape Girardeau were making their way to the podium.

"I'll talk to you later," Allison said. "I'm supposed to sit in one of the seats on the stage."

As she worked her way toward the platform, she spotted Clive Faulkner. To her surprise, he was standing next to Diedra Binzinger.

I guess I shouldn't be shocked, Allison thought to herself. *They aren't required to avoid each other, just because they broke up.* She fought the immediate instinct to be jealous of Binzinger. *How can I be jealous when I don't even understand my own feelings about Clive? Get a grip!*

She caught Faulkner's eye. "May I mention the Board's decision publicly?" she asked.

He nodded. "Just don't say it's a done deal yet."

Allison hurried to her seat as the mayor launched into effusive remarks welcoming Mark Windfoot to the city. He spoke about the history of Indian Park and the legendary hospitality of Louis Lorimier's "Red House" as a mecca for American Indians.

As the mayor droned on, Allison took the opportunity to study the crowd. Four-hundred people filled the park. Five separate television crews were covering the event. The audience consisted mostly of whites and African-Americans, probably locals, but a significant number of American Indians were scattered throughout the crowd. She spotted Harry Sullinger near the back. He waved at her and she waved back. She was sure he was studying faces, looking for suspects in Joey Red Horse's death. Would the killer have the chutzpah to show up at Joey's award ceremony?

Unbidden, the words of Louise Red Horse bubbled up from the back of her mind: "Have you figured out who killed my Joey?" Ironically, several people with potential motives were present at this big event: Mark Windfoot, Bear Smith, Lolita Smith, Marge Tappinger, Rex Tappinger, Clive Faulkner, and Diedra Binzinger. She had spotted all of them here today.

Polite applause followed the mayor's speech as he gave way to the morning's main speaker, Mark Windfoot.

As the handsome President of ARROW moved to the microphone, Allison considered how his organization had benefited from Joey's death. The theft had brought nationwide attention to the battle between ARROW and private museums. Joey's murder had increased its national exposure tenfold. Was it possible ARROW funneled money through Bear Smith for Joey's defense? Had Mark Windfoot helped plan the theft? Had ARROW been involved in the killing? Windfoot certainly had many zealous followers. But would they cold-bloodedly kill one of their own? Was there some reason they considered Joey expendable?

"ARROW stands for Angry Reformers Resisting Oppressive Whites," Mark Windfoot began. "We are a nonviolent organization dedicated to redressing wrongs committed against American Indians and improving the lives of our people. We at ARROW deliberately come up with ways to be provocative. We want to be rebellious. We want to be in your face. We don't want to be ignored."

Several young people whooped. Allison's eyes rested on one of them, Lolita Smith. She was wearing her CUSTER DIED FOR YOUR SINS shirt and was gazing at Windfoot with rapt admiration. Next to her, Bear Smith stood with his arms crossed, a satisfied expression on his gnarly face. Father and daughter each had a motive to kill Joey. She, out of jealously; he, out of anger and a sense of betrayal. The law books were filled with cases where a relationship starting with love ended with prison.

"If you read most American schoolbooks," Windfoot was saying, "you would think Indians were a people who vanished from the face of this earth. You would think we didn't exist today. But, ladies and gentlemen, we're still here. Many of our forefathers were shuffled off to reservations. Many others were murdered. But more than five-hundred-seventy federally recognized American Indian tribes still exist in the United States of America. We are proud of our heritage as the First Citizens of America!"

Several people applauded.

"We have many goals at ARROW," Windfoot continued. "The main one is regaining for American Indians the rights secured by the treaties signed by the United States government. Hardly a treaty was written that hasn't been violated by the United States government!" This comment brought widespread applause from every American Indian present.

"You tell 'em, Mark," a younger man with long black ponytail yelled.

Allison spotted the Tappingers near the podium. They were standing next to each other, but they didn't seem to be talking. Marge's pregnancy still didn't show. She was listening intently to Mark Windfoot. Rex Tappinger was scanning the crowd, a look of bemused contempt on his face.

Mark Windfoot lowered his voice. "White Americans are not aware how often and how violently those treaties have been broken over the years, and how they are still being broken today."

"Right on!" the ponytail yelled. Allison saw Rex Tappinger roll his eyes.

"Another goal," Windfoot continued, "is to wipe out the word 'redskin' from the English language, to remove it from all sports teams, all toys, all textbooks, all jokes, and all consumer products of any kind. When it is a dead word, we will have been such successful reformers that we might not even be angry anymore!"

A chorus of yells and applause forced Windfoot to wait several seconds before resuming. Allison wondered whether the crowd's reaction was completely natural or if Windfoot had planted his own cheerleaders throughout the audience. He was slick enough to pull a stunt like that, she decided.

"Another goal," he said, "has been to undo some of the hurt to our people caused by archaeologists and museums who dug up and displayed the human remains of Native Americans over the past two centuries. We are here today because one man and one lawyer in this Bootheel community were instrumental this past year as advocates for our noble cause!"

The crowd applauded politely. Allison hoped the applause was genuine. After all, it was partly for her. She glanced at Clive Faulkner. He was not applauding. Was it possible this enigmatic man had something to do with Joey's death? He had been out of town, but he could have paid someone to do it. But Joey's death had not ended the bad publicity for the Heartland Mound Builder Museum. In fact, it had turned the bad press into an avalanche. If Faulkner had done it to curtail the pressure on the museum to return the bones, his plan had badly backfired. Diedra Binzinger stood near Clive Faulkner. Did the artist have anything to gain from Joey's death?

"Nor is it a coincidence," Windfoot continued solemnly, "that ARROW chose this date, October 4, to present our awards. I'll bet that not one single person here knows why October 4, 1894, was a happy day for American Indians. Does anybody know?"

He made a show of searching the faces of the crowd. Allison's gaze landed on Harry Sullinger. He winked at her. She looked away.

"I thought not!" Windfoot shouted. "Ladies and gentlemen, October 4 was the day John Chivington died."

A smattering of applause came from some of the American Indians.

Allison glanced back at Harry Sullinger. He was once again studying people in the crowd.

Mark Windfoot wagged a finger. "I'll further bet that not one in ten of you has even a clue who John Chivington was!" He surveyed the crowd, as if waiting for someone to raise a hand.

"Colonel John Chivington," he said, the volume of his voice rising, "was the man who led his soldiers in an attack on the Cheyenne camp at Sand Creek on November 29, 1864. This outrage was overshadowed by other events of the era. The white man's battle of Gettysburg took place sixteen months earlier. President Lincoln was assassinated just five months later. And, after all, why should Sand Creek get big headlines nationwide? The people killed there weren't human beings to the national media when they died. They were just a bunch of 'redskins.'"

The crowd was completely silent.

"Colonel John Chivington," Windfoot whispered into the microphone, "was a man who, next to George Armstrong Custer, epitomizes better than anyone else the horrible injustices inflicted upon American Indians by white men. Chivington was a man who should've known better. Before the Civil War, he was a Methodist minister in a town just two-hundred-forty-eight miles from here, La Grange, Missouri, in Lewis County, up above Hannibal. He was a man of the cloth. Yet, to him, American Indians weren't human beings. They were animals. They were 'redskins.' Before he led his group of six-hundred Colorado men on the attack of Chief Black Kettle's peaceful Cheyenne camp at Sand Creek, he was warned by real soldiers, men guided by a sense of conscience, that a raid on the women and children in that camp would be 'murder in every sense of the word.' Chivington responded by saying, 'Damn any man who sympathizes with Indians! I have come to kill Indians, and believe it is right and honorable to use any means under God's heaven to kill Indians!' He spoke with the passion of a zealot about 'collecting scalps' and 'wading in gore.'"

Windfoot's voice rose. "His death squad did indeed wade in gore and collect human scalps. They attacked the sleeping camp at dawn, blasting tepees with artillery, and firing rifles and pistols at unarmed men, women, and children as they fled in terror. Black Kettle flew a United States flag outside his tepee, demonstrating his loyalty to The Great White Father in Washington. The peaceful chief also ran up a white flag to show his people's lack of resistance. White Antelope, another chief, an old man of seventy-five, approached the soldiers unarmed, confident they would stop firing when they saw the American flag and the white flag. Instead, he was shot down. Soldiers executed women and children who were begging for mercy. They hacked them to pieces with sabers. Soldiers later admitted scalping dead Cheyenne, mutilating bodies, and using body parts as decorations and souvenirs. In many instances the private parts of females were cut out and worn as hatbands. White Antelope's genitals were slashed from his body, and a solder bragged about making a tobacco pouch out of them."

Several people in the audience gasped. Allison noticed that Diedra Binzinger had placed her hand over her mouth.

"Many soldiers with Colonel Chivington later confessed these atrocities," Windfoot said. "Eyewitness accounts come from the soldiers themselves. But what happened to Colonel Chivington, the man responsible for massacring hundreds of people in America's worst act of genocide? Does anyone know?"

Absolute silence greeted the question.

"Nothing!" Windfoot shouted. "Like most white people who committed atrocities against American Indians over the years, nothing happened to him! Not a thing! He lived out his natural life and died of cancer on October 4, 1894."

Several people in the crowd applauded. Others booed.

"Well, I take back my statement that nothing happened to John Chivington," Windfoot said. "Even though he couldn't be court-martialed for his atrocities at Sand Creek, an Army judge who investigated the matter declared publicly that Sand Creek was 'a cowardly and coldblooded slaughter, sufficient to cover its perpetrator with indelible infamy, and the face of every American with shame and indignation!'"

The applause grew louder.

"We at ARROW," Windfoot continued, smiling grimly, "like to think something else happened to John Chivington. We like to imagine his horror and shock when his soul traveled to the next world, and he discovered the error of his ways. By golly, the creatures he killed were human beings, real people, even though they weren't good Methodists like him, even though they weren't ministers of the cloth like him, and even though they didn't have white skin like his! We like to think he is getting a taste of his own medicine in the next world!"

A loud blast of applause greeted Windfoot's remark. Even Clive Faulkner and Rex Tappinger were clapping.

Mark Windfoot raised his hand. "Now, we aren't here to criticize Methodists. Geronimo himself converted to Methodism at the end of his life. We American Indians don't blame an entire church for the actions of one man. In fact, in 1996, the Methodist Church issued an apology for the conduct of its wayward minister. But because his name will forever be clothed with infamy, we believe it is fitting and proper that we gather here on October 4, the anniversary of the date John Chivington departed this world to meet his Maker and settle accounts for what he did to American Indians."

He stood silently at the microphone for several seconds, waiting for the noise level to die down before continuing. Allison glimpsed Detective Paul Burns videotaping the crowd. If Burns and Sullinger intended to identify every person present, they had a daunting task ahead of them.

"Not all outrages committed upon Native Americans by the Europeans who came to this continent were as bold and blatant as the actions of John Chivington," Windfoot was saying. "Many were sneakier, like those who forced, often at gunpoint, American Indians, to whom the ownership of property was a foreign concept, to sell their homeland for pennies per acre in treaties usually broken by the American government before the ink was even dry. Other outrages were inadvert, or well intentioned, like digging up the bones of Americans Indians and putting them on display in museums and carnivals."

Windfoot pointed a finger at the crowd. "Do you know how much the United States government paid the Osages for the land we stand on today? Less than a penny per acre!"

Several people in the crowd booed.

"It is estimated that as many as three-hundred-thousand to two-million sets of human remains of American Indians are housed in federal, state, and private museums across this country. The Smithsonian Institute alone had eighteen-thousand dead Native Americans on its premises. But who really cares that the bones of these human beings occupy boxes and crates in museums instead of peacefully resting in graves? After all, they weren't people! They were just redskins! We have been fighting hard for the right to repatriate these bones to the proper tribes for reburial. Our cause was aided by the federal government in 1990 with the passage of the Native American Graves Protection and Repatriation Act. It requires museums receiving federal money to voluntarily list their human remains and make efforts to work with tribes to repatriate them. Much has been accomplished by this act. But it has a loophole. It doesn't apply to private museums. That's why the Heartland Mound Builder Museum in Cape Girardeau has been able to continue to insult American Indians by displaying the bones of the man called Bootheel Man and thirty-seven other sets of human remains at the museum. Bootheel Man and his silent brothers and sisters constitute a drop in the bucket of the number of human remains that still need to be repatriated, but they are a well-known and highly-publicized drop. We at ARROW care about them!"

Clive Faulkner was standing close enough to the stage for Allison to see the blush creeping across his face. His expression betrayed no emotion, though.

"We at ARROW," proclaimed Mark Windfoot, "are here today to recognize the bravery and vision of one young Osage, Joey Red Horse, who courageously brought attention to this issue by risking his own freedom and his own life by breaking into the Heartland Mound Builder Museum and taking one of the most well-known Native American burial artifacts and repatriating it by throwing it into the Mississippi River. His dramatic act was done with bravery and spirit that Crazy Horse himself would admire. As we all know, Crazy Horse was one American Indian who never bowed to the white man's ways. Yes, ladies and gentlemen, Joey Red Horse's brave deed has won him this year's Crazy Horse Award."

The crowd applauded politely. Allison guessed that fewer than a half dozen people present had known Joey personally. Many had probably never even heard of Crazy Horse.

"As you know," Windfoot continued, "Joey Red Horse was murdered while he was out on bond awaiting his trial. He cannot be here today to accept his award in person. But his mother made the trip here from Pawhuska, Oklahoma. Louise Red Horse, please come forward."

As the audience applauded, Louise Red Horse shuffled to Mark Windfoot's side. He presented the plaque to her and invited her to say a few words. As she nodded, he adjusted the microphone to her height. She stood in silence for a moment before she finally began. Her voice was soft but easily heard because of the respectful silence.

"Joey was a special person," she said. "He was a spiritual boy, even while growing up. When he saw wrong, he tried to right it. When he saw injustice, he tried to fix it. That's just the way he was.

He would thank ARROW for this award if he were here. He isn't, so in his place, I thank you."

The crowd applauded politely.

"Before I sit down," she added, "I would like to make a plea to the people here today and to those watching on television or listening on the radio. If you know who killed my Joey, please come forward and tell the police. Or call Joey's dedicated and honorable lawyer, Allison Culbertson. Please help. I won't rest until we get justice for Joey."

Mark Windfoot patted her back. "Thank you, Mrs. Red Horse. We at ARROW join your request that anyone who knows anything about Joey's death should come forward."

Windfoot picked up the other plaque. "Speaking of Joey's dedicated and honorable lawyer," he said, "this year's Legal Eagle Award goes to Allison Culbertson. She was the one who came up with the claim-of-right defense. She was prepared to argue that because Joey reasonably believed that as a member of the Osage Nation he had a better right to possession of the burial artifacts of the Mound Builders than did the museum, he had a complete defense to a charge of criminal stealing. ARROW believes she would have won Joey an acquittal had his case gone to trial. Her skillful advocacy of Joey's cause in the courtroom did much to advance the cause of repatriating the bones of American Indians across this nation. Allison Culbertson, thank you for your hard work!"

Allison appreciated the applause that greeted her as she accepted the award from Windfoot and moved to the microphone.

"Thank you, Mr. Windfoot. I'm delighted and honored to receive this award. It was my privilege to represent Joey Red Horse. He was a passionate man who believed strongly that whatever happened to him, the personal risks were outweighed by the importance of his cause. Not everyone is brave enough to dive off the Mississippi River bridge." Her eyes landed on Harry Sullinger. He was grinning. "Or even jump," she added.

Sullinger's grin widened.

"Joey risked his life to do his small part to try to return to American Indians the bones and burial items in this museum and in other private museums across the country. Joey behaved heroically. He truly did have the indomitable spirit of Crazy Horse."

The loud applause seemed more than merely polite. Allison was pleased. Both Marge Tappinger and Lolita Smith were openly crying. *Perhaps Joey had a little Casanova in him, too*, Allison thought, but she kept the unbidden insight very much to herself as she waited for the noise to die down. Her gaze landed on Diedra Binzinger. The artist, too, was weeping. *Not her, too*, Allison thought. *Surely, Joey, you didn't!*

When the applause dwindled, Allison continued: "I am authorized today to reveal a promising bit of news. Clive Faulkner, the director of the Heartland Mound Builder Museum, has told me that he is willing to begin sincere negotiations with the Osage Nation about the return of every single bone and burial artifact in the museum's possession. Current law doesn't require the museum to do it. But they intend to do it because they have come to realize it is the right thing to do." Allison glanced at Joe Black Dog and then looked to the sky. "Joey once told me that the Osage believe the Milky Way is the passageway to the next world. Joey, when you pause on your journey across the Milky Way, look back for a moment and revel in what you have accomplished!"

As the crowd applauded, Allison shook hands again with Mark Windfoot.

"Thank you, Miss Culbertson, and congratulations." He waited for Allison to take her seat, and closed with a fund-raising pitch.

"I want to remind each of you that ARROW exists only because of generous contributions made by people who want to see American Indians achieve their dream of true freedom and their rightful place as the First Americans. Please visit our website and consider making a contribution to our cause. Thank you."

As Allison watched Harry Sullinger watching Bear Smith watch Mark Windfoot, she felt a tap on her shoulder.

"You did good, Miss Culbertson," Louise Red Horse said. "Wherever he is, I'm sure Joey's still bragging about how good his lawyer is."

Chapter 46

Allison Culbertson was having trouble adapting to being a gun-toting moll. She went to the firing range with Sullinger twice a week and was becoming proficient at handling her Beretta, but now that she was licensed to carry a concealed weapon, she was finding the carrying and the concealing easier said than done.

One problem was legal. Most businesses and government offices posted signs forbidding concealed weapons. Carrying guns into those places was illegal. Allison was mortified by even the thought that she might accidentally violate the law and become a public spectacle. She could imagine the headline: ATTORNEY CHARGED WITH VIOLATING CONCEALED-CARRY LAW. A lawyer, of all people, could not plead ignorance of the law. As a result, she was constantly taking her gun in and out of her purse and often leaving it in the console of her car.

The other problem was physical. Allison was not a big person. The Beretta was not a tiny gun. It was a difficult thing to hide on her petite body, particularly with her current wardrobe. An ankle-holster didn't work with any of her clothing, a shoulder holster reminded her too much of *Dragnet* reruns, and a hip-holster produced way too much of a lump under even her baggiest outfits.

She had settled for carrying the gun in her purse to and from work and hiding it in her desk drawer throughout the day.

Sometimes she asked herself why she didn't just quit carrying it altogether, but she knew the answer. The carefree feeling she'd enjoyed prior to witnessing Joey Red Horse's death was gone forever. She was no longer a sheep in denial. Now, alone on the sidewalk at night, walking from the front door of her office to her car or navigating the short distance from her driveway to her door at home, she was keenly aware of the existence of the wolves. She could never forget the possibility that the person who killed Joey might have undergone a change of heart about letting her live and might be lying in wait for her. Allison knew her chance of getting off even one shot at a killer who ambushed her was infinitesimally small, but simply carrying the gun in her purse made her feel less helpless.

She was glad the Beretta was in her big Prada purse as she locked the front door of her office shortly before midnight a week after she received ARROW's Legal Eagle Award. She'd been working late on a trial brief in a driving-while-intoxicated case, cobbling together a halfway feasible argument that her client's blood sample had been improperly drawn. By the time she was ready to go home, it was late and dark. Since her parking space was on the lot at the back of the building, right across the street from the floodwall, she faced a nice little hike to get to the Jeep Cherokee.

She carried her purse, unzipped, under her left arm. She knew she could get into it quickly with her right hand, if necessary. The click of her heels on the empty sidewalk made a lonely sound. *I am a sheepdog*, she told herself, *not a sheep. I am a sheepdog, not a sheep.*

Main Street was quiet as she neared the turn down Themis Street. The silence reminded her of the night Joey Red Horse had been killed. She tried not to think about his awful death-dance.

Behind her, she heard a motorcycle start up. It seemed to be sitting still, revving its engine. She quickened her pace, involuntarily. She reached the corner of the building and turned down Themis toward the floodwall, her hand slipping into her purse and settling comfortably on the gun grip.

God! Was the rest of her life going to be like this? Getting jumpy at every little noise? She chastised herself for her faintheartedness.

Behind her, she heard the motorcycle roar to life. It sounded like it was coming south down Main Street, the same direction she'd come. *But that's why they call it Main Street*, she told herself, *because it's the main drag. Lots of traffic. Nothing to get worked up about!* But as Allison walked onto the parking lot behind her building, the motorcycle turned down Themis Street, following the exact route she'd taken. It was only fifty yards away and closing in on her.

Casting decorum aside, Allison ran the last thirty feet to her Jeep Cherokee. She put the vehicle between herself and the motorcycle as her pursuer roared onto the parking lot. The driver was dressed in black clothing and wore a black helmet with tinted glass.

Allison pulled her gun and held it at her side, next to her thigh. She pushed off the safety with her thumb.

The motorcycle rolled to a stop near her. Using both hands, the cyclist removed the shiny black helmet. In the light of the streetlamp, Allison saw Lolita Smith's face.

Allison felt rather awkward and mildly embarrassed, standing in the parking lot with a fully loaded Beretta semiautomatic pistol gripped in her hand, facing a lone high-school girl, but she didn't put it away. What was Lolita doing, approaching her outside her office at midnight? Where was Bear Smith?

"I saw your car," Lolita said. "I figured you were working late. I thought maybe we could talk."

"Your father made it clear he didn't want us talking," Allison said.

"I know. That's why I had to sneak around to find the right way to meet you."

"Why lurk outside my office? Why not call or ring the door-bell?" Allison asked. "I've been inside for hours."

Lolita turned off the engine of her motorcycle, still straddling its seat.

"I don't know," she said. "I've been sitting out here for thirty minutes or so, trying to decide what to do. I bounced back and forth about whether I should talk to you at all."

Allison studied the Osage girl, clad all in black. Black sweat pants. Black jacket. Was it possible Lolita was the person who shot Joey? Allison hadn't been able to gauge the killer's size or shape. She couldn't rule it out.

"I don't really feel comfortable, talking at midnight on a park-ing lot," Allison said.

"Obviously," Lolita said, nodding at the gun.

Wordlessly, Allison flipped on the safety and put the Beretta back into her purse. She studied Lolita's face in the purplish light. The girl looked even more frightened than Allison.

"If we're going to talk, let's go back to my office."

"I'd rather not leave my motorcycle parked out here by your car. My father doesn't know I'm here, but if he happened to come looking for me, I wouldn't want him to see it."

Allison glanced around. Her gaze landed on the nineteen-foot-wide gaping entrance to the concrete floodwall. They would have a great deal of privacy on the river side of the wall, standing on the cobblestones near the water.

"Walk your motorcycle over to the other side of the floodwall. We can talk in private over there, out of sight. Your father would have to be looking pretty hard to find us."

Lolita nodded.

They walked across the street, Lolita pushing the small Harley Davidson and Allison walking quietly next to her. On the river side of the floodwall, concrete steps and cobblestones completely covered the fifty-foot slope from the floodwall to the water's edge. Lolita leaned the motorcycle against the concrete wall.

"Thanks for talking to me," she said. "This must be sort of creepy for you, my showing up unannounced in the middle of the night."

"I'm becoming accustomed to creepy," Allison said, noting that the sound of the river lapping against the cobblestones added to the discomfort of the moment. Perhaps coming to this side of the floodwall had not been a good idea. They were alarmingly close to the treacherous depths of the river should anyone pop out of the darkness and try to hurl either or both of them into the flowing water.

"I thought you should know," Lolita said, "that I found out where my father got the fifty-thousand dollars he gave you for Joey's bond money."

"You did?"

"He got it from Mark Windfoot and ARROW." Somewhere in the night, an owl hooted.

"How do you know that?" Allison asked.

"When Mark Windfoot was in town last Saturday to present the awards, he met with my father. I heard them talking. My dad was returning the unused part of the fifty-thousand dollars, the money left over after your attorney fee."

"That means Mark Windfoot lied to me," Allison said. "He specifically told me he had never met your father until Joey's funeral. He claimed his organization didn't put up Joey's bond money. Why was ARROW providing the money? What does it mean?"

Lolita shook her head. "I don't know. I thought it might be important, though. I thought you should know. You're the only person who really has Joey's best interests at heart. You want to find out who killed him. I do, too. I just hope it's not," she paused, a flicker of despair crossing her face, "someone close to me."

Allison studied her face. "Like your father? Could he have done it?"

"I hope not. He was sure mad, though. When he found out about Joey and me, he went ballistic. And this whole thing about ARROW putting up Joey's bond. Why the big secret? Why didn't he tell me? I've been sick to my stomach the last couple of days, thinking about it. You were the only person I felt I could talk to. Tonight was a home football game." She tapped the Central High School tote bag tied to her motorcycle. "I was cheerleading. My dad didn't go to the game. It seemed like the perfect time to talk with you if I could find you. I tried your house first, then spotted your Jeep down here. I don't want to get my dad in trouble, Miss Culbertson, but something I don't understand is going on. I'm really scared."

"What exactly did you hear them say?"

"My dad thanked Mark Windfoot for the bond money for Joey. Windfoot thanked my dad for keeping his name out of it."

"Could you tell whether your father or Mark Windfoot helped Joey plan the theft of Gazing Woman?"

"Not for sure."

"Did they say anything about Joey?"

"Mark Windfoot said Joey had served the cause well. Those were his exact words. Served the cause."

"Did they talk about Joey's death?"

"Windfoot just said Joey had become a true martyr and that the votes might be there this year in Congress to get NAGPRA expanded to cover private museums."

Lolita's cell phone rang. "I'd better get this," she said. "Hello? Hi, Dad. Yeah, the game's over. We beat Poplar Bluff 38-21. Oh, I stopped at Taco Bell. I'll be home soon. Five tacos? Aren't you worried about getting fat? Okay. I'll get 'em. Love you, too. Bye."

After the phone call, Lolita Smith was agitated. "Great, now I really do have to stop at Taco Bell! My dad said to bring him five tacos. I'd better go."

She put on her helmet.

Allison touched the girl's arm.

"If you hear anything else, Lolita, let me know."

"I will," she said, starting the motorcycle. "Besides me, you're the only person who really seems to want to know who killed Joey. Whoever did it ruined my life. They're gonna be sorry."

With that, Lolita Smith roared off into the night.

Chapter 47

Harry Sullinger sat at his office desk on a Friday morning, listening to his voice-mail messages. He was delighted to hear Allison Culbertson as his third message. She wanted him to call. Just hearing her voice brightened his day. She sounded excited, saying it had to do with Lolita Smith. *Interesting*, he thought, as he listened to the next message, realizing as he did so that in the hierarchy of messages to be returned, it was unlikely any subsequent message would supplant Allison Culbertson's at the top of his list.

As he played a long message from a Missouri Highway Patrol sergeant about a pending leaving-the-scene-of-an-accident case, one of the legal secretaries at the prosecutor's office stuck her head in his door. It was Callie, a cute redhead. She had the face of a porcelain doll and the observational powers of a Nazi sentry on speed.

"The boss wants to see you," she said.

"Where is he?"

"In his office. He tried to buzz you but your line's been busy. He sent me to get you."

Sullinger hung up. The rest of the messages could wait.

"What were you smiling about?" Callie asked.

"When?"

"Just now. While you were listening to that message, you were smiling like a monkey with a mirror."

"That was Shane Tucker from the Highway Patrol. I wasn't smiling."

"No, the one before. A woman's voice. Was it a girlfriend?"

"I don't have a girlfriend."

Callie put a hand on her hip, striking a pose that showed off her curves. "Now, Harry," she chided, "you can tell me. Who was she?"

Callie had worked at the prosecutor's office for three months. She was straight out of Metro Business College, not a day over nineteen. From her first day at work, she had made it her mission to find out about Sullinger's personal life. It must have been the five divorces that intrigued her. He was unclear whether she was flirting or honing her skills as an office gossip. Either way, he enjoyed dodging her questions.

"I don't have a girlfriend. Five divorces will inoculate a guy from that sort of thing."

"Yeah, right," Callie said. "Girls don't interest you. By the way, the boss sounded like he might be mad at you."

"What?" Harry said.

John Marshall Plimpton was usually an easygoing boss. If he was angry about something, it had to be important.

"What's he mad about?"

"Search me, but he was cussing up a storm about you being on the phone when he needed you."

"You're kidding!"

John Marshall Plimpton almost never cursed. This must be something really bad. Sullinger took a mental inventory of things he might have screwed up recently. Nothing really terrible jumped out at him. There were a couple of small things he hoped Plimpton didn't know about.

He glanced at Callie. She burst out laughing. "Gotcha!" she giggled. "I'm kidding. He said to send you to him. Didn't say what it was about. Didn't seem mad. Man, are you easy to punk!"

"Very funny," he said, watching the sassy roll of her hips as she laughed her way back to the reception area. Muttering, he headed down the hallway to Plimpton's office.

He found the prosecuting attorney sitting at his desk, its surface looking like a snow-covered mountain range, white peaks and valleys created by stacks of papers and files of varying height.

John Marshall Plimpton pointed to a large accordion file on a corner of his desk. "Got a question for you, Harry."

"Yes, sir. What's up?"

"You recognize this file?"

Harry glanced at the accordion folder. It was the file from the coroner's inquest into his shooting of Jesse and Carrie Torrence more than ten years earlier. The memories cut into him like a knife.

"Yeah," Harry said.

John Marshall Plimpton leaned back in his chair. "Any idea why Allison Culbertson would have requested a copy of the testimony from that particular inquest?"

Harry was speechless for several seconds. Finally, he spoke, essentially thinking aloud. "That case was over and done with years ago. The coroner's jury ruled the shootings justifiable. The family sued me civilly, but it was settled. I can't imagine why she would be interested."

Plimpton frowned. "Well, she wrote a letter a few days ago. Wanted a copy. It's public record, and she was willing to pay for the copying, so I sent it to her. I thought maybe you'd have an idea why she wants it."

"No," Harry said. "I don't."

He was hurt that Allison hadn't simply asked him to track it down for her. Maybe he didn't know her as well as he thought. Maybe she hadn't believed what he had told her. Maybe she was checking up on him. Maybe she was wanting it for some other purpose, something she didn't want him to know about.

"I don't know why she didn't mention it to me," he said. "I've talked to her several times the past few days."

The prosecutor picked up the thick accordion folder and thumbed through it, then shrugged. "Well, I thought you should know," Plimpton said. "I've tried to think of possible reasons she might want a copy, but I'm not coming up with anything. I guess I should've asked her, but I thought I'd check with you first. Why would Joey Red Horse's lawyer want a copy of this particular file, Harry?"

"I don't know."

"Do I need to take you off the case?"

"No. I'll talk to her today. I'll find out what's going on."

"Do that," Plimpton said. "Let me know what she says."

When Sullinger got back to his desk, he called Allison Culbertson's office.

"Hi," she answered, when Rita put him through. Her voice sounded cheerful and excited, exactly the opposite of how he felt.

"I got a message you called," he said.

"Lolita Smith came by to see me last night," she said.

"Oh?"

"She told me that Mark Windfoot was the one who gave Bear Smith the money to bond Joey out of jail."

"Really." The gears in Sullinger's brain started whirling. He processed the new information, even while a part of him still wondered why Allison Culbertson had gotten a copy of the coroner's inquest into his shooting of Jesse and Carrie Torrence.

"How does Lolita know?" he asked.

"She heard them talking when Windfoot was in town. Bear Smith returned the leftover money to Windfoot."

"Did Windfoot know in advance that Joey would burglarize the museum? Did he put him up to it?"

"She didn't know. But she said Windfoot made the comment that Joey had served the cause well. Those were the exact words, 'served the cause.'"

Sullinger was taking notes. He underlined the words "served the cause."

"Guess I'll need to reinterview Miss Smith," he said.

"Harry, do it when Bear Smith is *not* around. Lolita's frightened. At this point, she's not even sure her father didn't kill Joey."

"She's over sixteen," Sullinger mused, "so I could interview her at the high school without involving her father."

"There you go," Allison said. "That's what you need to do."

Harry paused. He wanted to ask Allison Culbertson why she had requested a copy of the Torrence file. Yet, it was the sort of thing that should be saved for a face-to-face conversation.

"Harry," Allison Culbertson said, "there's something else I wanted to talk to you about. Could you come by my office this afternoon? Say about four o'clock?"

"Sure. Should I bring my lawyer?"

"What?"

"Just kidding," he said.

Before the morning was over, he and the school resource officer had taken a supplemental statement from Lolita Smith at the high school. She verified the things she'd told Allison Culbertson.

When he got back to the office, he added Lolita's supplemental statement to the fat three-ring binder containing the evergrowing

376

police reports in the Joey Red Horse murder investigation. Afterward, he sat thinking about the case for a long time.

It bothered Harry Sullinger that Bear Smith's own daughter was no longer 100 percent certain that her father was incapable of murder. She ought to know him better than anyone else. If she was frightened, maybe she had reason to be.

It bothered him that phone records showed calls from Joey Red Horse's telephone to ARROW's telephone prior to the museum burglary. Were Mark Windfoot and the ARROW secretary lying about not talking with Joey beforehand?

It bothered him that both Bear Smith and Mark Windfoot had apparently lied about not knowing each other. One of his favorite law-enforcement axioms was that a provable lie was the next best thing to a confession. Why would they lie, if they weren't hiding something incriminating?

Had the whole museum burglary been a conspiracy between the three men? Had two of the conspirators decided to kill off the third? If so, what was the motive? There was an old saying that three people could keep a secret as long as two were dead. What was the big secret? Was someone else going to die before he figured it out?

On a completely unrelated matter, it bothered him that Allison Culbertson had tracked down a copy of the Torrence file. Even more, it bothered him that she had not told him she was doing it. He had hoped the two of them had something special starting. He felt undeniable sparks when he was around her. Big sparks. It bothered him that once again he was interested in a woman who was not being honest with him. It was the story of his life. Five divorces in twelve years. His track record was embarrassing, no matter how much he joked about it. In a way, it was too bad that what he'd said to Callie wasn't true. Maybe he would be better off if he were inoculated against attractive women. Certainly, nothing good was likely to come from falling in love with a lawyer who was already sneaking around gathering information about him behind his back. Talk about red flags. At least his previous wives had saved their sneaking around until after the marriage! She was, when all was said and done, merely a witness in a case he was investigating.

He needed to throw cold water on himself and quit thinking of her as an attractive woman and just see her as a witness.

This whole deal about her requesting the Torrence file was disheartening. Was it possible she was looking for a way to discredit him if she ever had to cross-examine him again? He'd find a way to ask her about it when he met her at her office later in the day. The conversation should at least be interesting.

Allison Culbertson greeted him warmly when he arrived at her office. "Hi, Harry," she said. "Thanks for coming."

They shook hands, and she seemed to hold his hand in hers for a moment longer than necessary.

"So," he said, eyeing her closely. "What was so important we couldn't talk about it over the telephone?"

"There's somebody I want you to meet," she said, "in my conference room."

Sullinger's antenna went up. Had she located another witness? "Is this a client of yours?"

"No. Come on. You'll see."

She led him to the conference room door and pushed it open. When they entered the room, he saw a teenage girl sitting on the other side of the long table next to a woman who looked to be about sixty. They regarded him with interest.

Suddenly, recognition exploded in his mind like a flare gun. This was Susan Torrence and her grandmother. He had killed this girl's parents. He had killed this woman's son.

"What's this all about?" he asked, looking at Allison Culbertson.

"Harry," she said, "I hope you don't mind, but after you told me what happened to Jesse and Carrie Torrence, and to you, I couldn't stop thinking about it. I tracked down newspaper stories. I read the testimony from the coroner's inquest. I read the official report from the Missouri Highway Patrol. I contacted Betty Clinkscale, Jesse's mother, and met with her. She introduced me to her granddaughter, Susan. I told them all about you, about the good work you do, and about how that long-ago tragedy still affects you. It was their idea to meet with you."

Sullinger glanced at Betty Clinkscale. The woman was nodding. Her face and neck were mottled with red marks, perhaps from nerves. Her eyes were watering, but she was smiling.

"That's right," she said. "Susan and I talked about it. We wanted to meet you. We never said a word to you before, back when all this happened. We didn't want to, frankly. You were the enemy."

Sullinger looked at the floor. "I'm sorry," he said. "I'm sorry for everything."

Susan Torrence was looking at him with wide eyes. She wore her hair in a ponytail. Her shapely torso was encased in a tank top. She was slender, with freckles on her bony shoulders.

"I want you to know," she said, "that I don't blame you for the death of my parents."

Harry stared at her.

She smiled timidly, a bulging wall of tears waiting to cascade from each eye at any moment. "I used to blame you, but I don't, anymore. I've read the police reports. I've read your testimony from the coroner's inquest. I've read the crime-lab reports. I've even," she hesitated, "read the autopsy reports. I watched the videotaped statement the police took from me when I was five. That was weird." Her lip quivered, but she forged ahead with her thoughts. "I realize now that you were trying to help my mother. I know you didn't want anything bad to happen."

The girl's shoulders began trembling. Sullinger ached for her.

"My grandmother told me about my parents' drinking problems, how they both would get abusive when they were drinking. I read how high their blood-alcohol levels were the night they died. My father was a good father, Mr. Sullinger. My mother was a good mother. I want you to know that. They both loved me, and I loved them. But they had problems, bad drinking problems. It was their drinking that killed them, not you."

Sullinger stared at her, dumbfounded.

"Miss Culbertson told me you still cry when you think about that night," Susan Torrence said. "Thank you for that." The walls broke. Tears coursed down both cheeks. "But don't cry for *me*," she continued. "I have a good life. My grandmother is the best person in the world. I'm a happy person, present appearances notwithstanding." She wiped her cheeks. "I have lots of friends. I'm in the band. I'm on the swim team. I give talks to grade-school kids about the dangers of drugs and alcohol. I make good grades. Next year I'm going to college. I'm going to make something of myself."

She sighed and looked directly into his eyes. "You did what you had to do. You did what you were trained to do. My father was pointing a gun at my mother. She was begging him not to shoot her. Miss Culbertson told me how it's no coincidence that a police badge is shaped like a shield. She said a policeman is like a knight from the old days, who would go out with sword and shield to serve and protect the people of his realm, to fight for justice. When you came to my house that day, you were a knight in shining armor, riding up to save my mother. Things didn't go like you planned, but I don't see how you could have done anything differently."

The grandmother spoke up. "We both feel that way, Mr. Sullinger. We've moved on with our lives. We want you to do so, too."

Sullinger's throat constricted to the point he found it hard to talk. He looked from Susan Torrence to Betty Clinkscale to Allison Culbertson.

"Thank you," he whispered.

Chapter 48

Allison Culbertson was deep in thought as she stood at the self-service gas pump, pumping the cheapest unleaded fuel in town into her Jeep Cherokee. She barely noticed as the meter on the pump spun higher and higher, a slot machine never destined to hit a jackpot for any customer. Oblivious to the world around her, Allison was wondering who killed Joey Red Horse, looking at it again from the angle of who had the most to gain from Joey's death.

Bear Smith? He was scary. He had reason to be mad at Joey because of the affair with Lolita. The motive for the murder could be that simple. Or it could be more complex. He and Joey were involved in drugs. The gun that killed Joey had been connected to drug-related shootings and the notorious drug lord Pablo Ramirez. Money and drugs went hand in hand. Maybe this was about drug money. Maybe Bear Smith and Joey Red Horse had been dealing more than peyote, and something went wrong.

Lolita Smith? Was it possible Lolita killed Joey in the heat of passion? The possibility seemed more and more remote. Lolita's fear that her own father might be involved rendered her rather less of a suspect herself.

Mark Windfoot? Now there was an intriguing piece of the puzzle. He had been on national television at the time of the shooting, so he had clearly not pulled the trigger. But why had he secretly posted Joey Red Horse's bond? When you looked for someone who benefited from Joey's death, Mark Windfoot fit the bill. His organization had reaped significant national exposure, and probably increased donations, as a result of Joey's high-profile death. His cause of battling museums over skeletal remains had been advanced. In his own words, according to Lolita, Joey had served "the cause" well. Had Joey been killed as a part of a public-relations gimmick? Or because Joey knew too much about Windfoot and his secrets? She couldn't rule Windfoot out. He could be a part of some conspiracy.

Marge Tappinger? Allison was leaning away from her as a suspect. Marge was carrying Joey's baby. She had just lured him back into her bed. It didn't seem likely she wanted him dead. Far from it.

Rex Tappinger? *There* was a man with plenty of reason to hate Joey. Nor did he have a good alibi. Joey's death removed a real threat to Tappinger's marriage. He had gained something significant from Joey's death: elimination of the competition. He or a henchman couldn't be ruled out.

Clive Faulkner? His museum had gained a ton of publicity from Joey's death, but not the good kind. Try as she might, Allison could not think of one positive thing Clive Faulkner gained from Joey's death. He may have disliked Joey for committing the theft of Gazing Woman, but Faulkner had gotten the famous statue back. He had no reason to kill Joey over it. Besides, she felt a connection to Faulkner. She liked to think she could never be physically attracted to a murderer.

Diedra Binzinger? Why did Allison keep thinking about her? Allison supposed that the artist had something to gain if Clive Faulkner decided to return the skeletons and burial artifacts to Native Americans. But Binzinger would profit from the repatriation only if the museum hired her to make the replacements. Faulkner said he planned to bid out the work. She couldn't be certain she would get the job. And, speaking of ancient art, why had the Binzinger chunkey-player figurine been thrust through her smashed window? Who left the note for Allison? Why warn her that she would be in danger if she did not stop asking questions?

And here she was, still asking questions.

The gas pump clicked off. The noise reminded Allison where she was. She disengaged the nozzle and returned it to its place on the pump.

When she turned back toward her Jeep to replace the gas cap, she found herself face to face with Bear Smith. The huge man was wearing black leather with lots of silver chains. His bearded head was topped by his Nazi helmet with the painted feathers on its sides. Allison took a step backward.

"I thought I told you to stay away from my daughter." His thumbs were hooked on his belt. His hands were massive.

"Hello, Bear."

"You didn't take my advice." His eyes glared at her from his swarthy face. She glanced around. They were the only customers at the gas station. Somewhere in the bulletproofed, iron-barred clerk's kiosk, a gas-station attendant might or might not be watching what was happening. Allison couldn't tell. Help from the person in the kiosk seemed rather unlikely.

I'm still worthless as a sheepdog, Allison thought ruefully, recalling the gun in her purse inside her jeep. *I have no clue when a wolf is approaching the flock. I'm always walking around in a fog. I'm one of those people whose gun will be taken away and used against her. A lot of good it's doing me now.*

"Maybe I didn't make myself clear," the big man said. "You are to have *nothing* to do with my daughter. Stay away from her."

"Why?" Allison heard herself ask. "Why should I stay away from her? What are you hiding?"

"I'm not hiding anything."

"Yes, you are."

"No, I'm not."

"Then why are you standing here threatening me? You should be glad that Lolita and I want to see the murder of Joey Red Horse solved. I thought he was a friend of yours."

Bear Smith stared at her, his face as hard as a granite statute.

"He *was* a friend of mine."

"Then act like it. I won't seek your daughter out to question her, but I'll be a friend to listen when she needs to talk. I'll be a shoulder for her to cry on. Perhaps *you* should listen to her, instead of scaring her."

"You don't know what you're talking about," Bear growled.

"Don't I? I know Mark Windfoot gave you the money to put up for Joey's bond. I know you and Mark Windfoot lied to me. What I don't know is why."

He didn't flinch. "Use your brain, Counselor."

"My brain tells me you had something to do with Joey's death. Either it was some publicity stunt for ARROW or Joey knew something you and Windfoot didn't want him to tell."

Bear Smith cursed. "You can't possibly believe that," he said.

"No? Well, it looks to me that Windfoot and ARROW have certainly benefited from Joey's death. The whole thing has been good for the cause, so to speak."

His eyes narrowed. "I knew she talked to you," he said.

A bolt of fear shot through Allison. Not for herself, but for Lolita. "If you weren't involved in Joey's death, then what are you hiding?"

He stepped close, lowering his voice. "I said to use your brain. If I were involved with Joey in planning the burglary, would I want anybody to know? Hell, no! I'd be guilty of burglary and stealing as an accessory. That carries prison time, especially for someone with my record. But that doesn't make me a murderer." He snorted and grinned, but the smile wasn't friendly. "We're just talking hypothetically, of course. I haven't admitted a damn thing."

He put a big hand on the window of her Jeep and leaned toward her, invading her space, towering over her. "And Windfoot?" he continued. "What if he *did* put up the bond? What if he *is* lying about it now? Maybe he thinks it would look bad for ARROW if he's the one who bonded Joey out. Maybe he was pleased by what Joey did, even if he didn't plan it in advance. Maybe he's even happy about the continuing media attention he's getting. But that doesn't make him a murderer, either." Bear Smith pointed a fat finger in her face. "All I know is, my daughter's been talking to you, and now she's afraid of me. My own daughter! I don't know what you've been telling her, but from now on, stay away from her. I mean it!"

Allison met his gaze, refusing to back down from the wagging finger. "What connection did Joey have to Pablo Ramirez?" she asked.

"I don't know what the hell you're talking about."

"Pablo Ramirez, the Colombian drug lord? Were you and Joey connected to him through drug dealing?"

"You're nuts! If that's the kind of thing you're putting into Lolita's head, no wonder she's acting paranoid around me!"

Allison stared up at Bear Smith. "All I want is the truth. I've read a lot about the Osage Indians recently. I know they value a brave man who tells the truth. Did you or Mark Windfoot have anything to do with Joey's death?"

384

Bear Smith stopped wagging his finger and let the hand drop to his side. "No," he said. "Joey's death took all the fun out of that burglary for me. And it had been fun, up until the night he died. I'd give almost anything to have him back." Bear Smith stepped away from the Jeep. He cracked his knuckles. "I'll tell you something else," he said. "If you find out who killed Joey, I'd consider it a personal favor if you'd let me be the first to know. I guarantee it will save the time and trouble of a trial."

He walked to his motorcycle and started it up. He gave her the finger as he roared off.

When she approached the booth to pay for the gas, she noticed that the clerk was watching television.

"Did you see what just happened?" she asked.

"Yeah, the Skipper pushed Gilligan into the water," the heavyset woman said, her eyes still glued to the small television screen, "and Mary Ann ran to get the Professor."

"No, I mean that man approaching me by the gas pump."

"What man?" the clerk asked, looking at Allison for the first time.

Sheep! Allison thought.

Once she was back in the front seat of her Jeep, Allison contemplated her suspect list. It was strange. Even though Bear Smith had frightened her, he had moved a notch or two down the list. She now had no doubt that Bear helped Joey plan the burglary. But he genuinely seemed to want to know who killed his friend. She didn't think he was involved in Joey's death.

She picked up the book lying on her passenger seat, one she'd been rereading: *Alfred Dennison and the Bootheel Man.* She flipped it over and studied the black-and-white photograph of the author. Clive Faulkner's smiling face almost seemed to be taunting her. Was there something she had overlooked about him?

She opened the book and thumbed through the pages. She'd read the book twice now, practically memorizing it. She flipped once again to the front of the book.

For the first time, she noticed the dedication. Instead of standing alone on a page to itself, it was crammed onto the same page with the Library of Congress cataloging information and copyright warnings. It consisted of merely two words: "To Carmelita."

Carmelita?

Chapter 49

Clive Faulkner sat alone at his office desk. It was ten o'clock at night. The Heartland Mound Builder Museum had closed two hours earlier. He was staying late, working on an article about Southeast Missouri's Mound Builders for *Anthropology Today*. He hit a button on the keyboard to save the pages he had written and slipped off his wire-rimmed glasses. He leaned back in his chair and found himself thinking again of the great love of his life—Carmelita Ramirez.

He didn't think of her nearly as often as he used to. When he allowed his thoughts to wander to memories of her, his heart was heavy with regret. The two years they had been lovers had been the happiest months of his life. He hadn't realized it at the time. Had he known then what he knew now, things would have been different. He would have married her, sociopathic brother or not. He would have married her, different countries or not. His life would have been completely different, better in so many ways.

He rubbed the bridge of his nose, feeling indentations left by his glasses.

There had been a time, right after Carmelita left him, when he thought of her at least once during every waking hour of every single day. It had astounded him how long it lasted, her overriding presence in his mind, the constant pain he felt from losing her, the constant longing to talk to her, to convince her to come back to him. He had never imagined anything could feel so bad. He supposed guilt was part of it. Guilt for thinking he was better than she, simply because of the outlandish immorality of her brother, the up-and-coming Colombian hoodlum. Guilt for balking at marrying her because of the harm an association with her criminal bloodline might do to his budding career. Guilt at the pure cowardice he felt at the prospect of becoming the brother-in-law of a coldblooded killer.

Their last argument was a knock-down-drag-out, no-holds-barred verbal slugfest. It started out when he admitted he had no intention of marrying her. She exploded, screaming that she had given herself to him expecting marriage. She vowed that if he wouldn't marry her she was going back to Colombia forever. He insulted her, saying things he didn't mean. She called him a filthy pig, packed her bags, and walked out of his life. His ears still burned when he remembered that last conversation. He had been so stupid, so very stupid. He had thrown away the best thing he ever had.

Helplessness was undoubtedly part of his heartache, too. He had let Carmelita walk away, confident he would easily forget her once she went home to Colombia, the same way he'd forgotten other girls, other friends, and other family members when he immersed himself in research and work. It shocked him when he discovered he could think of nothing but her. It took him weeks to realize his mistake.

Once he realized it, he wrote her, but the letters came back unopened. He called her, but her telephone was disconnected. He even swallowed his pride and traveled to Colombia and tried to contact her through her brother, the same sleazeball he had criticized to her so vociferously and so often. Through Pablo Ramirez, he learned she'd joined a convent. She left a note for him with her brother, just in case he came looking for her. In it, she said she was absolutely serious. She never wanted to see him again. She never wanted to talk to him again. He should not try to visit her at the convent.

He had not heard from her since.

The days turned into weeks turned into months turned into years. He no longer thought of her every single day. Sometimes two or three whole days went by without feeling the pang in his chest. But when it came, the memory of her washed over him like a summer rain. First he would savor the images of her beauty, of her intelligence, of her zest for life. Then he would ache with the knowledge that he had lost the love of his life because he had been a fool. He had not realized what he had when he had it. He had stupidly thought that love, true love, was a fungible item that could easily be replaced. He had been wrong.

He dedicated his book to her when it was published, hoping she would notice, be moved by his act, and get in touch with him.

He'd even sent a copy to her brother, certain it would make its way into her hands. But he heard nothing from her but silence.

He tried to contact her every time he traveled to South America for an archaeological dig or conference. He was surprised the DEA didn't have him profiled as a drug dealer, as often as he had visited the infamous Pablo Ramirez over the years. But her drug-lord brother always told him the same thing. *She never wants to see you again. She never wants to talk to you again. She wants you to leave her alone.*

When Pablo Ramirez finally told him that he, Pablo Ramirez, was *ordering* him to quit trying to communicate with Carmelita and to quit asking questions about her, Clive Faulkner finally gave up. When people disobeyed an order from Pablo Ramirez, they tended to end up dead.

It was truly hopeless. He would never see Carmelita again.

Still, he thought of her. He wondered if she ever thought about him. He wondered how she spent her days, how she spent her nights. He so desperately wished he had done things differently!

Other women had come and gone from his life, most recently Diedra Binzinger and, potentially, Allison Culbertson. But none had replaced Carmelita Ramirez in his heart. She was the love of his life. Even this last thing, this plot with her brother to provide the art-loving Colombian drug lord with a number of one-of-a-kind, genuine Native American artifacts, had been motivated in part by the notion that he might somehow see Carmelita again.

Sitting at the desk, he heard what sounded like a footstep. He glanced at his closed office door.

The knob was turning.

His blood went cold as he watched it move. When the door opened, he found himself staring at the man in black. The Colombian wore a black shirt, black pants, black Nike tennis shoes, and shiny black gloves. He held a black gun in his hand. He entered the room silently and closed the door behind him.

Allison Culbertson glanced at the caller ID on her telephone as she answered it on the second ring. The call came from Binzinger Studios.

"Hello?"

"Miss Culbertson, this is Diedra Binzinger."

Allison glanced at a clock. It was past ten o'clock at night. "What can I do for you?" Allison asked.

"I need to talk to you."

"I'm listening."

"No, I mean in person. I need to show you something, here at my studio."

"I can come by first thing in the morning," Allison suggested. "Would 8:00 work for you?"

"No, it won't. I really need to talk to you tonight. I need a lawyer. Right now. I expect to be arrested."

"Arrested? For what?"

There was a pause on the line.

"Well, it's theft-related. Don't worry, I can afford to hire you."

"I'm sure you can, but I don't see why it can't wait until morning."

"I need your advice about how to go about turning myself in."

"I still don't understand why it can't wait until tomorrow."

"Miss Culbertson, I'm knee-deep in art fraud. I've been bouncing back and forth for weeks about turning myself in. I've finally decided to do it. If I wait until tomorrow, I might chicken out. I don't want to change my mind. I want to do the right thing. Please come over. I need your help. I want to tell the police everything. I want to name names. I want you to negotiate the best deal you can get for me. I expect to go to prison, but I'm hoping you can help me cut my losses."

Allison's mind raced. Art fraud! Prison! She had been curled up on the couch, watching a rerun of *To Kill a Mockingbird*, her favorite movie. She smiled wryly. She knew Atticus Finch wouldn't force a desperate client to wait until morning. The noble lawyer wouldn't stay on the sofa watching television.

Alarm bells rang in Allison's head. She needed to clarify something with Diedra Binzinger. "Look, Diedra," she said, "before I agree to meet you I've got to ask you one thing, to make sure we're not wasting our time."

"Okay."

"If you had anything to do with the killing of Joey Red Horse, I'd have a conflict of interest in representing you. I don't mean to sound accusatory or insulting, but there's no point in meeting with you if your interests would conflict in any way with my intention to work with the police to solve Joey's murder."

"Don't worry," Diedra Binzinger said. "That's one of the reasons I want you for my lawyer. I want his murder solved, too, and I have an idea who might have done it. I didn't tell the police quite everything I know. Please come over. I'd rather talk about it in person. I've got things to show you."

Allison was pacing, the phone gripped in her hand.

"Okay," she said. "I'll be there as soon as possible. It'll be a while. I need to get dressed."

"Thank you. I'm on the second floor of my studio, in the loft. I'll leave the front door unlocked. Thank you so much."

Allison hung up the telephone and stared at it for a few moments. *Knee deep in art fraud.* Was Diedra Binzinger talking about something going on at the Heartland Mound Builder Museum or was this totally unrelated? Was this art fraud somehow connected to Joey's murder? Allison felt a thrill of excitement. The pieces were wanting to fit together.

Suddenly, she was hit with the memory of lying face down as bullets from Joey's killer shattered her Jeep's windows. She broke into a sweat as she recalled the passenger door opening, the feeling of utter helplessness as the killer stood over her. She wished she hadn't told Diedra Binzinger she'd come right over. She had a bad feeling about this. She was reluctant to go to the studio at night. She would be so close to the place where Joey had died. She would be so vulnerable.

Still, she had promised Diedra Binzinger she'd come. Binzinger needed a lawyer's advice. Allison had that law degree hanging on her wall, right next to the Lincoln quote about a lawyer's time and advice being the only valuable commodities a lawyer had to sell. Well, it was time to peddle some advice.

She hurried to get dressed.

"How did you get in?" Clive Faulkner asked, trying to make his voice sound calm.

"Easy," the Colombian said. "I hid in the bathroom right before the museum closed. You and I have been alone in the building for quite some time."

The man in black was named Carlos. Faulkner had never known his last name.

"Are you going to kill me, Carlos?"

"I don't know for sure. Not yet, anyway. Ultimately, it will depend on the choices you make."

"What choices?"

"Pablo has a plan for you, Faulkner."

"Pablo ordered you to kill Joey Red Horse, didn't he?" Clive Faulkner asked.

"Yes."

"Why? He didn't have to kill him. He could've just stolen the fake Gazing Woman statue from the police evidence locker before any experts had the chance to examine it closely. That's what I asked him to do!"

The man smiled grimly. "Pablo and I talked over your request. You don't appreciate how hard it is to steal something from a police evidence locker. It takes a lot of money, plus detailed knowledge of police personnel and their weaknesses. You have to know who is corrupt. Pablo considered it, but the United States is not like Mexico. Police corruption is the exception up here, rather than the rule. It was much easier to simply kill Joey Red Horse. His death ended his prosecution and allowed the evidence to be returned to you, with no one the wiser. To this day, not a single soul suspects that venerated museum Director Clive Faulkner has been hypocritically selling his priceless collection piece by piece to a Colombian drug lord, all the while replacing the artifacts with fakes, making himself a millionaire in the process. You're a good actor, Faulkner. Really, you are."

"I wouldn't have done it if I'd known Pablo would kill anybody," Clive Faulkner said. "I'm not a murderer."

"Maybe not, but Pablo Ramirez is. So am I. You knew who you were dealing with. The death of Joey Red Horse was a business decision. If an expert looked closely at the fake Gazing Woman, your thefts would be discovered. You would've been caught. Pablo was not convinced you would keep his secrets if you were facing prison time."

"I could've," Clive Faulkner said.

"He's not sure you can keep a secret now."

"I can."

"Pablo is worried about this Binzinger woman, the artist you paid to make the replicas. He's worried she will talk to the police."

Clive Faulkner felt drops of sweat trickling down his chest, under his shirt and tie. He shook his head. "She won't. She's reliable. She's in it too deep herself. I paid her a fortune to make those fakes. She just finished the fake Bootheel Man. Pablo and I agreed Bootheel Man would be the last thing he gets. It'll all be over then. We'll go back to our original plan. He gets the real Bootheel Man, I replace it with Diedra's fake, then I stage a burglary and report all of the fakes stolen at once. They'll disappear forever. No one will ever know that over the past few years Pablo has been getting the real artifacts one at a time."

The man made a show of examining his gun.

"Pablo doesn't trust the Binzinger woman. He believes she'll turn informant. He has a good feel for that sort of thing. That's why he's lasted so long in the business. He's right. She's a loose cannon. She has to be eliminated."

"She won't tell on me. She could go to prison for years."

"She suspects you of murdering Joey Red Horse. I was watching her the night she went to Allison Culbertson's home and broke out the window. I didn't realize until later what she was up to. She put one of her fake statues inside the lawyer's house. She's sending messages, practically crying out to be caught. She'll take you down with her, Faulkner. Quite frankly, Pablo is worried that you might drag him down, too."

"I'd never do that," Clive Faulkner said. "Pablo should know I can be trusted. We've known each other for years."

The man smiled again, his thick lips parting over yellow teeth.

"Pablo has the answer, as always."

"What?"

"He wants you to kill the Binzinger woman. If you have blood on your own hands, he's confident you will keep quiet about the blood on his."

Clive Faulkner felt his world spinning even farther out of control. It had seemed so logical at the beginning, so easy. Once it looked likely that NAGPRA might eventually be extended to cover private museums, it appeared to be only a matter of time before the Heartland Mound Builder Museum would be forced to return its skeletons and funereal objects to American Indians. Faulkner had known for years that Pablo Ramirez coveted Native American artifacts for his private collection. If the artifacts were going to be lost to the museum anyway, where was the harm in getting rich? Together, Clive Faulkner and Pablo Ramirez cooked up the plan by which Faulkner would steal several coveted pieces from the museum, one at a time, replacing each with a fake made by Diedra Binzinger. The culmination was to be a staged theft. Faulkner would report all of the items stolen at once. The fakes would be disposed of. The crime would go unsolved. Faulkner would retire shortly thereafter and travel to some warmer climate to enjoy his millions.

Joey Red Horse had inadvertently unraveled the entire plan by stealing the fake Gazing Woman, thinking he was stealing the original. The reason Joey had not been able to find Bootheel Man on the night he broke into the museum was because Diedra Binzinger had it at her studio, working on its replica.

"I can't kill Diedra," Clive Faulkner said. "I can't kill anyone."

The man shook his head sadly. "Pablo thinks you can. I told him you were too weak. I told him we would need to kill you both. Pablo is convinced that once you kill the Binzinger woman, you will eventually come to Colombia with your millions and hook up with his sister. I told him you didn't have the balls."

"His sister?" Clive Faulkner said. "He mentioned Carmelita?"

"Yes, I know she is your former girlfriend. She never married, you know. She went into a convent. Became a nun. But she's home now. Apparently she wasn't cut out to be a nun. Too much woman, I guess. She's not going back to that life."

Once again, memories washed over Clive Faulkner. Was it possible he could be with Carmelita again? For years, he had been going through the motions of living. Was there a chance he could be truly alive again? Was it possible they could take up where they left off?

The Colombian held up his semiautomatic and flipped off its safety. "It is your choice, Faulkner. Either you and I go kill Diedra Binzinger tonight, or I kill you right now and then go kill her myself. Which is it going to be? Either way works for me."

Clive Faulkner felt the abyss open underneath his soul.

"I'll come with you," he said.

Chapter 50

Allison Culbertson debated whether or not to call Harry Sullinger. On the one hand, she would feel safer if Sullinger knew about this meeting, and even better if he could be part of it. Agreeing to meet Diedra Binzinger alone at her studio in the middle of the night was looking more and more like a seriously reckless thing to do. On the other hand, if Binzinger was going to be her client, her first obligation was to Diedra Binzinger. What if Sullinger rushed down to the studio, barged in like a bull in a china shop, and spoiled Diedra's plan to turn herself in? What if he botched up any chance for Allison to negotiate a deal for her? What if he showed up before Diedra had the chance to explain what this art fraud was all about? What if Sullinger's arrival spooked her out of telling Allison who she thought killed Joey? What if her client blurted a full confession to Sullinger before Allison had a chance to cut a deal for her? Clearly, Allison's obligation to Diedra was to talk to her client first, hear the facts, and help her decide what to do next. It wouldn't be right for Allison to bring a police officer to her initial meeting with her client, even though her potential client was already talking about turning herself in to the police.

Still, what if she went to this meeting and disappeared off the face of the earth? Things like that happened. Nobody ever found Jimmy Hoffa, for example. Maybe the Teamster boss should have told somebody where he was going, and with whom. Allison squeezed her eyes tightly shut. *Maybe I'm not cut out to practice criminal law,* she thought. *Maybe I should stick with civil cases.*

She made a compromise with herself and dialed Sullinger's number.

Her relief at hearing his voice faded when she quickly realized she had reached his answering machine. At the beep, she left a message: "Hi, this is Allison Culbertson. It's about ten-thirty Wednesday night. I'm on my way to meet Diedra Binzinger at her studio. It's late for a meeting, I agree, but it looks like she may end up being a client and she claims it's urgent. She insisted we meet tonight. She says she may have information for the police. I can't tell you any details at this point, but just in case I disappear, I wanted to give you a head start on finding my body! I'll be the one right next to Jimmy Hoffa. Ha, ha! Bye."

Allison wondered if she went too far with the Jimmy Hoffa part. Even to her own ear, her attempt at flippancy rang pathetically false. There was no getting around it. She was scared. So scared, she was fastening her holstered gun to the belt she was wearing with her jeans. Her black suit jacket would cover it.

I can't believe I'm doing this, she thought. *I feel like a gangster.* She recalled once again her conversation on the firing range with Harry Sullinger. She wasn't sure where she fit into his classification of wolves, sheep, and sheepdogs. *If I'm a sheepdog*, she thought, *I'm a wimpy sheepdog. If I'm a sheep, I've at least got a gun under my wool.*

Harry Sullinger, fresh out of the shower, was walking through his house, toweling his hair, when he noticed his message light flashing.

The moment he heard Allison Culbertson's voice he grinned. He had just been thinking about her. His smile turned into a frown as he listened to the message. When it ended, he played it a second time, then a third.

He glanced at the clock. He had barely missed her call. He could try to call her back, or he could simply show up at Diedra Binzinger's studio in thirty minutes. Maybe it would be a good idea if he just happened to drop by. If he called Allison Culbertson and caught her, she might tell him not to come. No, he wouldn't call first, but he wouldn't merely sit at home awaiting her call, either.

He hurried to the bedroom to get dressed.

Allison Culbertson took a deep breath when she reached the front door of Diedra Binzinger's studio. She knocked but got no response. Remembering that the artist had told her the door would be unlocked, she tried the knob. The door swung open.

Allison stepped into the studio. The lights were on, both in the lower art-shop level and in the upper art-studio level.

Allison stood quietly by the front door. She clutched her purse under her left arm, right above the holstered gun on her left hip. She was right-handed, so she had positioned the gun backwards on her left hip, where she could pull it with her right hand. It all seemed so melodramatic, so extreme, and, hopefully, so unnecessary. As a practical matter, she would probably end up feeling embarrassed once she and Diedra started talking, should Diedra notice she was carrying a gun. Still, she was glad she had it with her.

"Diedra?" she called out.

The long, narrow building was completely silent.

"Diedra," she said louder, "I'm here."

Everything seemed quiet on the lower level. Everything seemed to be in its proper place. The paintings all hung cleanly on the walls. The ceramics were all displayed neatly on tables and cases throughout the store. The counter and its quaint cash register stood silently at the back of the long room, a silent reminder that this was a business, not an art museum.

Allison wondered if she should just leave. Something didn't seem right. For Diedra Binzinger to invite her over late at night but not to be waiting for her, this was strange. Alarming, even. If she just left, Diedra could always call her and they could make other arrangements to get together. But what if Diedra was merely in the bathroom or something? Allison would look decidedly sheeplike if she just ran off.

Before she could determine whether to leave, she heard a noise from the upper level. It sounded like a chair scooting. Or maybe it was a toilet-paper-roll dispenser being used. She definitely heard rustling noises. She knew Diedra had a tiny bathroom upstairs. Unfortunately, she could not see anything on the loft level.

"Diedra," she called out, making up her mind, "I'm coming up." She crossed the room to the spiral staircase.

She thought about pulling her gun, but how bad would that look if Diedra came out of the bathroom and ended up looking down Allison's gun barrel? Wouldn't *that* get the potential attorney-client relationship off on the wrong foot! It was troublesome enough that Allison was *packing heat*. She already felt like a would-be Annie Oakley, even without charging up the steps with her weapon drawn.

When Allison reached the top of the steps, she stood still, letting her gaze wander over the studio. Most of the works-in-progress were draped with protective cloth, like shrouded ghosts. The curtain over the back window had been closed, completely covering the big glass window that overlooked the river. The door to Diedra's corner bathroom was also closed. Allison walked toward it.

"Diedra," she said. "I'm here."

She had just started for the bathroom door when Clive Faulkner rose up from behind one of the cloth-covered tables.

"Hi, Allison," he said. His voice was cheerful, as if they were meeting on a bike trail in a park.

Allison felt the hair on the back of her neck rise. She stopped and stared at him. He was wearing his normal tweed sport coat and bow tie. "What are you doing here?" she asked.

"I was about to ask you the same thing."

"Diedra called me thirty minutes ago," Allison said. "She said she wanted to meet here."

Faulkner knitted his brow. "That's funny," he said, "she did the same thing to me. I hurried right over, but she isn't even here. The place is empty."

Allison studied him. He seemed nervous and distracted. His casual air seemed contrived. His forehead glistened with sweat.

"Why didn't you say you were up here when I came in the front door?" Allison asked. "You must have heard me calling."

He shrugged. "You were calling for Diedra. I'm not Diedra. Besides, I'm confused about what she's got up her sleeve. I can't figure out why she called us both to come meet her here and then didn't show up herself. It's all very peculiar."

"Isn't it, though?" Allison said.

Allison looked again at the room full of drop cloths covering art projects. It reminded her of how her living room looked when the ceiling was being painted.

"Diedra claimed she had something she wanted to show me," Allison said. "Did she say the same thing to you?"

"Yes."

"Have you found whatever it is she wants us to see?"

"No. Frankly, I got here right before you did. I was just about to leave when you showed up. I sort of panicked. I can't imagine why she wanted both of us here. I thought maybe she was trying to embarrass us in some way. I thought it might be better if I just kept quiet and we went our separate ways."

Allison studied him closely. Diedra said she had an idea who might be behind the murder of Joey Red Horse. Was it possible Clive Faulkner was her suspect? Was he a killer? Was he involved in this big art fraud?

"Where is Diedra, Clive?"

"I don't know."

On the far side of the room, an object large enough to be a standing human being was covered by a drop cloth. It stood near the riverfront mural that ran the length of the far wall. Surely Diedra wasn't hiding under the drop cloth. Allison crossed the room, glancing at Clive Faulkner as she did so. He was watching, but said nothing.

When she reached it, she yanked off the cloth. She found herself staring at Bootheel Man. Her eyes lingered involuntarily on the axe embedded in his skull. It was the first time she had been this close to a human skeleton.

"What's Bootheel Man doing here?" she asked, turning to face Clive Faulkner.

"That's not Bootheel Man. It's a replica Diedra is making for the museum. I told you about it. We're going to return all of the skeletons to the American Indians and replace them with replicas. Diedra's making them for us."

"No," Allison said, "you told me that Diedra was *not* getting the job, that someone else would be hired to do it. You were bidding it out. How could Diedra have made such a good replica so fast?"

Allison pulled the drop cloth off a nearby table. Gazing Woman, or an exact replica of the famous piece of art, sat on the table amid several skulls and flint-clay figurines.

Art fraud! Diedra Binzinger's words came back to her. *I'm knee-deep in art fraud.* Somehow, some way, and for some reason, Diedra Binzinger and Clive Faulkner had been involved in stealing ancient American Indian artwork, probably from the museum itself.

"You and Diedra were stealing from the museum, replacing the real objects with things she made, weren't you?"

"Allison," he began.

"Don't lie to me!" She was furious, remembering the admiration she had felt for him and for his passion for the museum. Had it all been an act? "Clive, how could you have been involved in something like this?" She pulled one drop cloth after another from nearby tables, revealing an assortment of ancient Native American art or very good fakes. Allison couldn't tell which. She glanced at him. He stood in the same place, his shoulders sagging.

When she reached the long counter under the riverfront mural and began pulling off another drop cloth, he called out, "Allison, no!"

As she yanked off the thin canvas cover, she froze. She was staring at Diedra Binzinger's lifeless body. Diedra was wearing her art smock. Something was horribly wrong with her neck. A wire garrot dug into the flesh of her throat. Her eyes bulged, wide and empty.

Allison tore her eyes away from the awful sight. When she looked back at Clive Faulkner, he was holding a gun in his hand and was pointing it at her.

"What are you doing!" she said.

"I don't know," he said. "God forgive me! I don't know. Things have gotten way out of control."

Allison thought about the gun in its holster on her belt. A lot of good it was doing her there. She would have no chance of pulling it without getting shot. In hindsight, she should have taken it from the holster while she was coming up the spiral staircase. Better yet, she should have just left when Diedra didn't answer the door! She just wasn't cut out for this sheepdog business.

Clive Faulkner was sweating. The hand holding the gun was shaking. But the black ugly hole at the end of its barrel was pointing directly at her.

"You have to understand," he said, "I didn't mean for any of this to happen. I didn't mean for anyone to die."

"I *don't* understand," Allison said. "Not a bit of it! But I want to. Tell me, Clive. Make me understand."

He swallowed, still pointing the gun at her.

"A few years ago, I realized it was probably inevitable that the federal laws would eventually be expanded to cover private museums, and that the Heartland Mound Builder Museum would be forced to surrender Bootheel Man and Gazing Woman and all of our other burial objects to various American Indian tribes. It made me sick to think about losing them. It would be the death knell for the museum." He took a deep breath. "I knew a man, a rich man, who collects Native American art. He lives in Colombia, the country. At one point I had been engaged to marry his sister."

"Carmelita?" Allison asked. "The one you dedicated your book to?"

A look of surprise shot across Faulkner's face. "Yes, Carmelita. Her brother is Pablo Ramirez, the drug lord."

Allison thought about the long hours she had spent trying to figure out how the gun that killed Joey Red Horse could be the same gun involved in drug-related shootings in Los Angeles and Miami. It wasn't a drug connection, after all. It was a connection to Pablo Ramirez.

"When I met Pablo," Faulkner was saying, "he was just one of many small-time Colombian drug-dealers. He hadn't yet become as successful and infamous as he is today."

The gun lowered an inch. If it discharged now, it was pointing more toward her legs.

"Pablo prides himself on being a man of culture. His compound has both a museum and a zoo. He always told me he'd buy anything I wanted to sell from any museum wherever I worked. I never thought I'd take him up on it. I was scornful of him. I regarded him as a common crook. I, on the other hand, was an honest man, a scholar. I remembered what he said, though, as I watched NAGPRA get passed by Congress. I considered what would happen to my museum, and what would happen to me, when the federal repatriation laws were extended to cover private museums. We'd lose Bootheel Man. We'd lose everything. I love the museum. I never would have done it had I thought the museum had a chance to keep its exhibits. But if the museum was going to lose them anyway, if the Indians were just going to bury these priceless objects in the dirt, where was the harm in replacing them with fakes? I contacted Pablo. He was still very interested in buying anything I wanted to sell. You wouldn't believe how much he was willing to pay. I'll be a multimillionaire when this is over. I never meant for anyone to die, Allison; you have to believe me."

"I do. I believe you. What went wrong?"

"Joey Red Horse. He screwed everything up."

"Was he part of the plan?" Allison asked.

"No. Not at all. He was the wild card who botched things up. I had the perfect scheme. I met Diedra Binzinger when I was wondering how I could get the fakes made. We started dating. She was hurting for money. She was a wonderful artist. I hired her to make the replicas for me, piece by piece. As she made each one, I'd steal the original from the museum and replace it with the replica. She knew what I was doing, and why. She was okay with it. We agreed it would be stupid to let the originals simply dribble back to the Osages to be buried. I was sitting on a fortune, one that was about to be given away. I had a chance to become rich without hurting anyone."

Faulkner shook his head. "Joey Red Horse created a huge problem for me when he burglarized the museum. His theft of the fake Gazing Woman was completely unrelated to what Diedra and I were doing. Unfortunately, what he stole was the replica. I'd already sold and delivered the original to Pablo Ramirez. I was okay, at first, because he threw the fake into the Mississippi River. No one would be the wiser. But when the fake was fished out of the river by those Water Patrol jerks, I had a problem. Somebody might decide to look at it closely."

He raised the gun again, pointing it directly at Allison. "You played a role in Joey's death, Allison. Inadvertently, of course. When you started talking about having an independent expert examine the fake Gazing Woman to give an opinion as to its value, I realized I was at a crisis point. If the police discovered it was a fake, my whole plan would be discovered."

The gun dropped down again. Allison wondered how long it would take her to physically pull her own gun, click off its safety, aim, and fire. She didn't like her chances. For both of their sakes, she hoped Faulkner would decide to let her go.

"Did you kill Joey?" she asked.

"No, I swear I didn't! No one was meant to get hurt. I contacted Pablo Ramirez and told him what happened. I suggested that he might use his contacts to steal the fake Gazing Woman from the police evidence locker. That would've solved everything. It wouldn't have been around to be examined. No one would ever realize it was a fake. I'd be home-free again. It never occurred to me that the murder of Joey Red Horse would also solve the problem. After I spoke with Pablo, I sat back and waited for the fake Gazing Woman to disappear from the police department."

Faulkner ran a hand through his hair. "The next thing I knew, Joey Red Horse was gunned down. It was obvious to me that Pablo Ramirez was behind it. I knew I had caused it. Later, one of Pablo's men explained to me that it was easier to kill Joey than to bribe someone at the police department. I'd never thought of it that way. I was a novice criminal, you see."

He smiled. It was a ghastly sight. His face had lost its color. His eyes were sunken.

"You must have been horrified when he was killed," Allison said, watching both his face and his gun.

"I was! It was my fault, all my fault. I've been sick about it." The smile left his face. "But still, it gave me a chance to pull this off. I tried not to think about Joey Red Horse, about how my shameful actions led to his death, about how terrible it was for you to witness his shooting."

He smiled again, sadly this time. "I meant it when I told you I was falling in love with you, Allison. I believed it when I said it. But I don't believe it now. I'm not capable of love, anymore. My heart has turned to stone. I don't feel anything anymore. I'm numb. Completely numb." The gun dropped another inch. "Actually," he continued, "when you suggested that I should go ahead and voluntarily return the skeletons and sacred items to the Osages, it was an answered prayer. I couldn't bring Jocy Red Horse back to life, but I could help make his death meaningful. It was a chance for me to atone to him, in a small way. I decided to move up the pace, to try to get Diedra to work faster on finishing the Bootheel Man replica. It was to be the last item. Once I stole Bootheel Man for Pablo, I'd stage a fake burglary, and this time the burglars would get away with all the fake items, including the fake Bootheel Man. They'd never be recovered. No one would ever know they'd been fakes. The plan would work like originally planned, except I'd have the unintended death of Joey Red Horse on my conscience."

Allison thought about the corpse lying on the nearby counter. Obviously, things had not worked out quite like he'd anticipated. "I guess Diedra quit cooperating," she said.

"Diedra was convinced I killed Joey Red Horse. I denied it until I was blue in the face, but she didn't believe me. She couldn't stand to be in the same room with me. She loathed me. I insisted I had nothing to do with it, but I could not convince her. I warned her to keep her thoughts to herself. I told her the penalties for art fraud, for the forgery crimes we'd already committed. I made it clear we would both go to prison if she didn't keep our secret. I never told her about Pablo Ramirez, though. If he found out I'd told her his name, he'd have her killed."

"What happened?" Allison asked.

"Pablo had a man watching me and watching Diedra. The man reported back to Pablo. They decided she was dangerous to them. Somebody even followed her on the night she broke out your window and left the chunkey-player statue. It's inexplicable to me why she did that. She must have been trying to give you some sort of clue that Joey's death had been connected to art fraud. Maybe she was trying to protect you, thinking you were getting too close to figuring out the truth. Maybe she was just trying to protect herself by scaring you off. I guess we'll never know. She always was a bit flakey. Typical artist."

It seemed strange to hear him talking about Diedra Binzinger in the past tense, in her own studio, with her dead body lying on a countertop just a few feet away. Would he be talking so dispassionately about Allison while standing next to her corpse in a few minutes?

Clive Faulkner's eyes glistened. "Pablo's man came to me tonight. He said the only way Pablo could be assured I would keep my mouth shut would be for me to kill Diedra. They made me do it, Allison. They'd have killed her anyway. It was my only chance to stay alive."

"Oh, Clive."

"That's right," he said. "I'm a murderer now. The ultimate sin. I did it right before you got here. I tightened that wire around her neck as the life rattled out of her. You caught me red-handed. I was just getting ready to load the rest of the fake artifacts into the museum's truck. When you came in that door, I was hoping you'd be smart enough to turn around and leave."

"Clive," she said. "You don't need to do this."

"I think I do," he said, raising the gun so it pointed at her face.

Chapter 51

Allison Culbertson winced, expecting a bullet to slam into her cheekbone at any moment. When it didn't, she opened her eyes again. Clive Faulkner was still pointing the gun at her, but he'd lowered it a bit.

"I'm so sorry, Allison," he said. "I never meant any harm to come to you."

Allison felt her heart pounding. She took a deep breath and tried to calm down. Her gun was right there on her hip, waiting to help her out of this mess.

"I know you didn't mean any harm, Clive. I know you don't want to hurt me."

He nodded. "I'm sorry I'm so weak, Allison."

She moved her right hand slowly to her stomach, just inches from the butt of the gun. She moved her left hand so it covered her heart. If he noticed the placement of her hands, he might think she was merely beseeching him.

"Please," she said, "stop right now and turn yourself in, Clive. Think about what you're doing. You're not a murderer."

"I am. I killed Diedra. I betrayed the museum. I betrayed my fellow archaeologists. I betrayed Alfred Dennison. I betrayed myself."

The hand holding his gun was shaking again.

"It's not too late," Allison said. "You can put an end to the killing. You can confess and throw yourself on the mercy of the court."

"Hah!" he said, without mirth. "I'm no legal scholar, but somehow confessing to premeditated murder doesn't strike me as a particularly good idea. Taking my millions and moving someplace nice sounds like a better plan."

Allison's right hand slipped under her jacket like a barn snake slithering between bales of hay. She felt the solid grip of the Beretta. She pushed the button, flipping off the safety. Still, her gun was in its holster, pointing straight down. His was aimed directly at her. She would definitely be at a big disadvantage. At least she would have the element of surprise on her side.

406

"You can undo some of the harm you've caused," she said. "You can help them recover the stolen artifacts. You can help catch Pablo Ramirez. You could testify against him. He's a big fish. Surely they'd make a deal."

He shook his head. "I wouldn't get any sweetheart deal. You don't get probation for murder. I'd go to prison. I couldn't survive in prison. I won't go to prison."

His gun lowered an inch. Allison prepared to make her move.

Suddenly, the bathroom door swung open, and a man dressed completely in black stepped out. He also held a gun. He was pointing it at Faulkner.

Allison caught her breath. This had to be the man who killed Joey. This was the wolf who came to the side of the Jeep as she lay inside it, paralyzed with fear. This was the boogeyman who stripped her of any sense of comfort and safety, even in her own home. This was the man whose ruthlessness had changed her life.

"Faulkner, you talk too much," the man said. "You should've shot her a long time ago. What if she's wearing a wire or a tape-recorder? You're an idiot."

Faulkner was still pointing his gun at Allison. The three of them formed a triangle.

"I was hoping she'd leave without finding us," Faulkner said. "I didn't want to hurt her."

"Yes, well, we're way beyond that point," the man said. "You told her about Pablo. She can't be allowed to live. Kill her."

"Clive, please don't," Allison said, her grip tightening on her gun.

The man in black looked at her for the first time. "I am sorry, Miss Culbertson," he said. "Perhaps it would have been easier for you had I just killed you the night I shot Joey Red Horse. You were no threat then, though. You were too afraid to even look at me. Such a lamb."

The man in black returned his gaze to Faulkner. The museum director was pointing his gun at Allison. The man in black was pointing his gun at Faulkner. Neither was aware that Allison gripped her Beretta tightly in her hand, readying herself to use it the first chance she got.

"Kill her," the man in black repeated.

Clive Faulkner glared at him. "Quit pointing that thing at me, Carlos. It makes me think you're going to shoot me the minute I shoot her."

"Maybe I should," Carlos said. "Pablo is tired of these loose ends. But I won't. Pablo wants Bootheel Man. We've got work to do yet tonight. Finish her off, and let's get back to the museum. I never liked you, Faulkner. You put on airs, pretending to be a scientist. You're nothing but a grave robber and a thief. We both know it. Now you're a murderer, too. You and I, we're exactly alike, hired killers on the payroll of Pablo Ramirez. The difference is, I know who and what I am. You still think you're something special."

Time slowed down for Allison. Everything that happened next occurred in slow motion.

Clive Faulkner swung his gun toward Carlos. Faulkner's eyes were wide with fear and anger.

Carlos' eyes widened as Faulkner's gun turned toward him. Carlos pulled the trigger of his own gun. Fire flickered from the end of the barrel. He repeatedly jabbed his gun toward Faulkner as he fired over and over. He was smiling as he fired.

Faulkner fired back, screaming. His shouts were incoherent.

Amazingly, neither man was falling. Each stood, shooting at the other, neither giving ground.

The gunfire went on and on. The noise was deafening. Gunsmoke was filling the room.

Allison pulled her gun. She assumed the stance Sullinger taught her, gripping the Beretta with her right hand and steadying it with her left. She took a moment to get a good view of Carlos over the white dot on the sight on her gun and began squeezing the trigger. She saw surprise register on Carlos' face. She saw him wincing as bullets from two shooters struck him simultaneously. She saw him trying to turn his gun on her. She saw him jerk as slug after slug struck him. He fell to his knees, his gun pointing feebly toward the floor. She kept firing. He jerked from the impact of bullets tearing through him. Mouth agape, blood pouring from a wound in his cheek, he careened forward and fell face-first to the floor. Her last shot splattered into the top of his head while he was down.

408

Hearing an empty click, she realized she was still firing, but her gun was empty. She had shot her entire clip. She had fired fifteen shots at the Colombian hit man, this killer dressed all in black, this man named Carlos who had snuffed out Joey Red Horse's life right in front of her terrified eyes.

She stood like a statue, the empty gun clutched in her hands.

Clive Faulkner remained on his feet. He had been hit more than once. One hand still held his gun. The other gripped his bloody gut. He was staring at her, dumbfounded. He staggered over to the downed Colombian and knelt next to him.

"He's dead," he said, picking up Carlos' gun. Faulkner stood and leaned back against the counter. He shook his head.

"You are full of surprises, Counselor. I never saw that coming. It never once occurred to me you might have a gun."

Allison realized sickly that her gun was empty and that Clive Faulkner now held two guns.

"Now, we just made a hell of a lot of noise," Faulkner said. "Somebody is bound to have called the police. We don't have very long to decide what we're going to tell them. There must be some way we could put all the blame for Diedra's death on old Carlos here."

Allison swallowed hard. Could she make him believe she would lie for him? "What do you want me to say?" she asked.

Harry Sullinger heard the sound of gunfire as he got out of his car. He pulled his Beretta and sprinted toward the sound. It was coming from Diedra Binzinger's studio.

No! Don't let me be too late! He ran toward the popping gunfire like a fireman running toward a burning building. *Please don't let me be too late!*

There were lots of shots. Too many to count. Someone was surely dying.

Please not Allison!

The sound of the shooting ended just as he reached the front door of Diedra Binzinger's studio. He took a deep breath and tried the door. Finding it unlocked, he slipped inside.

The lights were on. The downstairs level appeared to be empty. The upstairs level was bathed in a cloud of thick gunsmoke. There were two ways to get upstairs, the spiral staircase or the fireman's pole. Neither seemed particularly safe from a gunman positioned above him. He decided to take the spiral staircase, listening as he went.

He distinctly heard Allison Culbertson's voice. *Thank God she's still alive!*

"I mean it," she was saying. "What do you want me to say?"

Sullinger crept up the spiral staircase, keeping his gun pointed at the spot where the shooter's head would appear should somebody upstairs hear him coming. He moved as quietly as possible, listening to the conversation, trying to figure out what was going on.

"You can't fool me, Allison," a man's voice was saying. "You'd never let me get away with it. You'd tell on me the first chance you got. My best hope is to shoot you with Carlos' gun. That would leave both you and me shot by *his* gun. He's shot with bullets from yours and mine. I'm the only survivor. I tell them we caught this guy killing Diedra and the three of us had our little gunfight. Admit it, Allison. It's my best option."

Sullinger reached the top of the spiral staircase.

He saw Allison Culbertson standing to the right, her face white, her Beretta in her hand. The man doing the talking was somewhere to the left, still not in Sullinger's line of vision.

Sullinger saw Allison Culbertson notice him. Bless her heart, she kept a poker face. Her eyes lingered less than a second before flicking back in the direction of the man doing the talking.

"Tell me, Allison," the man was saying, "would you have shot me if Carlos hadn't come out of that bathroom?"

"It's hard to say, Clive. I like to think I would have."

He grunted. "I love your spunk, Allison."

Sullinger moved up another step. He was still on the spiral staircase, but now Clive Faulkner came into view. The museum director was pointing a gun at Allison Culbertson. Another man lay at Faulkner's feet.

"Police!" Sullinger shouted, pointing his Beretta at Faulkner. "Drop your gun! You're under arrest!"

Sullinger hesitated to shoot. Faulkner was still pointing his gun directly at Allison. If Sullinger shot Faulkner, the museum director's gun might go off, injuring or killing Allison.

"Come on, Faulkner, drop it!" Sullinger yelled. "Don't make me kill you!"

"Okay," Faulkner said. "Take it easy. I give up."

Faulkner dropped the gun. Sullinger heard it hit the floor.

He stole a glance at Allison Culbertson.

"Are you okay?" he asked, at the exact moment Allison was shouting, "Watch out! He has two guns!"

Faulkner was already firing when Sullinger's eyes went back to him. Sullinger's gun was knocked from his hand as a searing pain shot from his fingertips up his arm. The gun clattered down the spiral staircase, landing somewhere below. Sullinger followed it, propelling himself backward, trying to get away from Faulkner, trying to catch up with the gun. He tumbled down the spiral staircase, head over heels, finally coming to rest on his back, halfway down, his feet still pointed up toward the second floor. His hand was bloody and throbbing. Faulkner's shot must have hit either his hand or his gun or both.

Sullinger kicked his feet, pushing himself down the staircase backwards. If Faulkner reached the top step while Sullinger was so exposed, he was a dead man.

Faulkner's face came into view.

Sullinger still had a long way to go before he reached the bottom of the steps. He kicked hard with his feet, feeling the metal steps slamming against his shoulder blades, back, and tailbone.

Faulkner was bringing up his gun. Sullinger realized he did not have time to make it all the way to the ground floor. His only hope was that Faulkner was not a good shot. Suddenly, he heard a noise. It was the sound of a magazine being snapped into a semiautomatic weapon, along with the metallic snap of a shell being chambered. Faulkner heard it, too.

Sullinger saw the look of shock on Faulkner's face as the museum director whirled back toward the place where Sullinger had last seen Allison Culbertson. She was out of Sullinger's sight, but he pictured her lining up Faulkner in her sights.

The rapid fire of the Beretta erupted again, and Faulkner jerked spastically. He lunged for the top of the spiral staircase as a bullet hit him in the side of the head, knocking off his wire-rimmed glasses. The gun flew from Faulkner's hand, bounced off a metal step, and fell harmlessly to the ground floor.

Faulkner's body slammed to the floor at the top of the staircase. His motionless head was tilted toward Sullinger. His lifeless eyes stared sightlessly, even as blood from the nasty wound at the side of his head flowed across his face and pooled in his left eye socket.

Harry Sullinger gripped the rail of the spiral staircase and pulled himself to his feet. Gingerly, he made his way up the steps. He examined his throbbing right hand. The end of his little finger was missing. *Ouch!*

"Are you okay, Allison?" he called out.

"Yes," he heard her say.

"Are you hit?" he asked. "Are there any more bad guys we need to worry about?"

"Not that I know of. The other one up here is clearly dead. His brains are leaking all over the floor."

At the top of the steps, Sullinger glanced down at Faulkner's body. In addition to the head wound, other perforations and expanding bloodstains spotted his tweed jacket.

Sullinger felt his heart twitch when he saw Allison Culbertson. Her beautiful face was ashen. She still gripped the Beretta in her hand, pointing down. But she was alive. She was standing there alive. She looked like a frightened deer, but she had acted with the heart of a lioness.

What can I say to her? he wondered. How could he possibly convey how worried he had been about her when he heard the gunfire, how much he cared for her, and how deliriously happy he was to find that she was not lying there dead? Words failed him.

He nodded toward Faulkner's body. "Nice shooting," he said.

Allison Culbertson gave him a faint smile. "He had it comin'," she said softly.

"I'll bet he did."

Sullinger crossed the room to the body of the man in black and pulled out a ballpoint pen. He used the pen to pick up the gun next to the body, slipping the pen through the trigger guard, carefully handling it in a way that would not disturb any fingerprints.

He glanced around the room and spotted the corpse of Diedra Binzinger lying on the countertop, something lethal still wrapped around her neck.

"Allison, I'm so glad you're alive," he said, turning his attention back to the only other living person in the room. "I think you can put the gun down now, though."

She holstered her weapon. They stared at each other as the sound of sirens drew closer.

"You were right about carrying that extra clip," she said. "You were right about a lot of things."

He moved across the room and took her in his arms, hugging her and holding her close. He pressed his nose into the part of her hair and kissed the top of her head. "When you feel up to it," he said, "I want to hear all about it, every single detail."

"I'll be ready to talk pretty soon," she said. "Just give me a second to see if I peed my pants this time."

Chapter 52

Allison Culbertson watched quietly as the coffin containing Bootheel Man was loaded into the hearse hired to carry him to the cemetery in Pawhuska. The door of the hearse closed. She knew she had seen the Midwest's most famous skeleton for the last time. He was on his way to the reservation, to a spot where his remains could rest in peace while his soul resumed its journey through the afterworld. Joe Black Dog had worked out the details for a tasteful ceremony once the hearse reached Oklahoma.

She was standing near the gazebo outside the Common Pleas Courthouse. Mark Windfoot had chosen the site for a short memorial service. It was the same place where Louis Lorimier, Cape Girardeau's founder, had conducted the funeral for his Shawnee wife, Charlotte, back in 1808. Windfoot's remarks had been eloquent. He'd talked about the Native American civilization that existed along the Mississippi River centuries ago, about the hopes and dreams of Bootheel Man and his contemporaries, about the continuity of the human condition throughout the centuries, and about life after death. He was giving a television interview now, no doubt condensing his thoughts into thirty-second sound bites.

She was surprised by the size of the crowd. At least five-hundred people turned out for the memorial service for Bootheel Man. The crowd had spilled onto Lorimier Street and covered the parking lot across the street. Some people even cried during Windfoot's remarks, shedding tears for a man they had never met, a man who had died one-thousand years ago, a man whose skeleton had been a tourist attraction for over a century. Allison wondered how many people had cried when the flesh-and-blood Bootheel Man was felled by the axe. Who mourned him then? Now, here he was, going off to be buried in Oklahoma, far away from the banks of the Mississippi where his friends and loved ones were undoubtedly buried. Was that really what he would have wanted? To be so far away from them? She supposed it beat being a museum exhibit.

"Miss Culbertson?"

414

Allison was startled to find Bear Smith standing next to her. Lolita was by his side. He nodded respectfully.

"I owe you an apology," he said. "I was rude to you. You were trying to help us. I should have welcomed your help, rather than trying to drive you away. I've never had a good experience with a police investigation. I guess I had some secrets I didn't want the cops to stumble across. I'm sorry for the things I said to you."

Allison made a fist and poked his arm. "Thanks, big guy. You're not so frightening, now that I know you're no killer."

He grinned. "Not this time, anyway."

"Dad!" Lolita said, shaking her head.

"Keep in touch," Allison said to Lolita. "You're a great girl. You're going to amount to something."

"Thanks."

Bear Smith and his daughter moved toward Mark Windfoot, who was still pontificating for the reporters.

Allison glanced again at the hearse. It was moving slowly down Lorimier Street. As it cruised down the hill and gradually disappeared from sight, she heard someone else talking to her. It was Marge Tappinger.

"We're repatriating all of the skeletal remains and burial artifacts, you know," she said. "The museum Board voted unanimously for it to be done as soon as possible."

"Good," Allison said. "Bootheel Man will have some friends joining him in Oklahoma, after all. I'm glad you're doing it. Joey would be very happy."

"I know," Marge Tappinger said. She put her hand on her stomach. Her pregnancy was beginning to show. "I left Rex," she said. "Something told me he wouldn't make the best father for Joey's baby."

"No, I don't suppose he would," Allison said. "Will you be staying on at the museum? On its Board of Directors?"

"Oh, yes," Marge said. "I'm going to be very actively involved in the nationwide search for Clive's replacement. We need someone creative and hard-working."

"Not to mention honest and non-homicidal," Allison said.

"Of course," Marge Tappinger said. "That goes without saying."

Allison saw Harry Sullinger crossing the green grass between the courthouse and the gazebo, coming toward them. The bandage was off his hand. She was glad the stub of his finger was healing so well.

"Oh, look, here comes Harry Sullinger," Marge Tappinger said. "He's so handsome. My hairdresser is one of his ex-wives. I think she still loves him. I can see why. He is such a fine-looking man."

Sullinger nodded to Marge Tappinger when he got to them. "Hello, Mrs. Tappinger. Mind if I steal Allison from you?"

"Why," she began, "we were just talking about the museum . . ."

"I knew you wouldn't," he interrupted, taking Allison by the arm and walking her to the front of the Common Pleas Courthouse.

"I just got off the phone with a buddy of mine at the DEA. Pablo Ramirez was killed in a shootout early this morning. The guy I talked to thinks the Colombian government might have recovered the real Gazing Woman. It could be months before she makes it back to Cape Girardeau, but there's a real possibility she'll be returning from Colombia."

"What about his sister, Carmelita?" Allison asked.

"No word about her," Sullinger said. "Nobody thinks she was actually involved in his drug dealing. The DEA doesn't have a file on her. Somebody said she's a nun, been one for years."

Allison pictured Carmelita Ramirez on her knees, praying for her brother, and for Clive Faulkner.

"What about Bear Smith? Is anything going to happen to him?"

"We've got no case against him. We suspect he had something to do with the break-in at the museum, but we can't prove it."

Allison nodded. "And Windfoot?"

"Ditto for him. All we've got are phone records. We can't prove anything. Plimpton's closing the case."

"What about me?" Allison asked.

"You? Did you miss the news conference right after the shooting? Plimpton called your shootings of Clive Faulkner and Carlos Estrada justified self-defense. Hell, Allison, you've lawfully killed more bad guys than most police officers."

"I didn't mean that," she said. "What about my future? What comes next? Am I always going to be remembered as the lawyer who gunned down two men?"

He shrugged. "That's better than being remembered as the lawyer whose body was found next to Diedra Binzinger's. Personally, I'm sort of glad you're still alive."

She slipped her hand into his, the one with five fingers. "What about us?" she asked.

"Us?" He smiled. "Well, after a lifetime of making lawyer jokes, I can't believe I'm actually saying this, but I'm starting to really like lawyers."

They kissed at the top of the Common Pleas Courthouse steps, a long and satisfying kiss. Beneath them, the picturesque brick buildings of downtown Cape Girardeau nestled behind the protective floodwall running parallel to the vast Mississippi River. To the south, the Bill Emerson Memorial Bridge stood tall and proud as it linked Missouri to Illinois. To the north, the hills on the Missouri side rose high above the river, as they had for centuries. In their shadows, the waters of the Mississippi flowed powerfully downstream, hurrying swiftly on a timeless rush to the sea.

Afterword

Best-selling author Dean Koontz once wrote that the best way to write popular fiction is to put your characters in terrible trouble on the first page and keep piling on more and more trouble, to keep your readers turning the pages. For the sequel to *The Gold of Cape Girardeau*, I wanted to write more "sugar-coated" history of Southeast Missouri, and I wanted to weave into that history another modern legal battle for fictional lawyer Allison Culbertson. With Koontz's advice in mind, I was delighted to discover so much real-life trouble in both the lives of the Mound Builders and the feud between modern museums and American Indians.

It is amazing how few Americans know anything whatsoever about the civilization that flourished in North America before the arrival of the Europeans. The vanished city at Cahokia probably boasted a population of 20,000 to 30,000 people. In 1150 A.D. it was larger than London at the time. No city in North America grew so large again until Philadelphia in 1800. Its tallest mound rivaled the pyramids of Egypt and South America. It was undoubtedly the center of power for a network of villages spreading across the Midwest, from the Great Lakes to the Gulf of Mexico, reaching its zenith of power somewhere around 1200 A.D. Exactly what happened to cause its inhabitants to abandon it will never be known.

The Mound Builders existed. They were not a vanished race of people, but rather the ancestors of the American Indians who still populated the continent when Europeans arrived three-hundred years after Cahokia's heyday. Exactly why they abandoned their huge city and broke into scattered tribes is a mystery. Whether flood, famine, earthquake, or rebellion broke up the budding empire, the lack of written records from these people hides the details of the fall of their civilization. But oral histories of existing Native Americans coupled with archaeological work at various Mound Builder sites help piece together the stories. My favorite books on this topic include *Cahokia: The Great Native American Metropolis* by Biloine Whiting Young and Melvin L. Fowler;

Ancient Cahokia and the Mississippians by Timothy R. Pauketat; *The Southeastern Indians* by Charles Hudson; and *Hero, Hawk and Open Hand: American Indian Art of the Ancient Midwest and South* published by the Art Institute of Chicago and Yale University Press.

The people at Cahokia probably practiced human sacrifice. The scenes portrayed in this novel are based upon actual archaeological work done at Cahokia. Most chillingly, fifty-three women, all between the ages of eighteen and twenty-three, were all killed and buried simultaneously in a pit near a man laid out on a bird-shaped bed of twenty-thousand white beads. Other bodies presumably belonging to various servants and sacrificial prisoners were buried nearby. It struck me that being one of those chosen girls would constitute terrible trouble. So would being a young man in love with that particular girl.

Thunder Runner, Dawn Breaks, and the other characters in the Mound Builder section of this book are fictitious, but the life I portrayed for them is realistic, based upon what we know. The game of chunkey appears to have been every bit as popular as depicted in this story. Wonderful artists like Dawn Breaks created outstanding pieces of art, much of it in museums today.

As a novelist seeking ways to create trouble for my characters, it was my lucky day when I stumbled across the fascinating and complicated issues involved in the legal conflict between museums and archaeologists on the one hand and American Indians on the other over the rights to skeletons and burial artifacts stored in museums across the country. This battle has been waging for three decades. It is far from over. It proved to be a timely legal mess to drop into Allison Culbertson's lap. My fictional Bootheel Man was inspired by two very special skeletons. One was a man's skull with a stone weapon lodged in his orbital area, formerly displayed in the Mesa Verde National Park museum in Colorado. The other was Kennewick Man, a well-preserved skeleton with an arrowhead embedded in his hip, whose bones produced a courtroom battle between archeologists and American Indians that made it all the way to the Federal Court of Appeals, one notch under the United States Supreme Court. See *Bonnichsen v. United States*, 367 F.3d 864 (9th Cir. 2004). My favorite books on the skirmishes between archaeologists and American Indians include *Grave Injustice: The*

American Indian Repatriation Movement and NAGPRA by Kathleen S. Fine-Dare; *Skull Wars: Kennewick Man, Archaeology, and the Battle for Native American Identity* by David Hurst Thomas; and *Repatriation Reader: Who Owns American Indian Remains?* by Devon A. Mihesuah.

I must confess that like most Americans, I did not have a full appreciation of the historical wrongs our white ancestors perpetrated upon our American Indian ancestors until I did the research for this book. American history has two sides: the story of the European conquerors, who wrote the first draft of history; and the story of the Native Americans, who were here first and whose land was taken away from them by force and unfair bargaining, who even today exist as sovereign nations within the borders of our great country. Unforgettable books on this topic include *Bury My Heart at Wounded Knee* by Dee Brown; *A History of the Osage People* by Louis F. Burns; and *Custer Died for Your Sins* by Vine Deloria Jr. A book vividly describing the tough and controversial road of the American Indian Movement in modern times is *In the Spirit of Crazy Horse* by Peter Matthiessen.

All of the characters in the modern story are fictional. The descriptions of the archaeological sites at Cahokia, Illinois, and Wickliffe, Kentucky, are factual, but all characters in this story, from the lawyers to the cops, from the crooks to the archaeologists, from the museum directors to the American Indians, are fictional. The only real human beings mentioned in the modern story are the scholars whose excellent books and publications are cited. No real Alfred Dennison ever existed, although many amateur archaeologists like him pilfered many a mound in Southeast Missouri, often with the best intentions. President Howard Taft really visited Cape Girardeau on October 26, 1909, but didn't request any artifacts from an Alfred Dennison. Rush Limbaugh really did grow up in Cape Girardeau, but never won any chunkey tournaments at my fictional museum.

Many people helped me as I researched and wrote this book. Dr. Susan Swartwout at the Southeast Missouri State University Press was the first person to suggest that a conflict between a local museum and American Indians might produce a new case for Allison Culbertson. A meeting with Director Stanley I. Grand and

Curator James M. Phillips from the Southeast Missouri Regional Museum not only gave me a reading list of background material, but also educated me about who might be stealing ancient art from museums, and how and why. (Not that these honorable men from the wonderful museum are suspects in any pending cases!) Telephone calls with Lieutenant Colonel Mike Smith and Wayne Talbert from the Missouri Water Patrol educated me about what the Water Patrol can do these days in regard to fishing things out of the Mississippi River. Detective Mike Alford of the Southeast Missouri Drug Task Force, knowing I was writing a book that included characters involved in a gunfight, referred me to the excellent book *On Combat: The Psychology and Physiology of Deadly Conflict in War and in Peace* by Lieutenant Colonel Dave Grossman and Loren W. Christensen, which inspired Harry Sullinger's observations about sheep, wolves, and sheepdogs, and parts of his other conversations in the book. The staff at the Osage Tribal Museum in Pawhuska, Oklahoma, was gracious and helpful. Director Kathryn Red Corn, Pauline Allred, Lou Brock, and James Elsberry went out of their way to assist me. Kathryn Red Corn and I spent some quality time in the museum's vault as tornado sirens blared while I was at the museum doing research. Kathryn Red Corn told me that she prefers the term "American Indian" to "Native American" since anyone born on American soil is a Native American, whereas not everybody can claim to be an American Indian. Dr. Andrea A. Hunter, who is both an archaeologist and an enrolled member of the Osage Nation, was kind enough to share some of her insights and wisdom with me. She made this a better book. Last but not least, Osage artist Gina Gray put her heart and soul into reading my manuscript and creating the painting for its cover. I am extremely grateful to all of these individuals for their time and assistance. Any mistakes are my fault and not theirs. Nor do my villains share any traits whatsoever with any of these wonderful people!

—*Morley Swingle*
Cape Girardeau, Missouri

About the Author

Morley Swingle is the Prosecuting Attorney for Cape Girardeau County, Missouri. He has prosecuted thousands of cases, from speeding offenses to death-penalty murder trials, including 69 homicide cases and 120 jury trials. Some of his cases have been featured on the *Oprah Winfrey Show*, *Dateline*, and *Forensic Files*.

Swingle is a member of Mystery Writers of America. His first novel, *The Gold of Cape Girardeau*, a historical mystery set in Missouri during the Civil War, won the 2005 Governor's Book Award from the Missouri Humanities Council for increasing "understanding and appreciation of Missouri's history and culture." His true-crime/humor book, *Scoundrels to the Hoosegow: Perry Mason Moments and Entertaining Cases From the Files of a Prosecuting Attorney*, was hailed as "engrossing" and "highly recommended" by Vincent Bugliosi.

Swingle lives in Cape Girardeau, Missouri, with his wife and two daughters.

About the Artist

Gina Gray is widely respected as one of the finest contemporary Native American artists working today. A member of the Osage tribe, she is recognized as a master artist whose work has won virtually every major award in the Indian art world. Renowned as a printmaker and painter, her innovative style and colorful works are featured in magazines, books, films, and public and private collections. Her honors include an appointment by the Secretary of Interior as a Commissioner for the Indian Arts and Crafts Board in Washington DC. Her work has been featured in a one-woman exhibit at the Wheelwright Museum in Santa Fe, New Mexico; in the collection of the Philbrook Museum of Art in Tulsa, Oklahoma; and in the Smithsonian Museum of the American Indian in Washington DC. She won the 70th Annual Santa Fe Indian Market Fellowship Award from the Southwest American Indian Art Association.

Gina Gray graduated from the Institute of American Arts in Santa Fe, New Mexico, and attended the California Institute of the Arts where she studied as a commercial artist.

Gina Gray lives in Pawhuska, Oklahoma, where she recently opened Gray Ink Studios, an art studio and teaching center. She is the mother of two and the grandmother of three.